"Have no fear."

His voice was low, almost a growl as his hand threaded through the thick mass of her hair. The sensuous friction of her breasts against his chest, rising and falling from her rapid breathing, intensified his craving to explore all of her. Thoroughly, relentlessly, and slowly. But though he held her far closer than necessary, his hands remained on her back and on her head, holding her steady instead of learning the tantalizing curves of her body.

She gasped when Mencheres sealed his mouth over her neck, sucking on it with slow, steady pressure. He didn't pierce her yet, but readied her for his bite, bringing that smaller, succulent vein closer to the surface. His eyes closed at the lemony nectar taste of her skin, the way her pulse leapt against his mouth, and at the shiver that raced all over her body. Her scent enveloped him, a mixture of apprehension, hesitation . . . and something else.

Excitement.

By Jeaniene Frost

ETERNAL KISS OF DARKNESS
FIRST DROP OF CRIMSON
DESTINED FOR AN EARLY GRAVE
AT GRAVE'S END
ONE FOOT IN THE GRAVE
HALFWAY TO THE GRAVE

Coming Soon

THE OTHER SIDE OF THE GRAVE

JEANIENE FROST

Eternal Kiss Of
Darkness

AVON

An Imprint of HarperCollinsPublishers

AVON BOOKS
An Imprint of HarperCollins*Publishers*
10 East 53rd Street
New York, New York 10022-5299

For my beloved nieces and nephews,
the closest I'll come to children of my own.
Wesley, Lauren, Patrick, Michael,
Matthew, Christopher, and Amy.
May all of you find your own happily-ever-afters.

Acknowledgments

I'll try to keep it short this time, but since there's truly a small army behind each book, I'd be remiss if I didn't at least acknowledge those on the front lines.

For holding me up even when I think I'm going to crash, thanks so much, Lord. For dealing with my deadlines, occasional talking to my computer, and a hundred other things, you're the best, Matthew. For giving me a background of unconditional love, thanks so much, Mom, Dad, and family.

Melissa, Ilona, Vicki, and Yasmine, whether it's critiquing my manuscripts, offering encouragement, laughter, or a safe place to vent, you ladies rock!

Nancy Yost, you make the impossible job of being an agent look easy. Erika Tsang, as always, your editorial input is invaluable for making my stories the best they can be. Thomas Egner, you delight me with each new amazing book cover. Amanda Bergeron, Pamela Spengler-Jaffee, Carrie Feron, Liate Stehlik, and the rest of the team at Avon Books/HarperCollins, I so appreciate the support you give to me and my novels!

Thanks so much to Tage, whose assistance has allowed me more time to write. Thanks also to all the members of Frost Fans; you make me feel like I'm at a virtual coffee-house chatting with friends when I'm on the forum. Plus, thanks to the ladies on the Charlaine boards; you humble me with your enthusiasm for my series. To the group from Vicki's boards, thanks, and I'm looking forward to more post-True Blood chats! To review sites, bloggers, booksellers, and readers who've spread the word about my series or offered a word of support: Thank you all so much. It means more than I can ever articulate.

Chapter One

Mencheres smelled blood even before he caught the earthy scent of ghouls clustered on the ground floor of the decrepit warehouse. They showed no concern when he walked inside. Another inhalation revealed it was vampire blood two of them stank of. The other four didn't have that coppery aroma clinging to them, but from the predatory gazes they leveled on Mencheres, they intended to rectify that.

"A young vampire went missing from this area recently," Mencheres said by way of greeting, ignoring the way the ghouls began to circle around him. They looked to be in their late teens, and from the energy in their auras, they were teens in undead years as well. "Short blond hair, tribal tattoos on his upper arms, silver piercing in his eyebrow. Goes by the name Trick," he went on. "Have you seen him?"

"Not smart to be out so close to dawn, vampire," the ghoul with the heaviest scent of blood drawled without answering Mencheres's question. Then the ghoul smiled, showing he'd filed all his teeth to points.

Instead of inspiring fear, the sight annoyed Mencheres. These ghouls thought they had the advantage because of the impending dawn, but dawn would only sap the strength of a new vampire. Even with his power level cloaked to where it would feel like he was only a young vampire, if the ghouls were wise, they'd wonder at Mencheres's lack of hesitation in confronting them.

Then again, if they were wise, they wouldn't have killed Trick in the same area they used as a home. It had only taken Mencheres an hour to track them down. Such stupidity wasn't only blatant disregard for vampire and ghoul law; it also endangered the secrecy of both their races. In another mood, Mencheres would have killed the shark-toothed ghoul without further conversation, then rounded up the remaining five for public punishment later. After all, Mencheres didn't require their confession to know they'd killed Trick. Not with the scent of vampire blood on them.

The ghouls were lucky, because today, he wasn't looking for retribution over Trick's murder. Perhaps it was a good thing he'd lost his visions of the future, Mencheres reflected. Otherwise, if he'd foreseen that *this* was how he'd end his eons-old feud with the corrupt Law Guardian, Radjedef, he'd question his own sanity.

But if he hadn't lost his visions, none of this would be necessary. Anger flashed in him. After four thousand years of seeing glimpses of the future, to suddenly have his visions gone was as crippling as it was unexpected. He'd long lamented the frustration of having visions that some people paid no heed to; but now that they were gone, for all his other powers, he couldn't protect those he cared for. A friend's recent, accusing words rang in Mencheres's mind. *Why now, when I need you the most, are you of no use to me?*

Radjedef might have hated Mencheres for millennia, but he was too clever to come after a foe who could counter most hostile moves before they were even made. Now that Mencheres's visions were gone, this was Radjedef's best chance. As both men knew, Radjedef wouldn't hesitate to use his considerable power as a Law Guardian to manufacture charges against Mencheres for crimes that had never taken place. Radjedef was no stranger to bending the law to suit his own purposes. It was something he'd done even before he had become a member of the powerful vampire ruling council.

His old enemy might relish the upcoming confrontation and all the bloody collateral damage it would doubtless involve before one of them emerged a victor, but Mencheres would end this before it started. It rather pleased him to imagine the frustration Radjedef would feel at being denied the opportunity to implement his elaborate plans for vengeance.

So when the six ghouls pulled out their silver knives, smiling in that cruel, anticipatory way, Mencheres simply stood there. This would get bloody, but he was no stranger to blood. Or to pain. Both had been his companions for far longer than these ghouls could even imagine.

He cast one look at the predawn sky, wondering briefly if the sun shone in the afterlife. Before the sun was high, either he or the ghouls would find out.

* * *

Kira walked down Ashland Avenue, the second-to-last street before hers. A sudden breeze blew her hair into her eyes. They didn't call Chicago the Windy City for nothing. She pushed stray pieces back behind her ears and shifted her heavy backpack onto her other shoulder. After all the times she'd toted her backpack to and from work, Kira would have thought it wouldn't feel as heavy as it did. Still, she was lucky her boss allowed her to use the company car on stakeouts, and besides, many people who lived and worked in the West Loop didn't own cars. They just didn't have to carry around the various cameras, camcorders, binoculars, and other necessary stakeout items that she did.

At least it had been a productive night. Her surveillance of her client's cheating wife finally paid off in the version of several incriminating photos that Kira dropped off at her office before she'd taken the Green Line back to her neighborhood. She could sleep in as late as she wanted to today, and even her exacting boss wouldn't have a thing to say about it.

Being a private investigator meant tuning in to her surroundings, which came naturally to Kira, but her focus sharpened even more when she rounded the next corner. Walking this particular stretch of road during the daylight was fine, but now, it made her uneasy. She was glad the sun had started to peek out. The line of dilapidated warehouses were supposed to be gone by now, but the lingering recession had slowed their razing and rebuilding. The stretch of unsightly buildings meant the rent in her building farther up the block was much lower than it would be once shiny new apartments replaced the graffiti-laced, abandoned units, but it also meant that she had to be watchful now. Muggings weren't uncommon in this area.

She was almost past the last of them when raucous laughter jerked her head around. It had come from inside one of the warehouses, and it sounded more ugly than amused. *Keep walking,* Kira told herself, patting the pocket of her backpack where she kept a gun. *You're almost home.*

That harsh laughter rang out again, this time, right on the heels of what sounded like a pained shout. Kira paused, listening hard. If it had been later in the day, the noise from cars and pedestrians would've drowned out anything coming from the warehouses; but with most people still sleeping, she next caught what sounded like a loud moan. Whoever had made that sound was hurt, and when it was followed by more of that ugly laughter, Kira knew the two were related.

She slipped her backpack off, pulling out her cell phone while walking faster toward the safety of her apartment building.

"Nine one one, what's your emergency?" a voice intoned after Kira punched in the numbers.

"I want to report a Code 37," Kira said.

"Say again?"

"Aggravated assault," Kira amended, surprised the dispatch operator hadn't registered the police code. She gave the address of where the warehouse was located. "Sounds like the bottom floor," she added to be more specific.

"Please hold while I transfer you to that station," the operator replied. Moments later, another voice asked what her emergency was.

"I'm reporting an aggravated assault," Kira said, not bothering with the code this time. She gave the address and information again, her teeth grinding in frustration as she had to repeat twice what she'd heard.

"So you never actually saw an assault?" the dispatch operator asked.

"No, I didn't go in there," Kira said stiffly, not walking now that she was close to her apartment building.

"Right," the now bored-sounding voice replied. "What's your name?"

"I prefer to be anonymous," Kira said after a pause. She had a history with the police that wasn't necessarily pleasant.

"We'll send a car around," the operator intoned.

"Thanks," Kira muttered, and hung up. She'd done all she could. Hopefully it would be enough for whoever'd made that awful noise.

But when she started to walk toward the front door of her building, her steps faltered. Instinct told her to turn around and head back to the warehouse. It would be five to ten minutes before the patrol car arrived. What if the unknown, injured person didn't have that long?

Never try to be a hero, kid. Leave that to the shields.

Her boss's admonition rang in Kira's mind, but instead of making her feel better, anger rose. If not for her ex-husband, she'd be one of those "shields." She'd aced the police academy, gotten her certification in law enforcement, and she was just two blocks away from that scream, not several minutes like the patrol car.

Mack's voice, deep and scratchy, sounded through her mind next: *Save one life.* That had been her mentor's credo. If Mack had been more like her boss, Kira might be dead. Not standing on a sidewalk debating whether or not to help someone in need.

Mack wouldn't have hesitated, badge or no badge. Who did she want to be like, her old friend Mack, or her jaded boss, Frank?

Kira spun around, heading back toward the warehouses and the source of that scream.

* * *

Mencheres let out a long moan when the silver knife slashed into his sternum. When the ghouls first started cutting him, he hadn't made a noise, and they'd drawn their blades even more slowly across his flesh, taking his silence as a challenge. So he grunted, moaned, and even shouted. It helped; they grew more excited, their cuts went deeper.

Soon, he'd have to choose between using his energy to cloak the fact that he was a Master vampire, or using his power to protect himself from the worst of the pain. He'd lost too much blood to keep doing both. But if his attackers had a grain of sense, revealing the extent of what he had coiling inside him might make them run away. No, he couldn't chance that. Pain it was, then.

Mencheres dropped the mental barrier he'd erected between himself and those relentless, seeking knives. Immediately, his body felt like it was on fire, the silver causing an intense, agonizing reaction as it sliced through him.

With his barrier to the pain down, a new problem arose. Every new cut or stab wound roused the swirling energy in him that craved retribution. Mencheres forced it back, concentrating on keeping his aura tamped down, fighting his urge to kill the ghouls even though his power demanded to be released.

"Stakes," Mencheres said, calling him by the name the others had used. "Are you inexperienced, or is this merely the best you can do?"

The ghoul snarled at the insult, hacking a deep line in Mencheres's thigh as a response. Another ghoul took hold of Mencheres's waist-length black hair and sawed a hunk of it off at the shoulder.

Mencheres's anger rose again, dark and deadly, seeking to merge with his power to be given form. He forced it back, knowing if he released his control for even an instant, all of the ghouls would die. And they hadn't served their purpose yet.

"Put the knives *down* and get away from him," someone gasped.

Mencheres swung his gaze toward the sound with the same amazement the ghouls showed. Had he been so distracted by his own thoughts—and the ghouls by their torture—that a *human* had actually managed to sneak up on them?

The proof stood on the other side of the room, posture in a classic shooting stance, gun pointed at the ghouls clustered around him. The woman's eyes were wide, her face pale, but she held her weapon in an unwavering grip.

This was a complication he didn't need.

"Leave now," Mencheres ordered. Her warm mortal body would be too tempting for the flesh-eaters to resist if she didn't flee at once.

"Well, well," Stakes drew out, leaving his knife embedded in Mencheres's thigh. "Look here, guys. Dessert."

A clicking sound indicated the woman's thumbing back the hammer. "I'll shoot," she warned. "All of you, put your knives down and get away from him. The police are already on the way . . ."

Her voice cracked as Stakes moved away from Mencheres. Most of what they'd done to him had been blocked from her view by the ghoul's body, but when Mencheres was fully revealed to the woman's gaze, she stared.

The ghouls charged.

Mencheres knew he should do nothing. Should stay lashed to the building's support beam, pretending to be helpless, and let the ghouls kill her. After all, he'd had an objective when he set out to this place, and it didn't involve saving a reckless human.

But in the single second that it took the ghouls to reach the woman, another thought rose within Mencheres, overcoming his practicality. She'd tried to save him. He could not let her die for it.

Power ripped out of him, slamming into the ghouls. The bloodied ropes around Mencheres began to unwind themselves, whipping about like snakes as Mencheres blasted more of his power into the six ghouls. The strikes were weaker than normal from his blood loss, but the sudden high-pitched shrieks coming from the flesh-eaters ended as abruptly as their attack on her. By the time the ropes all fell away, and Mencheres strode over to the woman, none of the ghouls could even move.

Mencheres kicked Stakes of out the way to reveal the woman underneath him. She was gasping, blood coming from her mouth in a thin trail, more pouring from the gaping wound in her stomach. His hesitation had been costly. The ghoul managed to wound her mortally before he'd stopped him. In mere minutes, the woman would bleed to death.

She stared up at him, anguish showing in her expression, followed by a horrified understanding as she glanced down at her stomach.

"Tina," the woman whispered. Then her pale green eyes rolled back into her head, and she passed out.

Mencheres didn't pause this time; he sliced his fangs across his wrist and held the wound to her mouth. No blood flowed. Of course—the ghouls had drained all his blood. He swept the woman up in the next instant, taking her to the pole he'd so recently been lashed to. Then Mencheres scooped up a handful of blood that pooled on the floor, forcing it into her mouth. Her pulse was now erratic, her breathing almost nonexistent, but he ignored that, making her swallow.

Sirens approached. The police were almost here, just as she said they would be. Mencheres scooped up another handful of his blood, rubbing it onto the gouge in her stomach. The woman's hot blood mingled with his, but only for a moment. Then her bleeding stopped, the edges of her flesh pulling toward each other as she began to heal inside and out from the regenerative effects of his blood.

Two car doors slammed. Mencheres left her on the red-smeared floor while he went over to the ghouls. Their eyes were the only things that could move as he stared down at them.

"If you had killed me at once, you might have lived another few days," Mencheres said coldly. Then he flexed his power in a short, controlled burst. A popping sound preceded six heads rolling away from the ghouls' bodies in the next moment.

Footsteps approached the warehouse. Mencheres paused, glancing over at the woman. She'd regained consciousness, and she was staring at him, her pale gaze riveted with shock and horror.

She had seen his fangs. Watched him kill the ghouls. She knew too much for him to leave her here.

"Police," a voice called out. "Anyone injured in here . . . ?"

Mencheres snatched up the woman and flew out of a broken window before the officers had a chance to gasp at the carnage they found inside.

Chapter Two

Kira knew she wasn't dreaming, or hallucinating, or crazy. And that was the bad news. It meant everything she'd seen was real, which meant the man who'd kidnapped her couldn't be human. As impossible as the notion was, it was the only logical explanation. Humans couldn't recover from the butchery she'd seen when she'd gotten her first clear look at the man lashed to that pole. Humans didn't have fangs or eyes that glowed fluorescent green. And humans couldn't *tear people's heads off* without even touching them.

Even if she wanted to rationalize that all of the above had been her hysterical misinterpretation of a traumatic event, humans sure as hell couldn't fly. Yet her kidnapper had flown away from that warehouse, then performed several impossible roof-to-roof leaps while holding her as if she weighed nothing.

Kira had always been afraid of heights, so that fear, combined with dizziness, shock, blood loss, and vertigo, proved too much. At some point during the roof-jumping, she passed out. Now she found herself awake in a very normal-looking bedroom, still in her ripped, blood-spattered clothes, her stomach wound miraculously healed and her kidnapper sitting in a chair across from the bed.

"Do not fear, you are safe," were his first words, spoken in an oddly accented voice.

Only Kira's survival instincts kept her from saying, "Bull*shit*." She glanced down at herself, but of course, her gun was nowhere to be seen. Not that it would have done any good against whatever he and the other creatures at the warehouse were.

"Where am I?" Kira asked, edging out from underneath the covers someone—he?—had pulled over her.

"A safe place," her kidnapper replied, eliciting another mental scoff from Kira. Sure. She was as safe as a skydiver with a broken parachute.

"How strange," the man murmured in the next moment. "I can smell your fear, but I can't hear a word of it."

Kira had been in the process of slowly edging out of the bed, but at that, she stopped. A cold thrill of adrenaline washed over her as she took her first real look at the person holding her captive.

Straight black hair hung well past his chest in some places, but was hacked to his shoulders in others. At first glance, his features looked Middle Eastern, but his light skin made her think mixed heritage. A wide mouth was curled in a slight half smile while black brows hung over equally black eyes. Where had that previous unearthly green glow gone? He looked to be in his midtwenties, judging from the lack of lines around his eyes. He still had blood spattered on his neck, but it looked like he'd put on a fresh shirt and pants. If not for the blood and the unevenly shorn hair, Kira would think him a young, suave executive if she'd run into him on the subway.

But she'd seen him sliced half to pieces just this morning, though no sign of injury was visible on him now. It was even more proof that whatever he was, it couldn't be human.

Why bother with pleasantries? Kira wondered. Both of them knew she'd witnessed something that would probably result in her being killed so she couldn't tell anyone about it.

"Fascinating," he said, almost to himself. "I cannot hear a *word* of what you're thinking."

Kira's hands instinctively went to her head, as if she could physically block him from trying to peer in her mind. His half smile quirked.

"That would do you no good under normal circumstances, but as I said, I cannot hear your thoughts."

"What are you?" she blurted. An alien? She knew the government was lying about that Roswell incident . . .

"Nothing you need to worry about, Tina," he replied with a shrug. "Soon, you can—"

"Why did you call me Tina?" Kira interrupted in a panicked whisper.

"Perhaps I just need more blood," the stranger muttered.

"You stay *away* from my sister," Kira snarled, rising. Whatever he was, he'd run from the police. That meant they must be able to hurt him, and if he had anything planned that involved Tina, she'd find a way to hurt him, too.

He held out a hand. "You misunderstand. You said

'Tina' right before you lost consciousness earlier. I thought it was your name."

Kira didn't remember that, but it made sense. When she saw how horrible her injury was, her last thought had been that no one else would be around to take care of Tina once she was dead. A wound like that should have killed her, yet the first thing Kira had noticed upon waking was that her stomach was healed. Incredibly, no mark even remained, and she felt fine, though her clothes were still torn and stained crimson with blood.

That made her give her kidnapper another slow evaluation. *He* must have healed her somehow. Did that mean he was being truthful when he said she was in no danger, or did this creature have something even worse in store for her? If he had no malicious intentions, why hadn't he left her at the warehouse with the police?

The dark stranger sat motionless, that single hand still extended toward her. Kira took a deep breath and sat back on the bed. She'd been in enough strange situations with her job to know that getting hysterical never helped anyone. True, nothing about being a private investigator had prepared her for *this*, but if she wanted to preserve even the smallest chance at surviving, she needed to keep her cool.

"My name is Kira." If he'd taken her belongings, he'd soon know that from her wallet, anyway. "I want to go home now. I'm not sure what happened this morning. When I try to remember, it's all so blurry . . ."

"You are lying," the man said with a scoff that somehow managed to sound elegant. Those coal-colored eyes narrowed. "I don't need to read your mind to know that. I can smell it."

Kira swallowed hard. "Wouldn't you pretend you didn't remember anything, if you were in my position?"

"I don't know," he replied almost musingly. "I've never been in your position. I always knew about Cain's children, even when I was a child myself."

Then he shook his head as if to clear it. "Why am I saying this to you? I *must* need to feed again. Come, let us get this over with . . ."

He was suddenly in front of her, his hands on her shoulders. How could he have moved so *fast*? Her heart began to pound while a sick franticness welled up in her. *Get this over with?* Was that how casually he referred to murdering her?

"Do not fear," the monster said softly. His eyes changed, glowing a terrible bright green as he forced her to look at him. Pressure began to build in her mind. Oh God, he was about to rip her head off, like he'd done to those other creatures back at the warehouse.

"Stop it," Kira gasped. "I tried to help you—"

"I know," he interrupted, brushing his fingers across her face. "It was very brave. Foolish, too, but brave nonetheless. Look into my eyes, Kira. *Nothing happened this morning.* You never went to the warehouse. You never saw me. You went home, fell asleep, and nothing else happened . . ."

His voice deepened until it vibrated with something more than his unusual accent. The pressure in Kira's mind intensified, but her head didn't feel like it was about to snap off her shoulders. Maybe he wasn't trying to kill her. It hadn't taken this long for him to kill the others at the warehouse. After several more moments staring into his impossibly bright eyes, Kira tried to reason with him again.

"That's exactly what I'll say. Whatever you are, whatever they were, I don't want to know about it. I just want to forget about it."

A frown creased his features. "Impossible," he muttered. His eyes brightened even more. "Nothing happened this morning. You walked home, you went to bed . . ."

"Got it," Kira said, blinking. Looking into his eyes was like staring into two green spotlights.

He was on the other side of the room before her next blink, looking at her with the same wary speculation she'd bestowed on him before.

"You are immune to my power." A short laugh came from him. "This is a memorable day, indeed. Perhaps it's because I gave you my blood to heal you. That could interfere with my mesmerizing you now. Once you get it out of your system, you will be susceptible again."

That didn't sound good. It sounded lengthy, like she wasn't getting away anytime soon, and things were forming a connection in her mind. *Blood. Mesmerizing. Fangs. Flying.* Only one creature had all those in common, but this stranger couldn't really be a *vampire*, could he?

"I might remember what happened this morning, but you can bet I won't tell anyone," Kira said quietly. "You don't have to wait for anything to clear out of my system. I'll go home and won't say a word about you, that warehouse, or anything else that isn't completely normal."

He stared at her, darkness replacing the green in his gaze. Then, very slowly, he shook his head.

"At this moment, you may believe that, but I cannot take the risk that you will change your mind later."

The sound of the door shutting was the only indicator that he'd moved. Kira ran to it, but though the knob turned, and she shoved against it, she couldn't open the door. Something very heavy must be on the other side of it.

How was she supposed to get away from him when he

moved so impossibly *fast*? Once again, the word "vampire" jumped into her mind. With all the other traits she'd seen, it seemed to be the frontrunner for what her kidnapper was. Then again, weren't vampires supposed to catch fire in the sunlight? He hadn't. The sun had been out when he'd carried her from the warehouse, yet her kidnapper hadn't suffered any ill effects. Plus, she had on a cross necklace, but that hadn't stopped him from carting her over half of Chicago's rooftops this morning, either. That shot a big hole in her "vampire" theory.

Some part of Kira couldn't believe she was contemplating what sort of supernatural creature he could be. None of those things were supposed to exist, let alone *kidnap* her! Disbelief battled with the memory of everything she'd seen. Even if she wanted to believe that her long night without sleep had made her see things that weren't real, her blood-smeared, perfectly healed stomach was a reminder that her eyes weren't playing tricks on her. She hadn't imagined the agony of her flesh being ripped open, either. Or the coldness that had seeped through every pore, the sense of fading away . . . and then the abrupt yank back to life just in time to see her dark-haired captor ripping the heads off several people when his hands hadn't even been near them.

It didn't matter what he was, Kira decided. The most important thing was getting away from him. She began to prowl around the bedroom, ignoring its lavish furnishings. No phone that she could see. An attached bathroom loaded with all the amenities, none of them useful for escape purposes. No computer. She went over to the window and stared out in frustration. Of course she'd be a few stories up without a balcony or trellis. She supposed she should be grateful that there didn't appear to be a moat around the property, or wolves baying around the perimeter. Was she still in Chicago? Or, when she'd been unconscious, had he managed to take her much farther away?

Kira sank onto the bed, fingering the fabric of the comforter. Frank probably wouldn't even notice she was missing until later tonight. Her boss knew she'd pulled an all-night stakeout; he'd expect her to sleep late today. Tina also wouldn't attempt to call her until later, and if Kira didn't answer, her sister would just assume she was working. Her only hope was that her kidnapper had left her backpack at the warehouse. The police would *definitely* investigate her whereabouts if they found her belongings at the scene of a grisly multiple homicide. Had he taken it with him when he grabbed her? She couldn't remember. Her backpack wasn't in this bedroom, that was all she knew.

Kira fisted the comforter, wanting to shred it out of frustration, but with its thick smoothness, it was probably a thousand-thread count and thus stronger than rope. All she'd do if she tore at it was break several fingernails.

All at once, Kira began to smile. *Improvisation is a necessary part of the job,* Frank had told her when training her to work as a P.I. He'd been right about that.

Kira went into the bathroom, dragging the comforter behind her.

Mencheres closed his eyes as he swallowed. Warm flesh pressed to his mouth, a sweet pulse vibrating underneath his lips. A haze of pleasurable thoughts blanketed his mind as he lightly dug his fangs in again, but they weren't his thoughts. They belonged to Selene, the human he fed from.

Yes, bite me again. Deeper. Ah, so good, don't stop . . .

Selene shuddered with an ecstasy Mencheres hadn't felt in centuries. He drew back after his next swallow, closing the punctures from his fangs with a drop of his blood while the bliss he'd so briefly felt turned to ashes.

Selene's passion was only due to the skillful way he'd bitten her, combined with the mild euphoria-inducing venom all vampires had in their fangs. He'd be able to give her mind-shattering orgasms with his bite, if he wished to, but any vampire could rouse the same sensations in her. If there was one thing Mencheres's long years had taught him, it was that being an instrument of pleasure wasn't the same as being truly desired.

Once he would have scoffed at that. When he was a human ruler in Egypt, it was considered an honor to share his bed, and Mencheres had welcomed many there. When he became a vampire, men and women flocked to him in the hopes that he'd transform them into vampires. Later, his power drew those looking for protection. Over time, being his lover was a status symbol among vampires. Even if Mencheres lived among humans, hiding what he was, his wealth seduced people to his side. After living that way for twenty-five hundred years, even the most sensual enjoyments began to feel hollow. Mencheres wanted more.

He thought he'd found it in Patra, the young Egyptian queen he married two thousand years ago, but that had ended in disaster. Back then, he'd been naïve enough to believe he could sate Patra's need for power by changing her into a vampire, sharing his vast wealth, and teaching her the deepest, most forbidden secrets of his race, but it hadn't been enough. Nothing he'd done had been enough, and a long-ago sin resulted in Patra nearly destroying everyone Mencheres cared about until she'd fi-

nally been killed last year. As depressing as the thought
was, everyone in his life had been drawn to him for an
ulterior motive, even those he trusted. Even those he
loved.

Oddly enough, the only exception was the human
locked upstairs in the bedroom. Kira had tried to save
him, acting without the influence of his heritage, status,
power, wealth, or charisma. She'd *risked her life* without
expecting a single thing in return. No one had done such
a thing for him. Ever.

As a result of Kira's baffling, selfless act, combined
with his inability to control her mind *or* hear her thoughts,
he hadn't been able to stop thinking about her. Even as
the day slipped into evening and he sent another vampire
to deliver food and refreshment to her room, Mencheres
couldn't banish her from his thoughts.

Kira. In Greek, her name meant "lady". In Celtic, it
meant "dark". Which fit her better? Her appearance fit
both meanings of her name—her face was delicate and
beautiful, except for that strong jaw that warned of stubbornness. Kira's eyes were pale green, but her brows were
dark, matching the deep hue of her hair before it lightened
to gold at the tips. Her hair was short for Mencheres's
tastes, falling to just above her shoulders, but it was so
lush, thick, and curly, it practically invited him to twine it
around his fingers.

Kira's body was another contrast of femininity and
strength. She was slender to the point of delicacy, but she
held herself with a fighter's stance, and her wide shoulders only served to better highlight her full breasts. She'd
squared those lovely broad shoulders *and* that stubborn
jaw when she'd snarled at him to stay away from her sister.
Even though Kira knew he wasn't human, she hadn't hesi-

tated to challenge him over the perceived threat to her family. *Dark lady, indeed.*

"Yes, please!"

The cry yanked Mencheres out of his musings. Gods, he'd been caressing Selene and unconsciously sending out strands of his power to stroke and stimulate her nerve endings. How could he have gotten so lost in his thoughts of Kira that he'd *forgotten* he still held Selene in his arms?

Mencheres pulled back his power and set Selene away from him.

"I've taken all I need," he told her.

Her eyes opened as she pressed against him. "Let me give you more than blood," she offered in a husky voice.

"No," Mencheres replied automatically.

As soon as he uttered the words, he reminded himself again that he didn't need to refuse. His wife was dead, so there was no more death sentence on any woman he took to his bed. If he wanted Selene, he could have her.

But it was ironic; after burning with unspent lust for longer than many civilizations existed, now, when he had a chance to indulge, he had no desire to. Selene was beautiful, willing, yet he didn't want her.

Kira's face flickered in his mind, but Mencheres wiped her image away before he allowed himself to dwell on it.

"No," he repeated to Selene in a tone that brooked no argument.

She left after one last lingering look that he pretended not to notice. Selene, like all the others, didn't only want him. She also wanted the power, security, and supernatural pleasure he could give, but somehow during Mencheres's extended, forced celibacy, that was no longer an acceptable trade.

Selene had only been gone a few minutes before

Gorgon, the only vampire Mencheres brought with him to this house, came into the library.

"Sire," Gorgon said. "We have a situation with the human you brought home this morning."

Mencheres rose, already striding up the stairs to Kira's room, when Gorgon's voice stopped him.

"Ah, sire? You might want to go outside instead."

Chapter Three

Kira dangled out the window on her makeshift rope, reminding herself with gritted teeth not to look down. It had taken hours to tie the bedspread, sheets, drapes, and shower curtain together until it was long enough to reach to the bottom of the house. Then she secured it around two corners of the bed, waiting tensely until after dark so she'd have less chance of being seen. It took another half hour of mental pep talking before she'd worked up the courage to heave herself over the window ledge, and she'd had a moment of sheer panic when the rope first stretched under her weight.

But the rope, the bed anchor, and her biceps had held. Slowly, Kira edged down, tangling the rope between her legs to slow her descent. *You're doing fine*, Kira told herself as she carefully began to climb down the side of the house. With luck, she'd be safely on the bottom in just a few minutes. If she had even more luck, it wouldn't take her long to find help. She doubted she was still in Chicago, judging from the lack of almost any houses or buildings within eyesight, but she had seen what looked like another home past the line of trees to the north. That's where she'd try first—assuming the rope or the bed didn't all of a sudden break.

When she reached the ledge below her window, Kira blew out a tight sigh of relief. One story completed, two more to go. So far, no one had sounded the alarm. Pretending to be a compliant captive had worked, it seemed. She'd even pretended to eat the food and drink the soda the blond-haired man with the scar running down his cheek had brought her, but in reality, she'd flushed them down the toilet. No way was she risking being drugged by touching that stuff. She'd swallowed some water from the shower when she cleaned off. That was more than enough to keep her hydrated, and she doubted they were clever enough to have drugged *that*.

Kira kept easing herself down the rope, amazed that her arms didn't feel shaky. She'd lost a lot of blood this morning, but for some reason, her arms were steady, handling her weight with ease. That was unusual enough to concern Kira, but she decided to worry about it later. Like, when she was far away from this house and at the nearest police station.

She made it down another story, holding her breath as her rope brought her dangling directly in front of a window. The light inside glowed against the glass, making the interior clearly discernible to her. Kira prayed the darkness outside would make her almost invisible by contrast. She lightly kicked off to position herself away from the center of the window, and lowered herself a little faster. Should she risk looking down to check how much farther it was? No, Kira decided. She'd done well to get this far, considering her fear of heights. No need to ruin that by looking down now.

When Kira finally felt solid earth underneath her feet instead of more emptiness and rope, she almost whooped in relief. She stuffed her glee back, though, pulling the rope to the left of the windows and securing it by tucking the end under a potted plant. With luck, no one would find it until morning, and she'd be long gone by then.

Kira began to run as fast as she could in the direction where she thought she'd glimpsed the other house from her bedroom window. It was dark as pitch outside, but she was pretty sure she was headed in the right direction. Her heart thumped with joy and exhilaration. She was free!

She made it twenty yards before she ran into a wall.

Mencheres had watched Kira climb down the house with a mixture of wonder and amusement. She certainly was a tenacious female, stringing together rope made from various materials in the bedroom—and were those *shower curtain* loops she'd used as anchor points for her knots?

"Want me to get her?" Gorgon asked, his voice too low for Kira to hear him.

"No," Mencheres replied. He was rather curious to see if she'd make it all the way to the bottom. If the rope broke or she lost her grip, he could easily catch her. But in the meantime, watching Kira maneuver down the side of the house was more entertaining than anything he'd done in the past several months.

"You may go back inside," he told Gorgon, his mouth twitching as Kira delicately kicked away from the window. She was being very quiet for a human; but of course, with his hearing, she made quite a commotion.

Gorgon nodded once before disappearing back into the house. Mencheres stood on the darkest part of the lawn, where he'd be invisible from Kira's sight, and continued to watch her. He tensed when the bed frame that the rope was anchored to creaked warningly, but her line held. When Kira made it to the ground, Mencheres smiled along with her. *Well done, dark lady.*

Pity he couldn't let her complete her victory by running away, however. A human telling the police tales of supernatural creatures was the last thing Mencheres needed. Radjedef would seize on that as more proof that Mencheres had broken their laws.

Radjedef. How odd that Mencheres hadn't thought about the vengeful Law Guardian since he left the warehouse this morning, but he would tend to his business regarding Radjedef later. First, he had to erase Kira's memories of everything supernatural. He could pass her off to Gorgon or another vampire in his line to mesmerize, but taking care of Kira himself seemed the least he could do to repay her for the kindness she'd shown him at the warehouse. Even if she regretted that kindness now.

He could always find another way to implement his plan concerning Radjedef after Kira's memories of that warehouse and him were gone. Mencheres hadn't seen Radjedef in over a week. No need to rush; he'd accomplish his objective soon enough.

Mencheres let Kira run for a few paces before he stepped in front of her. She collided with him hard enough to knock a scream out of her, but he absorbed the impact as if she were a butterfly.

"That's two brave yet foolish things you've done today," Mencheres noted.

Kira's breathing was labored, but her aim was steady as she punched him squarely in the chest. "Damn it! It's *you* again, isn't it?"

He could see her clearly in the dark, but she'd be almost blind with the lack of lights on the lawn.

"Yes, it's me," Mencheres replied. He didn't comment about the punch though he couldn't remember the last time a person had actually *struck* him.

"You watched me the whole time, didn't you?" Kira demanded. Bitterness wafted from her, changing her scent from lemons and sea spray to something harsher. "Why? Did you think it was funny, seeing me try to get away?"

In fact he had been amused, but only because he knew she was never in real danger. The angry desperation in her tone made him pause, however. He might have known that Kira wasn't in jeopardy, but she hadn't. In truth, he had told her nothing to truly reassure her that she had no reason to fear, whether she was inside the house or dangling on a rope outside of it.

"I apologize." Mencheres dropped his hands from her shoulders, where he'd steadied her after Kira had barreled into him. She didn't attempt to run away once he released her. She just stood there, gulping in breaths and glaring at him.

"What are you? And *what* do you intend to do with me since it's clear you won't let me go?"

Mencheres hesitated for a moment before giving a mental shrug. Soon enough he'd erase her mind. What did it matter if she knew more in the interim about him?

"The modern word for what I am is 'vampire.'"

Kira's heart had already been pounding, but at that, it skipped a beat.

"Vampires don't exist," she said, even though she

sounded as if her words were a last attempt at denial instead of a true statement of disbelief.

"That's exactly what humans are supposed to think, except you've seen too much to hold on to that fabrication any longer," he replied steadily.

"But you were out in the sunlight this morning, and my cross . . ."

Mencheres reached out to touch the emblem hanging from Kira's neck. Merely touching silver wouldn't hurt him. Its burning, draining effects were dormant unless silver broke a vampire's skin. "The effects of sunlight, crosses, wooden stakes, and holy water are red herrings my people deliberately planted along the millennia. Our real weakness is not something we allowed to become common knowledge."

"Silver," Kira said.

His brows rose. She couldn't see it, but she must have sensed his reaction, because she shrugged.

"That must be what those other, ah, vampires were using on you this morning. The knives didn't quite look like steel, but of course, they were so bloody . . ."

Her voice trailed off again and she looked away, biting her lip. Amidst the shocking silence of her mind, he caught a changing of her scent into something that reflected an emotion he was well acquainted with.

Regret.

She did wish she hadn't stepped in to help him this morning. Mencheres couldn't blame her, but to his surprise, he found that it actually . . . hurt.

By the gods, was he really saddened over what a stranger thought of him? He was over forty-five hundred years old! Perhaps it truly was time that he passed on from this world. Before he manifested other forms of what had to be undead senility.

"Those other men were not vampires," Mencheres corrected her coolly. "They belong to another race known as ghouls, or flesh-eaters."

It sounded like Kira gagged. "This morning I walked in on ghouls, who eat flesh, hacking away at a vampire who drinks blood. Is that what you're telling me?"

"Yes."

Now fear sharpened Kira's scent, and a fine tremble went through her limbs, but her spine stayed straight. "Is that what you're keeping me here for? To drink my blood?"

Mencheres couldn't stop himself from glancing at her throat with its temptingly rapid pulse before he replied.

"No. I told you—you have nothing to fear from me. I would have already returned you to your home except I am unable to erase your knowledge of this morning yet. Once my blood has left your system, and I can clear your mind of this, you will be freed. Until then, you will be unharmed. I give you my word."

That tremor slowed, but her heartbeat didn't stop its racing. "This is like a bad dream," Kira whispered. "You might promise not to harm me, but someone else brought me dinner, and I'm guessing he wasn't human, either. If you mean it when you say you don't want me harmed, you have to let me go. If not, I'm only safe until one of the other vampires around me gets an appetite."

Mencheres couldn't stop the snort that escaped him. "My word is law among my people. No one would dare to touch you without my permission, and I've expressly forbidden it. You are quite safe from anyone getting an 'appetite' around you, Kira."

She was silent for several moments. Mencheres concentrated on her mind, but it remained frustratingly elusive to him. Her scent wavered between mistrust and shock, though, telling him as much about her internal struggle to digest this information as her thoughts probably would.

Kira's distress was to be expected. Considering she'd started the day knowing nothing about the creatures that existed alongside humanity, then had almost been murdered by some of those creatures and was now held against her will by others, she'd shown remarkable strength. Mencheres had seen leaders of nations reduced to incoherent sobbing under lesser circumstances.

"Even if my life isn't in danger, I can't just stay here waiting for my mind to become malleable again," Kira said at last. "I have a job, and, ah, other very important responsibilities. Please don't misunderstand, I'm more than relieved that you're not intending to eat me, but I can't just disappear for several days. If you let me go, I'll go home, and I won't breathe a word to anyone about any of this."

"Is that where you were intending to go when you ran tonight?" Mencheres asked, his hand shooting out to stop Kira as she started to turn away. "And do *not* lie to me again."

Kira's face flushed as she met his gaze.

"I was headed for your nearest neighbor's house to call the police," she replied softly.

Mencheres dropped his hand from her face. "And that is why I cannot let you go while you remember anything about what you've seen."

"But that was *before*," Kira said insistently. "When I still thought you were going to kill me, so yes, the police sounded like my best option. But you've proven that I can't run off without you knowing, and you could clearly overpower me anytime. I can't imagine you'd go through the effort to lie to me this much if you just intended to kill me. And if you're not going to kill me, then you must not be the insatiable murderers legend paints you to be, so I don't need to warn humanity about you. Yes, you killed those people who were torturing you; but that's justifiable homicide in any court, so there's no need for me to tell anyone anything."

Kira's voice had risen in her agitation, and her pulse accelerated again. Mencheres said nothing, knowing she was trying to reconcile the facts out loud more than anything else. It was always frightening for humans when they realized their belief in the superiority of their race was false. When they realized how vulnerable they truly were to the other species that shared the dark with them.

"Besides," she said at last, expelling the word on a ragged sigh. "No matter how many people I'd tell, who would believe me? I'd never believed any of the clients who used to talk about weird, impossible things, and I heard more than a few of those stories as a private investigator . . ."

Kira's eyes widened even as she stopped talking in midsentence. Mencheres couldn't hear the thoughts form in her mind, but from her expression, she was realizing some of the stories she'd summarily dismissed might have been true. Then she looked around the darkened yard as if seeing it with new eyes, her breath hitching.

Mencheres watched with pity, knowing it was the moment Kira truly accepted that all of this was real. The small part of her that still hoped there was another explanation had finally given up. He'd observed this same mental surrender in humans before, too many times to count, and though Kira might believe she could return to a normal life with this information, Mencheres knew she couldn't.

"You do not want this knowledge," he said, his voice

quiet but firm. "It will destroy your life. You will see every shadow in a different way, and every strange sound will make you wonder—is that a person, or a monster? Humans who are not part of a vampire's or ghoul's line do not do well with this information. Time has proven that repeatedly."

What he didn't tell Kira was that time also proved that such humans usually ended up dead. Eventually, those mortals tried to make *someone* believe them about the supernatural world, and an unclaimed human spreading tales about the undead was a threat to both species. Both vampires and ghouls did claim a certain number of humans as property, but those humans were specially chosen, then removed from their own world. They lived with their undead protectors in full knowledge that if they spilled the secret about either species to mainstream society, they would be eliminated.

Such knowledge wouldn't reassure Kira, however, so Mencheres kept it to himself. He really didn't want her climbing out of any more windows in the future.

"You'll let me go unharmed?" she asked at last, seeming to come to a decision.

"As soon as I remove these memories from your mind," Mencheres promised.

She gave him a measuring look. "I'll need to call my boss, make some excuse about missing work. I can't afford to get fired."

"I'll see to it that your employment situation is taken care of." But Mencheres wasn't about to let her call her employer even under his watchful eye. Kira worked for a private investigator; the line could be traced, or she could use code words indicating danger that Mencheres might not recognize. He would like to hope that Kira wouldn't do such a thing in light of her new capitulation, but he was too jaded to trust in hope.

"I need to call my sister." Her voice hardened in a way that it hadn't when Kira spoke of her job. "She's not well. I can't let her worry my disappearing without telling her something."

Mencheres inclined his head. "I will make arrangements for you to speak with her tomorrow."

Kira took in a long breath and let it out slowly. "All right. How long should it take until you can erase my memories?"

He mentally calculated how much blood he'd given Kira. It had been several swallows at least, and his blood was very potent. "A few days at minimum, a week at most."

She winced but didn't reply. Again, Mencheres was impressed with her fortitude. Kira had attempted to run away and had repeatedly argued with him to let her go, but she hadn't resorted to begging or hysterics. What sort of person was she, to make her so unusually strong in the face of such trying circumstances?

If he still had his visions, he could look into the future and see exactly what kind of person Kira was. Nothing revealed character more than seeing the culmination of a lifetime's worth of decisions. But Mencheres couldn't see the future anymore. He drove back his immediate flash of anger at that. Railing at the gods over what they gave— and then took back—was useless.

"All right," Kira said again, bringing his attention back to her. "I can't believe I'll be spending up to a week with *vampires*, but . . . all right."

Mencheres hid a smile, his mood lightening as he saw the wry way Kira shook her head. She wasn't the only person surprised at this recent turn of events. A part of him also couldn't believe he'd just committed himself to being housebound with the same human who had ruined his plans this morning.

"Are you ready to go inside now?" Mencheres asked, offering her his arm.

Kira's mouth curled as she took it after a moment of hesitation. "I guess so. Tell me, vampire, what's your name?"

What was one more thing to erase from her mind? "Mencheres."

"Sounds Spanish," she murmured, looking him over as best she could in the dark.

"Egyptian." Yet another detail he'd have to erase from her later. What was it about Kira that made him so uncharacteristically talkative?

"Ah." She smiled then, the first one he'd seen that didn't look forced. "So, Mencheres the Egyptian vampire, are you really old, or are you as young as you look?"

He gave her a sideways look as he began walking back toward the house, feeling the oddest pang as he contemplated their age difference. "I'm older than dirt," he answered dryly.

"A vampire with a sense of humor. I *really* didn't know that existed," she quipped with equal dryness.

Mencheres didn't answer. First, he was telling her things he had no reason to reveal, now he was joking about his age. How strange. He'd thought his sense of humor had expired a long time ago.

"I suppose putting that room back together will give me something to do for the next few hours," Kira noted with a sigh.

"That is not necessary, you'll . . . stay in another room."

Mencheres almost tripped as he bit back the words that had so nearly crossed his lips: *You'll stay in my room.* What possessed him even to think such a thing? He hadn't found his sense of humor—he'd lost his mind.

Undead senility. There weren't very many vampires left who were older than he was. Maybe it was an actual condition after all.

Chapter Four

Kira awoke with her heart pounding, her arms lashing out against an attacker who wasn't there. For several panicked seconds, she couldn't seem to merge reality with the image of that *thing* tearing open her stomach. Then she fell back against the pillows, panting. *Just a nightmare, only a nightmare.*

Except it was more than that. Kira willed her breathing to slow as she counted backward from thirty. By the time she'd reached one, her heart had stopped racing, and she was no longer gasping. Another set of backward counting took care of the tremble in her hands. By the third set, Kira could get out of bed without constant images of the ghoul's face bombarding her mind. *He's dead, he can't hurt you anymore,* she reminded herself firmly.

Besides, though the circumstances were different, this wasn't the first time someone had attacked her, yet she'd survived. Those awful memories might show up again in her dreams, but she wasn't about to give her attacker's ghosts—either of them—power over her once she was awake.

And soon, her memory of this recent assault would be erased, courtesy of a strangely formal, lethally powerful vampire named Mencheres. Of all the assaults she had to stumble upon on the way to her apartment, who would believe she'd come across one involving creatures who weren't supposed to exist? *No one, that's who,* Kira thought darkly. Hell, she'd *seen* it, was living proof with her stomach miraculously healed, and still she had a hard time grasping that all of this was real.

Vampires. Ghouls. What other creatures existed that weren't supposed to be real? Kira shuddered. Maybe Mencheres was right. She'd probably live a much happier life if she didn't remember any of this.

Oddly enough, she *did* expect to get out of this alive. After their exchange last night, Kira believed Mencheres when he said he'd let her go. It could just be part of vampire allure, but all of Kira's instincts said that Mencheres was trustworthy, and her instincts had never been wrong—even when she'd desperately wanted them to be.

Vampires who didn't murder innocent people. It was almost as incredible a revelation as vampires' existence. Ghouls seemed to be a much crueler species, at least from what Kira had seen. What those creatures had done to Mencheres had been horrifying, and they'd certainly shown her no mercy. If Mencheres hadn't stopped them, then healed her, she wouldn't have lasted five minutes after walking into that warehouse . . .

Kira froze in midstride to the bathroom as a question that had been buried under an avalanche of shock finally surfaced in her mind.

If Mencheres could stop those ghouls so easily, why hadn't he done it *before* she arrived?

Mencheres felt Gorgon approach before his image appeared through the haze of water above him. He gave a mental sigh as he rose from his comfortable position at the bottom of the swimming pool. Being underwater was one of the few times he could enjoy relative quiet. The layers of water muted the sounds from the mortals in his house, and being enclosed in it had become a sort of meditation.

"Sire," Gorgon said, once Mencheres had surfaced. "Your human is requesting to speak with you."

Mencheres's gaze flicked behind Gorgon to Kira, whose expression said she didn't care for the term "your human." Once again, Mencheres probed at Kira's mind, and once again, he came up against a thick wall. The barest hint of confusion threaded through her scent, but the bewildering, impressive barriers that prevented him from hearing Kira's thoughts as easily as he heard her heartbeat were still there.

"Bring her forward," Mencheres said, balancing his arms against the side of the pool.

"Tinted glass," were Kira's first words as Gorgon beckoned her forward. "I thought you said vampires had no aversion to sunlight?"

Mencheres glanced around the enclosed pool area with a slight shrug. "Sunlight does not harm us as legends claim, but prolonged exposure does sap our strength, and we tend to sunburn easily."

Why am I explaining that to her? he wondered in the

next moment. Every word he uttered to Kira would only be erased from her recall later. It was as senseless as speaking to the wind.

She sat a few feet from the pool's edge, folding her legs underneath her as if she were at a picnic. "Why not have real walls around your pool? Concrete blocks a lot more sunlight than opaque glass."

Mencheres gave a small, grim smile. "Because sometimes I enjoy things regardless if they are beneficial to me or not."

Speaking to Kira was another of those unbeneficial things he seemed to enjoy, because here he was, still answering her questions despite there being no sense in it.

Kira tilted her head, the muted sunlight highlighting the gold in her hair. She had on denim pants and a collared blouse that was a fraction too tight. Mencheres made a mental note to arrange for new clothes for Kira during her stay. She was wearing some of Selene's now, but Selene's breasts weren't as generous as Kira's.

Mencheres's gaze lingered on her chest until Kira crossed her arms over it with obvious annoyance. She gave him a pointed look as his gaze traveled upward to meet hers. He glanced away, almost chuckling at this unexpected absurdity from him. How many centuries had it been since he'd been caught ogling a woman's breasts? A woman's *clothed* breasts, no less. His co-ruler, Bones, would fracture a rib laughing if he knew.

"Some things must never change," Kira muttered under her breath.

Mencheres found himself smiling. "It appears they do not."

Kira brushed a hand through her hair, giving him another feminine, censuring look before her expression became serious.

"Why didn't you stop those ghouls yesterday before I showed up? You–"

"Quiet," Mencheres said instantly. Gorgon had walked away out of eyesight, but he could still hear her.

"I've thought it over, but it makes no sense," Kira went on, completely ignoring his order to be quiet. For a stunned second, Mencheres didn't know how to react. It had to be centuries at least since a human had dared to ignore his commands. "You didn't even need to touch them to—whoa!"

He'd vaulted out of the pool to physically stop Kira from uttering more damning sentences by putting his finger to her mouth. Water dripped onto her clothes, and her pale green eyes widened as he loomed over her.

"Never speak about that again," Mencheres said, his voice soft but steely. He couldn't mesmerize her into silence, but if need be, he would gag Kira so Gorgon didn't find out about Mencheres's thwarted plan with the ghouls yesterday.

Her heartbeat had accelerated the moment he leapt from the water, and it stayed elevated when she looked away from his face at the rest of his body. Then she gasped.

Her warm breath vibrated against the finger he still held to her lips. Kira gasped again as her gaze dragged from his shoulders to his feet, then became fixated at the point between his legs. Abruptly, Mencheres's dark mood over her nearly spilling his secret changed to amusement when Kira didn't seem to be able to tear her eyes away.

When the vampire burst from the water to crouch over her, Kira's first thought had been, *Uh-oh.* She hadn't even seen him move before he was upon her, black eyes blazing with warning, water dripping down onto her. That single finger to her lips felt like a mini hammer, and Kira reminded herself that on the food chain, he was a preda-tor, and she was prey. *He* really *doesn't like this topic, so I'll shut up now,* had been her very logical decision.

Then she'd looked down—and forgotten what she'd started to ask him about. Beads of water caressed down the hardest, tightest body she's ever seen. Mencheres's chest, arms, and stomach were corded with an intricate pattern of muscles that seemed too flawless to be real. His lightly tinted skin only emphasized how black his hair was, dripping in dark rivers past his shoulders. At some point since yesterday, he'd cut the uneven pieces so it was all the same length now. Her gaze swept lower, reveal-ing that his legs were as deliciously sculpted as the rest of him. Nothing interrupted her view of his taut, rippled flesh, either, because Mencheres had been swimming naked. Kira was surprised to see that he was hairless ev-erywhere, even between his thighs . . .

Kira's eyes fastened there, widening. *Oh. My.* If the vampire hadn't still had a finger to her lips, she would have licked them in reflex.

"Some things must never change," a deep voice noted, as his finger left her lips to raise her chin.

Kira reluctantly tore her gaze away to meet Mencheres's dark eyes. They were devoid of his former anger, and the corners of his mouth twitched. Her distracted mind fi-nally translated that he'd repeated her earlier chastising remark, and she laughed.

"Guilty," she admitted, resisting the urge to drop her gaze again. No wonder the vampire didn't wear swim shorts.

He smiled as he sat back. "One could argue that I had it coming."

He reached behind him, pulling a white towel off a nearby chair and settling it around his hips with a casual unhurriedness that said the action was more for manners than modesty. Kira gave her head a slight shake. At least now with him covered below the waist, she should be able to keep her train of thought.

Of course, her initial train of thought was what had sent him catapulting out of the pool to silence her. Something about yesterday had Mencheres so spooked, he refused to discuss it with her. Was it simply that he'd been so close to being eaten by ghouls? Did he not want to remember how helpless he'd been? He hadn't seemed embarrassed about it yesterday when she'd first woken up, but maybe that changed. Delayed traumatic reaction, or something similar. She'd had experience with that before.

Either way, it was clearly a delicate subject, and though all her investigative instincts were burning with curiosity, she wanted her freedom more. It seemed common sense that keeping in Mencheres's good graces was directly related to his letting her go, so she'd drop the subject of his bewildering failure to free himself before. Getting back to her life was more important than finding out why a frighteningly powerful vampire had almost died at the hands of several ghouls that he'd later killed without even needing to touch them.

"You said that I could call my sister," Kira reminded him, changing the subject.

He rose with the same quicksilver grace that all his movements seemed to have. "So I did. Come."

Mencheres held out his hand, and Kira took it, letting him draw her to her feet. She glanced down at her borrowed shirt and pants, feeling them stick to her in places from the pool water Mencheres had dripped onto her.

He held out his towel without the slightest hesitation that it was the only thing covering him. "Please, use this."

Just like when she'd dangled from that rope outside the house, Kira told herself not to look down. "Ah, no thanks. I think you need it more than I do."

His mouth quirked again, as if he were fighting back a smile. Kira felt that touch of surrealism once more. She couldn't *really* be standing by a pool next to a naked vampire who was offering her his towel so she could blot her damp jeans and shirt, could she? So much of what had happened in the past thirty-some hours had a dreamlike quality to it. All she needed to make this scenario more unbelievable would be for leprechauns to come somersaulting out of the nearby garden.

Or for the gorgeously bare vampire to give her a sensual massage while feeding her peeled grapes. Then she'd *know* this was a dream. But because Mencheres was belting the long towel back around his waist instead of throwing it to the ground while he went in search of fruits and scented oils, Kira supposed this was reality. A bizarre, sometimes terrifying, sometimes titillating reality, but reality nonetheless.

And her memories of it would only be temporary. In some ways, that was the strangest part of this whole thing. How could she simply not remember *any* of this in a week? Wouldn't some lingering knowledge remain? Like, she'd experience déjà vu whenever she saw a vampire movie in the future?

"There is no need for you to be concerned," Mencheres said quietly. "Your life will continue on without any ill effects from this experience."

"Are you able to read my mind now?" Kira asked, feeling embarrassment rise. "Because if so, about that massage . . ."

His brow ticked upward. "I still cannot read your thoughts, but your scent and expression led me to surmise that you were thinking about your future. I would, however, like to hear about the massage."

"I've, um, got a kink in my shoulder," Kira said, glancing away.

A soft laugh. "Humans emit a distinct scent when they lie, and you, Kira, smell of that scent now."

Kira turned back around with a challenging look. He wanted the truth? All right, then. Mencheres might be a powerful vampire; but she was a grown woman, so she wasn't about to act like a timid, *blind* virgin.

"Dead or not, you must be bored with women telling you how you look like the hottest, most exotic wet dream they've ever had. No wonder the thought of you, grapes, and some scented massage oils crossed my mind—and if you drop that towel again, I'm going to need a cold shower."

Kira expected a smug smile in return. Maybe a knowing glance down and a wink, too. But Mencheres's expression could only be described as . . . surprised. Then it became carefully blank.

"You know nothing about me."

She stiffened. Was that his way of telling her she was shallow? Oh please, he'd flaunted his looks by walking around naked—now she was cheap because she'd noticed them?

"Don't worry. I think Mount Everest is gorgeous, too, but that doesn't mean I have any intention of trying to climb it."

"I do not understand this analogy," Mencheres muttered.

Kira let out a sigh. "Let's just keep this subject in the same 'do not discuss' category you want your actions yesterday under."

Pinpoints of green flared in his charcoal-colored eyes, reminding Kira that what she'd said was akin to yanking a tiger by the tail. But for the strangest reason, Kira wasn't afraid of Mencheres. He might be a predator who could kill her with laughable ease, but Mencheres also had an aura of complete control about him. Even when he'd leapt from the pool to shush her, she'd been startled, but every instinct said he wouldn't break his promise not to harm her.

Although, if he hadn't given his word about that, Kira would be terrified of him. All that astonishing ability combined with an iron will made Mencheres more than deadly—it practically made him a force of nature. Someone who could rip the heads off other supernatural creatures without using his hands, who could heal her life-threatening injury, could fly, *and* make her forget that any of it had happened? Mencheres might not frighten her as much as he should, but knowing that power like his existed was scary.

What if all vampires could do the same things he could, but they weren't as disciplined as Mencheres about not killing humans? The ghouls yesterday would've made lunch out of both of them, so clearly, not all supernaturals operated under a strict moral code. Those missing-person case files with strange stories attached to them flashed in Kira's mind. What if those disappearances weren't just related to sinister human activity but something else?

Kira glanced up to see Mencheres studying her with palpable intensity. Was he trying to see into her mind again? Was he succeeding? She almost hoped he was. If he could read her thoughts, then erasing her memory couldn't be far behind, which meant she could go home.

"Any luck tuning in?" she asked.

Chapter Five

Kira paced around her room. Tina hadn't answered when she tried calling her earlier. She could just be out, but what if something happened and her sister was too ill to get the phone? Kira debated asking Mencheres to send Gorgon around to Tina's apartment to check on her. According to Mencheres, the blond vampire was already stopping by her office today to somehow mind-manipulate Frank into believing that Kira was unable to come into work because of the flu. Kira had her doubts that the vampire could make her hard-nosed boss okay with her suddenly taking a week off, but Mencheres seemed confident in Gorgon's abilities.

Her gut wasn't sensing any menace from Gorgon, just like it hadn't with Mencheres, but maybe that was part of a vampire's natural camouflage. Nothing helped predators more than their prey's thinking they were harmless. Kira wasn't about to risk exposing her sister to a vampire, even if Gorgon was harmless and it would set her mind at ease to have Gorgon report that Tina was fine.

She'd just have to try calling her sister later. Mencheres didn't seem to be so draconian that he'd only allow her one call, regardless if she reached Tina or not. For an undead captor, in fact, Mencheres was turning out to be pretty accommodating. He'd told Kira she could have free rein of the house, pool, and the surrounding garden—as long as she didn't try to make any unsupervised calls, e-mails, texts, or attempt to run away again. Her shackles would be velvet-lined, apparently. How odd. She'd been in harsher captive circumstances when she was married.

Kira brushed aside the thought as quickly as it had come. That chapter of her life was closed, and everything she'd seen in the decade since had just served to reinforce that she'd done the only thing she could. *Survival.* Sometimes it wasn't noble or pretty, but it was necessary.

Her stomach growled, reminding Kira that she'd only had a banana for breakfast and nothing at all to eat the day before. Mencheres told her to help herself to whatever was in the refrigerator, actually sounding apologetic when he said she'd have to prepare her own food.

Velvet shackles, indeed.

Kira strode out of the bedroom, heading for the kitchen. Time to see if Mencheres meant it when he said she'd have free run of the house.

She went down the staircase, pausing on the landing of the second floor. Her bedroom was on the third floor, and though there were two more doors in her hallway, she hadn't heard anyone else on her floor. If Mencheres was up there, he was very quiet. Or was his room on the second floor? Aside from her, Gorgon, and Mencheres, she hadn't seen anyone else in the house. Were they the only ones here? If so, why did Mencheres need such a big place, if it was normally just him and Gorgon?

And either Mencheres was the most unsentimental person *ever,* or he hadn't been here long. The house had no personal photos or memorabilia that Kira had seen, and it had that cold, model-home perfection that spoke of habitual emptiness. If this wasn't Mencheres's main home, why was he here now? And where did he live when he wasn't here?

Laughter jerked Kira's attention away from curiosity over her mysterious captor. It had a distinctly feminine lilt to it, correcting Kira's assumption that she, Mencheres, and Gorgon were the only ones in the house. Kira went down the last flight of stairs almost cautiously, hearing a masculine chuckle next. A peculiar twinge went through her. Was that Mencheres? If so, who was the woman he was laughing with? His girlfriend?

Or wife, perhaps? The vampire wore no wedding ring, but who knew if that meant anything? Maybe vampires didn't do ring exchanges.

Kira squared her shoulders and followed the sounds. At least they came from where she was already headed—the kitchen. No need for an excuse to go in there; her growling stomach would explain her presence. But when Kira caught her first glimpse of the people clustered around the dinette table, she didn't recognize any of them.

Conversation stopped as Kira entered, and they looked up at her. From the food in front of them, Kira surmised that the two men and one woman were human. More witnesses kept against their will? Kira wondered. Good Lord, did Mencheres have a stable of people held captive who'd inadvertently found out about vampires? A tremor went through her. Maybe everything Mencheres had said was a lie. Maybe he had no intention of *ever* letting her go.

"Hi," the blond woman said in a cheerful way, waving over at the stove. "There's some eggs and bacon left over, if you're hungry."

"'S up," the dark-haired male said, to an accompanying friendly grunt from the sandy-haired guy whose mouth was full.

Kira blinked at their greeting. If these three were prisoners, they sure seemed relaxed about it.

"Thanks," she managed, heading over to the stove more for something to do as she pondered this new development. Kira glanced around. No signs of Gorgon or Mencheres, but that didn't mean they weren't nearby.

She scraped the leftover eggs and bacon from the two pans onto a plate, then sat at the remaining empty chair at the dinette table. Three sets of eyes regarded her curiously.

"I'm Kira, by the way," she said, wondering how to discreetly find out if they were being held against their will.

"We know," the black-haired guy replied, with a slight grin. "Name's Sam, and this is Selene and Kurt."

Kira chewed some eggs, trying to appear casual. "You know, huh?" she remarked once she'd swallowed. "What do you know?"

"That you're not staying here long, and that you're not thrilled about the time you are spending here," Selene summarized with that same sunny smile.

Kira swallowed another bite of eggs before replying. "And you are, ah, thrilled about the time you spend here?" she asked carefully.

"Beats working a nine-to-five," Kurt said, speaking for the first time.

The three of them laughed at that. Kira blinked. They

were here willingly? Did they not know what Mencheres and Gorgon were? Mencheres had sounded so confident about his ability to mesmerize humans under normal circumstances. Was it possible that these three had no idea their other "roommates" were vampires?

"So, are you three self-employed, then?" Kira asked, wanting to keep them talking.

More chuckling. "You could say that," Sam replied. He leaned back, balancing himself on the back two legs of his chair. At a glance, Kira guessed he was in his early twenties. All of them looked younger than she was, in fact.

Come to think of it, so did Mencheres, despite his "older than dirt" comment. Maybe she was wrong. Maybe these three weren't human. They were eating regular food, yes, but so far most of Kira's assumptions about vampires had proven to be wrong. Maybe vampires ate three square meals a day just like everyone else—except they followed up those meals with a blood chaser. Kira looked them over as surreptitiously as she could while she pushed her eggs around on her plate. Selene, Kurt, and Sam appeared normal in every way . . . but so did Mencheres. Right up until he started moving like greased lightning or ripping heads off people.

"How did you meet Mencheres?" Kira settled on asking.

Selene shrugged. "I was turning tricks for meth back in 'Frisco several years ago when Mencheres rolled up on my pimp knocking me around. He drank him, then asked me if I wanted a new life. I did. So Mencheres took me with him, got me off the drugs, and here I am."

Kira had heard far-more-sordid tales as a P.I., but she almost gaped at how casually Selene relayed a tale of drug addiction, prostitution, and murder to a complete stranger. Before she could even say anything, Sam spoke up.

"I was a Legacy. Used to belong to Tick Tock, but he died in the war over a year ago. Mencheres was Tick Tock's Master, so he inherited all his property when Tick Tock died, me included."

"Master? Mencheres considers you his *slave*?" Kira blurted, aghast.

Sam gave her a look. "Not Master like that, lady. Master of the line of vampires Tick Tock came from. If you're a human who belongs to a vamp, you're considered their property, but I can walk away from this anytime I want to. I'm no one's damn slave, got it?"

"I'm more like you, Kira," Kurt said, breaking up the tense moment. "Didn't know about vampires until I stumbled across some by accident, but I decided to stay because they were safer than the gang I ran with."

Kira's mind spun with this new information. Selene, Sam, and Kurt knew exactly what Mencheres was, yet they all stayed with him willingly. Or did they? Had Mencheres manipulated their minds to make them think they'd *chosen* to be here? Was he waiting to do the same thing with her? What if she were thinking Mencheres's ability to erase her memory was her ticket home, but in reality, she was giving him the ability to lock her up forever?

It was such an ugly thought that Kira felt bile rise in her throat. Her instincts, which had been her flawless compass for the past dozen years, might not be trustworthy when it came to Mencheres. If vampires could manipulate minds, then it stood to reason they could alter someone's gut reaction to them, too.

Kira looked around at the kitchen and the three people seated in it. On the surface, everything was the picture of

normalcy, but scratch the surface, and all of that disappeared.

Just like her trust in the instincts that assured her
Mencheres meant it when he said he'd let her go.

Kira stood up, barely managing to keep her hands from
shaking. "Nice to meet all of you," she got out.

Then she quickly left the kitchen to go into the garden,
feeling as if the walls were closing in on her.

Mencheres strolled past the pool toward the garden, drawn
toward Kira's heartbeat as if it were a beacon. She was on
the far edge of the garden, sitting in the lower branches
of a tree, of all things. A breeze carried her scent to him,
that lemony fragrance tainted with fear, confusion, and
anger.

He sat on a concrete bench at the opposite side of the
small garden, wondering what caused Kira's sudden shift
in mood. She'd seemed fine this morning as he listened
to her move about her room. Then nothing in the conversation he'd overheard between her and the others in
the kitchen should have alarmed her, but Kira had gone
straight into the garden afterward and stayed there the
past three hours. Was it normal chafing at the circumstances that necessitated her being here? Or was it something else?

He shouldn't care. It was utter madness that he'd come
out here to sit on this bench in the hopes that Kira would
tell him what was bothering her. After all, if he were
being logical, he'd concern himself with crucial matters
instead of with a woman who would soon not remember
him.

That breeze lifted her scent to him again, tantalizing
him with the invisible caress of her on his senses. *Then*

again, what was the harm in a little pleasant madness?
Mencheres decided, breathing in Kira's fragrance. At
this point in his life, hadn't he earned the right not to
make *every* last decision based on cold, unfeeling logic?

His attention snapped away from Kira when something else swept over Mencheres's senses. Something old,
strong, and vindictive. He straightened, already coiling
his emotions back into their familiar, impermeable shell
by the time he heard Gorgon answer the door.

"I am here to see Mencheres," an all-too-familiar voice
stated.

"Guardian," Gorgon replied, with the proper amount
of respect his enemy's station warranted. "I shall let him
know you're here."

Laughter rolled from Radjedef like quiet thunder. "He
knows, boy."

Mencheres kept the anger that flickered in him tamped
down to undetectable levels. Radjedef could only guess
that his derisive treatment of his people angered him; if
Mencheres gave him proof, the Law Guardian would increase his insulting behavior. Radjedef knew the protec-
tions his status gave him and exploited every one of them
when it came to Mencheres.

If he wouldn't have been the very *first* suspect in Radjedef's disappearance, Mencheres would have done away
with his old enemy thousands of years ago. But that was
the problem. Their history went back so far, everyone
knew about it.

And if Radjedef were anything except a Law Guardian,
Mencheres would have risked it regardless.

Gorgon came into the garden. Radjedef, as expected,
followed after him instead of waiting to be announced.

"Sire, you have a visitor," Gorgon said.

"Thank you," Mencheres replied. Gorgon turned

around, heading back to the house before the Law Guardian could bark at him to leave. This wasn't the first time Gorgon had dealt with Radjedef.

"Menkaure," Radjedef said, calling Mencheres by the name he'd been born with. "I am surprised you didn't try to hide your location from me."

"I weary of our games, Radje," Mencheres said, using the abbreviated name Radjedef had hated as a boy.

His enemy's lip twitched so subtly, no one else might have caught it. But Mencheres did, and he gave an inward smile. After four and a half millennia, Radjedef still couldn't quite let go of his childhood insecurities. If he had, they might have met today as friends instead of adversaries.

"No one delights in games as much as you," Radjedef replied coolly, taking a seat next to Mencheres without invitation. His hand swept in the direction of the house. "Such squalid accommodations. Are you doing some form of penance by staying here?"

Mencheres lifted a bored brow. "Even you would not come merely to mock my current residence."

Radjedef smiled. "I have been speaking to many sources, my old friend. Such terrible things they say about you. Repeated theft of property. Murder. Imprisonment. Witchcraft. How many laws do you think you've broken this year alone?"

"If you had credible sources, you would be asking me this in front of the council of Guardians, not by yourself," Mencheres replied in an even tone. "You cannot prove any of this. You never could. Find a new pastime, Radje. I hear Wii is extremely entertaining."

"Everyone knows you killed your wife by raising wraiths through black magic and sending them after her," Radjedef said sharply.

Mencheres just shrugged. "If everyone says that, then your proof should be easy to obtain."

"You know that all those who witnessed Patra's slaying are loyal to *you*," Radje said with a flash of naked bitterness.

As for Mencheres using wraiths to kill his wife . . . it hadn't exactly happened that way. But the fact that the most serious charge Radjedef could bring against Mencheres was mostly true, yet it benefited Radjedef nothing, was almost enough to make Mencheres smile.

Almost.

"What will you do, Radje, when I am no longer here for you to center your hatred on?"

A gleam appeared in Radjedef's black eyes. "I have no intention of killing you, old friend. That would not give me what I seek—and it would be too merciful for you."

"You might find me gone regardless if it is what you seek," Mencheres muttered in a rare moment of unguarded honesty.

Radje smiled. "My heart twists in my chest at the thought."

Not as much as it would if I struck silver through it, Mencheres mused darkly. But such a thought, while tempting, would carry with it too many repercussions. Law Guardians were the highest ruling body among vampires. Mencheres might be able to kill another Master vampire with only the risk of war between himself and that vampire's allies, but if he killed a Law Guardian, *all* vampires would have cause to unite against him. After the last few wars he'd been in, Mencheres had too many enemies who would relish his making such a stupid mistake, but he wouldn't. Not when Bones and others he loved would have to face the consequences.

"I *am* weary," Mencheres said. In that moment, he felt

the weight of all his years pressing on him; the countless strife, guilt, and toil swelling with merciless relent-
lessness. Suddenly, he wanted Radjedef to know that his
schemes for an elaborate vengeance would never come to
pass. "You should have struck at me before, old friend.
When I still had the desire to give you the fight you
sought."

Something passed across the Law Guardian's face, as
if he just now realized Mencheres wasn't feigning his
apathy.

"You would never abandon your people, Menkaure."

Amidst his mental exhaustion, Mencheres felt a glim-
mer of satisfaction. Did Radje finally grasp that his
chances for revenge were slipping away?

"That is true, which is why I gave Bones the gift of my
power when I merged my line with his."

"Power that should have been *mine* to begin with!" Radjedef exclaimed, showing more emotion than Mencheres
had seen from him in centuries.

"Still you lament that?" Mencheres scoffed. "It was our
sire's choice who he gifted his additional power to, just as
it was my choice to give my power surplus to Bones. Even
now, Bones grows more into his strength, and his wife
Cat's powers grow as well. Radje, Radje . . ." Mencheres
allowed himself a small, thin smile. "You waited too
long."

Radje stood so violently that the concrete bench crumpled beneath him. He paced in a short, furious stride
before stopping with the same abruptness.

"You lie," Radje said, perfect control in his voice now.
"You seek to deceive me as you have always done, but I
know you. You would never do such a thing."

If Radje had made such a statement even a year ago,
it would have been true. But with Mencheres's wife

dead, Bones strong enough to lead their combined lines, Cat transitioned into the rarest type of vampire, and Mencheres's visions gone . . . he had no reason to stay. His death would end his cold war with Radjedef, denying his enemy the opportunity to bring down Mencheres's line along with him.

For thousands of years, Radje had sought to hurt him through his people, but his attempts had been hampered by Mencheres's visions. With those gone, the Law Guardian would attack those belonging to Mencheres without mercy. But Mencheres had no intention of letting that happen. He'd leave this world knowing he'd secured his people's safety and thwarted Radje in one stroke. It was something he almost looked forward to.

Except for Kira. She alone remained to keep him alive, but the sands ran ever faster through that hourglass as well. Soon, Kira's memories of him would be gone—and then he would be free to go. In his rest, Mencheres would achieve a victory over Radje for all eternity. It made his smile widen as he stared at the Law Guardian.

"You know me, Radje? Then you should fear."

A branch snapping brought Mencheres's attention back to Kira. She'd abandoned her perch in the tree to slide down the trunk to the ground. She glanced in their direction, her heart rate accelerating. Guessing, no doubt, that her descent had been overheard.

"Who is that human?" Radje snapped, whipping around to glare at Kira.

Mencheres chuckled. "You are so arrogant that you just now noticed a woman in the garden with us?"

"That heartbeat could have belonged to a dog, for all that you love to surround yourself with curs," Radje said coldly.

Mencheres stiffened at the insulting way Radje referred to Kira. Then he forced himself to relax when he saw the Law Guardian's eyes narrow. Too late. Radjedef had noticed.

"Bring this human forth," Radje said, staring at Mencheres.

Refusing would make Radjedef even more intrigued about who she was. Mencheres assumed a bored expression as he called out, "Kira! Come."

She slowly made her way through the garden toward them, glancing around as if seeking out possible exits. Mencheres showed no reaction as Radjedef slid his eyes over Kira in a way that left no curve of her body missed.

"Pretty," Radje said, drawing the word out. Then he smiled. "Not as pretty as your dead wife, though, is she?"

Mencheres kept his face blank and his limbs loose, appearing as relaxed as he was when he rested on the bottom of the pool. Thankfully, Kira didn't rise to Radjedef's bait. She looked at the other vampire for a long moment but didn't say anything.

"Don't you speak?" Radje asked, losing his patience.

"Sure," Kira replied in a perfectly neutral tone. "But you weren't talking to me before."

Her scent betrayed her nervousness, but aside from that, Kira was the picture of assurance as she stood before the glaring gaze of the ancient Law Guardian. From the narrowing of his gaze, Radjedef didn't like her cool composure.

"I suddenly find that I'm thirsty," Radje said, his voice lowering to a menacing purr. "This human will do."

Radjedef moved, his hand closing around Kira's arm before she could even flinch . . . and then his whole body froze.

Mencheres slowly tightened his power around the Law Guardian until nothing twitched on his old enemy except his mouth. Kira's eyes were wide as she stepped away from Radje, but she didn't run. Smart.

"You dare to assault me?" Radjedef hissed.

"If I assaulted you, you'd be missing your head," Mencheres responded coldly. "Yet I am well within my rights to stop you from putting your hands on one of my people without my permission, *Guardian.*"

Radje's gaze burned with the promise of vengeance, but both of them knew it was futile. He wasn't strong enough to break Mencheres's hold, and the laws were on Mencheres's side. He allowed himself another moment to enjoy Radje's helplessness before releasing him from the hold of his power.

As soon as he could move, Radjedef backed away from Kira as though she were a snake. Then he caught himself, glaring at both of them.

Mencheres smiled. Kira hadn't moved since she'd detached her arm from Radje's frozen grip, showing more poise than the ancient Law Guardian. From Radje's furious expression before he schooled his features into blankness, he knew he'd been shown up by her.

Radjedef flicked his hand in a dismissive gesture at Kira. "I've seen enough of her."

Mencheres glanced at the house, and Kira turned around without a word, leaving the garden. His respect for her grew once again. If she'd panicked before, or argued with the Law Guardian over his deliberate, baiting treatment of her now, Mencheres might have been forced to punish her—which was what Radjedef wanted. But her poise left Radjedef with nothing to do but simmer in his own impotence. The very laws he could have invoked to punish Kira kept him from being able to do anything now.

And once Kira was safely back home and Mencheres was gone, both of them would be forever past Radjedef's bitter reach. Mencheres smiled again at his old enemy.

"You know the way out, Radje."

Chapter Six

Two days passed. Kira watched more TV than she'd seen in the last month, plus sunned by the pool, something she hadn't done in, well, she couldn't remember how long. Who would've thought this was how she'd spend her time as a prisoner in a house with *vampires*? Still, she didn't have much else to do. Every time she left her room, she knew she was being politely shadowed by Gorgon, which was equal parts unnerving and annoying. She hadn't seen Selene, Kurt, or Sam since that afternoon in the kitchen. Kira hoped they hadn't gotten into trouble for talking to her. None of them had seemed to be afraid of their circumstances, but again, Kira had only seen the surface of life among the undead. Much more might be lurking within the depths, and chances were, a lot of it wasn't pretty.

Kira also hadn't seen Mencheres since the day he'd had that ominous visitor. She shivered at the memory of Radje, as Mencheres had called him. So much for her thought that all vampires gave off a calming aura as part of their camouflage. As soon as she'd seen Radje, her instincts went into overdrive with alarms of "danger, danger!" Her short time in the garden with him had been like standing near a rabid pit bull—any sudden moves, her gut warned her, would result in a vicious attack.

And that was *before* the cold-eyed bastard had tried to bite her. Kira was beyond relieved that Mencheres made good on his vow that no one could touch her while she was with him. When Radje stared at her while Mencheres somehow managed to freeze him into place, she'd felt waves of malevolence pouring off him. He hadn't just wanted to bite her, she could tell. He'd wanted to hurt and humiliate her even though she was someone he'd never met before.

Even though she hoped never to see him again, coming across Radje had relieved some of Kira's anxiety. Even staring at him from her perch in the tree before his vicious display in the garden, something about Radje had put her off. That proved her instincts could still transmit danger warnings, even with vampires. It gave Kira hope that Mencheres wasn't just lying to her in anticipation of the day when he'd use her memories to enslave her. After all, he shouldn't care if Kira liked her captivity or not. Someone as fast and strong as a vampire didn't need to worry about consent.

It might be frightening to admit it, but Kira was already powerless when it came to her circumstance. She'd just been deluding herself by thinking that Mencheres would need to control her mind to force her to remain here.

On the plus side, she'd finally managed to reach her sister on the phone. Kira told Tina the same cover story Gorgon claimed to have given Frank—that Kira was home sick with the flu. Tina had been concerned, but both of them knew she couldn't risk visiting. Not while Kira supposedly had a contagious virus that would weaken Tina's already-compromised immune system. It didn't escape Kira's notice that each of Tina's laughs ended on a coughing fit, and her voice was thicker, her words heavier. At twenty-nine, Tina was already in the autumn of her life expectancy, as unfair as that was.

The thought was so depressing that it drove Kira out of her room. She'd just spoken to Tina yesterday, but now she wanted to talk to her again. She needed to assure herself that for the time being, Tina was still here, still part of her life.

Kira went downstairs, looking for Mencheres or Gorgon. If she just picked up a phone without checking with one of them, for all she knew, alarms would go off. Then they might not believe that she'd been innocently trying to reach her sister and think she'd decided to call 911 after all. Annoyance flared in her. She might understand why vampires would be protective of their secret existence among humans, but she was still the one paying the price for that for the next few days. At least, she hoped that was all the time she had left to pay the price for unwittingly discovering their existence.

She reached the first floor and did a quick check of the living room and kitchen. No one around. Next Kira went out onto the patio, but the pool area was empty. So was the garden. Kira came back inside, about to check the laundry room next, when a voice right behind her made her jump.

"Were you looking for someone?"

She whirled around, taming her galloping pulse, to see Mencheres. He hadn't been here a second ago, as if she needed a reminder of how blazingly fast he was.

"I should put a bell on you," Kira said before she could think.

Instead of being annoyed or confused, Mencheres tilted his head. "Forgive me, I did not mean to startle you."

So perfectly formal. So rigidly in control of the situation at all times—except for that morning at the warehouse. Which was the real Mencheres? *Do you really want to know?* an inner voice questioned.

No, she probably didn't. Especially not in these circumstances, when she was his pampered prisoner.

"I wanted to call my sister again." A part of her hated to ask permission to do such a simple thing, but the other part reminded her that if Mencheres were a more ruthless person, she wouldn't even be alive. *Dead investigators tell no tales of vampires,* Kira thought wryly.

"Certainly," Mencheres said, as if there was never any chance that he would refuse.

Kira released the breath she hadn't been aware of holding. What a strange scenario this was, being a captive who was treated like a guest—most of the time. Radje's hawkish features flashed in Kira's mind. She hadn't been treated like a guest in front of him. In fact, she'd felt like more of an insect under Radje's cold, pitiless gaze.

"Will you be expecting that vampire to return anytime soon?" Kira asked, phrasing her words carefully.

Mencheres arched a brow. "I assume you're not speaking of Gorgon?"

"No, I'm talking about the one with the dark straight hair who looks a little like you."

"Radje," Mencheres murmured. "No, I do not expect him to return here in the near future."

"Good," Kira muttered. "He gives me the creeps."

A tiny smile touched his mouth. "Yet more proof that your youth doesn't preclude you from being wise."

Kira felt an answering tug of her lips. "I'm thirty-one. In my species, once a female is over thirty, she's considered to be well on her way to middle age."

Mencheres laughed, startling Kira, and the sound rolled along her spine in a shivery caress. It was the first time she'd seen him laugh, and his relaxed expression combined with his wide smile changed his features from striking into stunning. *God, you're gorgeous,* she thought, glad the vampire couldn't hear that in her mind—or know how hard it was for her not to stare.

"Such foolish human notions that women are only beautiful in the first flush of youth. My wife was thirty-five in human years when we married, and she was ravishing . . ."

Just as abruptly, his laughter vanished, that familiar look of impassivity settled over his face.

Kira reached out to touch Mencheres's arm. "Radje said that your wife was dead. I'm sorry."

A strange, sad smile flickered on Mencheres's mouth. "As am I, but not for the reasons you think."

A dozen questions instantly sprang to Kira's mind at that mysterious comment, but Mencheres changed the subject in the next moment.

"Come, place your call now. The library should be the most comfortable for you."

You don't like that topic at all, do you? Kira thought, her investigative instincts still urging her to find out more about the obviously unusual circumstances surrounding Mencheres's late wife. But Kira tamped them down. She wasn't on a case here; she was a captive, albeit a well-treated one. If she asked Mencheres about his wife, and he became defensive, he might not let her call her sister. Tina ranked higher than Kira's curiosity.

"The library sounds good to me," was all Kira said, and let him lead the way.

Mencheres waited in an adjoining room as Kira made her call. He'd let her have the illusion of privacy by leaving her alone in the library, but both of them knew he was listening.

He marveled at how Kira's voice changed when she spoke to her sister. It became softer, gentler, with an undertone of protectiveness. Kira's love for her sister shone through each syllable, and for these brief times that Mencheres listened to their conversations, that love was strangely soothing to him, even though he wasn't the recipient of it.

Why a woman who would soon have no memory of him could affect his mood with just her voice was bewildering. Soon Kira would be gone, and once she was, Mencheres intended to live only until he could find another convenient way of getting himself killed. He should be spending his final days with the vampires he'd sired, or old friends, or even by asking forgiveness from his co-ruler for the manipulation that had caused such a breach between him and Bones.

Instead, he found himself staying in this house with his thoughts occupied by Kira, even though he tried to give her as much space as possible. It must be her novelty that made her fascinating to him. Kira had known nothing about him when she rushed to his aid at the warehouse, and what she had learned about him since then should only have terrified her. Yet the look Kira had given him the other day when he crouched over her by the pool had been filled with heat. Then she'd casually admitted to her attraction to him, as if that hadn't leveled him where he stood.

It made no sense. Since Mencheres had wanted as much solitude as possible in his last days, but couldn't be completely alone without arousing suspicion, he'd chosen this small, modest house. Gorgon and the humans had been given strict instructions not to tell Kira anything about him, so Kira couldn't know about his status among vampires, how rare his abilities were, that his wealth was far beyond Fortune 500 standards, or any of the other things that had enticed so many others before her. That she would find him desirable based on mere flesh and bone, nothing else, made him equal parts enticed and incredulous.

If things were different, Mencheres might have acted on the draw he felt toward Kira, the first woman in thousands of years—possibly ever—to want him without ulterior motives. But his time was almost finished.

Of course, Kira's flattering comments could also have been an attempt to sway him to release her. Kira hadn't hinted at any desire for him since that day by the pool. It was entirely plausible that she'd first sought to charm him into letting her go, realized it wouldn't work, and thus ceased. Mencheres felt a pang as he contemplated that. *Yes. That was far more likely.*

"Treatments again?" Kira's voice interrupted his musings. It sounded like she took in a deep breath as her pulse sped up. "Well, those do help, and I should be able to go with you . . . I told you, I feel better, and I've been on antibiotics for days now . . . Yes, my phone's still acting up at home . . . well, I fell asleep and forgot to charge my cell. Sorry I missed your call. I'll call you tomorrow. Promise. Love you, Tiny-T."

A click signaled that Kira had hung up, but Mencheres

stayed where he was. The sudden raggedness of her breathing said she was fighting back tears. Kira hadn't been prone to overreactions thus far, so her sister must be quite ill. Mencheres felt a twinge of guilt that he forced back. Whatever her sister's condition, it didn't sound as if it were new, and Mencheres *couldn't* let Kira leave with her memories intact. With luck, she would only be here another day or two.

"I'm done now," Kira called out, her voice throatier than normal.

Mencheres rose, glad she hadn't tried to covertly make another call. That showed caution and intelligence, two things undervalued in modern times, from what he'd observed. When he came into the library, Kira's eyes were dry; but a frown stitched into her forehead, and her scent was deeper with worry.

He hadn't tried mesmerizing her in the past two days. Maybe enough time had passed that he could erase her memories, even if he still couldn't hear her thoughts.

"Kira, I will attempt to breach your mind again. If I am successful, you can return home tonight."

She gave him a glance that was both hopeful and wary. He found that he had mixed feelings about this as well. Logic stated that the faster Kira was gone, the better it would be for both of them, but despite that, he knew he would . . . miss her.

The stupidity of missing a woman who wanted nothing more than to forget she'd ever met him was so enormous, he'd find it funny if the jest weren't on him.

"All right," Kira said, standing up.

Emerald blazed from his eyes as he locked them with her light green ones, compelling her not to look away.

"Kira." Her name was barely a whisper, but seething energy filled that single word. "Come to me."

She did, taking the hands he held out to her. Her heart-beat, breathing, and blood rushing through her veins were a symphony of sounds calling to him. But her mind remained quiet, secluding its secrets behind a wall he couldn't penetrate.

"Open your mind to me," he breathed, releasing more of his power.

"I'm . . . trying," she gritted out, her hands flexing in his grip.

That mental wall flickered, but didn't fall. Mencheres released her hands and stepped back.

"It's still too soon," he said, more disturbed by the knowledge that he was relieved he wouldn't need to say goodbye to Kira tonight than by his inability to breach her mind yet again.

"It's been almost five days since that morning at the warehouse," Kira said, spinning around in frustration. "Five days of being trapped here. I don't know how much more of this I can take. Come on, let me go."

She had no qualms about wanting to forget him forever—or at best, never to see him again. If only he felt the same single-minded detachment over her.

"Your sister believes you to be recuperating from the flu, and your job is secure. I know this situation is not of your choosing, but it will be over soon."

Kira's fists clenched, and her natural sweet scent soured. "My sister isn't well."

"Is she in danger of dying in the next few days?" Mencheres asked bluntly.

Kira hesitated, biting her lip. "No."

"Then I cannot justify the risk."

"Look, she's scared!" Kira snapped. "I don't suppose that happens very often with vampires, but it does with the rest of us. These hospital stays are hard on Tina. They beat on her back to loosen the mucus in her lungs, then give her treatments to help her breathe easier. She's my little sister, I told her I'd be there for her." Kira's voice wavered, becoming huskier. "I told her she could always count on me."

Mencheres closed his eyes. Kira didn't know it, but loyalty was one of the qualities he prized most. And he understood, all too well, the sense of responsibility Kira felt toward someone she considered hers. He studied her strong, lovely face and the curve of that stubborn jaw. Any manipulations Kira might have tried on him were justified. Mencheres would have done the same himself, if he were her.

"There is one thing that might hasten my ability to erase your memories."

Kira's expression became hopeful and she took a step toward him.

"What? Whatever it is, I'll do it."

Would she still say that once she heard what it entailed? "Your blood would give me greater power over you. For humans with very strong minds, drinking them is sometimes necessary before they can be mesmerized. You are very strong-willed, Kira. Perhaps more than my blood in your system is preventing me from manipulating your mind."

Kira paled as she digested what she'd have to do. Mencheres watched her, keeping his expression blank. Was her protectiveness for her sister greater than her fear of offering her throat to a vampire?

She swallowed hard, then gave a short nod. "Okay. Let's do it."

He was surprised by her quick capitulation. "You realize this means I will bite you and drink your blood?" he asked, just in case she hadn't understood.

Kira let out a small laugh. "You're a vampire. I didn't think you'd use a needle and a straw."

"You're not afraid?" he challenged.

Her pale green gaze was steady even as her pulse began to race. "You promised not to harm me. So then I have nothing to be afraid of."

Loyalty. Bravery. Determination. Kira's attributes were like a torch shining on all his dark years of ruthlessness. Long-dormant emotions rose in him, and his eyes flared green. He couldn't remember the last time he'd met someone of her quality, and her blood would become part of him when he drank from her. When Kira pulled back her hair and came to stand only inches away, he found that he wanted her blood inside him so badly that he dared not touch her lest he injure her with his urgency.

She shivered, glancing over her shoulder. "It feels like something just brushed up against me . . . do you feel that?"

It was his power uncurling and wrapping around her in all the ways he couldn't allow himself to. Mencheres tempered it, only letting his aura caress hers without that coiling energy stroking along her skin like dozens of hands.

"Come closer," he rasped, still not trusting himself to touch her. It had been *so long* since he'd felt anything this strong for a woman. The unexpected surge of need snaking through him had his skin humming with energy. If this was how he felt in anticipation of biting Kira, what would it feel like to possess her body? To make those full, red lips part with a slow, rapturous scream as he drove his flesh deeply inside her?

A sound escaped Kira, almost a gasp. Mencheres

reined himself back in again, trying to squelch the sudden flare of lust that resulted in his unconsciously flicking his power along the most sensitive cluster of her nerve endings. The depth of his response to her was astounding, as if something long asleep in him had unexpectedly awakened with a roar.

"Like this?" Kira asked, tilting her head to the side with her eyes closed.

The smooth line of her neck with its vibrating pulse was almost his undoing. Mencheres clenched his fists, drawing himself back under control with great effort. *Slowly. She's never been tasted before.*

The knowledge that he'd be the first to claim her blood aroused a primal instinct in him. He enfolded Kira in a smooth, strong embrace. Her pulse thundered beneath his lips as he brushed them over her neck. Her flesh was so soft, her scent mingling with his as he drew her close. She didn't speak, but her breathing came in small, unsteady puffs that warmed him where they landed. His arm slid down her back, pulling her even closer, smothering his moan at the feel of her body flush against his.

"How much . . . will you need to take?" she whispered unsteadily, her heart rate jumping when Mencheres grazed her throat with his fangs.

"Have no fear."

His voice was low, almost a growl, as his hand threaded through the thick mass of her hair. The sensuous friction of her breasts against his chest, rising and falling from her rapid breathing, intensified his craving to explore all of her. Thoroughly, relentlessly, and slowly. But though he held her far closer than necessary, his hands remained on her back and on her head, holding her steady instead of learning the tantalizing curves of her body.

She gasped when Mencheres sealed his mouth over her

neck, sucking on it with slow, steady pressure. He didn't pierce her yet, but readied her for his bite, bringing that smaller, succulent vein closer to the surface. His eyes closed at the lemony nectar taste of her skin, the way her pulse leapt against his mouth, and at the shiver that raced all over her body. Her scent enveloped him, a mixture of apprehension, hesitation . . . and something else. Excitement.

A dark thrill of triumph washed over Mencheres. She might not be aware of it, but a part of Kira yearned for him to bite her for reasons that had nothing to do with her sister. *You want to be claimed this way*, he thought, flicking his tongue across her neck once more. *And you shall be. Now.*

His fangs sank into her flesh in the next instant.

Chapter Seven

Everything in Kira froze at the feel of those sharp fangs puncturing her skin, but she wasn't prepared for what happened next. Instead of pain, a cascade of pure sensation flowed over her. Sweet, luscious warmth seemed to spread slowly from her neck, down her shoulders, and lower, until it felt like her body was submerged in heated chocolate. All her worries drained away in such a rush that she felt dizzy, only realizing how heavy the stress had been when it was no longer there to weigh her down.

Something thick and silky threaded through her fingers. After a hazy moment, Kira realized she'd raised her arms and was now gripping Mencheres's hair. He made a deep, guttural sound that vibrated against her neck as he swallowed. *My blood. Mencheres is swallowing my blood.*

The thought should have frightened her, or at the very least, made her uneasy, but Kira found herself pressing closer to him instead. Shards of pleasure spiked in her as his fangs slid deeper in response. The heat spreading through her began to swirl and concentrate in one spot, making her gasp at the sudden intense need in her loins. Her hands tangled tighter in his hair while a dark, inexplicable urge had Kira rubbing her neck against his mouth.

Pleasure stabbed into her with enough impact to make her gasp as his fangs slid into her again. She heard herself moaning. Felt another dizzying sweep of heat. How could a *bite* be responsible for so much bliss?

Mencheres lifted his head all too soon, leaving cool air on her throat instead of the hard, sensual pressure of his mouth. The firm caress of his hands on her back and head vanished, too, resulting in disappointing emptiness instead of the feel of him gripping her.

She didn't even think before she yanked his head back down to her neck. "Don't stop," she gasped.

A harsh noise escaped him as his tongue slid a long, slow path across the spot on her throat where he'd bitten her.

"You don't really mean that."

Like hell she didn't. She needed more of that wonderful, seeking heat flooding all through her. More of *him* touching her. Her breasts rubbed against the muscled wall of Mencheres's chest as she tightened her grip on his head, keeping him cradled in the crook of her neck.

His hands reached up, clasping her wrists in a gentle yet unbreakable hold as he lifted his head away from her. That clawing need in her began to ebb, leaving behind a warm, light-headed lethargy, as if she'd just emerged from a hot tub after breathing nitrous oxide.

Kira swayed as a tingling wave of dizziness overtook her. Mencheres lifted her, then she was placed on something soft. She opened her eyes to find that he'd moved them over to the couch. She expected his mouth to be stained red, or to see crimson trails zigzagging down his face, but nothing marred his strikingly handsome features. His eyes were still bright emerald green, meeting hers with an intensity she couldn't name.

And she had not the slightest idea of what to say. The uninhibited feelings that had led her to shove Mencheres's head to her throat, *demanding* that he bite her again, had faded, leaving Kira torn. Was her impassioned reaction just what happened to everyone Mencheres bit? Was that why he'd said she didn't really mean it when she'd told him not to stop?

Or had she not wanted him to stop because the vampire's bite was an excuse to act on the desire she felt toward him? She certainly wouldn't let her unhealthy attraction loose under any other circumstances. No matter how well-intentioned his actions were, he was still her captor—her *inhuman* captor. She wasn't about to further complicate an already-twisted situation.

"Are you feeling better now?" Mencheres asked, none of her discomfiture coloring his tone.

Kira looked away, taking in a deep breath. She noticed her heart wasn't racing anymore. In fact, it had the same relaxed cadence as if she'd just woken up.

"Fine." Then she forced herself to ask, "Is that whole 'more, more!' response common when you bite someone? Or do I owe you an apology?"

Mencheres moved away from her before he answered. "It is very common."

His tone was so stiff that Kira shot a glance at him. His face was utterly closed off, as expressionless as a statue. *Why would you expect anything different?* she asked herself. This might be a new experience for her, but Mencheres must bite a different person every day. The only reason he wasn't yawning was probably because he didn't need to breathe.

Then abruptly, he was kneeling in front of her, his hand cupping her face and his green eyes blazing into hers.

"Nothing happened, Kira. I did not bite you. You did not come back to my house. You went home from work Tuesday morning, and you have been ill in your bed ever since."

A strange thickness pressed on her mind as his voice seemed to vibrate through her. For a split second, Kira felt elated. It must be finally working! But just as quickly, dismay swept over her. If it was, then she would forget Mencheres. She'd never even realize she'd met him . . .

She blinked, and that insistent pressure vanished from her mind. Mencheres's eyes were still locked onto her, so bright they didn't even seem real; but she no longer felt the urge to fall inside their glow.

"It's not working." The strangest feeling washed over her. *Regret? Relief?* Kira let it go before she could determine which.

Mencheres was across the room with his back to her before her next blink. Nothing from the square set of his shoulders gave her any indication of what he was thinking.

"We try again in two days," he said.

That would make it a week since that fateful morning at the warehouse. The maximum amount of time Mencheres said it would take for the effects of her drinking his blood to wear off. Kira bit back the question that immediately popped up in her mind.

What if in two days, he still couldn't erase her memories? And if Mencheres couldn't make her forget everything she'd learned about him and the other vampires . . . would he *ever* let her go?

Mencheres lay on the bottom of the pool, the rays of the late-afternoon sun shining mutedly through the opaque glass. He'd been down here for over an hour in the artificially warmed water, yet even this normally relaxing pastime did little to soothe him. He kept thinking about how Kira's skin had felt under his mouth yesterday, how she tasted, and how her scent assumed a richer, deeper fragrance with her arousal.

He knew that arousal was only due to how he'd bitten her. Kira's response had been the same Mencheres had encountered from countless women and men he'd fed from before. What was so different was *his* response. When Kira moaned for him not to stop, for a moment, he was tempted. He could drink from her the entire time he took her, draining only the smallest amount of blood but giving her the same incredible sensations from his bite—and more. His desire had been so great that it caused physical pain for him to set Kira away. Mencheres couldn't remember the last time he'd wanted anyone with such intensity. Perhaps never.

And yet it was more than lust. When he'd been unable yet again to penetrate her mind, the relief that filled him was undeniable. He couldn't help but wonder if reluctance on his part played a role in his inability to erase Kira's memory. Yes, there was another possible reason for his inability to alter her thoughts, but the truth was that he didn't want her to leave. It was a pleasure seeing Kira's face each day. Her voice was something he found himself straining to hear whether she spoke to him or not, and her close proximity occupied his thoughts far more than he would ever let her know.

It was ironic; he held her captive, yet she'd captivated him.

Mencheres rose from the pool, abandoning this futile pursuit of tranquility. One thing would make him feel better, and it had nothing to do with basking underwater. He would have Gorgon pull all of Kira's information, discreetly and thoroughly. Mencheres had already decided to claim her as his so she would be left in Bones's care once he was gone. Now all he needed to do was ensure that Bones knew whom to look after once that day came.

The fact that this was one of the few items he was prioritizing didn't escape his notice, but he didn't care. He could pretend that Kira hadn't become important to him, or he could accept it and find a way to proceed regardless. Denial had never assisted him in the past.

"Gorgon!" Mencheres called out. He didn't even wait for the other vampire to come out onto the deck before he spoke again. "I have a task for you."

Mencheres could hear Kira pacing in her room. She'd been doing that for the past two hours. Doubtless, she was again chafing at her circumstances, for which he could not blame her. Her time with him had gone on longer than either of them had anticipated. Still, in her sixth day since drinking his blood, he did not catch even the slightest glimpses of Kira's thoughts, which he should have been able to do by now.

He could no longer pretend that his blood was just taking an unusually long time to wear off in her system. It was time for him to make a decision. And he dreaded it.

"Screw it," Mencheres heard Kira mutter before she shut her door and came down the stairs. He stayed seated in the living area, keeping his expression composed, as if he hadn't been tuned in to her every nuance for the past few hours.

"I need to call my sister," Kira said as soon as she saw him.

He raised a brow at the urgency in her voice. "Is something wrong?"

"I hope not," Kira muttered. "Library phone okay again?"

"Yes," Mencheres replied, watching Kira as she almost ran toward there. What had her so agitated? When she'd hung up on her sister last night, Kira had been fine. Worried, but otherwise calm. Now she acted as though she'd just walked on her sister's grave.

Mencheres heard the mechanical beeps that signaled Kira dialing, then her tense breathing as she waited. After a dozen rings, Kira let out a curse, then hung up and dialed again.

He came into the library just as Kira muttered another curse and hung up again. Her face was pale.

"She's not answering. Something's wrong."

Mencheres didn't reach out to her, but to his bafflement, his first inclination had been to stroke her in a comforting way.

"You've been unable to reach your sister other times before, yet nothing was amiss," he noted.

"This is different. Ever since later this morning, I just . . . felt that something was off." Kira shot him a pensive look. "You'll think it's crazy, but sometimes I just *know* things. Call it instinct, gut reaction, whatever, but I've had it all my life."

On the contrary, he was one of the few people in the world who could relate to knowing things based on an unusual inner gift. Or at least, he used to relate.

"Concentrate on this feeling. Focus," Mencheres stated.

She looked surprised at his instruction, but then her brow furrowed, and she began to pace in a slow stride. Silence and concentration had sharpened Mencheres's gift when he was younger and unused to it. Then over time, he'd honed his ability to call visions forth at will. He'd even been able to use his power to locate people over countless miles, especially if he'd tasted that person's blood.

Until his visions abruptly ended and all he saw was darkness. Symbolism was often a part of his visions, and Duat, the underworld where his soul would travel to await judgment by the god Anubis, was a place of uniform darkness. Death was coming for him, but Mencheres would choose his own end. One that best served his people.

"If I'm right, and something bad happened, Tina would be in a hospital. I need to make another call," Kira said. She went to the phone and started dialing, not waiting to see if Mencheres objected. He said nothing, watching as her fingers twisted together in agitation.

"Mercy Hospital and Medical Center," he heard the operator's voice intone.

"I'm checking to see if my sister has been admitted," Kira said, taking in a deep breath. "Her name is Tina Graceling. She might also be in the emergency room."

"One moment." Hold music filled the line for several seconds, then the operator's voice again. "Yes, Tina

'Graceling is a patient here. Please hold while I connect you to the nurses' station."

Mencheres didn't speak as Kira was transferred and another voice explained to her that her sister was in critical but stable condition. From what he deduced, it wasn't due to an accident but a recurring medical ailment.

"Thank you," Kira said before she hung up. Then she met Mencheres's gaze.

"She's in intensive care." Her voice was raw, her scent swirled with fear, agitation, and guilt. "She hemorrhaged and was brought to the hospital by ambulance this morning . . ."

None of this should matter to him. Kira's sister was in a hospital; there was nothing more she could do to help her, and an unknown mortal's poor health was truly not his concern.

But Kira cared, and because of that, he did, too. Regardless of all the reasons why she shouldn't matter to him, Mencheres found that he couldn't bear to see Kira in pain.

Yes, he cared far, far too much.

He'd kept Kira here with the original intention of protecting the secrecy of his race, but as the days passed, Kira's greatest threat wasn't to the vampire world—it was to him. She made him feel things he couldn't allow himself to feel at this point in his life. No matter how hard it was, it was time for him to remove that threat. He had no other choice if he intended to stay the course he'd set.

"Come," Mencheres said, holding out his hand.

Kira's brow furrowed, but she took it. *Beautiful dark lady,* he thought. *I wish I didn't have to do this.*

He had Kira locked in an unbreakable grip before she could even gasp.

Chapter Eight

Kira's breath whooshed from her lungs when Mencheres set them down in the parking lot. It took a second for her legs to stop trembling enough for her to let go of him, but the hospital gleaming so close ahead gave her the needed strength to start walking toward it.

"Why didn't we drive here?" she asked, her heart still hammering.

"It would have taken three times longer," Mencheres replied. "More, if we were caught in traffic."

Sure wasn't any traffic in the skies, Kira thought, still a bit dazed from her recent flight. Mencheres had swept her up, hurtling them through the night skies, before she'd even realized what he was doing. The vampire's ability to fly in a dizzying blur of speed was both exhilarating and terrifying. She didn't think she would *ever* forget the sight of the buildings from her vantage point of being zipped along above them. *Superman and Lois Lane, eat your hearts out.*

But Kira pushed her residual wonder aside when she entered the brightly lit hospital. Somewhere on the floors above, Tina was fighting for her life against a disease that left no survivors. The hospital attendant gave her a sympathetic look as she assigned Kira a visitor's pass.

"You're just in time. ICU visiting hours end in thirty minutes."

Kira shot a grateful glance at Mencheres even though the vampire wasn't looking at her. If they'd driven instead of flown, she wouldn't have made it.

"Only family members are allowed in intensive care. Is he family, too?" the attendant asked.

"Yes," Kira replied at once. She wasn't about to repay Mencheres's kindness in bringing her here by making him cool his heels downstairs.

The attendant gave a single, doubtful glance at Mencheres. Kira couldn't blame her. She and Mencheres looked nothing alike, with her blondish brown hair and light eyes in striking contrast to his darker coloring and Arabian features.

"Driver's license, please," the attendant said to Mencheres.

He leaned forward across the counter, the flash of green in his eyes gone so quickly, Kira wasn't sure if she really saw it.

"Given. Now, hand me the pass," Mencheres directed in a smooth, low voice.

The attendant handed over the visitor's pass with a glazed smile on her face, not even writing a name on it. Mencheres took it and turned to Kira.

"Let us go."

Kira looked back at the attendant, who still smiled in a frozen sort of way, before she followed Mencheres to the elevators. Once they were inside, she finally found her voice.

"That's how easily you can control people's minds under normal circumstances? A one-second glance with a little bitty flash of green?"

Mencheres gave her a sideways look. "Perhaps now you can appreciate the rarity of your resistance to my power."

"Because you gave me your blood," Kira murmured pensively, looking at the floors light up as the elevator passed them. "And possibly my stubbornness," she added with a limp smile.

Mencheres almost seemed to sigh. "There is one more possibility. A very small percentage of humans are naturally immune to vampire mind control. In my lifetime, I've come across only a few dozen humans with that immunity, but there are those who must have a form of genetic mutation that prevents—"

"You *never* told me that before," Kira interrupted, dread filling her. "You knew this whole time that it might not just be your blood that's prevented you from erasing my memory?"

Sick fear boiled up in her. Was this Mencheres's way of telling her he'd never let her go?

The elevator doors slid open, revealing the nurses' station to the intensive care unit. Mencheres said nothing, which Kira took as a damning admission.

But she couldn't talk more about that now. She only had half an hour to see her sister, and that took precedence even over her fears of Mencheres's new revelation. Kira's gaze flicked around the clear doors of each room until she found the one marked Tina Graceling. Then she flashed her pass at the nurse before approaching her sister's room, not even looking to see if Mencheres followed her.

Tina looked to be asleep, her petite body connected to machines that seemed to dwarf her from their perches around the hospital bed. She was almost as pale as the sheets around her, dark shadows circling her eyes the only spots of color on Tina's face. She looked so frail, so broken, like a beautiful doll some child had carelessly discarded. A clear plastic tube was taped in place over Tina's mouth, the steady compression of the nearby ventilator sounding like a wheezing accordion.

Tears filled Kira's eyes, making her sister and all the machines blurry. Tina wasn't asleep; she was unconscious and on a ventilator. One of Tina's greatest fears was being on a vent. Her sister had often said that once her lungs deteriorated to that point, it was all over.

And Tina was probably right.

A sob escaped from Kira before she could stuff it back. She'd known this day would come. Thought she'd even prepared for it, but the sizzling pain that wrapped around her heart when she saw Tina alive only by the assistance of machines made her knees give out. She sat in the nearby chair, unable to tear her gaze away from her unconscious little sister.

"What disease does she have?"

Mencheres's soft, deep voice startled Kira for a second. She'd almost forgotten the vampire was here. He circled around Tina's bed, looking down at her sister with his usual hooded expression.

"Cystic fibrosis," Kira rasped. "She was born with it."

The irony of that stabbed a fresh spurt of pain in Kira. According to what Mencheres just revealed, Kira might also have been born with a genetic mutation, but though hers might steal her freedom, it wouldn't grow deadlier until it killed her, like Tina's.

"She is dying," Mencheres said, still with that same indecipherable expression.

"Don't *say* that."

Kira gave the vampire a look filled with all her impotent rage over her sister's condition as she stood up. She knew it was true. All her instincts warned that this time, Tina wouldn't recover. She'd felt that dread growing in her all day even though she'd tried to discount it.

His black eyes were hard. "As she is now, that is fact, but what are you prepared to do to change that fact?"

Did he mean . . . ? Kira looked at Tina, at Mencheres, then at the EKG machine monitoring her sister's weak pulse. A pulse that Mencheres no longer had.

"Nothing quite that drastic," Mencheres said, with the barest hint of a nod at the heart monitor. "My blood healed your injuries. It cannot cure your sister's disease permanently, but it could heal the complications that cause her to be in this condition."

Hope smashed through Kira as she stared at Mencheres. His blood *had* healed her—from a mortal injury, no less. Even if it didn't cure Tina's cystic fibrosis, could it heal Tina enough to get her off the ventilator? Maybe even out of the hospital?

"You'd do that?" It took everything Kira had not to beg as she waited for his response.

"Yes. For a price."

Her knees felt weak again, but this time, with a different sort of dread. Of course the price of Mencheres's help would be for Kira to accept the loss of her freedom . . . forever. After all, he'd repeatedly said he wouldn't let her go until he could erase her memory of vampires. Six days later, he still couldn't manipulate her memories or hear her thoughts. Kira didn't hold out much hope that tomorrow would magically make any difference. *Genetic mutation. Natural immunity.*

She looked back at Tina. If his price for getting her to accept her fate as a permanent captive was to heal her sister enough to give Tina another chance at living, she'd agree. She might not have a choice about losing her freedom, but she could see that Tina benefited from it. A thousand times, she'd wondered, "Why her?" about Tina's condition, and yet not once had she ever heard Tina echo that sentiment. Her sister had accepted her fate with an ice-cold bravery that Kira had long been in awe of. Now, it was Kira's turn.

"I can guess your price," she said, straightening her shoulders. "And I'll agree, *if* you heal Tina more than this one time. Do it enough times to give her a normal life span, and I'll stay locked up for the rest of mine. A life for a life."

Mencheres stared at her in silence for so long, Kira wondered if she'd dared to demand too much. Was he angry by the condition she had added to his price? Amused? Scornful? None of the above? It was true Mencheres could just hold her hostage forever *without* helping Tina, but if wanted her to be as docile as Selene, Kurt, and Sam were, then this was what he had to do.

"Call the nurse," Mencheres said.

That wasn't really an answer, but Kira didn't press. She went to the nurses' station and within minutes returned to the room with Tina's nurse.

Mencheres looked up at the woman and his eyes flashed that bright emerald glow. "Bring me a syringe."

The nurse's expression immediately changed into the same obedient, placid one the visitor registrar's had. Once again, Kira marveled at how effortlessly Mencheres could control other people's minds as the nurse left the room. Less than a minute later, she returned with a syringe and handed it to Mencheres.

"Leave now. You gave me nothing. You remember nothing about me," Mencheres said to her dismissively. The nurse walked away without a backward glance.

Kira would've commented about how eerie that whole exchange was, but she was too busy concentrating on Mencheres as he slid the needle into his wrist and slowly pulled the plunger out. Red liquid oozed into the syringe until it was full.

She glanced behind them at the nurses' station. No one was looking their way. Kira glanced back to find Mencheres staring at her. He now had the needle inserted into the IV line. She didn't look away as he pressed the plunger down, turning the tube that fed into Tina's hand red with his blood as it absorbed into Tina's vein.

Kira held her breath until the syringe was empty and out of the IV line. Mencheres capped it and slipped it into his coat pocket. The only trace that anything unusual had happened was the residual pink fluid at the end of the IV line where the catheter was secured into Tina's flesh with tape.

"Stay here," he said before walking out of the room.

She didn't ask where he was going. Kira sat by the bed and traced her hand along her sister's pale, motionless arm. How long would it take for his blood to counter the merciless damage Tina's disease had inflicted on her? He'd only given her one single syringeful. Maybe that was all he intended to give her to start, but then he'd inject another few syringes' worth of blood into Tina in the next day or so. Maybe he didn't have enough blood in him now to give more. That could be where

Mencheres was headed; to find an unknowing donor and refill . . .

Tina made a gagging sound. Everything in Kira froze as she saw her sister's eyes open. Tina blinked several times before gagging again, her head turning. Her sea-green gaze met Kira's in question, but not confusion. Tina was awake—and lucid. Then the limp arm Kira had been stroking lifted, her sister's hand moving up to tug at the tube in her mouth.

That was all Kira saw before her gaze blurred, and she choked out a single word.

"Nurse!"

Mencheres watched Kira say goodbye to her sister. Her face was still flushed with happiness as she leaned down to kiss Tina's cheek.

"I'll try to come again soon," she murmured. "Love you, Tiny-T."

"Love you, too, sis," Tina replied, her voice soft, but lacking the scratchiness Tina should have had after her ventilator tube had been removed.

"It's just *miraculous* how fast she responded to the new antibiotics," the nurse marveled to Kira as she accompanied her out of Tina's room.

"Oh yes. Miraculous," Kira echoed, but she looked up at Mencheres as she spoke.

He gave her a faint smile. The healing effects from vampire blood—specifically blood as old and powerful as his—would indeed seem miraculous to the nurse, who didn't know better. Kira did, though. She took his hand once she drew near, then she brought it to her lips.

"Thank you," she breathed as she placed a kiss upon it.

Such a simple gesture. The same one countless others—human, vampire, and ghoul—had made to him over the course of thousands of years, yet it seared through Mencheres with more force than a thunderbolt. All too quickly, the brush of Kira's mouth and the soft pressure of her hand were gone, leaving him feeling colder without her touch.

By the gods, this mortal was *so* dangerous to him.

"We need to return now," he said, relieved that his voice didn't betray the emotion raging inside him.

Kira glanced back toward her sister's room and nodded, some of the happiness leaving her face.

"I'm ready."

Mencheres didn't speak as they took the elevator to the ground floor of the hospital. Neither did Kira. When they were in the darkened corner of the parking lot, he opened his arms, and she stepped into them, her warmth enveloping him as he catapulted them into the sky. In moments, they were high above the hospital, then high above all the other buildings, too, invisible against the night with his black coat wrapped around them. Kira's heartbeat drummed against his chest, her body molded so closely to his, he could scarcely think of anything else. The wind rushing around them stole away her lemony scent, but he knew he'd smell it on him later. He might not wash this shirt or coat again, lest he lose all trace of her scent from them.

All too soon, he saw the outline of their destination ahead. His mouth tightened. It was time to eliminate the threat Kira posed to him. He had no choice.

Mencheres set them down on the building and let go of Kira as soon as she gained her balance. She looked around the roof with confusion stamped on her lovely features.

"Where are we? This isn't where you live."

He steeled himself, locking down his emotions behind an unreachable wall. "No, this is where *you* live."

Kira glanced around again, her eyes widening as she recognized the cityscape surrounding her apartment building. "Did you want me to pick up some of my things before we go back?" she asked in confusion. "I don't have my keys with me . . ."

"You aren't going back," Mencheres said in a cool, steady voice as he handed her the keys she'd left in her backpack the day they first met. Then with a mental push, the roof door gaped open. "I still cannot hear anything from your mind or control it, so it is obvious you are naturally immune to my power. I told you at the hospital that my blood came with a price. My price for healing your sister is your silence on all things you've learned in the past week. Speak of me, and them, to no one."

Her mouth opened in disbelief, those naturally red lips taunting him with their fullness. "But you said as long as I knew, I could never leave—"

"And you said I could trust you," Mencheres interrupted softly. "So I am trusting you, Kira, and letting you go despite your knowledge."

She had no idea how difficult this was for him. When Kira offered herself willingly in exchange for healing her sister, Mencheres had almost seized on it. The chance to see her each day, learn more about her—and seduce her to his bed—had filled him with a primal, hungry purpose. He wanted to show Kira things she hadn't even imagined, take her to places she'd only heard of, and lavish on her extravagances that would shame a queen. It made no sense; he barely knew Kira, yet something in her called to him in a way that almost overpowered him. The last time he'd felt this strongly about a woman, kingdoms had fallen in his wake.

But the darkness of the underworld loomed before him, mocking him that his time was almost over. Kira had a future. He didn't. He had to free her, both to let her live out her life and to let him finish what was left of his.

She came toward him with that strong, fighter's stride that was at odds with her feminine slenderness and grabbed him in a fierce hug.

"Thank you," she whispered. This time, she kissed his throat, not his hand, and the brush of her soft, warm lips there almost broke his control.

He had to leave. Now.

Instead of returning her embrace, Mencheres reached into his coat and pulled out a bag.

"Take this," he said, thrusting it toward her. "Undead blood will not degrade with time. Use a quarter of each tube every time your sister's condition worsens. You can either claim it's an herbal supplement and inject it into her, or slip it into a beverage strong enough for her not to taste it."

Kira opened the bag, her eyes growing shinier when she saw the dozens of vials filled with his blood. He'd mesmerized a nurse to provide the tubes while Kira had been busy with her sister. The contents of the bag should be enough to counter Tina's disease to give her a normal mortal life span. As promised.

"Does this mean . . . that I'm never going to see you again?"

Kira's voice cracked faintly as she asked, causing pain to slice through him. Did she feel something for him as well? She'd admitted to lust before, but did her emotions run deeper than that? Would she have *wanted* to see him again, even though with those vials, she didn't need him in order to keep her sister well?

It mattered not, that black void whispered. Whatever might have been with Kira could never be. All he had left was to make sure his death best served those he was responsible for—and thwarted Radjedef.

"Goodbye, dark lady," Mencheres murmured. Then he flung himself up into the night.

Chapter Nine

"Graceling!"

Kira's head jerked around to see Frank wearing his usual scowl as he threaded through the desks separating them. Her boss had missed her while she was away, sure, but not in a lovey-dovey way.

"Are you finished with those reports?"

"Almost," Kira replied. The stack on her desk was reduced by three-quarters since she'd returned to work four days ago—and that wasn't counting the new things Frank dropped on her desk that she'd completed on a daily basis.

"Good. Clients can't be neglected just because you get sick," Frank said, dropping another inch-thick stack of papers on Kira's desk. "I need these back by the end of the day."

It's a recession economy, jobs are hard to come by,
Kira mentally chanted as she forced herself to smile. If
the employment market were better, she'd be tempted to
tell Frank to bend over so she could get those reports back
to him *now*.

"Will do," was what Kira said.

Frank tapped his finger on her paper stack. "If everything's caught up before the weekend, I'll put you in line
for the next missing-person account we get. I know how
you want one of those."

It was Thursday afternoon. Kira would have to work
until after midnight tonight and tomorrow to accomplish
that, but Frank was right. She did want more serious as-
signments than catching cheating spouses, worker's comp
surveillance, or serving subpoenas. Her old mentor's
motto rang in Kira's mind: Save one life. *Well, Mack,*
Kira thought, remembering Tina's smile as she checked
out of the hospital the day before yesterday, *I think I did.*
Maybe if she were assigned a missing-person case, Kira
could make it two lives.

"I'll have everything finished," she told Frank.

He gave her his version of a friendly smile, which
still had a mercenary edge to it. "Ol' Mackey told me I
wouldn't regret hiring you."

And he told me you were a prick, Kira mentally
added. Mack hadn't been wrong about his former partner, but Frank did display the occasional hint of kindness beneath his normal slave driver mentality. He
didn't have to let Kira use the company car on assign-
ments. He could've just hired someone else who had a
vehicle. Kira knew she more than made up for use of
the car in unpaid overtime, but still. Frank deserved a
nod for that.

Her coworker, Lily, leaned over the space between their desks once Frank left the room. "First time you've taken off sick in over three years, and he has to make sure you regret it." Lily's mouth curled downward. "If there's a God, Frank'll be stricken with hemorrhoids. The pain in the ass deserves 'em."

Kira gave her a smile. "It's all right. A little more liquid incentive will help me get everything finished."

Lily frowned, the lines deepening in her forehead. "Coffee isn't supposed to be a substitute for sleep. You've got dark circles under your eyes, girl. You need to take care, or you'll get sick again."

"I'm all right," Kira said. She couldn't tell the sweet older lady that the circles under her eyes weren't from flu recuperation but because thoughts of a *vampire* kept her awake. Despite its being several days since he let her go, Kira didn't seem to be able to get Mencheres out of her mind.

It shouldn't come as that much of a surprise. In the six days she'd been with Mencheres, he'd shown her that two other species existed alongside humanity, saved her life, saved her sister's life, fascinated her, tempted her, bitten her, and against the best interests of his kind, released her. Why *wouldn't* she be thinking about him? Every time she saw or spoke to her sister, Kira was reminded of Mencheres, let alone every time she walked past that warehouse on her commute from the subway to her apartment. His impact on her life had been enormous, and now that he was gone, Kira felt an acute sense of loss.

She still couldn't believe he'd actually let her go. The first couple days, she'd expected Mencheres to pop up out of nowhere and say she had to come back. Some small, twisted part of her maybe even wanted him to, even though her common sense knew that was seriously unhealthy. Any situation where one person had complete power over the other wasn't just wrong; it was sick. The bottom line was that she'd been Mencheres's captive. A well-treated captive, perhaps, and even one for a good reason, but still. Prisoner and warden was *not* the right circumstance for a romantic interaction, even a casual one.

Though Mencheres didn't seem to be interested in any type of interaction with her, romantic or otherwise. He let her go, the one thing that opened up the possibility of Kira exploring the draw she felt toward him, vampire or not, but then he'd given every indication that he wasn't coming back. If he wanted to see her again, he would have said so. He wouldn't have given her all that blood, enough for her to have no reason to contact him again—not that she had any means to contact him. She didn't know exactly where Mencheres had kept her for that week, and he hadn't left his phone number before he jetted off into the night. *Face it,* Kira thought bleakly. *You've been dismissed.*

On the bright side, he was probably too old for her by hundreds of years, and really, a human and a *vampire*? That never worked out. Look at all the *Dracula* movies. Or *Buffy.*

"Are you listening to me at all?" Lily's amused voice asked.

Kira yanked her thoughts from the darkly enticing vampire back to her coworker. "Sorry, I . . . my mind wandered off," she said sheepishly.

"Told you that you need some sleep," Lily said. "But since I know you won't listen, let me at least get you some coffee. That way, you'll be able to get through the rest of the day without nodding off in front of Frank."

"Thanks, you're an angel," Kira said with a grateful smile. She did have a long day ahead of her still, and thinking about Mencheres wouldn't make the pile of papers on her desk get any smaller.

Coffee would help that paper pile get smaller, though. Lots and lots of coffee.

Eight hours later, Kira stepped off the transit car, pushing her hair behind her ear in weariness. It had blown free from its low bun sometime during her walk from her office to the L station, and she hadn't bothered to clip it back. At least it wasn't long enough to obscure her vision as she walked up the steps to the street above. In fact, with it trailing inches past his shoulders, Mencheres had longer hair than she did . . .

Stop thinking about him, Kira reprimanded herself. She turned down the first of the three streets that led to her apartment, picking up her pace. It was one thing to be grateful at the strange twist of fate that had made her path cross with Mencheres, because though she had almost died, she'd also garnered the ability to keep her sister's disease at bay. But she wasn't musing about her sister's condition when she kept thinking about him.

She remembered how his black eyes could glitter with humor, how graceful and stealthily he moved, how mouthwatering he'd looked naked, and how she wished she'd spent more time learning about him when she'd been incarcerated at his house. Mencheres was the only person she'd confided to about her instincts and how strongly she took them. To her surprise, he hadn't found that the slightest bit laughable or unusual. Instead, he'd advised her to focus on them. To listen to them. Apparently, her inner compass hadn't seemed at all odd to someone who could fly and manipulate things with his mind.

Though if she listened to her instincts now, they'd keep repeating the same thing that had nagged at her the past several days—that she'd lost something important when Mencheres disappeared into the night. Was there something more she could have done to prevent him from going? Like, telling Mencheres she *wanted* to see him again instead of just asking if he was leaving for good without stating her preference in the matter?

Kira was so preoccupied with her thoughts that it took several seconds before she saw the dark form in the shadows by the front of her building. She tightened her hand on her backpack strap and kept going, pretending not to notice him even though every muscle tensed. When she was almost at the front door of her building, a hand shot out toward her. Kira's adrenaline surged as she ducked and swept out a hard kick to the man's ankle, slamming her heavy backpack into him next. Graduating from the police academy followed up by self-defense classes made her actions more reflex than planned.

"Ouch!" her would-be attacker yowled, staggering and hopping on one leg. "Kira, what the hell?"

She stopped herself just in time before she rammed her foot into his groin next. "Rick?"

The man straightened, overhead streetlight revealing her half brother's face. "Yeah, it's me. Goddamn, you hurt me!"

Her heart was still racing from thinking he was a potential mugger she had to fight off, making her voice sharp. "It's after midnight, and you're lurking around wearing a damn hoodie and jumping out at me. You're lucky I haven't gotten a new gun yet, or I might have *shot* you!"

"I was just trying to get your attention." He sounded more petulant than apologetic. "You almost walked right past me."

That was so like Rick; not thinking before doing something stupid. Kira heaved a sigh. She didn't feel up to lecturing her little brother right now.

"What're you doing here this late?"

His gaze darted around the street. "I tried your cell for days, but you didn't answer. I couldn't remember your work number, so I thought I'd come by and just hang out until you got home. Didn't think it would take you this long."

Of course her cell didn't answer. Mencheres hadn't given it back to her when he dropped her off on the roof with only his blood and her apartment keys, and she hadn't gotten a new one yet. She assumed he still had her backpack, too, since that was where he would've gotten her keys. Unless he'd thrown everything away right after he unloaded her that night.

"Come on in," Kira muttered. So much for her plans of showering and going right to sleep once she got home.

Rick smiled, his dimples making him look younger than his twenty-five years. Despite knowing better, Kira felt some of her irritation lessening. Maybe Rick *had* just been worried about her when he couldn't reach her, and that's why he was here.

Bullshit, her inner voice whispered.

Kira hoped that was her tired cynicism talking and not her instinct. It would be nice to think Rick was here without ulterior motives.

"You hungry?" she asked, as he followed her inside

the building. "I have some frozen pizzas you could heat up."

"Um, I don't think I'm going to stay that long," Rick hedged, glancing away.

Her hopes plummeted. *Told you,* that inner voice whispered.

Kira didn't go into the elevator even though the doors opened. She dropped her backpack and gave her brother a tired, hard stare.

"I told you, Rick, I'm not going to keep doing this."

"I just need a couple bucks," he said, meeting her gaze now. His green eyes, darker than hers, widened in that beseeching way he'd perfected. "It's been really hard trying to find work, and—"

"Maybe if you could pass a drug screen, you'd have an easier time getting a job," Kira said coolly.

Rick waved a hand. "I quit, I swear. I just smoke a little weed now and then, that's all. Look, Joey says he's going to throw me out if I don't give him a hundred bucks by tomorrow. I've got an interview lined up in the morning, and it looks really good, but if I'm hired, I still won't get paid before Joey throws me out."

"Bullshit," Kira said, echoing her inner voice. "It's after midnight already, no way you're going to an interview tomorrow morning. Even if you did have one set up, you'd just end up sleeping through it. You can't keep coming to me for money. I told you before, I don't have a lot of it, and—"

"And what you do have, you give to Tina for her bills," Rick interrupted bitterly. "You wouldn't think twice about handing over a check if this was *her* asking."

Kira felt anger rising, covering her weariness. "Don't you dare. Tina's disease keeps her from working a regular job, not laziness like you, and she almost *died* last week.

Not that you'd know because you hardly keep in touch with her anymore."

Rick dropped his head, having the grace to look ashamed. "Sorry," he mumbled. "She better? Still in the hospital?"

Thanks to Mencheres, Tina was even better than she knew. Out loud, Kira said, "She's home now. You should call her. She'd like to hear from you."

"Yeah, yeah, I'll call her tomorrow," Rick said at once. "You know I'm not as close to her as I am to you, but I still care about Tina even if she's not my blood."

Their parentage did make things more complicated. Kira's parents had been former flower children who were all about free love, even after they got married. Kira and Tina shared the same mother, but different fathers. Kira and Rick shared the same father, but different mothers. Technically, Rick and Tina weren't blood related, but Tina had always considered Rick to be her brother despite that, and despite their not growing up in the same house like she and Kira had.

"I swear, this'll be the last time I ask you for anything," Rick went on, giving her more of the puppy eyes. "And I'll pay you back, I promise."

If Kira had a dollar for every time she'd heard that, she might have been able to buy herself a car. But on the off chance that Rick really *had* kicked his habit and was trying to turn his life around . . .

"This is the last time," she told him, pulling out her checkbook. "I mean it."

Rick smiled in the way that reminded her of when they were children, and she was so excited to have a little brother. It had almost taken away the sting of her parents splitting up and her dad moving to another state when he fell in love with someone else.

"You're the best, sis."

Kira wrote out of the check for a hundred dollars and gave it to Rick. He pocketed it immediately, then shuffled his feet while glancing away.

"You don't happen to have a twenty so I can catch a cab back to my place, do you? It's kinda late to walk it. You know that neighborhood. Besides, my ankle hurts. You kicked it pretty hard."

Kira gritted her teeth. If she hadn't seen where Rick lived, she would have flatly refused this second donation, but it *was* a scary neighborhood.

She handed over a twenty, which disappeared into Rick's pocket as fast as the check had.

"Love ya, sis," he said, giving her a quick kiss. Then he headed out of the building, whistling.

Kira pressed for the elevator, ignoring that inner voice telling her she'd been swindled by her brother yet again.

Mencheres quietly leapt onto the roof across from Kira's building, sitting down on the cool concrete floor. How close he'd come to murdering Kira's brother, neither of them would ever know. *Perhaps* now *you'll cease this insanity of following her night after night*, he berated himself.

When he saw the man reach out for Kira as she approached her building, he'd already jumped down from the roof, intending to tear the throat out of whoever threatened her, when her attacker called her by name. Kira and her brother were both oblivious to the dark form careering toward them from above, or how it had abruptly swooped to the left when Kira also addressed the boy by name. If either of them had been silent for just a few seconds longer . . .

Though the boy's death would not have been a great loss, from what Mencheres overheard of their conversation. The boy's scent confirmed he was lying about the interview, lying about being off drugs, and lying about the taxi, as he proved by sauntering off on foot down the street instead of calling for transportation. If Mencheres hadn't heard the miscreant call her "sister," he would have killed the boy on principle after he'd deceived Kira out of her money. By her own admission—and from Mencheres's observation—Kira did not have adequate funds to support herself, her dishonest sibling, and her ill sister. To see her kindness taken advantage of made anger burn in him. *You are lucky you share her blood,* Mencheres thought at the foolish youth still strolling down the street. *Or I'd be sharing yours with the gutters tonight.*

In the next minute, the window in Kira's apartment glowed with soft light. Mencheres relaxed. She was safely inside now. He caught a glimpse of her as she passed by the window on her way to her bedroom. Even if she went to sleep immediately, Kira had less than seven hours until she would be at her desk again. Her long work days bothered him. She hadn't returned home before ten o'clock even one night this week, and tonight, she had stayed out even later. It wasn't right that she toiled such long hours at her job.

You must stop *this,* his common sense railed at him. Here he was, perched like a gargoyle on a roof staring at a woman who had begged to be free of him. There was an appropriate modern word for his actions: "stalking." He didn't even bother to pretend that he'd only shadowed Kira these past several nights to ensure that she kept her word not to reveal what she'd learned about vampires. He knew he was here for one reason—he wanted to see her again even if he didn't alert her to his presence.

Though Kira was no longer under his roof, she still managed to dominate his thoughts to a dangerous degree. Even now, he wondered what she would do if he appeared at her door. Would she welcome him into her home? And if she did, would he be strong enough to leave? Or would her nearness, her tantalizing scent, and the smooth melody of her voice be enough to make him abandon all his careful planning in favor of the chance to be with her?

Better not to find out. Kira made him want to live, to fight Radjedef to the bitter, bloody end regardless of the consequences, and he couldn't afford that sort of thinking. His *people* couldn't afford it. They'd suffered enough the last time he'd let his emotions for a woman sway his actions.

Mencheres forced himself to turn away though the soft glow at her window proved that Kira was still awake. He had to cease this madness. From what he'd seen the past several days, Kira had settled back into a life of working hard and caring for her sister, similar to how his time was spent on duties related to his people. But even if it looked lonely—another thing they had in common—it was still her life, and it didn't include him.

He gave himself up to the embrace of the wind as he flew away. This would be the last night he followed her. It had to be, but he would do one tiny, additional thing before he purged Kira from his life completely.

Chapter Ten

Kira mentally groaned as she heard Frank's voice cut through the usual cadence of sounds in the office. Next to her, Lily gave Kira a sympathetic glance.

"At it early today, isn't he?" Lily muttered.

"Where's Graceling?" Frank called out.

Before Kira had a chance to reply, Frank came through the door. She plastered a limp version of a smile on her face, bracing for whatever had made him seek her out before nine in the morning.

"I'm caught up on the reports from last week and I should be done with the new ones by the end of today," Kira said, heading Frank off before he could bark out a demand for her status.

Frank dropped something onto Kira's desk that for once wasn't a stack of papers. She looked at the car keys in confusion.

"Did I leave those here? I thought I had them in my bag . . ."

"They're my set of keys for the company car," Frank said. He beamed. "I'm giving it to you. You deserve it."

Kira's mouth fell open even as she heard Lily drop something that sounded like her coffee cup. "You're *giving* it to me?" she repeated, glancing at the calendar. No, it wasn't April Fool's Day—unless Frank was getting his prank in a couple weeks late.

"Plus, I'm giving you a raise," Frank went on. "And I want you out of the office by six o'clock every night that you're not on surveillance. You work too hard."

One extravagantly good deed from Frank, Kira could chalk up to his trying to balance his bad karma or something. *Three* extravagantly good deeds . . . either he was high, or this was his idea of a joke.

"I'm waiting for the punch line," Kira said cautiously.

Frank laughed, loud and hearty, confirming her guess that he'd been joking. She wanted to smack him. That man had a real sick sense of humor.

Then Frank slapped an envelope on her desk. "Open it."

Kira broke the seal, glancing once at Lily for moral support before she pulled out the contents.

It contained two pieces of paper. One was the title for the company car, signed by Frank and made out to her as the new owner. A check for two thousand dollars, also made out to her, was the other piece of paper.

"I made your raise retroactive," Frank said, still in the same cheerful tone she'd only ever heard him use with clients. "Good job, Graceling."

Kira just stared as Frank walked away. She was too stunned to even say thank you.

"What the hell just happened?" Lily whispered. "I mean, you *do* deserve all that, but Frank's so cheap, I can't believe he *did* it!"

Neither could Kira. Frank must've been visited by the Ghost of Christmas Future or something. Otherwise, his abrupt transformation from miserly Scrooge employer to gleeful generous benefactor was nothing short of miraculous.

Miraculous.

"Oh my God," Kira whispered.

"What?" Lily asked.

"I . . . nothing."

Kira swiveled her chair around, taking in several deep, uneven breaths. Frank hadn't experienced a miraculous change of heart after a visit from the Ghost of Christmas Future. No, he must have experienced something just as unusual—a visit from a mind-controlling vampire sometime between yesterday and today.

Mencheres. Her heart began to hammer. *What are you doing?*

Kira put another stack of folders in the trunk of Frank's car—make that *her* car—and paused to wave at Lily across the parking lot.

"What're you doing with all those, girl? You're not supposed to leave at a decent hour just so you can work all night at home," Lily called out.

"These are for, um, a side project," Kira stammered. A *very* side project.

"Some people call dating a side project, too. You should try that instead," Lily cackled.

Kira almost flushed. *If Lily only knew . . .*

"Good night, see you tomorrow," was what she said with another wave.

It took about the same amount of time to get to the West Loop by car as it did by walking and taking the Green Line, as Kira found out. Still, it was infinitely nicer not to heft that heavy backpack around, or to tense at every shadowy patch along the streets she walked when she worked late. She'd just have to get a treadmill or a gym membership for her exercise from now on.

Once she pulled inside the garage of her apartment building, Kira couldn't help but look around. Was Mencheres nearby? The thought sent a thrill of excitement through her. Or had he mesmerized Frank at the office without anyone's noticing him? It was possible. Mencheres moved so quickly, he could have been in and out without Kira, or anyone else, seeing him.

And *why* did he do it? Whimsy? Boredom? Or as a hint that he wanted her to find him? Mencheres knew she worked for a private investigator. He knew she'd had cases where clients spoke of strange happenings that she'd previously dismissed . . . but now realized might have been true. If mesmerizing her boss into giving her a car and cash was Mencheres's way of dropping bread crumbs to see if Kira followed them, it worked. The chance to see him again, *not* as his captive, but as a woman, made more slivers of exhilaration course through her. She had a thousand good reasons why seeing him would be a mistake, but instinct over-ruled those whenever she thought of him. *All right, Mencheres. I'm taking the bait.*

Two trips from her car to her apartment later and she had all the boxes of files spread out in her living room. Each case contained some sort of occurrence that might be paranormal in nature, be it outrageous witness testimony, odd evidence left at the scene, or rumors of involvement in something freakier than the occult. Kira intended to go through all of them until she found a common denominator. Mencheres might have stayed in his house most of the time that she'd been with him, but she had a feeling being homebound wasn't his normal pattern—or the pattern of most vampires.

Time to follow those gut feelings. With luck, somewhere in these files, she'd find something that would lead her to Mencheres. If that didn't work, she'd search the Internet next.

Or she could always tape a bat image to her apartment window right above a Welcome sign, but Kira thought that might be pushing it.

She picked up the first folder. *Follow the bread crumbs.*

Gorgon appeared in the bedroom doorway, but Mencheres didn't bother to open his eyes. He knew who Gorgon had come to announce. He'd heard him arrive.

"Tell him I'll be down momentarily," Mencheres said.

"Yes, sire," Gorgon replied.

Mencheres opened his eyes once Gorgon shut the door. He stared at the ceiling for several long seconds, not seeing its pale patterns but trying to see into the future, hoping something had changed. Perhaps the new vigor for life Kira had somehow wrought in him would alter the vision of the future he'd seen before.

His power reached out, piercing the veil that separated *now* from *later*, but instead of images of people, places, or happenings, all Mencheres saw was a blanket of ebony as vast and fathomless as the universe.

The underworld of Duat, waiting for him. Just as before.

Mencheres got up from the bed. His fate was still death, but instead of the acceptance he'd felt when he first saw that looming endless void, now it angered him. Death had become a bitter defeat instead of a coolly logical way to thwart Radjedef while releasing the burdens he'd long carried, and it was all because of Kira.

He clenched his jaw. How cruel the gods were to send her into his life. She made him want to live when he had no time left.

And even less time for complaining about his fate, Mencheres reminded himself. He took the manila envelope from his nightstand before he swept out of the room. Some things he still had control over, even if his future wasn't one of them.

Mencheres went downstairs to the front hall. A vampire stood near the door, his dark curly hair cut close and his lean frame encased in casual black pants and a fitted pullover shirt. For a moment, Mencheres stared at him. *My co-ruler. My heir.*

And his wife's murderer.

"Bones," he said in greeting. "Thank you for coming."

Dark brown eyes met his with a coolness that still stung even though Mencheres knew he had earned it. "You said it was urgent," Bones replied, a British accent coloring his words even after centuries.

"I don't trust this to be passed even through members of our line," Mencheres said, not bothering with any formal pleasantries. Bones had always preferred getting right to business. He held out the manila folder that contained all of Kira's personal information. "Put this with my other Legacy items."

Bones arched a brow as he took the folder that was meant to be opened only in the event of Mencheres's death. He didn't know it, but by taking it, Bones had just assumed responsibility for Kira once Mencheres was gone.

"Still think you're soon to be shriveled, grandsire?" Bones asked with a hint of a scoff. "Vision impotence doesn't necessarily mean impending death. It might only be a temporary loss."

Bones knew that Mencheres's visions of the future were gone, but Mencheres hadn't told his co-ruler that the one thing he did see ahead of him was darkness. He also hadn't told Bones that his cold war with Radjedef was heating up. Bones would feel obligated to act on both pieces of information, and Mencheres didn't want that. He'd settle his own affairs in the time he had left.

"It is foolish not to be prepared for any eventuality," Mencheres said with a shrug.

"Indeed. Speaking of preparing for any eventuality, we might have a problem with some ghouls. I've heard reports that Masterless vampires have gone missing in recent weeks, with ghoul gangs as the primary suspects."

Mencheres hid a grim smile as he thought back to the morning of the warehouse. "I've heard the same thing."

"Could be nothing more than a few sods needing to be taught a lesson," Bones went on. "But it also could be Apollyon stirring things up with more of his rot about my wife's being a threat to the ghoul nation. I'll be checking into it. Thought you'd want to know."

Another reason why Mencheres was frustrated by his impending death. Bones would be left to handle this threat without him if he was right, and Apollyon was involved. His death meant he'd be leaving his co-ruler when Bones needed him the most. Once again, Mencheres cursed the looming darkness in his visions.

"How fares Cat?" he asked, forcing back his anger at his fate.

"Quite well," Bones replied. His lip curled. "She said to send her regrets for not coming today."

Mencheres gave Bones a dry smile. "Yes, I'm sure she deeply regrets not seeing me."

"You erased her memory of a vampire who kidnapped her and coerced her into marriage when she was only sixteen," Bones said softly. His eyes glinted green. "And then you didn't bother to tell either of us about it until that vampire came after her again a dozen years later, or tell us the reason why he wanted her so badly. That sort of betrayal tends to linger."

"Walk with me," Mencheres replied, not addressing that. He went out into the garden, stopping by the small reflecting pool, waiting until Bones was next to him before he spoke again.

"The future is like water. All our actions ripple over it, changing its reflection. If I had told either you or Cat what was to come, you would have altered your actions, making the reflections of who you are different than who you were meant to be. We would all like to change our future to the simplest path, the straightest line, the road of least regrets"—Mencheres paused to smile sardonically—"but then the final outcome wouldn't be the same."

"Easy to say when you're the bloke who could see that final outcome in advance," Bones replied with an edge to his tone. "The rest of us had to wonder if those we loved would suffer or die because of our actions."

"We all wonder," Mencheres said quietly. "Even if we *know,* we still wonder."

Bones didn't say anything. Then he picked up a small pebble and absently threw it into the reflecting pool.

"Something I've wanted to ask you, grandsire. You said you'd seen before I was even born that I'd be the one you'd share your power with. Why didn't you change me into a vampire yourself, then? You were there that night. Yet you let Ian sire me instead."

"To keep you safe. Patra searched my people for the one I'd prophesied would murder her. My wife thought it would be someone I had sired myself. You were unusually strong, Bones, even as a young vampire. If I'd changed you over, you would have been even stronger—too strong to stay unnoticed by Patra for as long as you did. So I let Ian change you. You were still of my bloodline that way, as I made Ian; but it gave you a chance to grow without rousing Patra's lethal interest until you were ready to defeat her. As I said"—Mencheres gestured at the water in the reflecting pool, which still vibrated from the pebble Bones had thrown into it—"the smallest ripple can change everything."

Bones gave Mencheres a look he couldn't decipher. "The power you shared with me increased my strength and gave me the ability to read humans' minds, all in the first night. It's been almost a year and a half since then. Haven't you wondered if anything else has popped up in the interim?"

Mencheres stared at Bones, unblinking. "I would think if you manifested more of my powers, you would tell me."

A smile ghosted across Bones's lips. "Perhaps. Unless, of course, it might cause a problematic *ripple* in future events."

Had Bones begun to manifest the power of visions? That was how it had started with Mencheres when he was not much older than Bones; he'd caught tiny, indistinct flashes that he'd first dismissed as imaginings and only later realized were slivers of the future.

Then again, it was also a possibility that Bones was just trifling with him. Bones knew that Mencheres's loss of visions disturbed him, and the cold part of Bones might think it was a fitting revenge to have Mencheres believe

Bones knew something about the future but wouldn't reveal it to Mencheres.

Just as Mencheres hadn't told him what he knew about Bones and Cat.

But if Bones wasn't just attempting to trifle with him . . . "Then I can only trust in the blood vow we made when we merged our lines," Mencheres said, his tone hardening. "Despite what happened in the past, I kept my vow to do everything that was best for you and for our line."

Boned nodded once at the reflecting pool before he turned away. "I don't intend to betray the vow I made when we forged our alliance. But mind those ripples, mate. They might surprise you with what they bring."

Chapter Eleven

Kira blew out a tight sigh as she stood outside a club named Around the World. This was probably another waste of time. Seven straight nights of going to bars, clubs, or even coffeehouses that were reported to have had unexplainable or supernatural events had so far resulted in nothing. Well, except her sleeping just as little as before, paying high cover fees, getting hit on by persistent men and women, and finding zero evidence of any vampiric presence.

Furthermore, Kira was starting to wonder if she'd read too much into Mencheres's gesture with her boss. If he'd truly wanted to see her again, he could have left a business card under her door. Called her. Returned her cell phone with his number entered into it, something *easier* to follow. Doubts crept into her. Mencheres knew where she worked and where she lived, yet it had been a week with neither sight nor sound of him since he'd mesmerized her boss. All she had driving her was a nagging persistence that said Mencheres didn't want to disappear from her life despite his very effective vanishing act.

Or her instinct was wrong, and things were exactly as Mencheres wanted them to be. He'd said goodbye, and he hadn't contacted her since then. Maybe it was time for her to take the hint and quit chasing her tail.

If this place turned up nothing, she'd have to reexamine her actions. She might want to see Mencheres again so much that it was clouding her judgment, making her think her gut was telling her something that it wasn't. *One last scouting mission,* she decided, heading inside the club. Too bad this place had been last on her list for establishments that Mencheres or other vampires might frequent. It was a strip club, and somehow she couldn't imagine the suave Mencheres paying to see women take their clothes off. As for other vampires. . . . well, they could mesmerize women into taking their clothes off if they chose to. Why buy the cow when you can get the cream for free, as the old saying went.

Kira paid the admission fee and was advised of the three-drink minimum bar tab. Once inside, she did a slow sweep of the interior, which consisted of several bars, a huge center stage with a runway, a VIP area cordoned off by glittering floor-to-ceiling strands, draperied alcoves, and a small dining area, to her surprise. The inside of Around the World was actually more high-end than she'd expected, but she didn't plan to become a regular. Applause signaled that a dancer had just taken the stage. Kira decided to find a seat and order a drink. This was her last night of reconnaissance, after all. She might as well stay until she'd gotten a good look at the club's clientele. It was only 9:00 P.M. Probably still too early for a lot of the regulars.

An hour and a half later, Kira had been approached by about a dozen men trying to buy her drinks, pick her up, or otherwise not pay attention to the women they were supposed to be focused on. Kira kept her rebuffs quick and to the point, causing a few of them to rudely state their speculation on her sexual orientation. She didn't care. Whatever made them feel better about being rejected.

A new blast of music announced the next dancer on the stage. Kira glanced over, her attention more focused on seeing if any of the people around the stage had that telltale pale skin or too-quick movements than on the dancer, when her gaze narrowed. That dancer looked familiar. If she'd just quit whipping her hair around so wildly while she gyrated next to the pole, Kira could get a better look at her face to be sure.

She got up from her seat, moving closer to the stage. The dancer performed several very athletic, erotic maneuvers that showed off her flexibility, but still didn't give Kira a good view of her face. Kira pulled some money out of her wallet and let out a loud whistle, ignoring the comments from a few of the males near her. If this girl was who Kira thought she was . . .

The dancer came over with a sultry smile, bending down and placing her gartered thigh very close to Kira's face. She didn't look at the girl's lower half, bare and close enough for Kira to feel uncomfortable. She searched the girl's heavily made-up features, comparing them to photographs she'd just went through in one of those missing-person files. Older, yes, and a damn sight less shy-looking, but this was Jennifer Jackson.

"Hurry up," someone barked at Kira.

She tucked a twenty into the garter belt in front of her.

Jennifer gave Kira a wink and strutted away, continuing on with the rest of her routine. Kira just stared at her, not even really seeing the explicit moves but concentrating on her memory of what was in Jennifer's file.

Disappeared three years ago when she was seventeen. Thought to have run off with an older boyfriend named Flare, real name unknown. Jennifer's record as a high-school dropout who'd dabbled in drugs reinforced the police's opinion that Jennifer simply left town to escape her parents' strict household. Jennifer's parents disagreed and hired Frank two years ago, but he'd gotten nowhere. Jennifer's disappearance was in Frank's "cold case" pile now. It ended up at Kira's apartment because of the interview Frank had with one of Jennifer's old boyfriends, who told Frank that Jennifer had come to see him asking him to help her escape Flare, who "wasn't human." Jennifer had set up a meeting with her old boyfriend outside Around the World, but then supposedly never showed.

Frank's interviews with Around the World's staff resulted in all of them saying they'd never seen Jennifer, yet here she was, dancing naked under the stage name of Candy Corn while still one year too young to legally even be let in the door.

Could Jennifer really have been hiding in plain, explicit sight this whole time? Or did those who noticed not remember afterward because Jennifer was right, and her boyfriend Flare really *wasn't* human?

Kira took in a deep breath. She'd only come here to get a foothold in the vampire world in the hopes of its leading her to Mencheres. Not to get involved in a case where a young girl might have become an unwilling stripper for a vampire. Jennifer had asked her boyfriend for help two years ago. That didn't sound like Jennifer wanted to be in this situation, but things might have changed. If they hadn't, and Jennifer was held against her will by a vampire, it would be damn hard for Kira to help Jennifer do anything about that, as she knew from experience.

Save one life, Mack's credo echoed in her mind. Mack hadn't taken the easy way out when it came to her over a decade ago. If he had, Kira probably wouldn't be alive. This situation was way over her head, yes, but Kira couldn't just walk away without even trying to see if Jennifer needed help.

She squared her shoulders and flagged down the next topless waitress who walked by.

"Who do I see about setting up a private lap dance?"

Kira sat in one of the private booths that were sectioned off from the rest of the room. After several minutes, the dark curtains parted, and Jennifer appeared, smiling seductively as she approached.

"Hi, beautiful," Jennifer crooned, running her hands up Kira's legs as she began to twist her hips. "I was hoping you'd be the one waiting for me—"

"Jennifer," Kira said quietly. "Jennifer Jackson."

The girl paused, her eyes darting around. Then she began snake-hipping again, leaning forward to brush her breasts against Kira's legs.

"How do you know my name?" she whispered.

This was an awkward way to carry on a conversation. Jennifer was naked except for an extremely small g-string, and she kept rubbing and swaying her body against Kira. Kira assumed the curtained booths were being monitored if Jennifer kept up the lap dancing even though she now guessed Kira wasn't just here for a thrill. Jennifer didn't seem to be afraid to verbally acknowledge her real name, though, so maybe the monitoring was only visual. Kira tried to fix an appreciative look on her face and ignore the softer parts Jennifer pressed on her as she spoke.

"I'm an investigator your parents hired," Kira whispered back.

Jennifer's face twisted even though her frozen smile still remained. "They can't help me. Neither can you. Get out before you're discovered or you might end up like me."

Poor girl clearly sounded like she was here against her will. Kira's resolve strengthened. Someone had forced Jennifer to disappear from her family's life at seventeen to become a stripper. What if Kira's little sister had been the one kidnapped so young, and someone who could have helped Tina didn't try because it *might* be too dangerous? She'd wanted to become a cop to protect the people who needed it. Well, here was someone who really needed it, and Kira might be the only one who knew enough about what held Jennifer to help her get away.

"Did Flare make people forget they'd even seen you when you tried to get away before?" Kira asked, taking the plunge.

Jennifer stopped in the act of straddling her. "Who are you? How do you know that?"

"Keep dancing," Kira hissed. Jennifer began her sultry squirming again even though her practiced smile had slipped.

"I'm someone who knows what kind of creature can make people forget things they've seen with just a look," Kira said, her confidence growing as Jennifer's expression changed from suspicious to hopeful.

She *would* hang a bat sign in her apartment window and shine a big light behind it to get Mencheres's attention if she had to. Or she'd take an ad out in the papers with her picture and a plea for someone tall, dark, and dead to contact her. Everyone but Mencheres would think she was just a crazy, horny female. Mencheres had kept Kira captive before, yes, but he'd been faultless in his courteous treatment of her. Kira couldn't imagine that he'd condone another vampire's snatching a teenage girl from her family and forcing her to strip.

"And I'm someone with a gun containing silver bullets right here in my purse," Kira went on. "If you come with me, Jennifer, I'll try to get you away from this. I—I know someone who might be able to help."

From how hopeless Jennifer had sounded before, she probably hadn't tried to escape in years. With luck, Flare wasn't here tonight, and any others who were supposed to keep an eye on Jennifer had grown lax. If she and Jennifer quietly snuck out a back entrance, they could be away before any of the bouncers or staff noticed . . .

The curtains snapped open, and a stocky male appeared. Both Kira and Jennifer jumped. A sinking feeling coursed through her as the young man's eyes changed from whatever color they had been to glowing, bright green.

"Why hello there," the vampire said. "And just who might *you* be?"

Kira's hand went immediately into her purse for her gun, but the vampire had her wrist seized before she'd even grasped the handle. Jennifer bleated in fear and jumped back, cringing against the curtained wall. The vampire hauled Kira up with her wrist still held in that painful grip.

Shit! ran through her mind over and over. She should have had the gun in her hand *before* she began talking to Jennifer. Maybe then she could've squeezed off a shot that would've disabled the vampire enough for her and Jennifer to get away.

The vampire grabbed her purse in a flash, yanking on Kira's wrist hard enough for her to feel like her arm was about to be ripped out of its socket.

"Don't move," he said, his eyes flashing green.

She didn't, but not because she had a sudden mesmerizing compulsion to stand still. If the vampire thought mind-control tricks worked on her, she might stand a better chance of escaping.

The vampire freed her wrist, making a band of hope arc through Kira. He was buying it! *Now just walk away and leave me alone while you rifle through my purse . . .*

He didn't, but Kira kept her face from showing her disappointment as he pulled out her gun and checked the clip.

"You really *do* have silver bullets in this," the vampire said musingly. "And you were trying to steal Jenny away. Who put you up to this?"

"No one," Kira replied, attempting to fix a glazed expression on her face even though her heart hammered with fear. Those ghouls had gutted her in a second. This vampire could do the same. Any moment, she might be looking down at a horrible lethal wound before she'd even realized the vampire moved.

The vampire frowned, grasping her chin in a grip hard enough to make her jaw creak.

"I said, who put you up to this? Only another vampire would know to send you here packing silver bullets. Whose pet are you, hmmm? Give me a name."

"No vampire sent me. I'm a private investigator. Jennifer's parents hired my firm," Kira replied in as much of a monotone as she could manage. If she was very,

very lucky, the vampire would flash more green in her eyes, tell her she'd seen nothing, assume that erased her memory, and send her on her way. She could redouble her efforts to find Mencheres and come back later with him to help Jennifer . . .

"You're really hot," the vampire said, looking her over. Fangs flashed when he grinned. "Too old for a job here, though. My customers like 'em young, real wet behind the ears still—and wet in other places."

He laughed at his crude joke. Kira didn't blink. *That's right, I'm too old to force into nude dancing, so just send me on my way.*

"But you sure are a sexy thing," the vampire continued. He grasped her wrist again, this time hard enough to make her bones grind together. "And you're lying your pretty little ass off," he whispered as he yanked Kira closer.

His breath smelled like alcohol fumes when he blew it out after a deep inhalation. "No scent of vampire on you, but you could've washed that off easy enough, and someone sure sent you here," he went on. "Someone who told you about silver and who fed you enough of their blood to make you immune to my gaze, or you'd have spilled who they were by now. Who is it, sweetie? And why did that person want you to steal my property from me? Tell Papa Flare all about it."

Despite the fear and adrenaline coursing through her, Kira thought of her promise to Mencheres not to tell anyone about him. She swallowed hard while her instincts warned her that she walked a razor's edge between life and death right now.

"I came on my own—"

Pain exploded in her face, so quick it stunned her. Her eyes teared, her head rang, and blood filled her mouth. As suspected, she hadn't even seen Flare move before feeling the effects of his striking her.

Flare smiled as Kira regrouped from the blow. It reminded her of the smile that ghoul had given her a couple weeks ago. Right before he'd torn her stomach open.

"So you need a little persuading before you tell me who it is, huh?" Flare asked. He sounded almost elated. "Well, we'll need a more private place to talk then, won't we?"

Chapter Twelve

Mencheres snapped his suitcase shut, taking a final look around the bedroom. It was the last time he'd see this tiny space with its unappealing décor. He wouldn't spare a thought about leaving under normal circumstances, but it was symbolic of his decision. He wasn't coming back. Not to this room, or this house, or this city. He'd lingered here too long already, loath to severe that final connection to the human who still haunted his thoughts even though he'd kept his vow not to follow Kira again.

Gorgon came into the room, his blue eyes somber. The Nordic vampire could sense his sire's moods, especially now with the normal shielding Mencheres maintained slipping as he looked around again. Selene, Kurt, and Sam had already left the day before. It was time for him and Gorgon to go. He could delay no longer.

"The plane is fueling?" Mencheres asked.

"Yes."

Mencheres gave Gorgon a dry smile. "You need not go with me, my friend. I have told you many times that you should occupy yourself with other things aside from my domestic duties."

Gorgon smiled back, stretching the scar that ran down the length of his cheek. "And I have told you that what I choose to do with my time is my concern."

Gorgon's loyalty was required as a member of Mencheres's line. His friendship was not. Neither was his genuine affection and concern. Some things simply could not be commanded by fear, respect, or power.

Mencheres didn't say it, but he was grateful to have Gorgon by his side, knowing the vampire cared for him beyond the bounds of obligation. If he told Gorgon how much of a comfort he'd been during the past several harsh centuries, it would add to Gorgon's determination to stay—which held Gorgon back from what he should become.

"Why do you refuse to ask me for freedom from my line? You know I would grant it to you. You are past the time when you should be your own Master."

Gorgon squeezed Mencheres's shoulder. "When you no longer need me, I shall leave."

That would be soon enough. The grave loomed ahead whether he sought it now or not. Perhaps he would stage his death to appear as though Radjedef had done it. The thought sent cold satisfaction through Mencheres. *You seek my end, Radje, but when it comes, I shall ensure that it brings you down, too.*

Gorgon's mobile phone rang. "Probably the pilot," he murmured, walking away.

Mencheres steeled himself not to take another look

around as he left the room and went down the hall of the third floor. The air was still faintly scented with lemon, Kira's essence lingering as if she were a spirit taunting him.

Mencheres walked faster, taking the stairs two at a time. When he was free of this house, he would be free of reminders of Kira, breaking the strange, hypnotic sway her memory seemed to hold over him. He had no time for this useless longing over a woman who was fated not to be his.

"Sire."

Gorgon's voice cracked through the empty house, filled with an urgency that made Mencheres spin around in midstep. He ascended the stairs without touching them this time, flying up to the third floor.

Gorgon's countenance was stony as he held out his phone. "You need to take this."

Kira watched Flare through one eye and a haze of pain. After he'd dragged her and Jennifer upstairs into a section of the club that was empty of anyone except two other equally abusive vampires, he'd continued to demand that Kira tell him what vampire sent her here. She refused. The beatings to her face grew more severe, but still, she wouldn't break her promise to Mencheres. Then Flare had taken her hand and slowly crushed it in his fist, smiling the entire time.

The agony from her bones splintering under that merciless grip had been more intense than anything she'd felt before. Flare kept his hand closed over her shattered one, continuing to squeeze, while his other hand began to yank up her skirt.

"How'd you like to be fucked while I squeeze your hand tighter with every pump, hmm, sweetie?" Flare crooned.

Kira thought she'd pass out from the pain, which would have been a welcome respite, but she stayed conscious. Everything in her rebelled against breaking her word, but this animal meant what he said. From his expression, Flare would enjoy it, too.

"Mencheres," she gasped out. "He didn't send me here, but . . . I know Mencheres."

Flare let go of her so abruptly she fell over, her vision blackening for several moments. When Kira could focus again, she saw Flare exchanging a wary glance with the two other vampires.

"That's a fucking problem," the bald-headed one muttered.

"If she's telling the truth," Flare countered. The cheerful expression he'd worn for the past hour slipped, and he began to pace. "Put her over there. I need to check this out."

The bald vampire hauled Kira up, sitting her in a chair. Everything swam in her vision for a few moments at the agony from her hand being jostled, but she took several deep breaths and kept herself from screaming. Jennifer edged a little closer to Kira's chair, not touching her but staring at her with silent sympathy.

Kira stayed quiet while Flare began making a series of phone calls, repeating to several people that he urgently needed to get through to Mencheres. She had no idea what sort of response Flare was getting, but every so often, he would throw a calculating, probing glance her way.

She wasn't sure which felt worse: the pain or her shame at breaking her promise to Mencheres. Still, she couldn't have allowed Flare to carry through with his threat. From what she knew of Mencheres, he'd understand.

"Finally got through," Flare said with a sharp glance at

her. "He's coming to the phone now. Moment of truth for you, sweetie."

Kira suppressed a shudder. Flare didn't need to add that what happened in the next few seconds determined whether or not she would die. She already knew that. The question that loomed in her mind was whether or not she could stand what Flare would do to her before he killed her.

"This is Mencheres?" Flare asked. "Yeah, sorry to bother you, but I have this human at my place who insists she belongs to you."

"I said I *knew* him," Kira corrected at once, coughing a little at the blood in her mouth.

A heavy hand landed on her shoulder, five fingers tightening in warning. Even that slight movement blasted more pain through her hand.

"Shhh," the bald vampire blew out threateningly.

"She's about five-five, dirty blond hair, pretty. Name on her driver's license is Kira Graceling," Flare went on.

He straightened from his easy slouch in the next moment, his expression turning grim.

"Uh-huh. Right. No, she's mostly fine . . . in a club called Around the World on State Street, Chicago Heights. Why don't we—"

Flare clicked his phone shut. "He hung up, and he said he's on his way," he told the room at large.

The bald vampire's hand left Kira's shoulder. "Shit, bro."

"I didn't fucking know!" Flare snapped. "I mean, what're the odds?"

Kira was weak with relief at hearing that Mencheres was on his way, but there was too much subtext going on for her to know if that meant she was out of danger or not. And she was having a hard time concentrating while mind-blistering pain continued to sear through her.

"You might want to fix her up," the vampire with the dreadlocks stated. "If Mencheres is coming to get her himself, then she's higher up on the food chain than just a blood snack to one of his people."

"Maybe not. He's gotta be local, since he said he'd be here in twenty minutes," Flare replied almost sullenly. "And if you're right, he'll be more pissed if she tells him I fucked her up, but he can't see for himself that it wasn't bad."

Not *bad*? True, compared to what the ghouls had done to her, Kira was in stellar condition, but how cruel Jennifer's time with him must have been if this is what Flare considered "not bad."

Jennifer. More shame swept through her. Some savior she'd turned out to be.

"How close are you to Mencheres?" Flare asked her suddenly. "You fucking him, or just feeding him?"

Kira turned her head away in silent refusal to answer. If she read the mood of the room correctly, Flare wouldn't dare beat her anymore unless Mencheres got here, then left her with Flare out of anger for Kira's breaking her word. But she didn't believe Mencheres would do that, no matter how upset he was at her for revealing that she knew him.

Though this was hardly the way she'd hoped to see him again.

"Not gonna answer me, huh?" Flare said, with a glint in his eye. "Smart girl, knows I can't touch her with the big dog coming to get her. But I can touch Jennifer, because she's *mine*."

Flare was behind Jennifer in an instant, his fangs cutting a thin red trail down her shoulder. Kira was on her feet before she even had a chance to wince at how much it hurt her to move.

"I'm not sleeping with Mencheres," she got out through gritted teeth.

Flare let Jennifer go. She stumbled off to the other side of the room, looking scared but not hurt aside from those two red scratches. Dreadlocks and Baldy made noises that sounded like relieved whoops.

"That's a load off," Flare muttered.

"Oh yeah," Dreadlocks said. Then he laughed. "Know how dead you'd be if you worked over the first woman Mencheres has taken up with in *how* long?"

"He'd be grinding your bones to make his fucking bread," Baldy joked, to more laughter.

"Scared me for a minute," Flare admitted, not looking afraid now.

Kira glanced away from them. Maybe if she concentrated very hard, she could focus on something other than their smirking laughter or the pain radiating up her arm. She leaned against the wall with her good side, closing her functional eye, taking in deep breaths and trying to mentally will herself away.

Unfortunately, even after several minutes of trying, no meditative technique Kira tried could hold up against the throbbing anguish in her hand. If Flare let her go, she could use some of the blood in those vials at her house to heal herself. But could she take some of that limited supply, knowing it might result in robbing Tina of a year or more of life?

"Do you feel that?" Flare muttered.

Kira opened her eye in time to see the two doors across the room explode outward, ripped off the hinges by some invisible force. They crashed onto the floor with a thud that seemed to reverberate around the room. Flare, Baldy, and Dreadlocks jumped, backing away.

Then a tall cloaked figure swept into the room, long dark hair swinging with his rapid stride, charcoal-colored gaze turned to blazing green.

Kira's heart felt like it skipped a beat. *Mencheres.*

His eyes seemed to meet hers without pausing over anyone else in the room. Then Mencheres stopped, his features hardening like sand turned to glass. The fury that emanated from him was palpable, making her heart skip a beat again.

Was her beaten condition the reason for his anger? Or was Mencheres that furious at *her*?

Chapter Thirteen

Mencheres crossed the room to Kira, rage erupting through him as he took in her battered face. One sniff revealed that though she'd been grievously mistreated, she had not been raped, which changed her captors' fate from a slow, tortuous death to merely a quick, painful one.

Then Mencheres saw Kira's hand—swollen, bloody, and misshapen—with shards of bone piercing her skin. *A slow, tortuous death it was, then.*

He didn't spare a glance at the three vampires as he gently took her into his arms. From their auras, they were too young and weak to pose any threat to him, even with his back turned. Mencheres's mouth tightened when he felt Kira flinch away from his touch. Was it from the pain she was in, or from fear of him?

He cut open his wrist with his fangs, holding the bloodied slash to Kira's mouth. She didn't attempt to turn her head away, to his relief, though she grimaced as she swallowed. Then a harsh gasp came from her.

"Your hand will hurt as it heals. It will quickly pass," Mencheres said, keeping his wrist pressed to her mouth. Even though his wound closed in seconds, drops of blood that Kira could swallow still clung to his wrist.

Something low clenched inside him as he felt her warm tongue flick across his flesh. Before his gaze, Kira's nose straightened back into its normal, lovely slope, her swollen eye cleared, her lip mended, and her hand stretched, fingers losing their twisted, crippled malformation until they became straight and smooth again. Even though more blood wasn't necessary, Mencheres kept his wrist to her mouth simply because he wanted to feel her lips on him for a few moments longer.

"Yeah . . . so you must be Mencheres," a voice behind him said. "I'm Flare, and this is Patches and Wraith."

He ignored them, focusing on Kira's eyes as the pain left her gaze and her breathing lost its raggedness. She sniffed, then coughed as some of the remaining blood from her previously broken nose went back up her nasal passages. Mencheres had no handkerchief, so he wiped Kira's face with his sleeve, removing his wrist from her mouth at last.

"Is the pain gone?" he asked.

"It's gone." Her gaze flickered to him before skidding away. "I'm sorry," she whispered. "I tried not to tell them your name, but—"

"But as soon as she did, I didn't touch her again," that same voice interrupted behind him. "Hey, you'd have done the same thing to someone who crashed your place and tried to make off with your property, right?"

Now the other vampire had his full attention. Mencheres

turned around, lasering his gaze on Flare. "Would I?" he asked, drawing the two words out.

Kira had been harshly abused out of loyalty to him, even though he'd only bid her not to speak of him or vampires to anyone *human*. He knew how much agony the injury to her hand would have caused with its abundance of nerve endings. Flare would have known that, too, and this fool expected him not to avenge her suffering?

"If I would torture a human for attempting an act she could not possibly complete," Mencheres went on, each word drenched in ice, "then what do you think I will do to a vampire who needlessly abused someone under my protection?"

Flare's expression became alarmed. The two other vampires began to edge away from Mencheres, but he slammed them into immobility with a flick of his mind.

"Now, listen," Flare began, holding out his hands. "She wouldn't say who she belonged to, and I couldn't control her mind to find out any other way."

Mencheres debated slaughtering them before any more useless words assailed his ears, but then decided against it. Kira had experienced enough violence tonight. Besides, these rooms were probably covered by security cameras, and he would leave nothing behind that might cause an issue for Kira later.

He'd kill these three another time, in a more private place.

"I only tried to help a young girl get back to her family," Kira said. She pointed at a human crouched in the corner. "He kidnapped her and forced her to strip here."

Flare shrugged. "She wanted to get involved in the vamp world. She got her wish. Can't help it if she's crying about it now."

Another reason to kill the fool. Young vampires who

gloried in abusing humans just because they could would cause even more trouble when they grew older and sought more challenging sport. It was a blatant lie that he'd had no recourse except torture to find out who Kira belonged to. They hadn't even attempted another way.

"We are leaving," Mencheres told Flare, his voice daring the other vampire to object.

Footsteps approached. Mencheres glanced up, expecting to see Gorgon, who'd come here by car instead of flying as Mencheres had. But the vampire striding into the room wasn't his loyal friend. It was his oldest enemy.

Radjedef smiled. "Menkaure, you look surprised to see me."

"Radje." Mencheres's voice was a barely contained growl. "You follow me now? How empty your days must be."

"I followed *him*," Radje said, nodding at Gorgon, who appeared behind him in the doorway. "You were a bit too hasty for me to track, but to my luck, he was not."

"My apologies, sire," Gorgon said, sounding both frustrated and contrite.

"Who's he?" the bald one Flare introduced as Patches asked.

Radje drew himself up to his full six feet. "I am a Law Guardian."

"Don't fuckin' believe it, a cop when you need one," Flare muttered.

"What do we have here?" Radje asked, coming closer. Mencheres shifted as if bored, but by doing so, he placed himself squarely between Kira and Radje. From his old enemy's smirk, the action hadn't gone unnoticed. "This same human again? Menkaure, do I detect an unusual interest from you?"

"If by interest you mean coming to collect my property, then yes, I am interested," Mencheres replied coolly.

Kira took in a sharp breath at being referred to as "property," but Mencheres didn't turn around to look at her. She was safer if Radjedef believed Kira was worth no more to him than any other human he'd claimed under his line.

Radje appeared to be mulling Mencheres's sincerity. "You are very protective of your people, even property. But there's something more here, I believe. You." Radje's gaze swung to Flare. "You implied that you were glad a Guardian was here. Why? What transpired with Mencheres and this human?"

Flare glanced at Mencheres before he spoke. "Uh, I grabbed that human when I heard her tell my girl that she had a silver-filled gun to take her away from me. Then she wouldn't tell me who she belonged to without prompting, but finally she says she's with Mencheres. I called him, he came, seemed pretty pissed at us for smacking her around, but it's not cool for someone to try and steal my property, right?"

Mencheres silently cursed himself for not ripping the heads off Flare, Patches, and Wraith as soon as he arrived. Radjedef would have nothing on him then. Only the other vampires' Masters would, if they chose to war with Mencheres over Flare, Patches, and Wraith's deaths.

Radje had a sly smile on his face as glanced from Mencheres to Flare, sensing the noose tightening. "Did Mencheres threaten you? Remember—I am a Guardian, so you must answer me honestly."

Flare shuffled his feet. "Not really. He was just about to leave with her when you showed up."

Radje laughed, so loud and merry, Kira jumped. "Oh, you poor fool. If he was leaving without even a harsh word uttered at you, he had no intention of letting you live to see the next moonrise. When my old friend is truly angry, he never bothers with words. He only kills."

Mencheres kept his expression impassive, but he did not bother to deny it. Radjedef knew him too well.

"These are serious charges against you, Menkaure," Radje went on, still in that same cheerful tone. "How do you plead? Do you admit that you sent your human to steal this vampire's property?"

"No, he didn't."

Mencheres swung around to face Kira. He'd been about to say yes, he'd directed *all* of her actions, but she'd spoken up before he could utter a word.

"Do not say anything else," Mencheres growled. Radjedef could only impose steep monetary penalties on him and damage his standing with the Guardian Council, but Kira was far more vulnerable to the Guardian's judgments.

"I'm not going to stand here and let you be blamed for my actions," Kira muttered.

"Do not—" Mencheres began.

"Silence!" Radje roared, all pretense of geniality gone. "I am the Law, and unless you choose to have the charges against you grow even more severe, Menkaure, you will not interrupt her again."

Frustration coursed through him. If he forcibly rendered Kira mute with his power, he'd be in direct defiance of a Guardian's order—with witnesses. Radjedef had been waiting countless centuries for Mencheres to make such a mistake. If he spoke at all now, his co-ruler and his people would pay for it, not just himself.

"I haven't seen Mencheres in over a week," Kira went on, her jaw set in that stubborn line. "He had no idea I was coming here. I'm a private investigator, and I recognized Jennifer from one of the case files at my job. She clearly wasn't here of her own free will, so I offered to help her escape. And yes, I told her I was armed. Mencheres only got involved when Flare caught me and called him."

"'S about right from what I know," Flare muttered. Patches and Wraith also murmured their agreement.

Radje looked disappointed, but it was all Mencheres could do not to roar with pain. Kira had no idea what she'd just done.

"Once he knew of your actions, Menkaure did nothing to reprimand you?" Radje sounded skeptical. "That's tantamount to authorizing your activities."

"We didn't get that far. I'm sure Mencheres is *very* angry at me." Kira glanced at him with those words, blind to the trap she'd dug for herself. "But you showed up right after he got here, so he didn't have a chance to do anything about it."

Radje let out a disappointed noise. "Very well, Menkaure, your human has exonerated you. Will you be killing her now, or shall I?"

Chapter Fourteen

Mencheres listened to Kira seal her fate as if he were trapped inside a terrible dream. For several frozen moments, he could almost see her death happening before him; Radje snapping her neck with a careless flick of his wrist. Or opening her jugular to leave Kira choking on her own blood as it streamed from her throat. What it would feel like to watch her die? Would it bring back the antipathy he'd had about living before he met her, making him once again view the impending darkness in his future as something to be welcomed?

If Radje were anyone else, Mencheres could kill him. He could slaughter every vampire in the room and hide all traces of their remains. He could raze *this entire building* so that even if his actions were recorded, they would never come back to harm him or Kira. All of these things he could do, were it not for the smirking Law Guardian across from him.

"Ah, my old friend, I do believe I've finally cracked that impenetrable sarcophagus of yours," Radje said with satisfaction. "This one did mean something to you, didn't she? How amusing."

A slow-building rage began to snake through him, throbbing beneath his skin, seeking to be released to wreak its will. *You could still kill them all,* it whispered. Suspicion would fall on him, but with no bodies as proof, Mencheres might yet avoid the punishment of the remaining Guardians raining down on him and Bones. *Let me free,* that rage urged in a tantalizing murmur. *You have kept me chained for far too long . . .*

"Hey, man, I didn't mean for it to come to this," Flare said, giving a nervous glance between Radje and Mencheres. "If he says he'll keep the human away from me and my property in the future, that's good enough for me—"

"But it is *not* sufficient for *me*," Radje snapped. "You lodged a formal complaint of attempted property theft against Mencheres by informing me of what his human did here tonight. If you had no wish to do so, then you should have stayed silent."

"I didn't know telling you was like filing a complaint," Flare muttered.

Radje smiled coldly. "Ignorance of the law is no excuse. Humans and vampires have that one thing in common. However, vampires are not permitted to steal from each other as freely as humans do, and most especially will I not be merciful to a *human* for stealing from a vampire.

Death is my sentence, so Menkaure, I ask you again, will you punish this mortal, or will I?"

"He kidnaps a teenager and forces her to strip for him." Kira's voice was calm even though her face was eerily white. "That's not considered a crime to you, but me trying to free the same girl merits a death sentence? You should be ashamed to call yourself the guardian of *any* law."

Radjedef did not even deign to look at Kira. "Kidnapping an unclaimed human is not a crime. Humans are our food; they don't have the same rights vampires do. Menkaure, your time to decide who carries out this punishment grows short."

Kira didn't reply to that. She didn't attempt to run, either, though the bald vampire grasped her shoulders as if he expected her to. Mencheres met her gaze, seeing horror and resignation swimming in those pale green depths, but no hope or pleading. She didn't expect him to help her. She expected to die at the whim of a man who had no real interest in her at all.

His rage began whipping around more urgently inside him, sensing Mencheres was close to letting it free. Kira's bleak acceptance of her fate was more than he could bear. No matter if it finished all of them, he could not let Radje condemn her to the same darkness that waited for him.

But he would not let the malicious power inside him free. It had ruined his life once. He would not give it another chance to destroy Bones *or* his people again.

"I shall carry out your sentence of death myself, Guardian," Mencheres said, watching as Radje's smirk deepened. "Yet afterward, I believe I shall bring her back from it."

Radje's smile fell. "Her sentence is meant to be a *punishment,* not a reward that improves her meager existence," he hissed.

"Her sentence is death, which shall be carried out for her crime. But as she is human, nowhere is it written that I cannot bring her back as a vampire after this sentence is completed. That boy might not know our laws, *Guardian*"—Mencheres gave Radje a cold smile as he emphasized the word—"but I am well versed in them."

"You haven't changed a human in almost a hundred years," Radje said, switching to the ancient Egyptian dialect that had been their first language.

Mencheres allowed a bemused expression to cross his face before he answered in the same language. "Has it truly been a century? Even more reason to change her. It has been too long since I refreshed my line with new blood."

"Your little mortal might not want to be your *new blood*," Radje taunted.

He turned toward Kira. Her breathing was jagged, and her pulse strummed loud enough to be heard even with the club's blaring music; but still, she did not beg for her life. Kira wouldn't have understood his recent exchange with Radjedef. She knew her sentence was death; what she wouldn't know was if she was to be brought back after that. Her green eyes seemed even paler with the overhead light reflecting in them as she stared up at him, powerless to control whatever fate Mencheres chose for her.

The bald vampire behind her released her with a little push toward Mencheres. Kira almost stumbled but regained her balance, casting a grim glance around at the other faces in the room before meeting his gaze again.

He didn't need to hear her thoughts to know what they would have been as she looked at the vampires surrounding her. *No hope, no reprieve, nowhere to run.* And she was right.

That blistering rage cascaded through Mencheres again, demanding another solution aside from violating Kira's mortality. But he knew what the only other solution was, and it could condemn his co-ruler for a crime he had no part in.

Mencheres cast a single glare at Radjedef. "Before this, you might have won our war without a battle from me," he said, again in their long-dead dialect. "But now, I will not go quietly into my grave. Instead, by the blood of Cain, I will drag you down to yours."

Radjedef gave him a measuring look. "I never wanted you to seek your own end. Why do you think I've been following you? After our last conversation, I feared you might kill yourself before you gave me what I wanted. And you *will* give it to me, Menkaure. Soon."

Mencheres knew what Radje wanted from him. The Law Guardian's slip at his house the other week was enough to betray his motivation, yet Mencheres had no intention of allowing him to obtain his goal. He thought of the dark void ahead of him. He had no idea how long he had until it enveloped him, but in that remaining time, he'd discover the means to finish Radjedef. Kira's mortality *would* be avenged. Both of them knew this wasn't a matter of law. The only reason Radjedef had demanded Kira's death was because he'd sensed it would hurt him.

It had, and Mencheres intended to make sure Radjedef felt the full measure of his pain, and Kira's, before he was finished. His eyes glowed green, and he pushed his rage back but allowed his power to uncurl. It filled the room, wrapping around each person in it, causing the other vampires to flinch and Radjedef to narrow his gaze. With his power spilling out until it enveloped the entire club, Mencheres was reminding him of the one thing the Law Guardian had always wanted but could never have.

Then he turned away from the sight of his enemy back to Kira. She didn't speak, didn't plead, but a single tear rolled down her cheek. Mencheres reached out, catching it before it fell from her proud, strong jawline. As soon as he touched her, Kira's whole body began to tremble.

"Make . . . make it quick."

Her voice was no more than a whisper, and she didn't look at him, but her spine was unbowed. Once again, her courage struck a chord in him. Kira had a warrior's spirit inside her sleek, feminine frame, for true valor was best revealed when defeat was inevitable.

His hand caressed her cheek, feeling her warmth soak into his fingers. Then he pulled her into his arms, hearing her heart rate triple as his head dipped to her throat.

"Mencheres—"

"Don't," he whispered, resting a finger against her lips as he held her in an unbreakable grip. "Don't tell me if you would prefer to stay in the grave, Kira, for no matter what you say—*I am bringing you back*."

Then he buried his fangs in her throat, right into the pulsating large vein that thrummed in unison with her heartbeat. Kira gave a gasping moan, her hands convulsively grasping his shoulders. Mencheres drew his teeth out, allowing a wealth of hot, sweet blood to fill his mouth through those twin punctures.

He swallowed that richness, his fingers moving from

Kira's lips into the thickness of her hair. Then he slid his fangs into her jugular again, deeper this time, sinking them to the hilt. Kira shuddered against him, the toxins from his fangs combined with blood loss making her sway on her feet. His arms tightened around her, holding her body and her tender throat closer to him as he bit her a third time, the three sets of twin punctures sending Kira's blood shooting into his mouth as fast as he could swallow it.

His entire body began to feel heated, heavier, and humming with the energy he absorbed with every crimson swallow. Despite hating the circumstances, feeling Kira's blood pour into him, merging them together more thoroughly than any sexual act, caused a heady exhilaration to flare through Mencheres. She would never be closer to anyone than she was to him in this moment, overflowing him with the life force that drained out of her, stitching them together with a bond that could never be undone.

When Kira hung limply in his arms, her heartbeat silent except for a few stubborn, intermittent flutters, Mencheres pulled away from her throat at last. Her eyes were closed, her mouth slightly open, those full red lips now palest pink without any breath stirring them.

Her penalty of death, paid. Now, to usher her into a new life.

Mencheres tugged Kira's silver necklace off, wrapping its thin chain around his fingers. Then he dug the long end of the cross into his neck, ripping it open. Held Kira's slack head to the wound and willed his blood out of him and into her. The silver burned his flesh, healing slower than a wound from any other material, as Kira's mouth filled with his—*their*—blood.

He could feel her body react to the blood even though not a muscle moved at first. Mencheres tilted her head back, sending that blood down her throat and deeper into her body. He dug her cross into his neck again, ripping another hole, willing more of their conjoined blood along with his power into her. This time, he didn't need to assist Kira to swallow his blood; her throat worked even as her heart fell silent for the last time.

Mencheres cradled her next to his neck, stroking her hair as he felt Kira's teeth bite down into the same spot he'd torn open with her cross. A sharp sting later, and she'd broken his skin, the life and power in his blood instinctively calling to her. She fastened her teeth harder into him and began to suck while great, wracking shudders enveloped her body.

He let his necklace-wrapped hand fall from his throat, using it to support Kira as he lowered both of them to the floor. None of the other vampires spoke as Mencheres sat with her in his arms, willing more of his blood into her while she tore and chewed at his throat with an ever-increasing hunger. The slight pain felt wonderful, because in each desperate swallow, Kira absorbed life from him just as he had from her. It was a darker way of life, yes, but a stronger one than the mortality that had slipped away with the fading of her heartbeat.

Live, Kira. Live.

When she swallowed more than the blood Mencheres had drained from her, he pulled her away, flexing his power to hold her when she would have fought to return to his throat. Her eyes were open but sightless, flashing with a darker, brighter shade of green, and two fangs curved out from Kira's previously flat upper teeth.

"Rest now," Mencheres whispered, holding her still.

A last shudder tore through her, then her eyes rolled back, and she slumped against him, her humanity murdered, her new vampire body unconscious but soon to rise.

Chapter Fifteen

Kira was trapped in a roaring inferno. She could hear the booming crashes of her apartment building collapsing around her, feel the agony of the flames as they ravaged her body, and she prayed for death to end the pain. And then death came, washing over her burned, broken body with sweet relief, easing the torment that seared her from the inside out. Cool, languid nothingness enveloped her, cocooning her from the fire that still raged around her.

She had to be dead, because the pain was gone, but oddly enough, Kira could still hear the crashing of her building and smell the fumes from the fire. What a strange thing, for her to so acutely hear and smell even though she was dead. Furthermore, she also could taste something incredible. Something so rich and succulent, it made even the sounds and smells fade into obscurity. She needed more of that, whatever it was. *Yes. More . . .*

Then that amazing nectar was gone, and lights smashed over Kira's gaze. The roaring of the collapsing building was back along with the choking fumes of gas that must have started the blaze, but something else was here, too. Kira whimpered. She must not be dead yet. Not yet, so any second, she'd feel the horror of her flesh being burned off her body again . . .

"*Kira.*"

Her name was an anchor that dragged her mind forward into reality. Suddenly, she saw Mencheres's face right in front of her, his eyes like black diamonds and his skin as perfect as colored crystal. She wasn't trapped in an apartment blaze. Something else had happened.

Mencheres. *He had killed her . . . and brought her back.*

That booming went off behind her again, the scent of gas rising above the darker, sweeter smell that was all around her. Kira tried to run from whatever had made such a horrible blasting sound, but Mencheres pressed her down. A jolt went through her as soon as his hands touched her skin. It felt like his entire body was electrified and shooting currents right into her.

"It is just the plane's engines, Kira. You are in no danger."

That blasting went off again, so loud and grinding, it couldn't be airplane engines. Kira looked around, but everything slid together in a blur until Mencheres grasped her chin and forced her to look only at him.

"Stay still. You have not adjusted to your new senses yet. They will feel overwhelming, but you will soon become accustomed to them."

Your new senses. Amidst the sizzling voltage that seared into her from Mencheres's hands, the crashing sounds around her, that oily-potent mixture of scents, and the flashes of light that seemed to burn her eyes, Kira's mind was seized with one single, unbelievable thought: She was no longer human.

"I'm . . . you . . . I'm not . . ."

She couldn't say it out loud. Shock blasted through her when she realized that though she'd used air to speak, she wasn't breathing. Almost blindly, her hand reached out to feel her neck. Nothing but smooth stillness beneath her fingers where her pulse should have been.

I'm a vampire.

Mencheres said nothing, his hand still cupping her face. Only then did her vision quit sliding enough to notice the rest of him. He was still wearing the same shirt from when she'd last seen him, but now, it had large red splotches on the front of it.

Was that her blood? And Radje . . . was the evil, smirking vampire who'd ordered her murder here, too? Kira's gaze swung around, but once again, everything started to blur together.

"Something's wrong with my eyes . . . who else is here?" she asked, panic starting to rise.

"No one but I, Gorgon, and the pilot are on this plane. As I said, you are safe."

Safe? Kira fought back a hysterical laugh. She supposed she was safe since she was already *dead*.

Mencheres sat in front of her, his dark gaze somber, one hand on her shoulder while the other cupped her face. She blinked, noting that he looked more—vivid. The striking planes of his face were more sharply defined, highlights of rust made Mencheres's hair a richer shade of black, his eyes were tinted with the faintest flecks of silver, and his skin . . . his skin was like sand in the sunshine, a gold-

and-cream mixture that felt electrified with the power sparking from him.

More than beautiful—magnificent. *Mencheres, her killer. Her savior.* It was too much for Kira to process.

"Don't touch me," she whispered, looking away.

His hands dropped. A sense of regret slivered along her emotions, gone so fast, Kira wasn't sure if she felt it or if it had been a hallucination, like the apartment inferno had.

That blasting kept going off all around them. She glanced to the side, things swinging less in her vision this time, to see that they were indeed on a small plane. A glance down revealed that Mencheres wasn't the only one with red splashed on the front of him. This wasn't the outfit she'd, ah, *died* in, but it was still covered in something purplish that smelled like liquid cotton candy.

Kira sniffed without thinking about it, her nose almost exploding at the rush of scents, too many to distinguish. Above all was the heady, addictive aroma coming from the red stains on her shirt. She'd grasped it and stuffed the material in her mouth before her next coherent thought, whimpering at the intense pain that flared through her chest.

Then something wonderful poured down her throat. Rich, intoxicating, vibrant, *necessary,* it cooled that instant flash of agony, soothing her from the inside out. She hadn't even been aware of closing her eyes until a smash of light and motion replaced the momentary peaceful blankness of her vision.

"What is *wrong* with me?" Kira managed to ask, trying to stop the crazy tilting when she glanced around.

Mencheres's features swam before they crystallized in the next moment. He was above her, his hair falling down around him in a dark curtain. If she was right, the hard, shaking flatness at her back was the plane's floor. Had she fallen down? She didn't remember doing that. Something wet coated her face and her mouth. Unable to stop herself, Kira licked it. A shudder of pleasure rippled through her, almost as intense as an orgasm. What *was* that?

"You are in the midst of the blood craze." His voice caressed her ears, making her shudder again. The sounds, sights, scents, tastes, textures . . . it was all too much. She felt like she was about to explode right out of her skin.

"It will lessen," Mencheres continued. Kira found herself arching toward his voice, as if it could physically touch her with the same effect that it stroked along her senses. "Until then, I cannot let you free. You would kill, Kira, and you would regret it."

"No . . ." she moaned, closing her eyes. *This isn't real. Isn't real.*

More bliss poured down her throat in the next moment, heavier than water, sweeter than syrup. She gulped, her back arching again, seeking to get closer to whatever the source was even though she couldn't move her hands to grab it.

"I will care for you," that silken, deep voice promised. "I will see you through this."

Isn't real, isn't real, isn't real, Kira continued to chant in her mind. *Nothing* this intense could be real.

And through the exploding sounds of the engines, the vibrations from the floor, that rush of pain and bliss ebbing and cresting within her, the liquid ecstasy streaming down her throat, and the shocks she felt each time Mencheres touched her, she heard his voice again.

"Forgive me."

Mencheres watched Kira's face as he lay next to her in bed. She hadn't stirred since dawn. The first rays of sunlight had caused her to fall deeply asleep, as it did to all new vampires. Her sleeping made it easier during their time in the human-laden areas, such as the private airport his plane landed in and the cars alongside him on the drive to his house in Jackson Hole, Wyoming. Mencheres had chosen this location with care. His nearest neighbors were at least a mile away in every direction, and Gorgon had attended to the immediate relocation of the humans staying there once they arrived. Fewer sounds, temptations, and restrictions near Kira was best as she dealt with her new condition.

Though it would still be hard on her. Normally, humans who were chosen to become vampires went through an extended period where they imbibed vampire blood in ever-increasing quantities. It gave them a glimpse of what their new hunger, senses, and increased strength would feel like, making the final change less of a shock. Kira had had no such preparation. Everything would be overwhelming to her at first.

And she had not chosen this transition of her own free will. That would be the greatest obstacle for her to overcome. Still, Mencheres knew he could not have acted differently. If it was a choice between Kira's death or her despising him, he would *always* choose to be the object of her hatred rather than the instrument of her permanent destruction.

Gravel churning on the driveway announced that Gorgon was back. Mencheres felt a twinge of relief. Kira had drunk almost all the blood bags he'd hastily stolen from a hospital on their way from the strip club to his plane. Animal blood would suffice in desperate circumstances, but he suspected that if Kira roused from her sleep to find herself feeding from a dead deer, she'd harbor even more resentment toward him.

"She awake yet?" Gorgon called out as soon as he entered the house.

"Not yet." Mencheres glanced at the ebbing rays of the sun straining through the crack in the drapes. She would rise soon. By nightfall at the latest.

Gorgon came into the bedroom carrying a Styrofoam cooler that he set on the floor. "This should last until dawn. I'll go back out to get more. Not a lot of hospitals around here, and I'd feel bad if I took their entire supply."

As would Mencheres, though again, the lengths he'd go to protect Kira superseded his concern for the trouble that might cause some unknown mortals.

"Secure fresh blood as well. Fly in some of my property to nearby hotels if need be."

"I will." Gorgon cast a glance at Kira's sleeping form. Mencheres had bathed and re-dressed her again, covering her with the thick quilt over that. It wasn't uncommon for new vampires to feel inexplicably cold as they adjusted to their altered body temperature, and even in spring, it was cooler at this higher altitude than it had been in Chicago.

"The Guardian was right. You do feel something unusual for her. When you're around her, your scent changes, and your shielding slips more than I've ever seen it do," Gorgon said quietly.

Mencheres pulled his emotions back inside the wall that cut off the other vampire's ability to sense them. "After what I've done to her, I would think it matters not."

"You had no choice. Once Kira accepts that and adjusts to being a vampire, she'll stop being angry at you." Then Gorgon smiled. "Though it might be fun to watch in the meantime. You've never had to work to seduce a woman before, have you?"

In fact, Mencheres had not previously needed to entice a woman into his bed with sweetened words or passionate pursuit. "Even if I had, considering my long state of celibacy, it would make me very *out of practice,* to use a contemporary phrase," he noted dryly.

Gorgon laughed. "Like riding a bike, some things you never forget."

Mencheres wished the only obstacle between him and Kira was the challenge of winning her. If that were so, he would relish the opportunity to gain her trust, affection, body, and—gods willing—her heart. But once again, that black void in his future was the true obstacle.

"I have larger concerns at present," was all Mencheres said.

Gorgon's smile faded. "Radjedef."

Mencheres sighed, closing his eyes. "I know what he wants, and I must ensure he does not find a way to force me to give it to him."

"You need to tell Bones."

His eyes snapped open. "No. And you will swear to me that you will not."

Gorgon looked dismayed, but he nodded. "If you insist. He's going to hear about Kira, though. I bet those three vampires at the club have already burned up the text-messaging and phone lines talking about it."

No doubt Flare, Patches, and Wraith *had* told others of the events last evening, but Mencheres wasn't concerned with Bones learning about Kira. He would have known of her importance to him as soon as he opened the Legacy envelope Mencheres left him. Now the only difference was that Bones would hear of Kira before that, but it was imperative that he not learn of Radjedef's increased hostility. Cat had only recently escaped a brush with death from one of the Law Guardians herself. Neither she nor Bones could risk angering another Guardian for a long, long time if they wished to stay alive.

Moreover, this fight with Radjedef had been brewing long before Bones was even born. Mencheres had no intention of letting his co-ruler fight this battle for him. It was his to win.

The currents in the room shifted and began to concentrate over the bed. Mencheres glanced at Gorgon, who wordlessly got out a bag of blood from the cooler.

He picked Kira up with one hand and took the bagged blood from Gorgon with the other, heading for the bathroom. Waking in a blood-soaked bed would do little to alleviate Kira's stress at being a new vampire.

Then again, waking in a blood-soaked bathroom probably wouldn't cause her to fare much better, but it was easier to clean tile than carpet and sheets, at least.

"You want me to wait, or leave now to round up more blood?" Gorgon asked.

Mencheres gave another glance at Kira, who was starting to twitch—the precursor to her roaring into awareness with a burning, mindless hunger.

"You may leave. I'll care for her."

And he would, during whatever time he had left.

Chapter Sixteen

Kira sat in the chair by the fireplace, hearing the crackling of the flames as acutely as if it were trees being chopped down. Still, she'd wanted the fire. Its warmth was a gentle cocoon, and it was softer on her eyes than the glare of the high-hat lighting or table lamps. She might be able to see in complete darkness now, but she didn't want all lights extinguished in order to be reminded of that. It was hard enough dealing with the intermittent chills, fangs stabbing her in the lip without warning, the clamor outside from the woods, and oh yes, her violent blackouts where she'd come to with blood running down her face and a burning desire for more of it.

She only had Mencheres's word that she hadn't hurt anyone during these blackouts. Well, that, and the cooler of rapidly dwindling blood bags. Mencheres said not to worry, that Gorgon would be back with more by dawn. The thought both disgusted and relieved Kira. No one needed to tell her that she was a threat to anyone—or anything—with a heartbeat right now, but though her body craved that red liquid with a boundless ferocity, Kira's mind still couldn't reconcile the fact that she was drinking *blood*. Human blood. She'd consider it a form of cannibalism, except she wasn't human herself anymore.

She leaned back—and the chair crashed beneath her, startling her. Even more surprising was that she wasn't sprawled on the wooden floor right now, but staring down at the broken chair with the afghan still around her shoulders. Had she leapt up before the chair fell? God, was she really that fast now?

A tingling along her skin announced that Mencheres had come into the room. He was almost soundless in his movements; only his scent and the faint rustling of his clothes would have betrayed his presence, if Kira couldn't *feel* him. She didn't even need to turn around to know how much distance separated them. The stronger that vibration grew along her skin, the closer Mencheres was.

Would all people feel as though they had their own form of an electrified force field around them? Or was that exclusive to vampires? Kira didn't want to ask. She wasn't sure she could handle more information right now.

"I don't know what happened, the chair just broke," she said. So much for getting a little time to herself. She hadn't been alone for ten minutes before the chair self-destructed on her.

"Leave it. I'll attend to it."

Even his voice sounded different than it had before she woke up undead. It was deeper, the nuances from his accent richer—and it seemed to curl around her like a thick, inviting fog.

"I can get it."

Kira went to pick up the largest piece of the chair when the wood splintered apart in her hand. She blinked and tried again, but the same thing happened. It was almost as if the chair disintegrated as soon as she touched it.

"What?" she began.

Mencheres moved next to her, close but not touching. Whenever she had an extended bout of awareness, like this one, he heeded her order not to touch her. She knew that wasn't the case during her blood-rampaging blackouts, but she couldn't blame him for that.

Of course, with his scent and tingling aura flowing over her, Mencheres might as well be touching her. Add in his voice, and Kira felt consumed just being near him.

"You are unused to your new strength." He reached down, grasping a chunk of the wooden armrest. It didn't dissolve into splinters like it had with her. He held it out to Kira.

"Try taking this, but *very gently*."

She grasped the wood—and it fell apart in her hand. Frustrated, Kira spun around, only to feel something stinging at her ankle. She looked down. Her right foot had gone through the wooden floor.

"What the *hell*?" she exclaimed, yanking her foot out. More of the floor came up with it, leaving a ragged hole.

"As I said, you are unused to your strength," Mencheres noted, no reprimand staining his tone even though she'd just ruined his chair and his floor. "This is another reason why you cannot be around humans until you have acclimated yourself to your new abilities."

She couldn't even rock back in a chair or stomp her foot

without causing massive damage? Add that to the blood-crazed blackouts every hour or so, and she'd been turned into a walking *death* machine!

Kira's eyes burned as if they'd been sprayed with Mace, her too-sharp vision turning pink and blurry. Would she ever be able to hug her sister again? Or would she crush Tina as easily as she'd ruined this chair if she touched her?

"Damn you for this," she choked, turning away from the sight of Mencheres. Then immediately, she wished she hadn't said that. It wasn't fair to blame him. He'd done his best to help her, both before Radje arrived and after, when the crooked cop made that lethal judgment against her.

From the corner of her eye, it appeared as though her words had no effect on Mencheres, but a wave of sadness ebbed through her consciousness. Kira stilled. She wasn't sad. She was angry and confused and starting to get hungry again already, but not sad.

Was that sadness from him? Could she actually feel his emotions now, like she could feel his power and the touch of his voice?

Kira remembered the last words she heard as a human: *no matter what you say—I am bringing you back*. Was Mencheres sad about being forced to kill her, or was he regretting his decision to bring her back as a vampire? Which were his real feelings: his previous, dismissive attitude about her to Radje yesterday? Or how caring he'd been when he first came to the club and healed her? He'd made no effort to see her after he let her go, but then Radje, after ordering her death, implied that he could tell Mencheres cared for her.

Before, wondering what the mysterious vampire

thought of her had been the source of Kira's dark, secret imaginings, but now, it was imperative that she know. Mencheres had altered her very existence and become a pivotal figure in her new life, but she had no idea if he regarded her as nothing more than a temporary irritant.

She looked up at him, noting that his usual impassive expression was firmly in place. Didn't matter. She wanted some answers before she lost her mind to another blackout or her consciousness to the coming dawn.

"Why did you mesmerize my boss into giving me a car and a raise?" she asked, almost tensing in her concentration to see if she could sense any emotions from him.

A faint tinge of surprise wafted across her subconscious before it vanished. Kira almost whooped. That *couldn't* be from her; she wouldn't be surprised by her own question!

"That's you, isn't it?" she asked, not giving Mencheres time to answer her other question. "Unbelievable, I can *feel* you now."

Just as abruptly, a wall seemed to slam in place around him, cutting off everything from Kira, even the tingling wave of his aura.

"You would be better served by concentrating on managing your strength and your blood consumption," Mencheres said, cool detachment in his tone.

She strode over, not caring that she felt the floors creak and bend beneath her feet.

"No you don't," she flared. "You don't get to wall yourself off from the only indicator I have of what you're thinking. You *killed* me yesterday and brought me back into an existence where everything is different, especially me. But what's almost as frightening is that I don't know if this means anything to you aside from a big, boring inconvenience. So give me something. It can be words, an unguarded expression, a flash of your emotions, whatever, but do it now, because I need a hint as to where I stand with you."

If Kira could still have breathed, she would have been panting with the emotions swirling in her, but she was as still as the vampire across from her as she waited for his response. Mencheres didn't lose his inscrutable mask, nor did that invisible wall around him collapse, but at last he inclined his head.

"You were working late into the night, and as it was more than proven the day we met, it wasn't safe for you to walk to and from your employment."

For a second, Kira didn't know what he was talking about. Then she remembered her original question to him, and disillusionment coursed through her. All that time she'd spent looking for Mencheres had been based on her assumption that his actions with her boss meant he wanted to see her again. How wrong she'd been. *Dead* wrong, in fact. It had been nothing more than a careless gesture made out of pity. *Be careful what you wish for,* she mused darkly. She'd succeeded in her quest to see Mencheres again, but it had cost Kira her life.

"Thanks," she said dully. "Now, tell me why you didn't let me stay dead?"

Mencheres glanced away, his face becoming even more unreadable if that were possible. "Radje's judgment was an abuse of his power. The only reason he sentenced you so harshly was because of his hostility toward me, so the least I could do was see that you did not remain dead."

Another pity gesture, Kira thought, shaking her head in disbelief. What a brilliantly wretched realization to know that her current existence was due to nothing more than one vampire's spite and another's twinge of conscience.

If she'd only stayed away from Mencheres once he let her go, she'd have a new car, a raise, a sister whose life wasn't cut tragically short, some friends, an irresponsible but somewhat loving brother, and an occasional social life. But no, she'd thrown that all away chasing after a vampire who probably hadn't spared her a thought since he dropped her off on that roof. *You fool,* Kira lashed herself.

"You need not fear that everything from your former life is lost to you," he went on, almost causing Kira to laugh. "In a few months, you should have enough strength after dawn in order to return to your employment. And in as little as a week or two, you should have control of your hunger and abilities around humans enough to resume seeing your family again—"

"You just don't get it, do you?" she interrupted him, recklessness rising up in her. "All of this—this suddenly being something *else* is bad enough, but to know the only reason I'm not in a grave isn't because my life meant anything to you but because you thought it would balance some imaginary set of justice scales . . . well, that *sucks*. And yes, I realize the irony of that statement."

Something wet slipped down Kira's cheek. She swiped at it, surprised to see pink liquid on her fingers. Were those tears? Could she still cry, even though she was a vampire now?

Before she could ponder that, a pain that was becoming all too familiar ripped through Kira. She bent over, holding her stomach as if she could somehow stuff her need for blood back down inside her.

The breeze lifting her hair was the only indicator she had that Mencheres left and returned in a flash of movement. He held two of those damn red bags in his hand, and the inner leap Kira felt when she saw them left her twisted with dueling urges. She wanted to throw the bags out of the window in repugnance. She wanted to tear them from Mencheres's hands and devour them with rabid gulps.

He held one of the bags out to her, but Kira looked away. She didn't want to drink more blood. It was wrong, gross . . .

Twin stings of pain in her lower lip told Kira her fangs had burst out of her upper teeth, resulting in a tease of that rich, coppery taste flavoring her mouth. More pain erupted through her body, that hated feeling of being burned from the inside out increasing to a ferocious pitch.

Mencheres had her in his arms in the next instant, holding the slickness of the bag to her mouth. "You must."

She only knew she'd torn into it when incredible relief filled up the previous torment inside her. Kira felt herself beginning to float away, her mind numbing from the rush of exhilaration and hunger, but before she lost herself to the blackness, something nagged at her subconscious. Something she'd been too distracted to pick up on when Mencheres first told her why he'd mesmerized her boss into giving her the car and the raise. *You were working late into the night . . .*

There was only one way Mencheres could know what sort of hours Kira had been working that week. He'd been following her.

Mencheres walked beside Kira in the woods. The air was pleasantly cool in the predawn hours, but Kira wore a thick sweater and pants as if it were much colder. She seemed preoccupied with the ground as she walked, her eyes flickering every so often to the sides only when nocturnal animals startled at their presence.

He said nothing, letting her become acclimated to the deluge on her senses from her surroundings. She'd woken a few hours before dusk on her second day as a vampire, insisting on showering by herself after she sated her hunger on the fresh bags Gorgon came back with. As Mencheres warned her, that did not bring positive results. Kira ripped the shower door off when she attempted to open it, then tore the faucet out of the wall when she tried to turn the water off after completing her doorless shower. Then her frustration at her inability to control her strength resulted in another attack of hunger, which was also no surprise. Anger and the urge to feed were tightly tied together for new vampires, and with all of Kira's emotions heightened to previously unexplored levels, she would be a swarm of volatility for the next few days.

"It doesn't seem right not to see the darkness," Kira said, finally breaking her silence. "I know it's night, but it looks like a sharper, overcast afternoon with a sun that doesn't hurt my eyes instead. There are no shadows anymore. Only spots of shade. How long did it take for you to get used to there being no darkness?"

Mencheres tried to recall his first days as a vampire. It was so long ago, it felt like the transformation had happened to someone else. He remembered the hunger when he first awoke; no vampire forgot that. But he couldn't remember what true night had looked like when he was human, so he could not recall how long it had taken him to stop missing it.

"Much of those early days, I've forgotten," he admitted.

"Because you're older than dirt, right?" Kira cast a slanted look at him. "So tell me, does it sound like a demolition site out here to you, too? Or did you learn to tune out background noise over the years?"

He briefly focused on the sounds that filled the forest. No, he had not bothered to pay them any heed, aside from discerning whether they were natural or a threat that needed to be eliminated. Had he simply learned to tune them out, as Kira described? Or was he so jaded that he no longer cared if the crickets sang, the leaves danced, the branches rubbed together while reaching out for one another, or the animals hunting for sustenance or companionship found their quarry?

"You learn to choose what you focus your attention on," he replied.

That was true. He might not have paid any notice to the sounds in the forest, but he could tell Kira every nuance of how her scent had changed as she walked alongside him. Or how many times her eyes had flared with emerald when she'd caught a glimpse of something with a beating heart in her vicinity.

Kira stopped walking, turning her face up toward the trees. "Fireflies. I haven't seen them since I was a kid. Tina and I used to go into the woods by our old house to try and catch them . . ."

Mencheres stopped as well, following her gaze to the lighted insects interspersed throughout the air. Her voice held another wistful note of remembrance he could not relate to. Even if he could remember his childhood, he'd had no siblings close to his age, and his homeland had been bare of such creatures as these.

But these memories held value to Kira, tying her to something lost from her youth. He glanced at her profile. Her head was tilted back, full lips parted slightly, pale line of her neck in stark, tempting relief against the backdrop of the forest. She looked so beautiful. Almost ethereal. Despite knowing better, he could not force himself to glance away.

He might not be able to share her memory of chasing fireflies as a child, but he could give her a new memory of the woods. One that no one else could replicate.

Mencheres sent wisps of his power along the ground, curling them around the blooms from several nearby patches of wildflowers. One by one, he plucked those blooms, until he had hundreds of pale purple, blue, yellow, and white flowers floating above the brush. Kira didn't notice. She was still staring at the fireflies.

Slowly, he drew his power back until the randomly interspersed blooms began to congregate into one large cloud.

Kira's eyes widened as she saw the mist of flowers sweep toward her on the ground. A shiver rippled over her flesh. "I can feel the energy coming from you. What are you doing with them?"

She didn't look at him as she asked. Mencheres didn't reply, but he sent his power out in another wave, grouping the flowers into a trailing comet that dipped and swooped around the tops of the trees in an intricate ballet. Kira made a sound between a gasp and a laugh, her face suffused with wonder instead of the pain and trauma from the past two days.

Still she didn't look at him, but kept watching the dancing flowers. Mencheres extended their former comet shape into one long swath. He sent that softly fragrant banner through a series of rising twirls before gathering the blooms into a circle several meters above Kira's head. Then he gradually widened the circle and brought it down around her, encompassing her inside a sheath of flowers.

She stared at the rings of wildflowers encircling her, reaching out her hands but not touching them. Then she finally looked at Mencheres, her green eyes lit up with a shade not unlike the fireflies she'd been admiring before.

"Let them go."

Chapter Seventeen

Kira held his gaze as she closed the distance between them. She'd gone on this walk meaning to confront him about following her. To find out if Mencheres had been motivated by suspicion or by the desire to see her again, but that wasn't necessary now. She could *feel* his craving for her. It seeped out from that wall he shielded himself with in ever-widening streams, until it was a tangible force, invisible but everywhere.

And it flared a hunger in her that almost brought her to her knees. She wanted to touch his skin, taste his mouth, and twist her hands in his long hair while he took her in his arms with something other than protectiveness. A throb took up cadence inside her as she came closer, almost within touching distance, impatient to feel him surrounding her with his body instead of just his power.

"Kira."

His voice was low, and he breathed in after he said it, as if inhaling her name. She reached out, her hands almost aching to connect with his flesh. Mencheres caught them, but he held her away from him, his aura of need changing to frustration.

"You don't really want this."

She almost laughed at the absurdity of that statement. Couldn't he sense the ache building in her, too strong to be called desire, too deep to be mere lust? If she could feel his emotion raging past his barriers, couldn't he feel hers, too?

"I want this. You. All of it."

She brought her body flush against his as she spoke, though he still held her hands away from him. The contact with his body, even covered in clothes, was enough to send a shock through Kira. She closed her eyes while a moan edged out of her throat. With his power sizzling into her everywhere they touched, he felt so good it almost hurt.

A harsh noise escaped him as well, so deep and primal, more heat flooded into her loins. Kira tried to free her hands from his grip with all of her uncontrollable strength, but Mencheres held her effortlessly, not even shifting his stance. His head dipped, his hair brushing her face and neck like sensual flicks of silk.

"This isn't what *you* feel. It's your new senses," he said, his voice dropping to almost a growl. "They make you feel things that might not be real—"

"I felt this for you before," Kira cut him off, need roughening her tone. "Even when you held me captive, but *especially* after you let me go. Don't tell me what I'm feeling isn't real, and don't even pretend that you don't want me, too."

She didn't care how challenging that sounded. With the same uninhibited, single-minded clarity she'd only felt before in dreams, all Kira knew was she wanted him and that he felt the same way about her. She tried to free her hands again. This time, Mencheres released her while his eyes turned from black to bright, blazing green.

Then he yanked her to him. Her nerve endings jumped in frantic response to the crush of his body against hers. She had time to wind her fingers into his hair before his mouth slanted over hers.

The jolt she felt at that contact seemed to go straight to her core, sending a ripple of shocks through her. His tongue raked past her lips to explore her mouth with blistering passion. He tasted like dark spices, rich and heady, exotic and intoxicating, filling her with heat. The erotic way he stroked his tongue along hers only increased when Kira's fangs burst free, inadvertently drawing his blood. Instead of pulling back, Mencheres kissed her deeper, holding her tighter, lifting her until her feet were off the ground and it was just his arms keeping her upright.

Her initial desire felt like only a vague whisper of longing. With Mencheres gripping her to him and his tongue ravening her mouth, she *burned* for him. Her hands left his hair to glide down his back, nails restlessly digging into him. Those hard muscles moved underneath her palms, taunting her with the rub of skin that was so close yet denied to her by their clothes.

Kira didn't want fabric between them. She wanted to feel his skin on hers. The steady pulsing between her legs built into a throb that demanded to be sated. She tried to tell him that, but his mouth continued to dominate hers with hungry, sensual insistence. She couldn't speak. She could barely even think.

Something soft brushed down her back and legs. Then,

somehow, her sweater and jeans were gone, and Mencheres was on the ground with her on top of him. She
didn't pause to wonder at the buttons that popped off his
shirt of their own accord before the fabric slithered away
from him. All she cared about was the incredible surge
she felt when their skin met. How hard, smooth, and tight
his chest felt against her breasts, and how it seemed that
he suddenly had a dozen hands, because she felt him
stroking every part of her.

The sensations bombarding her were just as intense as
when Kira first awoke as a vampire, only this time, they
weren't frightening. Her skin felt feverish, her body trembling with need and shuddering with ecstasy just from
the feel of him. A loud moan broke free when Mencheres
slid his mouth down from her lips to her throat, grazing
her skin with his prominently extended fangs. Instead of
biting her, he licked and sucked the highly sensitive spot
where his fangs had pierced her two nights before.

The electric feel of his mouth shot a path of blind,
aching need from her neck to her loins, making everything inside her tighten.

"I want you so much," she gasped, grinding herself
against him.

Mencheres tore away from her throat with a groan that
seemed to echo all through him. She gripped his hair,
desperate to have his mouth on her again, and then felt the
aching bliss of him molding her to him before he kissed
her once more.

Her desire rose to a painful level. Kira curled her fists
in his hair, almost tearing it out in her impatience to bring
his mouth closer. When his hand slid up her thigh, she let
out a smothered groan at the tingling trail it left. Then he
cupped her sex, his palm sensually grinding against her

clitoris with firm, circular strokes, his fingers devastating her with their skill even through her panties.

Molten heat blasted through Kira as all her lower nerve endings felt like they'd been struck by lightning. The sensation was so intense, so fierce, it overwhelmed her. She cried out at the sudden convulsive tightening within her, ecstasy blasting through her in uncontrollable waves that rippled from her core and spread out to the rest of her body.

Mencheres reveled in the feel of Kira's orgasm. The intoxicating sweetness of her mouth, the torturous ecstasy of her skin against his, her body shuddering on top of him while hoarse cries vibrated against his mouth—it was a memory he would replay many times in the future, however short that future might be.

But he'd already taken more than he should. If he were honorable, he'd have assuaged Kira's need without laying hands on her. He'd used his power for those purposes in the past with other new vampires he sired, but always at a distance, where it was impersonal. All vampire urges were too overwhelming to control at first, and lust was no exception. But when Kira told him she wanted him, when she reached for him . . . Mencheres could not bring himself merely to satisfy her with his power. He had to have his hands and mouth on her, feel her next to him, no matter that it was as painful as it was magnificent.

With the greatest reluctance, he ended their kiss, licking his lips to savor Kira's taste one last time. Then he sent his power out to gather up the sweater and pants that he'd hastily stripped from her before.

Her head dropped to his shoulder, those soft, full lips seeking out his flesh. A tremor went through him as her tongue flicked out, teasing and stroking his skin from his shoulder to the hollow of his throat.

Ah, gods, if only things were different.

"Kira. We must stop."

Mencheres forced himself to sit up, to set her back until her lovely face was staring at him in confusion instead of being pressed to his flesh.

"What's wrong?"

Everything about her was an enticement for him to forget his principles. Her breasts strained against her bra, her lace underwear was more alluring than concealing, and her lemony scent was both sweeter and muskier with her lust. He closed his eyes. If he even allowed himself to imagine that she tasted as good as she smelled . . .

"We cannot do this. You are impaired from your new senses. Later, you would rightly be angry at me for exploiting your condition if I took you."

Kira let out a sound between a scoff and a disbelieving laugh. "You're just intending to *stop* because you think I don't know what I want?"

He tried to remember the things he'd said to other people he'd sired when he was in a similar scenario, but he'd never wanted them with the same fierce need that clawed at him now. It was hard to form logical words when his attention kept being distracted by Kira's scent on his skin, how near she was to him, and how ravishing she looked in her miniscule undergarments.

"This isn't what you would choose of your own uninfluenced will," he managed to grit out. If this were any more difficult, he'd call it torture.

Kira jumped up in a single leap, grabbing her pants and sweater from the ground nearby.

"Unbelievable. Do you always do other people's thinking for them? Or is this something you've reserved just for me?"

The acid in her tone was unexpected. Did she believe that he refused her out of lack of desire? The notion would have been laughable if he wasn't suffering so strongly at the moment.

"I've had experience with new vampires. Right now, your new senses are directing your actions instead of your will. To assume you mean what you say under these circumstances is tantamount to—"

"You really *do* just make up other people's minds for them," Kira interrupted, yanking on her pants. "Wow, that must piss them off. It's got me infuriated, too. Congratulations, you win. Now I *don't* want you anymore."

"You never offered yourself to me before this," Mencheres snapped, his controlled façade cracking under the weight of his frustration. "You stayed under my roof for a week when we met, yet all that time, you only spoke of your desire to leave. Not of any longing for my attentions."

She strode over, her jeans not all the way closed because she'd ripped them when she pulled them on.

"When we first met, I thought you were going to kill me, then, when I knew you weren't, you were still holding me *captive.* I wasn't about to indulge in a smutty case of Stockholm syndrome by telling my captor how hot he made me—although if you remember, I did tell you something to that effect one day. Then when you let me go, which was the one thing that made it possible for me to act on what I felt toward you, you just *vanished.* I thought you could care less about me. If not for what you did with my boss, I never would have even gone looking for you . . ."

Kira stopped abruptly, turning away and yanking on her sweater next. It, too, ripped beneath her strength, hanging on her like a poncho from the tears. Mencheres leapt up, grasping her arm and spinning her back around. Something twisted inside his chest. *What was this?*

"You came looking for me? When?"

A harsh laugh escaped her. "The very next night after you mesmerized my boss. I went to all the places in my old case files that might have a paranormal association. You know why I was in the strip club that night? I wasn't there investigating a missing person's case; finding Jennifer was an accident. I was there looking for a connection to *you* because I wanted to see you again without that whole captor/captive thing between us."

For several moments, Mencheres could not speak. She'd been at the club that night searching for him? Spent other nights seeking him out as well? Could Kira truly have felt the same inexplicable, insistent draw to him that he'd felt for her? It defied reason that she would have sought him out for any other purpose. Her personality wasn't compatible with humans who flocked to the undead merely to seek the sometimes dangerous thrill of a vampire's company, and she hadn't needed him for anything else. He'd made sure of that when he gave her all the blood she would require for her sister before he'd left her.

She stared at him, moonlight reflecting in her green eyes. "Say something. Even if it's to tell me I was an idiot for chasing after you and I deserved to end up as a vampire over it. At least that's better than silence."

Her naked honesty was so unlike his normal, guarded speech. Reason warned him to tell Kira she was right. That a human plunging herself into the vampire world without a protector usually did end up suffering serious consequences, but he couldn't utter that statement. Nor could he tell Kira the other thing that would be better for her to believe, even though it was a lie: that he cared no more for her than any of his other property. Under the weight of her gaze, however, all of his cool logic crumbled and he found himself responding with the same raw honesty she'd shown him.

"I am Master of a large line of vampires and humans, and yes, I often do people's thinking for them. Moreover, I have betrayed almost everyone I've loved, including participating in my wife's murder and withholding important information from my co-ruler. My other sins are too numerous to list, and I have certain death looming in my future, so as soon as you are able to control your condition, Kira, you would do well to forget me."

She kept looking at him with that level, penetrating stare, no disgust or shock on her face. Mencheres waited, expecting any moment for his words to sink in and her reaction to change, but the minutes ticked away, and still her expression didn't alter from thoughtful contemplation.

"I'm getting hungry," she said at last, turning away and starting back through the woods toward his house.

He gazed at her retreating back in astonishment. Where were her reprimands? The castigation of his character that so many others would be quick to oblige him with were he to have said the same to them? Furthermore, he didn't sense an oncoming attack of hunger from Kira, but perhaps she was shielding it. Or learning to anticipate her cravings.

He gave his head a slight shake and followed after her, leaving his shirt behind on the ground. He'd already have too many memories of tonight without a tangible memento to torment himself with.

Despite that, he licked his lips one more time, absorbing Kira's taste and remembering the feel of her shuddering in pleasure on top of him. If he'd known she'd searched for him, that her desire was not wholly based on her new, uncontrollable senses, would he have had the strength to refuse her before?

No. The answer reverberated all through him, followed immediately by another taunting question.

Now that he knew these things, would *he* have the strength to stay away from *her*?

Chapter Eighteen

Kira forced herself to set the mug down even though there was still a swallow left in it. She slid it across the table to Gorgon.

"I'm done."

The words were perhaps the hardest she'd uttered, yet she felt an accompanying swell of pride even through the howls of hunger that demanded she snatch that mug back and lick every drop from it.

Gorgon grinned at her. "Only your fifth day undead. You're a strong one, aren't you?"

Kira allowed a tight smile to cross her face. "Years of dieting make lots of women tough when it comes to controlling our appetites. Who knew that saying no to desserts would turn out to be boot camp for becoming a vampire?"

Gorgon laughed, taking her cup and rinsing the remaining blood out in the sink. Kira noted that he never drank from the bags that compromised the entirety of her meals, but he did disappear several hours each night. She hoped he varied his donors, or that their nearest neighbors weren't anemic.

He tossed Kira a bottle of water from the refrigerator next. She drank it, grimacing at how it tasted now, but having already been warned that drinking water was important during her first couple weeks as a vampire. It seemed her new body burned through all the sustenance it received from blood without leaving anything left over to keep her from looking like a grape left too long in the sun. Kira hadn't asked how it was possible that she could drink or eat, but no longer had any need for a toilet. Some vampire mysteries she wasn't prepared to have explained to her yet.

On the plus side, she'd never have to deal with her period again, but having motherhood yanked out from under her was rough. Still, Tina had weathered the same inability to get pregnant due to her disease. Kira wouldn't let herself fall into a slump over her similar new childless state, especially since she could always adopt, way in the future when she'd come to terms with everything her new existence entailed.

"Now." Gorgon turned around, holding out an egg carton. "Let's try this again."

Kira eyed the egg crate with a mix of frustration and determination. A simple rule for new vampires was that if they couldn't handle egg cartons without breaking the eggs, then they couldn't be around humans without running the risk of inadvertently crushing them with a casual touch. In the past several days, Kira had demolished more egg crates and had her hands coated in more yolk than she wanted to remember. She still felt like she had some of that sticky substance stuck between her fingernails no matter how she scrubbed, but she was getting better. She managed not to rip doors off anymore, or leave holes instead of footprints in the floor, and the last egg carton she'd handled only had one broken egg in it when she was done.

Kira walked over to Gorgon, chanting "gentle, gentle" in her mind as she reached for the carton. When she managed to take it from Gorgon's open grasp without any egg guts streaming out onto her hands, she grinned.

"Ha!" Looked like the fiftieth time was a charm.

Gorgon's smile was proud. "Now, if you can open it and take some eggs out without breaking them, you're almost ready to be around humans again."

Very slowly, Kira opened the container and touched the top of an egg. It didn't break, to her relief. Now all she had to do was take it out.

In her peripheral vision, she noticed Mencheres walk by. That was how she'd mostly seen him lately—out of the corner of her eye. He hadn't been completely avoiding her, but he always seemed to be busy doing something else aside from spending time in the same room with her. It wasn't done in a rude way. Instead, it almost came off as though Mencheres wanted to avoid her but couldn't bring himself to totally stay away. The motivation behind his there-but-not-quite-there presence pricked her curiosity. Was this admittedly far older and sophisticated Master vampire actually feeling *awkward* about what had happened between them?

"Take the egg out," Gorgon prompted her.

Kira put three fingers around that cool oval shape, pressing as softly as she could to lift it. The egg trembled but didn't explode. *Think of Tina,* she urged herself. This wasn't an egg; it was her little sister's hand, and she was going to clasp it *without* hurting her when she saw her again . . .

The egg cleared the container in one piece. Gorgon whooped. Kira almost jumped in excitement, but smashing through the floor would ruin the moment. She looked up, the egg cradled in her hand, to see Mencheres watching her. He had a pleased expression on his face that quickly turned impassive once her eyes met his.

Still playing Mr. Cool, hmm? she mused, returning her attention to the egg crate. "I'm going to try for another one," she told Gorgon.

He grinned. "Go for it."

As she reached for another egg with her free hand, her thoughts returned to Mencheres. After his confession in the forest, Kira mulled over whether he was really as despicable as he'd made himself out to be. After all, she was the last person to think, "Oooh, *sexy!*" when a man admitted to being a controlling, ruthless bastard. She'd been through that kind of relationship before, so she knew there was nothing romantic or sexy about it. But though Mencheres had painted an ugly picture of himself, on reflection, his actions were in contrast to his words.

When he'd kept her with him that first week they met, he'd gone out of his way to give her as much freedom as possible. Then he'd let her go despite the risk to the secrecy of his race, plus given Kira the means to treat her sister's disease so Tina would have an average life span. Then when Flare had her, Mencheres had come for her and healed her without the slightest hesitation.

Faced with that ultimatum from Radje, Mencheres did the only thing he could for her: He'd brought her back from death. Since she'd first woken up on that plane, he hadn't placed one condition or limitation on her that wasn't solely to prevent her from killing innocent people. She had complete freedom to do anything she wanted, including call anyone, check her e-mail, or even shop online so she could have something other than borrowed clothes to wear. And Mencheres had repeatedly stated that once she was in control of her hunger and her new strength, she was free to go. Again.

"Almost there," Gorgon said encouragingly, as Kira began to pull out another egg. A slight crack appeared on its white surface. She pursed her lips but kept going. After another couple seconds, the egg lay in her hand, a tiny zigzag crack marring its smooth surface but its contents still safely contained.

"Put 'em back without smashing them, and I think you've got it," Gorgon said, winking at her.

Kira split her attention between returning those eggs to their container and on everything Mencheres *didn't* say or do. She'd felt his need the other night, but though she'd practically demanded he have sex with her, he'd refused on the grounds that she might be under the influence of her new senses. Then he'd told her terrible things about himself almost as if he wanted her to reprimand him. Mencheres didn't act like someone who had little regard for others. He had extraordinary power, but he didn't flaunt it. In fact, she'd only seen him use them when it benefited other people. If she were him, she'd use those powers all the time. Like teleporting her blood or water to her while sitting on her butt relaxing—and God help everyone if Kira ever had the ability to move objects when someone cut her off in traffic.

No, there was far more to Mencheres than the way he'd

so harshly described himself. Despite his admonition for her to forget him once she regained control of her new condition, she had no intention of doing that.

Out of the corner of her eye, Kira watched Mencheres walk into the next room with his usual gliding stride, his posture straight and regal, his ass filling the back of his pants with a sexiness that was sinful.

No, he wasn't scaring her away that easily. She would wear down that shell he'd erected around himself when it came to her. And then she'd see if the connection between them, the same one Mencheres seemed to be trying so hard to avoid, was as strong as she suspected.

Kira got the eggs back in their cardboard cradle, smiling at her accomplishment and already planning her next move.

Game on.

Mencheres heard the door to his bedroom open, but he didn't open his eyes. The hot water in the bathtub was soothing. He was loath to break the temporary peace of soaking beneath it for something as trivial as Gorgon dropping off his laundry. Even though he'd told his friend that he could see to his own menial tasks, Gorgon insisted doing them himself.

And in truth, it might take Mencheres a few minutes to figure out how to operate a modern washing machine. He usually had a large vampire and human staff in every house he stayed at, so others had handled such tasks for him. Perhaps Gorgon thought his efforts now would be in lieu of needing to replace Mencheres's entire wardrobe later.

But then a tapping noise snapped his eyes open. He looked through the veil of bathwater to see Kira framed in the doorway, her slim fingers drumming on the frame.

His head cleared the water in the next instant, alarm ringing through him. "Is something wrong?"

"No," she said, coming into the bathroom to lean against the countertop. "Gorgon left to take a walk— which I assume means find his dinner—and I was feeling a little lonely."

Her green eyes were clear and guileless, but Mencheres rather doubted the veracity of her statement. Never before had Kira even entered his bedroom, let alone surprised him while he was in his bath. She had a method to her actions. What method, he did not know. Yet.

"Lonely?" he repeated, raising a brow.

She shrugged. "Everyone I know is sleeping at this hour, and there's only so much TV a person can watch before it drives you insane. Since I'm just barely getting a handle on my hunger and my strength, I thought it was a good idea to talk to you instead of stressing myself just pacing the floors until Gorgon got back. Was I wrong?"

That guileless gaze again, but with a hint of challenge this time. Mencheres felt his mouth twitch. She was daring him to tell her to leave with the implication that it would set back her admirable progress. He was curious to see where she intended to take this.

"Please. Do stay."

He settled himself back against the edge of the large tub, lacing his fingers behind his head. Kira's gaze lingered over his chest before it flicked lower to the bathwater, paused, and then a slight grin broke out across her face.

"Bubbles. On a scale of one to ten, a bubble bath has to rank a zero as far as things I'd expect an older-than-dirt, bad-ass vampire to indulge in. The only thing that would surprise me more was if you pulled out a rubber ducky."

He fought another, stronger twitch of his lips. "Bath

toys are reserved only for the oldest, most lethal vampires. I have a full century to age and another thousand men to kill before I reach that hallowed landmark."

Kira laughed, a feminine, throaty sound that made things tighten in him, reminding Mencheres of why he'd tried not to linger long in her presence the past few days. A harsh tingling began in his groin, the silent demand from his body urging him to send his blood there. He ignored that, glad he had control over such things instead of his loins doing as *they* pleased.

"So how am I doing?" Kira asked, propping herself up to sit on his countertop. It creaked at the first touch of her hands, but she hadn't exerted enough force for it to break. Again, admirable progress.

He closed his eyes. Perhaps it would be easier to continue ignoring the urges of his body if he didn't keep looking at her. It was torment enough to have her scent filling the room, teasing him with her nearness.

"You are progressing very well. In another few days, we will show you how to feed from humans. When you're able to do that without assistance, you will have no need to remain here."

"I don't want to feed from humans," she said at once, that previous lightness fading from her voice. "I'll stick to the bagged blood. Heated up and in a mug, I can pretend it's really thick coffee. Biting into someone's skin . . . no, I don't want to do that."

Mencheres didn't open his eyes. "You must, even if it's not your preferred method of feeding. If hunger strikes when you're in a place where bagged blood is unavailable, better to know how to feed without injuring a human than to accidentally maim or kill one out of your own inexperience."

He could almost hear her chewing on her lip. "You have a point," she said at last.

Mencheres didn't bother to inform Kira that once she'd tasted blood straight from the vein, it was doubtful she'd return to her bagged alternative. There was no comparison in taste between fresh blood and bags of plasma. Even the energy derived from fresh blood was more potent than the substitute.

"That crooked cop Radje, what does he have against you?" Kira asked, the change of subject surprising him enough to open his eyes.

He almost sighed. Even if he could sum up several thousands of years' worth of antagonism between him and Radjedef into a short explanation, he didn't want to. However, since their bitter feud had resulted in Kira losing her mortality, it wasn't fair to refuse to answer.

"Radje came from a line of rulers where each heir was allotted a certain number of years to reign over their human subjects. At the beginning of each reign, the heir was turned into a vampire, granting the chance for immortality, but also ensuring that the heir could have no living children. Consorts were provided for the heir's wife, and of the children they bore, one was chosen as the new heir. This system was honored for many generations, until Radje. He was bitter after giving up his allotted time to reign. When his successor mysteriously died before the end of his reign, the responsibility of choosing a new heir fell to Radje. He delayed naming another and sought to retake power instead. An heir was chosen despite Radje's objections, but then he refused to relinquish control, citing concerns over the new heir's ability to rule. When attempts were made on that heir's life, Radje's sire interceded and forcibly removed him from the kingdom. Later, a gift of power originally intended for Radje was given by his sire to the new heir instead. Radje's hatred has burned ever since."

Kira stared at him, her face reflecting sympathy, understanding, and a touch of anger. "You were the other heir, the one he tried to kill."

Mencheres inclined his head. "Yes."

That green gaze didn't waver. "And what was the gift you got instead of Radje?"

"It would vary depending on the individual, but what I received was additional strength, the ability to read human minds, visions of the future, and the power to locate and control people or objects with merely a thought."

She let out something like a laugh. "Oh, *those* trivial things. It's his own fault, but since he's too ruthless to admit that, no wonder Radje hates you. World wars have been fought over lesser jealousies."

Yes, and if he told Kira how many of the wars fought between humans over the centuries had stemmed from feuds spilling out between other Master vampires, she'd be amazed.

"So, before you became a vampire, you were some sort of chieftain?"

Mencheres gave her a slight smile. "Something like that."

"No wonder you're used to doing other people's thinking for them," she murmured. "Just like politicians today."

He stifled his laugh at the wryness in her tone. " 'Absolute power corrupts absolutely,' " he quoted.

She jumped off the counter, wincing as the floor creaked when her feet landed, but looking relieved when the tile remained unbroken beneath her.

"And Radje took his bitterness and became the vampire version of a cop instead. Seems like an odd choice."

Mencheres lifted one of his raised shoulders in a half shrug. "Law Guardians are in the position of highest rule among vampires. Radje was denied one form of power, so he assumed another."

Kira looked thoughtful. "I wanted to be a cop. It didn't work out."

He was intrigued. She had proven herself to be a very determined woman. What had been enough to deter her from this goal?

"What happened?"

She gave him a look. "If you want me to tell you, then I'm soaking my feet in your tub. I'll need something to relax me for *this* trip down memory lane."

Now he was truly intrigued. Mencheres inclined his head at the side of the tub. Kira took her shoes off before carefully seating herself on the flat ledge. He moved his legs to allow her more room, but it wasn't necessary. He'd deliberately chosen a large tub so it would encompass his entire body when he rested underwater.

Kira let out a noise of enjoyment as her feet, then her calves, disappeared into the water. Mencheres kept his gaze on her face, not on the lovely thighs that were all too bare and close given the way she'd slid up the edge of her dress to well above her knees.

"I told you I get feelings about things. When I was seventeen, I had a feeling about my friend's older brother, and that feeling was *danger*. On the surface, there was no reason for it. Pete was athletic, popular, he came from a whole family of cops, and he'd just become a cop himself shortly after graduating high school. I think the only reason Pete noticed me was because I avoided him whenever I hung out with his sister."

Mencheres couldn't contain a mild snort. "Of course, it had nothing to do with your intelligence or beauty."

She gave him a slanted look. "Pete had lots of girls after him just as smart and pretty. But he started putting the charm on me, and I ignored that warning feeling about him because I hadn't learned to trust my instincts yet. We began dating. Things were good at first, but then Pete's jealousy started worrying me. He hated it when I spent time with my friends. Couldn't stand any other guy even looking at me. Right before graduation, I broke up with Pete. He was starting to scare me."

In the bedroom, Mencheres's mobile phone began to ring. She glanced over. "Do you need to get that?"

"It can wait."

He thought of the manila folder he'd given Bones. It contained all of Kira's information—details Gorgon had gathered that Mencheres refused to look at with the notion that the less he knew about Kira, the simpler it would be to purge her from his thoughts. Now he would let nothing, not even the ring tone indicating that it was Bones calling him, interrupt him from hearing about this part of Kira's past.

"My mom contracted bacterial meningitis a little after we broke up. Before Tina and I knew it, she was just *gone*. We were devastated. Pete stepped up and helped with the funeral, took care of things—he was amazing. He apologized for everything before, said he'd realized his mistakes and even wanted to marry me. I wasn't sure, but . . . the Department of Children and Families was sniffing around Tina. She was just sixteen, my dad wasn't *her* dad, and her real father didn't want her. If I married Pete, Tina would have what they considered a 'stable home environment,' and she wouldn't go into foster care. So even though I'd just turned nineteen and I still had doubts, I married him."

She paused to give Mencheres a dry smile. "As you can imagine, Pete had *not* miraculously changed. His possessiveness grew worse. Soon I had no friends, college was put off, and the only family I saw was Tina because she lived with us. I was miserable, but I decided to wait it out until Tina turned eighteen before I left him. I think Pete suspected what I intended. His fits of anger got worse, and he started beating me."

Mencheres said nothing, but in his mind, he was already ordering Gorgon to duplicate the information he'd gathered about Kira so he could find this Pete and kill him. Yes, he knew the sort. No, they never changed.

"I tried to hide the bruises from Tina because she was already dealing with enough hell from her disease. Then one day, when I was cleaning in the attic, I found a few bags of white powder and a pile of money stuffed in a box. It didn't take a genius to figure out what Pete was doing. I called his partner, hoping he'd step in, but that was a mistake. Pete denied it, said I was crazy, his partner buried the information, and Pete beat me unconscious. Threatened to kill me if I ever breathed a word about the money or drugs to anyone again. Strange people started showing up at the house at all hours after that. I knew Pete was dealing or worse, and it scared the hell out of me because of Tina. I had to try and get help again, no matter what he'd threatened me with. There was an old cop, Mack Davis, who I'd met at my wedding. Pete said he was with Internal Affairs. So I went to see him."

Her voice changed from the flat, emotionless tone

she'd used in her retelling to something softer and richer. That alone told Mencheres that Mack Davis had not failed her.

"Mack believed me. Set up a sting on his own to catch Pete because he knew that with the long line of cops in Pete's family, someone would probably tip Pete off if Mack went through normal channels. Inside of a month, Mack had all the proof he needed from video, recordings, and things I gave him to go straight to the DA. Pete and a couple other officers involved were arrested for running drugs. I was one of the star witnesses at Pete's trial. The judge locked him up for thirty years, but Pete was killed in prison within a year of his incarceration."

Kira paused to look straight into Mencheres's eyes. "I knew how former cops were treated by inmates when I testified against him. I even knew, deep down when I first went to see Mack, that it would result in Pete's death. But though a part of me still loved him, I did it anyway. Pete's family calls me a murderer, but I didn't kill him. He chose his actions, and *that* sealed his fate. I regret his death, but I don't regret saving myself and my sister."

She glanced away then with a self-deprecating shrug. "After I saw how one good cop like Mack could reverse the damage so many bad ones had caused, I went to college, got a degree in criminal justice, and went through police academy. Aced it, too, but despite getting my certification in law enforcement, no police agency would hire me. Some of Pete and the other cops' friends blackballed me. So instead of being a police officer, Mack got me a job to train as a private investigator. It's not much beyond chasing cheating spouses and a ton of paperwork now, but it has potential later for making a difference in people's lives. Mack died a year ago. His credo was to save one life, every chance he got. He ended up saving a hell of a lot more than one, and now it's my goal to do the same."

Chapter Nineteen

So many emotions ran through Mencheres. Satisfaction that the man who'd abused Kira was dead. Admiration for her icy bravery at such a young age. Gratitude toward the human who'd interceded for her. Anger at the policemen who'd denied Kira a job out of loyalty to those who'd disgraced the law. Above every emotion, however, was empathy. He knew the agony she'd felt being the cause of death to someone she'd once loved, even if Kira hadn't been the actual instrument. Yes, he was all too familiar with the pain of making that choice, then having to carry it through to the bitter, bloody end. Few people would ever know how heavy a weight that was to carry.

Of all the people in the vicinity of that warehouse three weeks ago, to have Kira be the one who'd followed his voice and come through that door had to be more than coincidence. It had to be fate.

But with that looming darkness waiting for him, could Kira be fated to be the cause of his death? In so short a time, her position in his life had risen to one of great importance. No one else in two millennia had been responsible for such a large change in his actions, thinking, and feelings. Cold reason was what had kept him alive throughout these many long, war-filled years, but whenever he was near Kira, reason left him. If he sought to stave off that impending dark void, his best chance was to cut Kira off from him. Those ruled by emotion instead of reason were so much easier to kill, as he well knew.

Yet, looking at Kira, he cared not about reason *or* death. Or his phone, which began to ring again.

Mencheres slid through the water toward her, drawn by the same inexorable compulsion that led moths to dance with flames. He'd had several lifetimes' worth of reason, cold machinations, and, ultimately, emptiness. Perhaps the moths knew what he didn't, that the joy of the flame was worth the price of destruction.

He intended to find out.

Kira's eyes darkened to a richer shade of green as he approached. He set his hands on either side of her, bracing against the ledge of the tub as he rose to his knees. Her legs brushed his chest, the water running down him soaking the ends of her dress, but she didn't draw away. Instead, her scent flared with desire as she slowly perused his body.

"I can almost feel your gaze on me," he murmured, heat winding into his loins as he sent his bath-warmed blood there at last.

"If you expected me not to look, Mencheres, you underestimate yourself."

Her voice was husky, lingering over the syllables in his name like she was caressing them. He moved closer, pressing his body against her knees until she either had to edge away from him or open them.

Kira parted her legs, careless of the water that soaked her as he brought his body flush against hers, savoring her moan as their skins met. She slipped her arms around his neck, her fingers separating his hair into several thick strands while she stared into his eyes.

"Not going to decide to stop halfway through again, are you?"

He dropped his mouth to her ear, licking the tender shell once before replying.

"I was separated from my wife for over nine centuries and forbidden by law from lying with anyone else. After her death, no one tempted me enough . . . until you."

A noise of astonishment escaped her as Kira drew back to look at him. "You haven't had sex in over *nine hundred years*?" She swallowed. "If you're trying to say you want to take things slow, wait until we get to know each other better—"

He laughed, pulling her down into the tub with him. "No. I'm warning you that I will show you no mercy."

He kissed her with all of the pent-up hunger that had been raging in him for the better part of a millennium. Kira's arms tightened around him, the taste of her mouth intoxicating, the caress of her tongue a sensual extravagance. Water sloshed from the tub as he pulled her dress off and flung it aside. Her bra and underwear were likewise discarded, until nothing interrupted the sleek smoothness of her flesh along his.

She moaned as she ran her hands down his body. He slid his mouth from hers, kissing that beautiful jawline before moving down to the fullness of her breasts. He filled his mouth with each of them in turn, sucking on her nipples until Kira's gasps became cries, and her nails raked down his back. Her touches became more frantic, and she curled her legs around his waist. The feel of her wrapped around was him magnificent, each luscious twist of her body inflaming, but he wouldn't rush this moment. He wanted to explore her more fully first.

He caressed her breasts as his head dipped below the water. That tight adornment of curls teased his mouth before his tongue parted her depths. Lust mounted with unbearable intensity at his first taste of her. Her slick softness was addictive, urging him to flick his tongue faster, deeper, until more of her honey flavored his mouth, and her cries had an urgent, rhythmic edge. Her pleasure only heightened his overpowering, aching need, tightening everything inside him with ravenous demand. He had to be inside her. Had to—

Mencheres shot from the tub with a snarl, only their centuries-long friendship stopping him from striking out with lethal force at the vampire who intruded. Gorgon stood in the bathroom doorway, his expression grim.

"If it weren't life or death, believe me, I wouldn't interrupt, but you need to see this. Now."

If Kira could still have blushed, her cheeks would have been fire-engine red. Staying in the bathroom and never setting eyes on Gorgon again sounded like a good plan to her, but the words "life and death" made it impossible for her to cater to her embarrassment. Mencheres had closed the bathroom door with a muttered apology when he stalked out to see whatever it was Gorgon interrupted them for, so she had a private moment to gather her shattered equilibrium—and a towel—before she followed him.

"I tried to call," Gorgon was saying as he went over to Mencheres's computer, of all things. "Bones did, too. He phoned me after he couldn't reach you. When I hung up with him, I ran back from town as fast as I could."

Mencheres stood with his arms crossed, still naked, water dripping onto the carpet beneath him. Kira noticed he had a tattoo on his back of a symbol she didn't recognize, but she didn't take the time to admire it with her attention fixed on what Gorgon was doing.

"You can't tell me what it is that's so urgent while you are preparing the computer?" Mencheres growled.

"That strip club from the other night was torched," Gorgon said while his fingers moved rapidly across the keyboard. "Those three vampires are dead, plus several humans as well. But that's not the real problem."

"Was Jennifer one of the humans killed? Jennifer Jackson?" Kira asked, taken aback by how coolly Gorgon described the deaths.

"It'd be better if she had been," Gorgon muttered.

Kira gasped at his reply. Mencheres drew her into the circle of his arms, his wet hair falling across her shoulders, mouth lightly brushing her temple.

"This news, while important, could have waited," he said to Gorgon in a hard tone.

Gorgon glanced up after a few more rapid taps of his fingers. "This can't."

The site for a Chicago news channel filled the laptop screen, video segment from the eleven o'clock news in the center of the page. Kira's eyes widened at the frozen image with the headline of VAMPIRE ROLE-PLAYING RESPONSIBLE FOR ARSON? It wasn't the headline that stunned her. It was seeing herself in the image, her head back, Mencheres's mouth latched onto her throat.

"Oh my God," she whispered.

Gorgon clicked play, and the news anchor's voice flowed out, talking about the grisly scene of burned bodies that firefighters found when they responded to the call. Surprisingly, the arson had happened the day before yesterday, not this past evening, but what had been discovered in time to make the eleven o'clock news was the security footage. The only set recovered from the scene, damaged, but some viewable segments still remaining.

" . . . don't have the names of the participants involved," the news anchor droned on in a professionally somber voice. "Police are still in the process of seeking their identities, but as you can see, there seems to be a bizarre imitation of a vampire—that's right, I said *vampire*—ritual taking place. Let's watch the footage, Robert."

Mencheres's grip on Kira tightened as she watched, speechless, while her death took place on-screen. When she saw Mencheres pull her necklace off and use it to cut open his own throat, her hand convulsively closed over her cross. *He must have replaced the chain*, she thought, feeling numb. She'd never even noticed a time when her necklace wasn't on her, but she'd been dazed from bloodlust that first day . . .

"You will regret this," Mencheres said on-screen to Radje after she'd finished slurping from his neck, and her body was motionless.

The Law Guardian folded his arms. "You threaten me?"

It seemed like the screen tightened to show a close-up of Mencheres's face. "I *promise* you."

The image faded to show the news anchor again. She asked anyone with information about the identities of the people on the video to contact the Chicago Heights police department, CrimeStoppers, or the news headquarters.

Kira still couldn't seem to form any words. *My sister*

might have seen this, she found herself thinking in a frozen, detached way. Or her brother. Or her boss, or Lily, any of the other people at her office—hell, the cops who had been at Pete's trial years ago might recognize her. In less than five minutes, all of her chances to return to some semblance of her former life were torched with the same ruthless efficiency as the fire that destroyed the strip club.

"Radje," Mencheres spat. "This is an unpardonable crime, even for him."

Gorgon gave him a steady look. "The Law Guardian's claiming *you* killed those people and burned down the club."

Mencheres stared at Gorgon, absorbing that information. His arms stayed around Kira, feeling the fine tremor that went through her.

"Was this all the footage recovered?" she asked in a raspy voice. "The video from that night is several days old. Wasn't there more recent tape available, maybe one that showed the real murderer and arsonist?"

Mencheres didn't need to see Gorgon shake his head to know the answer to that. He'd guessed that the rooms in the club were videoed. Radje obviously had as well, and the Law Guardian would have made sure nothing that incriminated him would have been left at the scene. No, Radje had only left images that looked very damning for Mencheres to anyone in their world who saw them.

"No footage was found dated later than this, and what you saw was an abbreviated version. The full clip isn't on the news-station site, but it's up on YouTube and various other places."

"Show me," Kira said at once.

Gorgon glanced at Mencheres. He gave him a barely perceptible nod. After a few clicks, the YouTube version began to play. It was significantly longer, starting when Mencheres first arrived to heal Kira and ending with him carrying her newly dead body from the room.

The cold part of him could admire Radje's cleverness. Saved on tape for all the world to see was Mencheres's veiled threat to the three vampires who'd injured Kira, his clear displeasure with the Law Guardian's sentencing, and his open threat to Radje at the end. Brilliant.

"Look at the comments." Kira's voice was hollow. "They're critiquing my death."

He scanned the commentary below the video box. Phrases such as "OMG that's so fake!" "Shoulda had more blood" "Worst actress ever" and "WTF is up with the lame glowing eyes?" were all he read before he shut the laptop with a flick of his mind.

Kira tugged at his arm and Mencheres released her. "I need . . . I don't know. I should call Tina. If she wakes up tomorrow and sees this, she'll freak, but what am I supposed to say?" she mumbled as she began to pace.

"You should get dressed," he said, gentling his voice to take out the anger and bitterness he felt toward Radje.

"Yeah. Dressed." Kira wandered out of the room, still plainly shaken. Mencheres could not fault her. He knew Radje had sabotaged more than his life with this ill deed.

He met Gorgon's blue gaze. "This is bad," Gorgon said, stating the obvious. "With Flare, Patches, and Wraith dead, plus the strip club burned, most vampires who see this video will believe Radje's assertion that you made good on your threats."

That wasn't the real concern, as Gorgon knew. Killing three Masterless vampires and a few humans wouldn't rouse the Guardian Council's interest. Leaving behind evidence of the vampire race for any human to download on the Internet? That would concern *all* vampires.

"Certainly, it would be easier to believe I did this than to believe a *Law Guardian* endangered the secrecy of the race this way." Mencheres's mouth twisted. "Nor do I have adequate proof of my innocence. The only people who know I was here during the fire are you and Kira."

The same ones involved in the crime. Radje had chosen his attack well.

"We need to leave at once," he stated. "Radje may have gambled that I was tending to Kira myself in her early days, away from most of my people and any alibi for the fire, but he also may have spies watching us. Even now, Guardians or Enforcers could be coming."

Gorgon gave him a somber look. "It's better if none of us were brought before any Guardians until you have means to prove that Radje did this. Radje wants something from you, but he has no use for me or Kira, and we're the only ones who could back up your claims of innocence."

Yes, the two of them would be Radje's first targets. Mencheres calculated their chances if they stayed together. He didn't like the odds. It was better if they split up while he rallied his allies. Otherwise, if one of them were caught, all of them were caught, and the truth might never be made public.

"Go," he said softly to Gorgon. "Do not tell me where. Stay hidden until this matter is over."

Gorgon clasped him by the shoulders. "You have allies who will urge the Guardians to listen to you. When the day comes that you need me, I will be there."

Mencheres briefly touched his friend's hands, the gesture encompassing the words he had no time to say.

"Go," he repeated.

Gorgon left without taking anything or looking back.

Wise. Time was of the essence, and what couldn't be carried in one hand wasn't worth the delay of taking.

He quickly pulled on some clothes, gathering only his mobile phone, his laptop, and his coat. Along with Kira, that was all he intended to leave with.

Chapter Twenty

Kira awoke to the sounds of people screaming and the whoosh of a train as it barreled closer. She shot upward in blind survival instinct to avoid the train's oncoming path, but hard arms seized her.

"Do not fear. You are safe."

Mencheres. How many times had she heard those words from him? A lot, it seemed.

She came awake enough to notice that they were in a bare room with several pieces of large equipment stacked against the walls. The machines hummed with their own internal racket while somewhere above them, that cadence of screams followed by the sounds of a freight train rose and fell again.

"What the—?" Kira managed.

He glanced at the ceiling. "We are underneath a roller coaster. Big Thunder Mountain, I believe it is called."

For a second, Kira didn't know whether to laugh or ask if he was kidding. Disneyland? *That* was where Mencheres decided it would be safe for them to flee to after leaving in such a hurry? He hadn't told her where they were going when he flew them away from the house, and falling asleep at dawn had prevented her from seeing where they were headed after several other stops and starts.

"First bubble baths. Now Disney parks. You're shattering every creepy vampire myth I've ever heard."

Mencheres shrugged. "It is an easy landmark to find, and we're meeting people here. Plus, you needed a safe place to rest. These theme parks have labyrinths underneath them, with many unused rooms such as these to keep the cleaning and running of the park away from guests' eyes."

Kira digested this. She hadn't known there was anything underneath Disneyland, which probably meant a lot of other people were unaware of that, too. This was safer than sleeping in a car or on a park bench, that was for sure. "Who are we meeting?"

"My co-ruler and his wife," Mencheres replied.

"Co-ruler." Her brows rose. "Does that mean he's a partner in a big vampire corporation you both oversee?"

His mouth quirked. "In essence."

"And you trust him?"

Kira felt his emotions flicker between sadness and resolve, an odd combination to feel at her question. "I trust that he will do what is best for our people and that he will speak the truth about his intentions, whatever they are," he replied at last.

"Why does that sound like you're not giving me a straight answer to my question?" she murmured.

Mencheres's slight smile deepened. "Because you are perceptive."

She glanced down to see that she was lying on his coat, several towels, pullover hoodies, and other soft items with various Disney character logos. They were the only buffer between her and the hard concrete floor. She shook her head. Her first trip to Disneyland was as a vampire hiding out under a roller coaster with another vampire. All of a sudden, Alice's adventures in Wonderland seemed normal by comparison.

Mencheres held out his hand to assist her up. Kira took it, used to the natural energy emanating from his flesh. The first few times she'd felt it might have seemed like mild electrocution, but now, she enjoyed the tingling sensations that touching Mencheres elicited. His pulsating power certainly had its unexpected advantages. After last night, Kira knew that his tongue felt like a vibrator set to the speed of Oh *Hell* Yeah.

His hand tightened on hers, and his mouth was suddenly brushing her neck as he inhaled next to it. Mencheres's scent intensified as well, that rich natural cologne of dark spices deepening and increasing. Something clenched inside her.

"You tempt me more than you can imagine." His voice was low but resonating. "Whatever your thoughts were at that moment, keep thinking them. They sweeten your scent in the most enticing way."

Kira almost sighed at the sensations running through her. He didn't even need to kiss her for her to feel aroused. Just being near him was enough to make her want him.

She traced her free hand along Mencheres's arm. "How long do we have until we're supposed to meet those people?" So much more than a question about their appointment hung in her words.

His mouth slid along her neck again, making her shiver at the additional tingles. "You deserve better than this," he said softly.

Kira could feel his lust battling with his sense of honor—and she wanted his honor to *lose*. "Dingy equipment room it may be, but for once, we're alone," she whispered back. "Let's not waste that."

His mouth teased her skin while more tingling ripples traveled over her body. She let out a short moan. She knew it was his power caressing her with a thousand invisible strokes, some of the touches shockingly intimate. Her fangs extended of their own volition, and a shudder went through her.

"Is that a yes?" Kira managed.

His lips slanted over hers in reply. Her mouth opened at once, stroking his tongue with hers and matching the urgency in his kiss. She moaned again as those phantom touches increased, the sensations fueled by the feel of his hands beginning to travel over her as well.

She reached for the buttons on his shirt, ripping them because she forgot to tone down her new strength. Mencheres stripped his clothes off without taking his hands from her, all the seams separating and pulling away from themselves until the remaining pieces dropped to the floor. Kira felt her own clothes fall away in the same manner, until the two of them stood naked with their ruined clothing at their feet.

A primal sound escaped her when she felt the hard length of him pressed to her belly. Then an almost painful clench of desire flooded her when she closed her hand over him and felt him grow even bigger. After all the starts and stops, the interruptions, she wanted him inside her now. The need was too great to delay with foreplay.

"Take me. Don't wait," she got out in a ragged voice once he freed her lips to trail his devastating mouth down her neck.

His fingers found her depths in the next moment, making her cry out at the sizzle of sensation. He stroked her far more slowly than she did him, her faster rhythm wringing deep, throaty groans out of Mencheres that spiked her lust.

"You are not ready yet. I would hurt you," he rasped.

She felt his need as if it were a living thing trying to claw its way out of him. The intensity, the overwhelming force of his desire fueled her impatience. Yes, that was how she felt. Like she'd die if he wasn't inside her *right now*.

"Wanting you hurts even more," Kira choked.

A harsh noise came from him right as she felt his careful control snap. The coolness of the wall met her back in the next moment, Mencheres parting her legs and lifting her. His mouth claimed hers in a torrid kiss as his hard, thick flesh pressed against her core.

Her nerve endings electrified at that intimate touch, then a cry wrenched from her when his thrust burned into her like a brand. She was wet, but not enough, not for his size. Still, Kira lashed her arms around him and arched toward him, her need rivaling the initial ache she'd felt.

"More," she moaned into his mouth.

The muscles in his back bunched beneath her hands, then another searing thrust brought him deeper inside her. She whimpered as the bliss combined with a quick-silver flash of pain, yet still, she didn't want him to stop. Nothing had felt this incredible as Mencheres raked her mouth with his tongue while his body stretched hers to its limit.

Another thrust made her head fall back as the pleasure drowned out those initial twinges of pain. She felt every rasp of the wall against her back, each stroke of his tongue, hands, and power while that hardness moved deeper inside her. Her hips twisted with a compulsion she couldn't control, urging him deeper still, until a groan tore through him and he buried himself completely with a hard arch of his hips.

She didn't need to breathe, but Kira was almost gasping at the bombardment of sensations. Mencheres's skin crackled with energy, every touch sending more tingles through her, until her body felt like it was vibrating with the same pulsating power his contained. That fullness inside her was overwhelming, making her nerve endings throb even as that hungry urgency demanded more.

He drew his mouth away from hers, staring into her eyes while he slowly pulled out of her. His thumb traced her lip as his other hand held her aloft, keeping their hips together. Deep, bone-melting pleasure surged through Kira's subconscious as he thrust forward again, almost causing her to shout at the crush of rapture filling her.

"That is what I feel when I'm inside you." His voice was low, eyes lit up with blinding green. "And you will feel every measure of the same, I promise."

A curtain fell over his emotions then, until the sensations Kira felt were hers and hers alone. She curled her hands into his hair, about to tell him to drop that wall so there were no barriers between them, but a clench of pleasure gripped her before she could speak. It cleared her mind of thought, wringing a cry from her instead of words. Mencheres slowly began to move, his mouth part-

ing as he stared at her while his body merged into hers.
Another clench of pleasure seized her, causing her to gasp
out his name while those rapturous bands inside her tightened.

He smiled, so sensual and beautiful, it was another
form of bliss just looking at him. Kira's hands unwound
from his hair to caress his back, growing more excited
by every flex of his muscles that meant another amazing
thrust inside her. His mouth closed over hers again, his
kiss somehow darker and richer. Their tongues twined together with the same silkiness as his movements within
her, Kira's heightened passion making her body able to
smoothly receive all of him.

His hands traveled over her while he slowly began to
increase his pace. Her moans were smothered by his kiss,
joining the hoarse, throaty noises Mencheres made as
they moved together. Each new thrust built the intensity
inside her, spreading it until her whole body throbbed instead of just her loins. Even her skin ached with a beautiful torment for more contact with his, making her grasp
him even more feverishly while her legs slid around to
encircle his hips.

He caught the back of her thigh in a strong grip, holding
her closer as his thrusts intensified. The waves of pleasure
cascading from her core had her crying out against his
mouth, her fangs cutting into his lip as her head began to
toss with growing urgency. His hand tangled in her hair,
keeping her steady, while his kiss became scorching, his
mouth ravaging hers with a hunger that was too fierce to
be contained.

Her nails dug into his hips as he began to move even
faster, shattering her reason with that ceaseless rhythm.
The sensual pressure built until it felt like she'd explode
if he didn't stop—and she didn't want him to stop. She

wanted him to take her past the edge, into the free fall beyond.

Mencheres tore his mouth free with a shout that echoed inside the small room. His pace suddenly increased to a degree that would have frightened Kira were it not for the ecstasy blasting through her. Her eyes closed while her loins finally convulsed from the overwhelming bliss, flooding a sensation far too great to be called pleasure through her.

Words spilled out of Mencheres's mouth in a language she didn't understand. She clutched him as the orgasm continued to throb inside her, shocking her with its intensity. She wanted him to feel the same thing she was feeling. To have him let go of that last bit of control.

"Come inside me," Kira gasped, her voice almost raw. "I need to feel you come now, Mencheres . . ."

Another slew of words she didn't recognize hoarsely tumbled from his lips, but then he kissed her with a passion that matched the burning demand of his body. She locked herself around him, moving with him, her mind sliding away from reality into pure sensation.

She felt the tremor deep inside her then, the shudder that passed from his body to hers. It flexed and contracted even as a harsh shout tore from his throat. Mencheres arched, thrusting inside her so forcefully that she gasped. His head fell back, dark hair fanning behind him as another, longer groan came from him. It matched the spasms reverberating within her, his climax thundering through her loins with powerful, rhythmic vibrations.

Her arms curled around his neck as she savored the tremors that still shook him. A profound sense of belonging filled her, as if something long restless inside her had found its home. For several extended moments, she didn't even want to speak, lest words break the rightness she felt.

Then she looked past Mencheres's face to see the pile of their clothes directly under them. Several feet under them, in fact.

"What?" she gasped. A glance around confirmed what her eyes first told her. That wasn't the wall brushing against her back anymore. It was the *ceiling*.

A low laugh shook him even as their distance to the ground began to dissipate, their bodies floating down slower than a drifting feather.

"Did you think I'd let you fall?" he asked huskily, kissing her throat with a languid thoroughness that took away her flash of anxiety. He settled them on top of the soft pile of clothes without once turning around to see where it was. It left her on top of Mencheres, her knees sunk into the pallet of fabric around them, his hair framing his face like black silk. His hands trailed along her back with firm, smooth strokes, pausing on the rounder part of her hips.

"I've heard the expression climbing the walls, but I never thought I'd experience it, let alone like that," she murmured, her mouth curling into what was probably a dreamy smile.

He smiled back, an unfiltered, wide stretch of his lips that reminded her how even more gorgeous Mencheres was without his usual impassive expression. She stroked his face, tracing her fingers over his high cheekbones, those dark thick brows, that full mouth, and his proudly sloped nose.

"What are you thinking?" she asked, leaning forward to brush her breasts against his chest.

"That I would stay like this with you always, if I could," he replied, his smile fading a bit.

Was the shadow that passed over his face due to their lack of time because they had to meet his co-ruler soon? Or because of Radje's frame job implicating Mencheres in murders he hadn't committed? She didn't want to ask. She wanted to keep this moment just between them, without other people or things intruding on it yet.

"Why did you close yourself off from me so I couldn't feel you?" she asked, resting her elbows on his shoulders.

His gaze slid over her breasts, compressed now against the wall of his chest. "It is a poor lover who ensures his lady's pleasure merely by letting her feed off his own," he replied with the hint of a grin.

Kira chuckled. "I don't think you need to worry about that. Ever."

"Then next time," he replied, his voice deepening, "we will share it together."

A rush of anticipation filled her, making her want to turn *next time* into *right now*. But another clench inside her, a more dreaded one, made Kira glance around the room in consternation. Aside from the machines, Mencheres's coat, and the Disney paraphernalia they were lying on, the room was empty. And she was getting very hungry.

Mencheres hadn't taken the blood cooler with them when they'd rushed to leave the house in the few hours remaining before dawn. She'd been so shocked by her death video and Mencheres's murder and arson framing not to even remember to ask him to bring that. The only thing she'd insisted on doing before they left was to call Tina, but in their hurry, all Kira managed to relay to her sister was that she was safe and for Tina to tell her brother not to believe anything he saw on TV. It wasn't nearly enough of an explanation, but it would have to do for now.

"Please tell me you stuffed a couple blood bags into

your coat before we left," she said, shifting uncomfortably as the clench in her stomach increased.

"I told you there would come a time when you wouldn't be able to cater to your feeding preferences. That time came sooner than expected."

Kira's mind revolted at the thought even as her stomach yowled in need once more. She swallowed. If she refused, tried to wait it out until they came across a hospital or blood bank, she might be thrown into the same mindless blackout hunger that had dominated her first couple days as a vampire. And if Mencheres wasn't right by her side when that happened, she could kill someone.

"How should I go about doing this?" she whispered. No way did she want to try winging it by herself.

He gestured to the pile beneath them. "We'll change into some of these clothes and go up to the park level. There are hundreds of adults there to choose from."

So saying, Mencheres gently rolled her over and sat up, pulling a T-shirt out from underneath him and slipping it on. He selected a pair of pants and donned them in the same careless fashion, completing the cover-up of his magnificent naked body, much to Kira's dismay. Still, she couldn't complain. If not for her, they could have spent more time making love in what was now her favorite room in the world.

Next he selected a hat from the pile, twining his long dark hair into a knot and placing a Disney ball cap over it. The effect on his appearance was startling. Somehow, in mere seconds, Mencheres went from looking like a striking, elegant man in his later twenties to a much younger tourist who might get carded if he attempted to buy a beer.

"You're like a chameleon, you know that?" Kira said.

He raised a brow. "Disguises are a necessary skill for vampires. It is not just a matter of changing clothes; it's affecting a new persona as well. Our faces have been publicized not only on the Chicago news, but also downloaded over the Internet. No need to chance any humans here recognizing us, even though our time will not be lengthy."

"You didn't say much about what our plan was when we left before, then, of course, I passed out at dawn. I don't even know how you managed to get us from Wyoming to Southern California. You couldn't have flown the whole way."

He shrugged. "It is easy enough to compel people to transport us where we need to go once I was certain we hadn't been followed."

And with Mencheres's hypnotic powers, none of those drivers would even remember their stint as a taxi driver. The thought made Kira pause. Did *she* now have that same ability to mesmerize people? Or was that something she'd grow into with time?

Another clench of her stomach reminded her that she didn't have the luxury of sitting here pondering the extent of her new abilities. She rooted through the pile of clothes until she found a T-shirt and some sweatpants, pausing to discreetly wipe away the remains of their passion with one of the torn pieces of her prior clothing. Then she tucked her hair inside a hat as Mencheres had done. It was unbelievable to realize that soon, she'd learn how to actually *bite* someone and drink their blood . . . all while wearing a Goofy ball cap and a Minnie Mouse T-shirt.

Her life had been blasted apart by Radje in every way possible, but right now, Kira wasn't thinking about that. Incredibly, she was happy, even though that happiness made no sense in light of the dire circumstances she and Mencheres were in.

He stroked her cheek when she stood up, staring with

more than casual interest at her mouth. Kira licked her lips. If only she'd thought to tell Mencheres to stuff some blood bags in his coat before they left his house. Then she might have been able to spend the next hour or so learning what made him moan the loudest instead of figuring out how to bite someone.

He inhaled, his eyes glinting with green. "I love your scent," he almost growled. "I love it even more now that it's all over my body."

The flat hunger in his tone made things low inside her clench, but unfortunately, her stomach refused to take a backseat to her rising desire. There went her plans for more ceiling explorations.

"Let's go now," she said. "Or I won't want to leave at all, and that will be dangerous for any person who comes into contact with me later."

Damn her need for so many feedings. That would lessen as time went on, she'd been assured, and she couldn't wait. It would be a relief when all she needed was a cup of bagged blood a day, and that was it.

"Yes. Now," Mencheres murmured. His lips brushed across hers for one last, seeking kiss, almost making Kira decide to forget feeding, but then he stopped, and they exited the noisy equipment room together.

Chapter Twenty-one

It only took a few flashes from Mencheres's gaze to make the employees they encountered forget that two unauthorized persons strolled through the underbelly of the park. When they reached the stairs that led to the park level, Kira's eyes were already tingeing with green and her fangs began poking out from her upper teeth. This was her first time around mortals after her transition. Their blood would be calling to her even louder than normal because of her hunger. Her hand tightened on his until she would have shattered his bones if his power hadn't automatically protected him.

"Don't let me hurt anyone." Her voice was hoarse, her fangs growing even longer.

He lifted her chin. "You won't. You are strong enough to handle this. It will feel overwhelming in the crowd at first, but don't focus on their heartbeats. Concentrate on the other noises. It will help."

Kira managed a short nod. Her fangs retracted a bit, and some of the glowing green left her eyes as she mustered her resolve. He waited until almost no traces of emerald remained in her light green gaze before he opened the door.

A bush trimmed into the shape of an elephant hid the side door from the view of the tourists as they came out. He drew Kira along with him to the main walkway, right in the midst of the crowd. Though it was past sundown, the park was still busy. The extended summer hours accounted for so much activity after dark.

A shudder went through Kira, and her eyes flashed green again, but Mencheres didn't stop. She needed to learn to control herself around a crush of mortals. It was far sooner than he'd let other new vampires brave a crowd, but this harsh crash course was necessary. While Kira slept earlier, he'd attempted to see into the future again, but nothing had changed except that the dreaded darkness seemed to be closer. His time was running out, and Kira needed to be ready when he was gone. That's why he'd deliberately thrown away the blood bags that he'd brought in his coat before she awoke, and why he didn't simply let her feed from one of the employees under the park.

"Lower your head," he directed her.

She dipped her head, shielding the flash of green in her gaze from any inquiring people around her. They passed through Frontier Land into New Orleans Square, where he procured Kira a pair of sunglasses. She gave him a grateful glance as she settled them onto her face. Now any green flashing from her eyes would be muted or probably thought of as a trick enhancement of the glasses.

Her confidence seemed to grow as they continued to

thread their way through the crowd, but though Mencheres knew she still struggled with her hunger, he couldn't feel it. Kira was turned vampire through his blood and power, so she was part of him and could sense his emotions whenever his shields were lowered. He, however, could only catch glimpses of her feelings the same way he had before; through her scent, her expressions, the tone of her voice, and her body language. All those were telling him that though her hunger continued to rise, Kira's strength did as well, matching the challenge of being thrust into this living feast around her.

"Do I just . . . pick someone, then find a bush or alcove to hide behind?" she whispered.

That would be sufficient, but he wanted her to learn how to feed even in plainer sight than that. He regretted the lack of time to ease her into this more gently, but Kira's ability to survive on her own was of primary importance.

"We will do it here," he said, pointing to the structure ahead of them on the hill.

She stopped walking. "You want me to bite someone while on the Haunted Mansion ride?" she asked incredulously.

He shrugged. "It is darker inside there than it is in most places in this park, and the other humans around you will be too distracted by the ride to pay attention to what you're doing."

She started walking again, but she shook her head. "Just when I thought I couldn't feel any weirder about this," she muttered.

Kira stood next to Mencheres as they proceeded through the first segment of the Haunted Mansion ride. They'd been hustled inside a small circular room. Then the

ceiling and the portraits stretched above them while a
faux-spooky voice went on about all the various ghoul-
ish delights awaiting the visitors. *Some more than others,*
Kira thought dryly.

She tried to focus on that recorded voice. Or the crank
of various machines and the overlapping music and
sounds from the rooms beyond. Anything except all the
blood-filled bodies around her. This room was packed,
with people brushing up against each other every few seconds. If she concentrated, she could drown out all those
tempting heartbeats under the commotion from the rest of
the noisy attraction.

When the doors to the room opened, she was relieved.
They went into a much larger room, onto a sort of conveyor belt where the caricatures of carriages called Doom
Buggies were being systematically filled with guests.
Much easier to control herself here, without being in a
small confined room with the equivalent of five-course
meals all around her.

Mencheres ignored the order of the line to stride up
to one of the ride's attendants. An almost imperceptible
flash of his eyes later, and the employee was all too happy
to seat them with a single rider instead of giving Kira and
Mencheres their own carriage. She found she couldn't
look at the young man in the Doom Buggy that the employee directed them to join. Only the steady pressure of
Mencheres's hand on her arm, leading her into the mechanical domed seat, kept her from fleeing altogether.

"Hey," the guy said in greeting when Kira sat next to
him, Mencheres on her other side. She couldn't bring herself to respond. Guilt and hunger competed in her. Could
she really *bite* this young man and drink his blood?

The attendant pulled up a metal safety bar, checked to
make sure it locked, then they were on their way into the

next section of the ride. A recorded voice blared out from speakers inside the carriage as the narrator continued to drone on. It wasn't dark to her eyes inside the ride, but with the various spots of shade, Kira knew the other guests would have a hard time seeing what occurred inside this aptly named Doom Buggy—except for the times when the ride deliberately twirled the buggies.

"I don't think I can do this," she whispered to Mencheres as the guy laughed and waved at his friends when the ride spun the carriages to briefly face each other.

His gaze was steady. "You must."

The pain spreading throughout her body with ever-increasing intensity seemed to agree. Mencheres was right. She was a vampire now. She still might not be used to the idea, and she certainly hadn't asked for this, but it didn't change the facts. Either she learned how to harmlessly take someone's blood, or she'd risk killing someone later when the need rose beyond her control, and there wasn't a plasma-vending machine conveniently nearby.

Mencheres leaned forward, catching the laughing young man's attention. His eyes flashed green before he spoke.

"Lean back with her into the corner. Say nothing. You feel no fear."

That familiar complacent look settled over the young man's face as he draped an arm around Kira and leaned them into the side of the carriage. She almost gasped. With half his body pressed to hers, his pulse seemed to drown out all the other noises around them, focusing her attention on that delicious, steady rhythm.

"The hand is safest until you have more experience. Then advance to the wrist, then the neck—but *never* bite the jugular unless you mean to kill," Mencheres instructed in a calm voice. The ride entered a faux ballroom filled with images of dozens of dancing ghosts dressed in eighteenth-century attire.

Kira looked at them instead of the young man's face as she slowly drew his hand to her mouth, reminding herself to exert no more pressure than she had when handling those eggs. If anyone could see them, all they'd notice was a couple huddled in the corner of the Doom Buggy, the man's hand over a woman's mouth as if urging her to silence. Her glasses hid her glowing eyes, and the young man's hand blocked her fangs from anyone's view when they popped out as that throbbing pulse beneath his thumb neared her mouth.

She closed her eyes, chanting "gently, gently" to herself as she pressed her fangs into the vein jumping against her lips.

The ambrosial flavor that immediately filled her mouth washed away her last vestige of hesitation. What she swallowed was richer than chocolate, smoother than cream, and it spread with luscious warmth all through her. Her mind hazily mused that this wasn't anything like when she'd fed from those bags. *That* always had a faintly acidic taste and left her with a sense of wrongness, but this felt entirely natural. Like she was part of an ancient chain of life that was at turns sacred and mysterious, dark and beautiful.

After her fourth swallow, Kira's eyes fluttered open. The young man's face was the first thing she saw. She braced for an accusing glare, but his eyes were slitted and a smile of pure bliss wreathed his face. He'd pressed closer to her, until his head lay on her shoulder and his body was an insistent brand against her right side.

One look at his lap revealed that he was enjoying this a little *too* much. Kira's gaze flew to Mencheres, but instead of jealous or censuring, his expression was faintly amused. Carefully, Kira pulled out her fangs, surprised when Mencheres gripped the boy's hand before she could even ask what to do next.

"One way to heal the punctures is to cut your tongue on a fang and hold it over the wounds before you remove your mouth," he said. "Or you could draw your thumb across your fang and press your blood across both holes. In either choice, preventing more blood loss and stained clothing is the intent."

She thought it was ironic that the ride took them through a singing graveyard as she followed Mencheres's directives. She opted to cut her thumb instead of her tongue, placing it over the twin punctures she'd made when Mencheres lifted his hand. Seconds later, when she checked, those puncture wounds were completely healed and so was the slice on her thumb. No evidence at all remained of what had happened, except the satiated warmth spreading throughout her body in place of that former gnawing hunger.

The guilt and shame Kira expected to feel was curiously absent. Instead, she felt better in a way that wasn't only due to her lack of hunger. All the heartbeats and the warm bodies inside this building no longer felt like temptations seeking to turn her into a murderer. The people around her felt like *people* again. Who would have thought that feeding from a human would make her feel more connected to her lost humanity instead of less?

"Take your glasses down," Mencheres said quietly. "Then look into his eyes and tell him he remembers nothing of what transpired except the entertainment of the ride."

She shot a glance at Mencheres. "I can do that . . . already?" She felt worlds better, stronger even, but not like someone who could alter a person's memory with a mere stare and a comment.

His mouth quirked. "Yes, already you have that ability."

Kira tried to muster her inner hypnotist as she slipped her glasses down her nose, directing her gaze at the young man who still leaned against her with a dreamy smile.

"So, ah, nothing happened except, um, you liked the ride," she stammered. God, that was a pathetic attempt at mesmerism. She'd have to do better to make this stick.

The young man sat up, that blankness leaving his eyes as the buggy started its trek toward a set of mirrors where the automated voice informed them that soon they'd see if one of mansion's ghosts had hitched a ride in their carriage. Mencheres reached over and pulled Kira to him, his arms encircling her in a loose embrace.

"That *worked*?" Kira blurted to him in astonishment.

He still had that faintly amused expression. "Of course."

She was overwhelmed with how smoothly everything had transpired when the young man turned to her with a grin.

"Look. You've got a ghost sitting on your lap."

She looked at the mirrors lining the wall across from them to see video footage of a plump bespectacled man superimposed over her in the carriage. The sight of the three of them with their grinning ghostly passenger only added to the surrealism Kira felt. Her first feeding as a real vampire was graced by a fake ghost.

The ride slowed as the next room revealed the disembarking platform with its large conveyor belt. An employee took down the safety bar in front of them and the three of them exited the carriage. The young man waved at his friends with the same hand Kira had bitten before he walked away, never realizing he'd been involved in a true supernatural event on the fake haunted ride.

Chapter Twenty-two

Mencheres and Kira were almost back at Big Thunder Mountain when he felt a shift of power in the air around him. For an instant, he tensed, but then that wave of energy struck a chord of recognition in him. *Bones.* How like him to be early.

"My co-ruler will be here momentarily," he told Kira.

She took her sunglasses off as if just remembering she didn't need them anymore. Her eyes hadn't flared once after her feeding, and her manner was far more relaxed. He hoped she'd recognize the wisdom of forgoing those plasma bags in the future. Not only would fresh blood taste better and make her stronger, it would also satisfy her hunger more thoroughly.

He saw Bones and Cat part through the crowd on the other side of the roller coaster. His co-ruler did not look happy.

"Bloody hell, grandsire," were Bones's first words as he approached. "You've left behind a wreckage of burned bodies, dead vampires, missing persons, threatened Guardians, and video evidence of our race's existence. Then you go on holiday. You really *do* have a death wish."

Kira's jaw dropped. Mencheres gave her hand a squeeze, noticing Bones's sharp brown gaze follow the gesture.

"Not anymore," he replied coolly. "I knew that establishment was being monitored; only a fool wouldn't expect those rooms were videoed. Yes, I intended to kill those three vampires, but not anyone else, and certainly not while leaving a tape behind with my actions documented. I did not do this deed."

"You were going to kill Flare, Patches, and Wraith?" Kira asked, shock plain in her voice. "I didn't believe Radje when he said that . . ."

Mencheres glanced down at her. "They tortured you. Of course I was going to kill them."

Cat cleared her throat in the tense silence that followed. "Uh, before this goes any further, let's at least introduce ourselves to your friend. I'm Cat, and this is my husband, Bones. We're part of Mencheres's twisted little fang family."

Kira shook the hand Cat extended to her after replying with her name. Bones shook Kira's hand as well, but with a far more speculative gaze than Cat bestowed on her. Mencheres met his co-ruler's gaze impassively, not answering the silent question Bones directed at him.

"Normally I would believe you, because you are the most patient, calculating person I've ever met," Bones said, getting back to the original topic. His gaze flicked to Kira again. "Yet in this instance, I'm tempted to believe

Radjedef's assertion that you were motivated to act without your usual careful planning."

"Is it safe to talk about this out here?" Kira asked, nodding at the families who passed by on their way through Frontier Land.

Mencheres gave Bones a challenging look. "It is if you weren't followed."

Bones let out a snort. "I was careful, grandsire."

"That 'grandsire' thing is too weird, considering you look older than he does," Kira muttered.

A dark brow rose even as Cat laughed. "You know, I never noticed, but she's right. Especially now, with his whole baseball cap and Disneywear thing going on. Quite a different look for you, Mencheres. Don't think anyone would recognize you like this."

"Yes, you're full of surprises, aren't you?" Bones agreed, with another pointed look at Kira.

"You told him you weren't the one who torched the club. If he doesn't want to believe you, we should just go," Kira said quietly, but with underlying steel in her tone. "I'm sure you have other friends who will be willing to listen to your side of the story."

Mencheres felt a swell of pride as Kira squared her shoulders and returned Bones's hard stare. She might have choice words for him later about his lethal intention toward those three miserable vampires, but all Kira showed now was her steadfastness—and her inability to be intimidated. She was a strong woman. Strong enough to survive this murky human and inhuman world once he was gone.

"That may be true, yet I don't see anyone of them here," Bones replied, encompassing the park with a wave of his hand.

"Nor will you see them. I'm meeting them without you," Mencheres stated calmly.

Both of Bones's brows went up. "Indeed? And why is that?"

"The less you know about my plans for Radjedef, the more that ensures the safety of our line if I do not succeed," Mencheres replied, his tone hardening when Bones's expression darkened.

"You know, I could really use a drink," Cat said, again breaking the tension. "Kira, mind keeping me company while I hunt for some gin and tonic?"

Kira glanced at Mencheres. "I won't be long."

It both amused and touched him that Kira felt protective of him. How long had it been since anyone felt the need to shield *him* from others?

"Gin and tonic, huh?" Kira asked as she walked away with Cat. "I've got some bad news for you. I don't think this park serves alcohol."

Kira's prediction turned out to be true, and her new companion settled for a lemon slush instead. She was about to head back to Mencheres, but Cat waved a hand at a nearby table and benches.

"Maybe we should give the guys a few minutes by themselves. That way, they can burn off some excess testosterone. Sit with me?"

Kira could still glimpse Mencheres through the passing throngs of people, even if all the surrounding noise made it difficult for her to hear him. She eyed the redhead warily, but Cat's smile was bland, devoid of any of her husband's thinly veiled antagonism. Cat slid her lemon slush across the table when Kira sat down.

"Enough sugar to make a dentist cry, but it's good."

Kira took a sip to be polite, but then was unable to stifle her grimace at the taste. It was like wet sawdust.

"Sorry, not my favorite," she managed, sliding it back over.

Cat took another gulp, unoffended. "Right, you're a newbie. Nothing will taste good aside from blood for your first couple weeks. Then your taste buds will even out."

Kira knew the woman across from her was a vampire; her lack of heartbeat had given that away the instant they met. She wondered how old Cat was. The tingle Kira had felt when she shook Cat's hand was far less than the vibe Bones gave off.

"Terrible, to be brought over without choosing it," Cat went on, still watching Kira with those clear gray eyes. "I saw the video. That Law Guardian was a real bastard. I don't blame you or Mencheres for being pissed—and if you ask me, those other three vampires had it coming, too. Torturing you? Kidnapping a teenager and making her strip for them? Burn, baby, burn. Mencheres did the world a favor by ridding it of those creeps."

Kira let out a laugh as understanding dawned. "Good cop, bad cop, right?" She nodded in Bones's direction. "He comes in acting all hostile, but *you* smooth things over and take me for a nice little chat. Was I supposed to be bowled over by your sympathy into confessing Mencheres's crimes? Sorry, try again. Something more original this time, I hope."

A smile played across Cat's lips. "Was I that obvious? God, I suck at subtlety. I suck at beating around the bush, too, so since you're obviously an intelligent woman, let's cut the shit and get right to it, shall we?"

"Yes, let's," Kira muttered. "It wasn't Mencheres. I've been with him in Wyoming ever since we left that club over a week ago. Yes, he could have snuck off while I was passed out from dawn until late afternoon, but the news station reported that the fire started after midnight. And Mencheres has been with me every night from the time I opened my eyes until dawn broke, so it *couldn't* have been him."

"See, that's the real scary thing right there." Cat leaned forward, her voice lower but more intense. "Mencheres clearly has a thing for you. That tape and seeing firsthand how he acts around you proves it. Normally, I'd say live and let love, but the last woman Mencheres fell for was an evil, murdering bitch. He couldn't bring himself to take her out until she almost destroyed everyone—and I mean *everyone*—close to him, me and Bones especially. So you'll understand if the sight of Mencheres making goo-goo eyes at you strikes fear in the hearts of me and anyone else who lived through what happened the *last* time that man had it bad for a woman."

Kira closed her eyes, hearing again the flat intonation in Mencheres's voice when he told her he'd participated in his wife's death. Was he still carrying guilt over whatever happened? She'd already surmised that the circumstances had been justified—if Mencheres was a casual murderer, he'd have killed Kira the first day they met. Cat's description of his ex only confirmed Kira's speculation. Mencheres clearly hadn't had a choice about killing her if he wanted himself and those he cared about to survive.

Just as Kira had had no choice about turning her husband in for drug dealing, knowing what would await him in prison.

"So you're worried that I might be another evil, murdering bitch? Maybe one who manipulated Mencheres into torching and slaughtering those people just to avenge what happened to me, is that it?" she asked, opening her eyes.

"You were tortured and killed." Cat's gaze flashed green for a second. "I've been tortured and almost killed, and let me tell you, I swore bloody vengeance against everyone who had a hand in it. If you did encourage Mencheres to torch that place and kill those vampires, I'd understand, but it seems he got overzealous. He does tend to lose his shit over a woman he cares about. Either way, both of you need to quit running and deal with the consequences before this problem gets any worse."

"It. Wasn't. Mencheres," Kira gritted out, her frustration rising. "It was that disgrace of a cop named Radje. He set Mencheres up because he wants something from him. Didn't you pay attention to *that* part of the tape? If you and Bones were real friends, you'd quit suspecting Mencheres, and you'd start helping him prove who really did it."

"If it was Radje, where is that young dancer?" Cat asked. "Jennifer, the one you tried to help? She's not among the dead, and she hasn't resurfaced with the police or her family. Isn't it odd that the person you originally tried to take away from the club might be one of the few people who walked away from the fire?"

Kira stood up, sick of arguing the same point. "Radje obviously knows how to do a good frame job. It wouldn't look as convincing if Jennifer ended up dead, would it? If for once you looked at this situation with the idea that Mencheres *didn't* do it, you might be surprised at what else you notice. And you might have wanted bloody revenge against those people who tortured you. Mencheres admitted he intended to kill them, too, but that's not me. I could kill in self-defense, but not in retribution. It's my goal to save lives, not destroy them."

Kira turned around, feeling those gray eyes bore into her back as she walked away. She doubted Cat had really heard a word she'd said. It seemed she and Bones had made up their minds about what happened before they even arrived. If these were Mencheres's closest allies, then they stood a better chance at defeating Radje without them.

"No," Mencheres said for the third time.

Bones ran a hand through his hair in frustration. "I'll take your word that you didn't do this. Your allies probably will, too. But you have many enemies who are seizing on this, spreading Radje's version of events high and low to rally opposition against you. If the majority of people are to believe you had nothing to do with this arson, then turning Kira in to the Law Guardians so she can support your claim of your whereabouts is your best chance. You know that."

"What I also know is that Radje will kill her or use her, and the other Guardians will not be able to protect her because they won't suspect him," Mencheres replied inexorably.

"Don't you see that hiding with her makes you look even more guilty?" Bones snapped. "You're claiming she and Gorgon are your alibi, yet all of you are refusing to present yourselves to the Guardians to answer Radje's charge."

"Radje is mainly demanding *her* presence in addition to my own. Does that not seem unusual? Why wouldn't he be as vocal in seeking out the other witness?"

"Yes, it's unusual." Bones's voice was sharp. "*I* believe that Radje's up to something. But you risk too much by not turning her in. You could be sentenced in absentia if you continue to defy them. Kira has a chance if she's relinquished to a Guardian you trust. It doesn't have to be Radje. Yet you greatly endanger yourself if you continue to act as though you are guilty. Grandsire." That sharp tone softened. "Please, don't do this."

Mencheres abruptly turned around and stared off toward the beverage stand. Kira and Cat no longer sat at the table next to it. He sent his senses outward and found a swell of inhuman energy behind a tall wrought-iron streetlamp. Mencheres fixed his gaze there, seeing Kira behind it. She flinched as she met his gaze, then pretended to tie her shoe in a poor imitation that she hadn't been eavesdropping.

"You're so busted," he heard Cat remark conversationally as she came up behind Kira.

"Mencheres," Bones prodded.

"I have nothing more to say on this subject," he replied, watching Kira give up the shoe-tying pretense.

"Radje's demanding that I turn myself in to testify?" Kira asked Cat.

She'd heard too much. Mencheres cast a hard look at Bones before he started toward her.

"Uh-huh," Cat was saying. "And Mencheres just said hell no. Told you he's unreasonable when it comes to a woman he's into. Oh, he's on his way over. Looks ticked, too."

Kira didn't turn around, but her shoulders tensed. Mencheres shot a warning look at Cat that she responded to with a little smile.

"You're nothing like she was, by the way," Cat went on to Kira, ignoring his glower. "And believe me, I mean that as a compliment."

Mencheres knew who Cat was talking about. Anger flared in him at the mention of his dead, deceitful wife. Was he always to be judged by Patra's actions? Would her sins continue to haunt him, a phantom he could never put to rest?

"Just because some of us make a mistake in love once doesn't mean we're doomed to repeat it," was what Kira replied right before Mencheres reached her.

His hand slid across her back even as her words took the sting out of his anger, lessening a guilt he hadn't acknowledged carrying. Yes, his heart had once been ensnared by a woman he knew had the capacity for great evil. He'd warned Patra that her dark actions would lead to her destruction. She'd chosen to stay on that path regardless, determined that she could alter her fate. Patra's demise had come just as Mencheres had foreseen—a silver knife twisted in her heart by the vampire Mencheres loved as a son, shared his power with, and elevated to the status of co-ruler in his line.

But just because that bitter fate had befallen him, it did not mean he was forever cursed to love those who would betray him. His hand slid down Kira's back once more. Cat was right. Kira was nothing like Patra, yet she'd captured his emotions even more firmly than his traitorous former wife had. This might be the end of his life, but he'd see that it was well lived.

"Our time with them is finished," he told Kira.

Bones circled around to stand next to Cat. "There's more that still needs to be sorted—"

"Finished," Mencheres repeated in a harder tone. Then he placed a hand on Bones's shoulder, meeting his co-ruler's obstinate brown gaze. "Protect the line. Until this is settled, it is yours."

"You can't do that," Kira said, shock in her tone. She must realize what he was giving up with those words.

"Wise lass, you should listen to her," Bones muttered.

"It is not permanent." Mencheres dropped his hand from Bones's shoulder and placed it on Kira's back again. "Radje has failed to defeat me in all of his many previous attempts. He will fail again now. I merely need time."

Bones opened his mouth, but Cat touched his arm. "Don't bother. You wouldn't give up your girlfriend either if you were him. Mencheres, you let us know what you need. We'll play dumb regarding your whereabouts with the Guardians in the meantime. Kira, pleasure to meet you. Bones . . . let's go."

Bones cast a long look at his wife. His scent still swirled with frustration, but then he lifted a shoulder in acquiescence.

"All right, Kitten. Grandsire, I sincerely hope you know what you're doing. Kira, perhaps next time, we'll meet under better circumstances."

Then the two vampires turned around and walked away, their striking looks the only thing that made anyone cast a second glance as they passed by. The air emptied of some of the energy in it, filled up instead with the softer vibrations that mortals gave off.

Kira faced Mencheres, her jaw set in that stubborn line. He cleared his expression back into an impassive mask as he waited for her to argue about his refusal to surrender her to Radje or the other Law Guardians.

Then, unexpectedly, her hands wound into the round collar of his T-shirt.

"Come down here," she said.

He bent almost cautiously, but his hesitation ended when Kira closed her lips over his. He savored the feel of her full mouth, then the delights of her tongue when she parted her lips. A slow heat began to build inside him. *So many hours left until dawn . . .*

She broke their kiss to stare into his eyes. "How long do we have before we're meeting your next set of allies?" she whispered.

A glint of emerald appeared in her light green depths, growing darker and brighter. He stopped stroking her face to curl his hand around hers. "Until tomorrow," he said thickly.

"Good." Kira's fangs had already started to lengthen with desire. "Then let's go back to the room now."

Power washed over the air in the next moment, whipping Mencheres around toward its source. Bones ran through the crowds, too fast to be observed by the humans as more than a rush of wind, Cat right behind him.

"Enforcers," Bones announced when he reached them. His eyes flashed green. " 'Round a dozen of them entering the park's main gates now. Don't know how they managed to follow me, but they must have."

It was **un**fortunate, but it wasn't a complete shock to Mencheres. Bones was smart and careful, but a vampire didn't become an Enforcer before turning five hundred years of age and completing a rigorous training process. They weren't the soldiers behind the powerful ruling body of all vampires because they were unexceptional. That was why Mencheres had chosen the park. It would be a relatively easier place to escape from.

"Go," he said with a growl. "If you fight them, you could be condemned by the Guardians along with me. Leave here and renounce me as a fool who would not listen to your urgings to turn myself in."

"I will not," Bones rasped.

Mencheres gave him a quick, hard glance. "Doing things you don't always want to do is the price that comes with Mastering a line. Now, protect our people and *go*."

He shoved Bones and Cat away from him then, with a blast of his power that hurtled them through the air far away from the park. Kira let out a shocked noise and a few humans looked up in confusion, no doubt their minds rejecting what their vision had just caught a glimpse of.

"We need to go, too," Kira said, tugging on his hand. "Come on, fly us away from here."

He would, but not just yet. "Wait."

A dozen Master vampires from the elite ranks of the Guardian Enforcers filed into the entrance of Frontier Land. Beside him, Kira's grip tightened on his hand.

"I won't be the cause of any deaths, Mencheres. It's my choice, and if you won't get us away from here, I choose to give myself up."

He uncurled her hand from his with a light tweak of his power. Then he spread his arms out to the Enforcers.

"If you want me, here I am."

Chapter Twenty-three

Kira watched the dozen vampires descend on them like it was something out of a nightmare. They moved past the people in the park as if they weren't even there, with a single-minded purpose that made her debate running over to them and giving herself up. She couldn't stand it if a fight broke out that left the park's innocent guests— men, women, and children—in the line of fire where they could get hurt. Or worse.

She gasped out something to that effect to Mencheres, but he escaped from her frantic grip and his reply to the Enforcers stunned her.

"If you want me, here I am."

The open challenge in his voice said that he had no intention of going quietly. Oh God, he couldn't mean to fight them! Not here with all these families around!

Kira let out a horrified noise as the advancing vampires, men and women both, drew shiny blades out of sheaths in their belts and quickened their pace. A few people paused to stare, but Mencheres didn't even flinch. He just stood there with his arms spread out and his feet squarely planted.

"Mencheres," one of the Enforcers called out, "by order of the Guardian Council, you will come with us."

A muted blasting sound followed by multiple showers of sparks filled the air in the next instant as all the lights went out in their section of the park. Even the emergency ones imploded with small popping noises, plunging Frontier Land into shadows for Kira but darkness for anyone human. Around them were various sounds of the park's rides grinding to a halt.

Several people gasped. Some children began to wail, but aside from giving Mencheres a dirty look, the Enforcers didn't react. They kept coming.

Kira attempted to run to them, trying to stave off a deadly confrontation by turning herself in whether Mencheres liked it or not. But after two steps, she found that she couldn't move. Her body felt like it had somehow been encased in a concrete block up to her neck. She could still turn her head, though, so she did, right in time to see Mencheres give her a censuring frown.

"That is not necessary. No blood will be shed tonight."

Then power flooded the air in a tidal wave, Mencheres standing at the center of it. All of the Enforcers abruptly began to slow; their quick, precise movements becoming sluggish. At the same time, the humans around them, adult and children alike, backed away in perfect, rapid synchronicity. Soon the area was empty of everyone but Mencheres, Kira, and the Enforcers, whose momentum had now slowed to the speed of a crawl.

"Release . . . us," the one who'd made it closest to Mencheres demanded in a strangled snarl.

He closed his fists in response. Another wave of power was released, resulting in all the silver knives the Enforcers held being yanked from their grip to land in a pile by Mencheres's feet. Then as one, the Enforcers were flung up into the night, past the height of the nearby roller coaster, before being slammed down onto the ground. Their impact broke the concrete and sent a shock wave trembling through their section of the park. Screams came from the perimeter even though few people would have been able to see what happened.

Just as abruptly, those dozen vampires were launched into the air again, this time slamming into each other instead of the street. Kira was stunned as she watched the powerful Enforcers reduced to looking like they were participants in some sort of kamikaze puppet show.

"You came to arrest me for a crime I did not commit," Mencheres said calmly below them. "Tell Radjedef I *will* present myself to the Guardian Council . . . once I have proof of who truly committed these acts."

Then the Enforcers were flung upward before slamming down into the ground again, and again, and again. Kira was too shocked by their macabre bouncing routine, which loosed more concrete each time to notice that Mencheres now stood at her elbow.

"We must leave."

Almost numbly, she nodded, putting her arms around his neck as he held her to him. Then Mencheres rocketed them away, the Enforcers still thumping solidly on the ground below them.

Mencheres kept one arm around Kira as he blasted them straight up into the sky. He kept half his concentration on the Enforcers below, trying to stun them as much as possible with the repeated impacts, but soon his power over them broke as the distance between them grew.

Once he felt that mental snap, Mencheres turned all of his focus on propelling them higher into the sky, farther up than he would have dared when Kira was human. After several seconds, the air chilled, and the lights below them became dimmer. Still, he did not ease up. He knew the mettle of the Enforcers. They would recover swiftly, then they would be after them.

Soon enough he felt another swell of power in the currents below them. He focused on it, sending a concentrated burst of force downward toward the source. He was rewarded by a muffled scream and the abrupt dissipation of that trailing energy. The Enforcer would probably recover before he hit the ground. If he didn't, mountains were now underneath them instead of the thousands of humans innocently gathered at an amusement park, and a hard landing wouldn't kill a vampire.

Two more sets of power rode on the air currents after them. Mencheres gave a grim shake of his head as he used more of his strength to deliver a pair of high-force impacts that sent them tumbling toward the earth. Killing them at the park would have been much easier, but Radje *wanted* Mencheres to kill them. Slaying even one of the Enforcers would ensure that all of the Guardians united against him. He couldn't do that, but that didn't mean he would allow them to capture him or Kira. The only surprise was that Radje hadn't come with the Enforcers to assist in their attempt to bring him in.

"Cold . . . too cold," Kira muttered.

Frost started to cover both of them, but he couldn't risk going lower. It took a great deal of his considerable power to keep them this fast and this high. Most of the Enforcers would not be able to match this height and velocity. It was their best chance of getting away without him resorting to slaying the ones who chased them.

A vast expanse of dark blue ran alongside the intermittent lights below them. Mencheres gave it a speculative glance. Perhaps there was another way to slip the Enforcers without depleting his strength on this altitude *or* those blasts of power needed to deflect his pursuers.

Mencheres swung them toward that continual stretch of blue, dropping their height until ice no longer began to crystallize on Kira's skin. At the same time, he felt the charge of three more Enforcers coming from below them. He let them get closer. Closer, closer . . .

He sent a triple blast of power that spun them back toward the mountains. A stretch around with his senses revealed that the other Enforcers were not nearby. Satisfied, Mencheres wrapped both arms around Kira and bulleted their bodies in a straight downward line toward that inviting indigo platform.

"Mencheres, no!" she screamed.

Their bodies torpedoed into the ocean a moment later.

The blast of impact shook Kira, sending sizzling pain through her body. For a few seconds, she was stunned. Then the pain dissipated, replaced instead by an inexplicable rush of panic. She had to remind herself there was nothing to be afraid of. She didn't need to breathe anymore, but a part of her still wanted to scream as Mencheres hurtled them deeper into the ocean. He was slower underwater than he'd been in the skies, but still so fast that she felt like they were being yanked downward by a great invisible chain. The water surrounded her with an ever-tighter embrace, the pressure increasing until she felt claustrophobic. Nothing but liquid was all around her, yet it compressed against her with the force of a fist slowly closing over her body.

Then their downward momentum stopped, and she was flying sideways through the depths. Water cleaved around them with the powerful bursts Mencheres used to propel them, slicing horizontally into the deep as though their bodies had morphed into a single torpedo.

Finally, that rushing sensation stopped. Kira held tightly to Mencheres, expecting another explosion of movement any second, but he remained still. She wasn't even aware that she had her eyes squeezed shut until salt stung her gaze when she opened them. Mencheres had them suspended in the deepest shadows she'd ever seen as a vampire, only the bright emerald flash from his eyes providing a welcome form of illumination.

Kira rubbed her eyes, but it didn't help the stinging. His grip on her loosened until only one arm held her to him. He looked upward, then back at her, and shook his head.

She supposed that meant they couldn't go to the surface anytime in the next few minutes, which, though she knew the odds were slim, still had been what she hoped would happen. The tight pressure around her added to the feeling that she was being smothered—even though she'd gone hours without a single breath every day for the past week. The murkiness also increased her unease, which made no sense. Just recently, she'd lamented that she'd never see darkness again, yet here was a decent substitute all around her, and she hated it. How quickly she'd gotten used to the ability to see everything around her with crystal-like clarity.

Kira wasn't wearing a watch, but she tapped the top of her wrist with what she hoped was a questioning look. Mencheres held up two fingers in response, almost leading her to attempt cursing while underwater. Two *hours* down here? If she saw a shark, she'd scream for sure, even though she had some sharp teeth now, too.

Something stroked across her back. Kira whirled with a silent shriek, but there was nothing but dark blue as far as she could see. That stroke came again, from her shoulders down to her lower back in a soothing, firm caress. She relaxed. *Mencheres.*

She turned back to face him, his face lit in the glow from her own gaze. His hair floated around him in a black cloud, his T-shirt edging up to reveal that taut, smoothly muscled stomach. The striking planes of his face looked almost eerily beautiful against the backdrop of that endless indigo canvas, the underwater currents gently rustling his hair. He was so stunning . . . and the amount of power he was capable of wielding was terrifying.

He'd knocked Bones and Cat out of the park as easily as brushing lint off his shirt. Then he'd disarmed those Enforcers. Moved people out of harm's way. Repeatedly slammed the Enforcers onto the ground as easily as a child bounced a ball—all without touching any of them. Then he'd taken her up to the limits of the sky before plunging them into the depths of the ocean while making it look effortless. Kira couldn't even grasp the magnitude of his abilities. She was already disconcerted about how she could control any human's mind with a flash of her newly bright gaze, and that was *nothing* compared to what Mencheres could do.

He watched her, his face wearing its usual hooded expression, but slivers of troubled yearning ghosted across her subconscious. Not her emotions. His.

Did Mencheres believe his jaw-dropping display would scare her away? On an abilities level, they *were* grossly disproportionate. He was easily a thousand years older than her, too, which was hard to even contemplate. Plus, he had that unfortunate tendency to do other people's thinking for them, as he'd admitted before and proved again when he wouldn't let her turn herself in to the Enforcers.

Yet for all of his staggering power, Mencheres still had a strong conscience. *Absolute power corrupts absolutely,* he'd quipped to her once, yet he'd repeatedly proven otherwise with his actions. For all of their power inequality, Mencheres kept himself on equal emotional ground with her, always giving her the freedom to accept him or reject him.

Her practicality warned her that their differences were vast enough to shatter them, even if they weren't in serious danger from Radje, the Enforcers, and the other Law Guardians. Yet her instinct said Mencheres was meant to be hers.

Kira found herself smiling at the thought. *Mencheres, hers.* She reached through the water separating them, stroking his face, feeling the spark of his power against her skin. *Mine.* It felt right. It felt more right than anything had before it, in fact.

He pulled her into his arms, emotions too strong for her to name brushing against her subconscious. Suddenly, the thought of two hours in the ocean like this wasn't unpleasant. Not if she could hold him and feel everything he hadn't allowed himself to tell her yet.

Chapter Twenty-four

Mencheres scanned the rows of houses in the valley below them. A slight breeze ruffled his hair as he narrowed his focus on each residence, seeking one that didn't contain a beating heart. Beside him, Kira was silent, but a slight shiver went through her. They were both still wet, and it was cooler here, much farther up the California coast than where they'd first entered the ocean hours before.

"There," he said, standing.

Kira rose, letting out a noise of relief. "I know it's wrong to enter someone's home while they're gone, but I can't wait to get all this dried salt off me. It itches."

He gave her an amused look as they started toward the empty residence. "The home has a FOR SALE sign on it. I doubt anyone occupies it. Would it ease your conscience if I later arranged to have funds sent to the homeowners to cover our brief stay?"

"It would, actually," she replied. "It still doesn't make breaking and entering okay, but then I wouldn't feel quite as much like a burglar."

"Consider it done." It was a small enough gesture to appease her sensibilities, even though he didn't intend for the residents or the Realtors to be aware that anyone had been in the home. Still, they had four hours before he was to meet his ally, and he didn't intend to spend that time with Kira wet, cold, and miserable.

They came upon the lawn of the house five minutes later. Mencheres burned out the motion-sensor lights with a flick of his mind once they neared the premises, then he disabled the lines to the alarm before unlocking a side door. He could have picked a more modest neighborhood to seek out empty homes in. Ones that might not have security systems, but this was closer to his meeting point. And Kira deserved a little more luxurious surroundings to make up for the squalid equipment room she'd woken up in yesterday.

The empty quietness of the home beckoned invitingly. Kira wasn't the only one who looked forward to resting for a few hours. He'd depleted a great deal of his energy between the Enforcers, the heights he'd flown to, navigating them through the ocean, then flying them here. He needed to feed as well, but that could wait until later, when they were safely with his ally.

"You could be the world's best bank robber if you wanted to," Kira remarked as she went inside the door he opened. No alarm sounded. Good. Some systems were more sophisticated than others. The home was furnished as well, but it had an empty feeling that spoke of weeks since it had been occupied.

"It gives me no pleasure to steal," he replied with a shrug. "Sometimes it is necessary, as with waiting here, or when I drink from humans who do not knowingly offer me their veins. Or when I compelled those drivers to bear us to our destination. But to take when the same thing can be purchased or freely given . . . no, that is not my way."

Kira gave him a long look before turning away. "I'm going to find a shower and hope the water's on so I can get this salt off me."

So saying, she climbed the shiny marble staircase and disappeared onto the second floor. Mencheres stared after her, measuring if there was additional meaning behind her words.

Much might have changed between them after the Enforcers charged the park. She'd obviously been shocked at the things he'd done, but then she'd held him in the dark depths of the ocean with tenderness while they waited to make sure no Enforcers would find them. Kira's voice also deepened ever so slightly when she said she was seeking a shower. He couldn't tell if her scent changed as well; she still smelled too strongly of the ocean for him to catch any faint nuances of desire. But her eyes might have glinted with emerald just a bit before she turned away.

He intended to discover if he was right.

Water turned on when Mencheres took the first step up the stairs. He climbed them slowly, listening to the rustle of wet clothing being removed, then the soft sound of enjoyment Kira made when she stood under the spray. He followed those sounds as he continued onto the second floor, stepping in the same damp footprints she'd made on the marble, drawn toward the bathroom where she was.

The bathroom with the open door.

Mencheres pulled off his wet shirt, leaving it on the floor. His shoes and sodden pants followed suit, the useless cell phone inside them making a soft thud as it hit the marble. Then he walked naked into the bathroom.

Steam enveloped him when he stepped into the enclosed shower. Kira stood under the spray, her back to him, her body softly glistening. The weight of the water turned her hair a darker shade of topaz as it dragged it down to coat her shoulders.

She leaned back into his embrace without hesitation, unleashing a feeling of profound relief in him. Not until that very moment did he realize how much a rebuff from her would raze him. His hands almost trembled as he slid them down the sleek, supple planes of her body. *My Kira. My strong, beautiful dark lady.*

He kissed the back of her neck, the water running over his face from the spray. A soft moan came from her. She attempted to turn around, but he held her where she was. In his impatience before, he'd neglected to explore her the way he'd wanted to. Slowly. Thoroughly. Until she writhed for him.

Mencheres spread Kira's arms out, bracing her against the shower wall with her body bent slightly forward. His hands caressed her front even as he dipped his mouth along her back, enjoying the small, sharp gasps that came from her. His power enclosed her as well, seeking all the curves of her body that his hands hadn't reached yet. When his mouth dipped to the slope in her lower back, he let his shields drop so Kira could feel his hunger. His anticipation and lust as he spread the globes of her cheeks to delve his tongue along their valley.

She shuddered, a harsh sound escaping her. He spread her legs wider, sinking to his knees, seeking her sweet center. His next lick found it, and he pressed her closer. She bent forward more even as her spine arched. A long ripple went through her.

"Please," Kira gasped. "I need to touch you."

Her knees trembled as his tongue swirled deeper inside her. He inhaled, reveling in her scent, her taste, and the tremors he felt vibrating against his mouth. His power held her upright while his hands continued to stroke her, the wetness on his tongue increasing even as Kira's moans grew into sobs. She leaned back, rocking in her ecstasy, inciting him to thrust his tongue faster and deeper within her. A primal triumph filled him as her juices began to cover his mouth even though the water still cascaded around them.

"Now, now, *now*," she all but screamed, letting go of the wall to clutch his hands.

Mencheres rose in a lithe motion, filling her in one powerful stroke. A cry tore out of her, but it wasn't edged in pain, and her walls clenched around his shaft in rapture instead of tension. A guttural moan came out of him as he grasped her hips and began to move with slow, deep strokes. She was so tight, but so wet, each twisting squeeze flooding his body with almost unbearable pleasure. His mouth latched onto her neck as he brought her flush against him, her back rubbing his chest and those deliciously full globes teasing his loins. Her head fell back while her arms rose to encircle him from behind, her hips matching the increasing pace of his.

Pleasure raced across every nerve in his body. It grew even as her cries became louder, the squeeze of her flesh around him tighter. The intensity increased until it felt like he burned from the inside out, his skin so tight and heated, even the continual spray of water from the shower was painfully erotic. He couldn't stop himself from moving faster, driving into Kira with an unrestrained hunger that demanded her response. Exultation filled him when she cried out, and spasms squeezed his shaft.

Her ecstatic inner clenching only sharpened his pleasure, making his whole body throb with an answering cadence. He wanted to bury his seed deep inside her, but even more than that, he wanted to feel the sweet clamp of her orgasm around him again. Right now.

She hadn't ceased trembling from her release when Mencheres pulled out of her, spinning her to face him, his mouth covering hers to capture her moan. Kira's tongue stroked his almost feverishly as he thrust inside her again, the remaining shivers from her climax vibrating along his flesh with endless sensuality. He lifted her, using his power to glide them from the shower into the bedroom before lowering her onto the bed. Another long, deep thrust had her legs curling around his waist while her nails dug into his back. Even through his haze of desire, he felt a flash of clarity. This was where Kira belonged— in his arms, sharing every emotion that rippled through him with devastating intensity.

Then he lost himself in the taste of her mouth, the rub of her skin, the strong grip of her arms, and the wet, tight embrace that flooded his body with indescribable pleasure. Her name left his lips in a groan as his mouth slid down her body, reveling in the scent and flavor of her silky skin.

"Don't stop," Kira urged, trying to pull him back up.

"I want to feel you come again," he all but growled.

She let out a breathy laugh. "Then come back here and give me a few more minutes—*oh!*"

The cry wrenched out of her as he sank his fangs between her legs, right into the heart of her sensitivity. A deep satisfaction filled him as Kira's soft flesh seized beneath his mouth almost instantly. Then he rose up and thrust inside her, a groan escaping him at the feel of her flesh convulsing around him.

Her back arched while those shudders continued within her. He moved faster, kissing her throat, her lips, and her jaw while he let his control slip away. That throbbing in him grew until it felt like his skin would split from the pleasure frothing inside him. It overtook him, drowning him in sensations that intensified until they exploded in a climax that left him clutching Kira hard enough to bruise her.

For several long moments, he stared at her while the last ripples slowly faded from his body. Her eyes were greener than he'd ever seen, and her fingernails still dug into his shoulders.

"I can't believe you bit me there," she finally said. "But what I really can't believe is how it *felt.*"

A smile curved his lips. "There are perks to being a vampire. That is one of them. I'll enjoy showing you the others."

"I can't wait," she murmured. Then her expression changed, losing its sultry lethargy to become serious. "There's something I need to tell you."

He pulled away, leaving the bliss of her embrace to lean back against the headboard. Kira sat up as well, pulling the outer blanket around her either out of chill or an attempt to put another barrier between them aside from the space that now separated them.

"I'm listening," he replied. Dozens of centuries spent concealing his emotions made his face blank and his voice neutral while his walls went up, keeping Kira from feeling any of his inner turmoil.

Her gaze was steady. "I'm in love with you. Yes, it's very soon. Yes, there's still so much I don't know about you, but this isn't infatuation or lust. It's real, and it's something that's been growing in me since before you left me on that roof."

Mencheres was stunned. He felt his mouth open, but he could not seem to make it form words. Reason at once rejected her statement. She couldn't love him. Kira had a clean heart. Not a spotless one—no one's heart was—but if she'd seen all the darkness in his life over the course of the years, she would run away from him.

Her gaze remained level. "Say something. I don't care what, just speak."

"I am a murderer."

The words came out without thought, but they were true. She deserved to know what he was, even though it would probably drive her away.

Her full, lovely mouth twitched. "I know that. I saw you knock the heads off those ghouls the day we met, remember?"

"Not just then." Mencheres met her gaze, waiting for it to cloud with revulsion at his next words. "Many times. More than I can remember."

"How many of those times had to do with protecting yourself or your people?" she asked, no change in her expression.

His brows drew together. She'd surprised him yet again. "Does it matter?"

"Yes," she replied with emphasis. "Your world operates by very different rules. I might not have seen much of it, but that part's clear. You're calling yourself a hardened killer, Mencheres, but I've seen you protect or save lives that shouldn't matter to you if you were such a cold person. I should know. Mine was one of those lives you saved, and at the time, you didn't even know me."

"I set my wife up to be killed. I watched her die and did nothing to stop it." His voice was flat.

Kira touched his face. "Cat told me she tried to kill

you and everyone else close to you. So you had no choice. Neither did I when I turned Pete in."

He set her hands from him. It was too difficult to say this next part with her touching him, but she needed to know exactly who it was she thought she loved.

"I killed Patra long before that day. You asked me if I ever took a life outside of protecting myself or my people. The answer is yes. Before Patra married me, she loved someone else. I slew her lover, and it was not in defense. I was a vampire, and he was merely human."

The memory of that murder rose within him, as it had done so often in the past several years while Patra edged ever closer to her fate. *Intef's broken body on the floor, his blood soaking into the pale clay, and the stunned faces of Mencheres's guards as they looked at him.*

"I told Patra her lover was murdered by Romans. We married a few years later, but eventually, one of the witnesses spilled my secret. I tried to explain the circumstances behind his death, but she didn't care. What I did caused Patra to hate me, and that hatred is what led her to attempt to destroy me and my people. All her actions can be laid at my feet."

"You killed him out of jealousy?" Kira asked, her voice raspier.

His eyes closed. "That day, the humans were warring. Soldiers injured Patra enough that I had to change her over instead of merely healing her. Then I went to fetch her lover as I'd promised. I felt no real jealousy toward Intef. He was one of many amusements Patra had indulged in during her unpleasant marriage, though he had a stronger hold over her because she did want him changed into a vampire, too."

"Weren't you worried that changing him over would

ruin things for you? You must have cared for her by then, or were you two not, ah, involved yet?"

Mencheres opened his eyes to give Kira a pointed look. "We weren't lovers yet. Patient I would be, share I would not. I cared for Patra then, but I wasn't blind to her nature. She was attracted to power and riches. I had both, Intef had neither. I knew she would soon choose me over him."

"So if it wasn't jealousy . . . ?" Her voice trailed off.

"The power to move things with my mind can be influenced by my emotions. That is why it requires absolute control, which is also why my sire knew Radje would have been a poor choice for it. I hadn't met Intef before that day, but when I went to fetch him, I heard his thoughts. He'd been using Patra to curry power, selling her secrets to her enemies. He was the one who'd sent the Roman soldiers to kill her, the same ones who'd injured her so badly I had to turn her. I heard all that, and my rage let loose my power." Mencheres's mouth tightened into a grim line. "He was dead before any of my people could speak to stop me."

Pink glistened in Kira's eyes. "You were wrong to kill him," she said softly. "But you know that, and you've served a nine-hundred-year sentence of guilt under it. I think that's punishment enough—and you are *not* responsible for what Patra did. If that's the excuse she used for all the misery she caused, especially considering he tried to have *her* killed, then I call bullshit. That man's death is on your hands, but everything she did is on hers."

Once again, Mencheres found himself in the rare position of being speechless. People just did not *love* him if they knew him. They respected him, were loyal to him, feared him, hated him, envied him, lusted for him, needed things from him, or felt a combination of several of those things. But no one simply loved him—most especially, no one like Kira.

She slid her hands along his arms, moving closer to him.

"For all your experience, I'm guessing this is one thing you're not very familiar with, so let me help you out," she murmured. "For starters, it doesn't require weeks or months to know what you feel is love. For another, this is something that even with all your power, you can't control. You don't have to echo my feelings, Mencheres, but you can't talk me out of them, either. I love you." Her smile was wry. "Deal with it."

She pulled his head down to her then, her mouth moving over his with such gentleness, he could have been a human she was trying not to bruise. He still couldn't summon the words to respond to her incredible statements, but this . . . this required no words.

He kissed her with everything in him that he could not form into speech, pulling down the barrier that prevented Kira from sensing his emotions. Her arms tightened, her fangs lengthened, and her body molded to his. A powerful need rose in him, stronger than lust, deeper than possessiveness. He let Kira feel all of it as he rolled on top of her, pulling away the blanket that was the only barrier between them.

Chapter Twenty-five

The black limousine waited ahead of them at the street Mencheres said it would be. Kira heaved a mental sigh of relief. They were late. Thank God his friend had waited for them.

She smoothed down the front of her makeshift toga, imagining that she looked as confident as Mencheres did in his matching outfit. However, while he seemed able to wear anything, even a bedsheet, while affecting an elegant air, Kira was pretty certain she looked like a frat-party reject.

If they'd thought to put their sea-soaked clothes through the washer and dryer, they would've had something else to wear. But Mencheres had proven to be insatiable, and so, to Kira's mild astonishment, had she. She wasn't sure if this was due to her new stamina as a vampire, or because Mencheres made love like he'd invented the act. If she wasn't already dead, the number of climaxes he'd brought her to might have killed her. And feeling his pleasure at the same time? She shivered. Good thing Mencheres finally remembered about the meeting. She wouldn't have.

Of course, that meant they'd had to rush out the door and the house, while furnished, didn't have any additional clothes in it. Kira was about to put on her wet, seaweed-stained clothes when Mencheres yanked a clean sheet from another bed and fashioned a sarong for her out of it, making one for himself out of another sheet. Thankfully, there were few people out on the streets now, less than an hour before dawn.

The window to the limousine rolled down when they approached, a handsome man with long brown hair and a closely cropped beard on the other side of it.

"Mencheres," the stranger said. "If anyone other than you had me fly halfway around the world just to keep me waiting while you were obviously lingering in bed, I'd have my driver run them over. Twice."

"Long flight?" Mencheres asked in reply, opening the door to let Kira in. She minded the edge of her toga as she sat down in the opposite seat from the brunet stranger, whose gaze flicked over her in a measuring way.

"Very long," he answered. "I was stopped twice at the airport for 'random' security checks, too. Just because I have long dark hair and a beard, I'm constantly mistaken for a potential terrorist. I suppose it's worse when you fly commercial. They must attempt a cavity search every time."

Mencheres's mouth curled as he climbed into the limo. "Those private body-search rooms do provide an easy opportunity to feed." Then he sat next to Kira, placing his hand on her shoulder. "This is Kira Graceling. Kira, Vlad Tepesh."

"Quite an honor," Vlad drawled, holding out a hand crisscrossed with what looked like old scars.

Her brow furrowed even as she shook the hand offered to her. That name sounded familiar. Where had she heard it before . . . ?

"Oh!" Kira exclaimed. Her eyes widened. "You're not the *real* Dracula, are you?"

"Does *no one* think to warn people before they meet me?" Vlad muttered, shooting an irritable look at Mencheres. "Though I suspect what made that detail slip your mind was the same thing that also made you late."

"You're being discourteous," Mencheres said in a reproving tone even as Kira shifted in her seat. It was true that showing up late wearing nothing but sheets wouldn't require much imagination to figure out what had kept them.

"It's fine, Mencheres. Though if you'd told me I was about to meet such a legendary vampire, I would have grabbed the nicer silk drapery to wear instead," she replied, meeting Vlad's coppery green gaze with an arched brow.

Vlad flashed her an instant's worth of a smile. "I can see why he likes you. Although, to listen to Radje, Mencheres doesn't just like you. He's fallen so in love that he's slaughtering vampires over you, defying the Guardian's attempts to bring him in, and generally acting even more crazed than he was at the beginning of his relationship with Patra, may she burn in peace."

Kira cast a glance at Mencheres. This was a discomfiting topic for more than one reason—and was *no one* sensitive about throwing up Mencheres's dead wife in front of him?

"You know I would not have been as foolish as to let myself get caught on tape at a place I later went back to and supposedly torched," Mencheres said. *Please,* his tone implied with heavy irony.

Vlad's lip curled. "No, you're very careful about video. Heard all the cameras at Disneyland were blown out yesterday after a reported Muslim extremist knocked out the lights, then detonated a small bomb before escaping."

"Muslim extremist?" Kira repeated, her jaw dropping. Of all the racial-profiling bullshit . . .

"No one was hurt," Vlad went on. "Though the families who were shaken up did get a refund of their admission tickets."

"Bones was followed by Enforcers," Mencheres said, shrugging. "It was an unfortunate incident."

Vlad grunted in a way that made Kira think he and Bones weren't close, but that was hardly her concern. A wave of lethargy crested over her. Dawn must be getting closer. She'd wanted to call Tina before she fell asleep, but now there wasn't time. It wouldn't reassure her poor sister that she was okay if Kira passed out in midsentence while talking with her.

"We'll need a safe place to stay for the next few days," Mencheres said. "Obviously, all of my residences would be the first place the Guardians looked for me, my people's homes and hotels being the next. But you're not of my line, and your people would fear your wrath more than the Guardians', if any of them revealed you were assisting me."

"I already have a place picked out for you." Vlad's gaze turned knowing. "But you must want more than that from me, to have me come all the way out here. Secret accommodations can be arranged over the phone."

"I will set up a safe, neutral place to meet with Veritas,"

Mencheres replied. "One that we can easily escape from if she's not inclined to come alone. I want you there as witness to what's said between us."

Vlad's eyes seemed to get a shade greener. "Veritas? Why, out of all the Law Guardians, would you assume she'd be the most sympathetic to your cause? I know you share the same sire, but Veritas almost had Cat killed for interfering in a duel just last fall."

"I've known her for most of my life," Mencheres replied.

Vlad grunted. "You could say the same about Radjedef."

"Who is the vampire who sired you, Mencheres?" Kira asked. "Will I ever meet him or her?"

"Not this side of the grave," Vlad muttered.

Mencheres gave Vlad a mildly reproving glance before turning to her. "Tenoch was my sire. He was an extremely powerful, respected vampire, and he died almost six hundred years ago."

"How did he die?" Kira asked before remembering that *natural causes* wasn't a possibility. "Oh, ah, never mind," she stammered.

"Tenoch died from the same thing that kills most extremely old, very powerful vampires," Vlad said. "Suicide."

"That has *never* been proved," Mencheres shot back in a hard tone.

"Tenoch had even more power than you do, yet I'm supposed to believe he was brought down by merely a quartet of Master vampires?" Vlad asked in an equally inflexible tone. "Those who don't know the details might believe that fable, but you and I know it was only four vampires against him, not fifty as reported. Tenoch set himself up. If he'd truly wanted to live, he could have killed them. Yet Tenoch was tired. He'd lost his most treasured anchors to this world, and the majority of his people didn't need him. He *wanted* to die. He only made it look like murder so his people didn't suffer guilt over it."

Mencheres's face was back in that impassive mask again, the walls around him closing up like a force field.

"I'm sorry I asked, let's just drop the subject," Kira said, thinking it was cruel of Vlad to press the issue. If Vlad was right in his description of the circumstances, then it did sound like Tenoch had committed suicide. Some depressed humans did similar things, like pointing an unloaded gun at police in a form of suicide known as Death by Cop. Death was bad enough, but suicide added an additional pain to those left behind. One Tenoch apparently tried to prevent by making his demise look like an ambush by enemies . . .

Her gaze swung back to Mencheres as horror slid up her spine. His expression was impenetrable, his dark gaze fathomless as he met hers.

The warehouse. The ghouls. They'd been butchering him, but Mencheres hadn't even moved to defend himself before she'd arrived, even though he could have killed them at any time—

"No!"

Kira launched herself at Mencheres. He caught her, holding her very close, keeping his arms tight around her.

At the same time, she could feel the sun rise, sucking all her strength out of her. She tried to fight the pull of those rays, to stay awake long enough to demand to know why he'd done it, but even before she could speak, the darkness came for her.

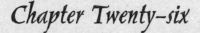

Chapter Twenty-six

"She seemed quite upset."

Mencheres looked up from Kira's newly sleeping form to meet Vlad's level gaze. "I have some explaining to do once she wakes," he replied dryly.

"You, explaining yourself to a vampire not yet two weeks old." Vlad shook his head. "From where I sit, Radjedef is correct in his claims that you've fallen recklessly in love."

"Does that make you wonder if his other claims about me are true as well?" Mencheres challenged.

Vlad's smile was wintry. "No. But I'm wondering why all of a sudden Radje decided to come after you this ruthlessly? Your animosity toward each other has long existed, but neither of you has openly acted on it. He didn't even back Patra during her war against you.

That's what your other allies are wondering as well. Why would a Guardian suddenly risk everything for an eons-old feud?"

"Radje did not back Patra because she meant to kill me, and he wants me alive," Mencheres replied, shifting Kira more comfortably in his arms. "Why now is because he fears if he tarries, I might forever slip his grasp, taking with me the one thing no one else can give him for a thousand years."

Vlad's brows rose. "And that is?"

"My legacy of power." Mencheres let out a soft grunt. "Many vampires raged when I passed it on to Bones, but none more than Radje. He feels it's *his* power that I unfairly stole, but if not for me, Tenoch would have given it to someone else. Tenoch knew Radje couldn't be trusted with such incredible power over vampires. Of course, Radje doesn't concede this point."

Vlad let out a snort. "I confess I was one of those vampires who thought I might be the recipient of that legacy. After all, you and I were close, and I was the last vampire Tenoch made, though he left you to care for me along with the rest of the dependent members of his line when he killed himself mere weeks after siring me."

"I was proud to call you one of mine until it was time for you to become your own Master," Mencheres said in a voice thickened from memories. "You know I care for you still. Fate chose Bones as my heir. I merely obeyed her choice."

Vlad's mouth dipped. "Yes, fate does have a whimsical sense of humor, doesn't she?"

Then Vlad's usual, jadedly amused expression settled back over his face. "I have no complaints. You saved my sanity more than once in my early years when I lost my wife, then my son to death. You ever have my loyalty and gratitude for that. Yes, I will stand as your witness in your meeting with Veritas, repeating all that transpires if need be. You, however, will have the hardest job. You'll have to get her to come."

Mencheres rested his head against the interior of the limousine. Convincing the staunchest member of the Guardian Council to meet with him secretly so Mencheres could accuse another Law Guardian of lying and betraying their race? And then ensuring that Veritas agreed to just let him leave after their meeting? Yes, that part *would* be a challenge.

Kira awoke with a sharp cramp in her stomach. She glanced around, but of course she wasn't in the limo anymore with Mencheres and the other infamous vampire. In fact, she was alone.

The room had no windows, but it was clearly a bedroom, as what she was lying on attested to. The residual sounds around her had a curious echoing quality to them, and the walls didn't look like plaster or concrete. They looked like highly polished rock, actually, and the air had an odd smell to it. Not unpleasant; just unfamiliar.

Another jab in her stomach took Kira's curiosity away from her surroundings. She hadn't eaten since feeding from that young man on the Haunted Mansion ride. Almost a day ago, her stomach reminded her with increasing insistence.

She rose from the bed, noticing that she was now wearing a maroon satin nightgown instead of the belted bed-sheet. Mencheres must have switched her clothes, but he was nowhere to be seen now. Kira did a quick inspection of the bedroom, which thankfully had an antique armoire in the corner containing male and female clothes. She slipped into a cardigan and slacks with a mental apology to whoever the clothes belonged to, but that rumbling in her stomach was starting to become ominous.

Once dressed, she left the bedroom in search of Mencheres. To her surprise, the hallway that she entered was very tall, with more of those odd walls around her. She passed another three doors on her way to the top of what looked like a narrow staircase. When she started down, Kira stared. The staircase was of polished stone, cut into steps, and it led to an impossibly large living area with a huge domed ceiling. Still, not a single window was in sight, and those grayish shiny walls were all around.

"Ah, you're awake," a lightly accented voice said from beyond her sight.

Kira went farther into the room, disappointed that the voice didn't belong to Mencheres. Vlad sat on one of the three sets of couches in the huge room, an open laptop in front of him, his hand idly stroking his bearded chin.

"Is Mencheres here?" Kira asked, that question more pressing to her than even the painful gurgles starting to build up in her stomach.

"No, but he should return soon. You're up earlier than we expected. The sun won't set for two more hours yet. Hungry?"

A flare of pain went through her even as she managed to say, "A little," in a tone that wasn't shaking.

"No trouble, I'll send someone in for you," he replied.

Some*one?* "Um, if you have any bagged blood, that would be better."

Vlad let out a short laugh. "*Bagged* blood? You haven't taken those training wheels off yet? Of course, when I was changed, there wasn't any bagged blood. Criminals or enemy soldiers were thrown in with new vampires during those first few days."

It only went to show how hungry she was that such a mental image didn't ruin her appetite. "If I can avoid treating people like food, that's my choice," she replied, bristling a little at the "training wheels" comment.

Vlad's cool gaze considered her. "You think you're honoring humans by not feeding from them, but you're actually hurting them. Animal blood won't suffice long term, and blood supplies are chronically low because not enough humans donate. Those bags you drink from might mean the difference between life and death for some humans in an emergency room, and if you have them, they don't."

He emphasized those two last words with a challenging cock of his brow. Kira found herself thinking that all the actors who'd played Dracula in the movies had it wrong. Vlad wasn't a pasty-faced dandy with a Euro-trash accent, nor was he an aging aristocrat with claws for nails and a monstrous appearance. No, Vlad was a thirtyish, striking man with a compelling presence who had a brutally honest outlook on things. One he wasn't shy about sharing, it seemed.

And he had a point. Her feeding preferences shouldn't endanger anyone, and if she kept her diet limited to plasma bags, they would.

"You're right," she said. "I'd appreciate it if you would send for whoever you have as a donor, then. I'm hungry enough that it's starting to concern me."

He smiled, making those stern features all the sudden charming. "Of course." Then he spoke into his cell phone, asking someone named Mordred to "send up Lewis."

Kira lingered where she was, unsure. Should she sit down? Or was there a special room she was supposed to feed in? The kitchen seemed like the obvious choice, but in this weird windowless vampire hideout with its stone walls, floors, and echoing acoustics, who knew if there was a kitchen?

"Are we underground?" she asked.

"Not quite. We're in the side of a mountain. This used to be an old mining station, but it's long been deserted. I renovated it a few decades ago for a more comfortable, yet private, environment."

If there were abandoned mine tunnels still underneath them, that would explain the echoes. "Where did Mencheres go?"

"To make an important call. Can't have him using my cell, then our location being traced that easily, not with whom he's calling."

That's right, Mencheres wanted to meet with the other Law Guardian, the one with the Latin name for truth: Veritas. Hopefully, Veritas would live up to her namesake and not attempt to ambush Mencheres if she did agree to a meeting.

Kira wondered if the other reason Mencheres wasn't here yet was because he was stalling. She had no intention of just *forgetting* about the fact that he'd tried to commit suicide-by-ghouls.

A russet-haired young man walked into the room from the opposite way that Kira had entered. He bowed to Vlad, which struck her as strange, then he knelt.

"Not me, Lewis. Her," Vlad said, with a careless wave of his hand toward Kira. "Have you done this before?"

She assumed the question was to her, since Lewis looked like a pro. "Once."

"Use the hand, then. Less chance for a mistake there."

Same thing Mencheres told me, Kira thought wryly. Was all of this Vampire 101? If so, what was in Vampire Advanced Courses?

Lewis smiled at her as he approached, holding out his

hand. Kira glanced around. The floor was stone, so she wouldn't ruin anything if she spilled a few drops.

"Let's, um, sit down," she said.

Vlad just watched from his spot on the couch, amusement decorating his chiseled features. Kira squared her shoulders. She could do this by herself. No sweat.

"Do you want to be put under first?" she asked Lewis as they sat down.

"Huh?" he replied in confusion.

Something like a cough came out of Vlad that jerked her head up. Vampires didn't need to cough. Was that a muffled *laugh*?

"You know." Kira's eyes flashed green at Lewis, and her fangs seemed to jump out of her gums. "Get bespelled so you don't feel or remember this."

Lewis appeared even more confused. "If that's what *you* want."

I will not ask for pointers from Dracula, she swore to herself. *I will not.* "Yeah, I'd feel better about that. So, ah . . . look into my eyes."

Another strangled sound came from Vlad's direction. Now Kira was sure it was a laugh. She determined to ignore him.

Lewis obediently stared at her, and Kira tried to make her voice sound confident. "You don't feel anything. You're not afraid."

"I am," came Vlad's immediate reply. "If you tell him wolves are the children of the night next, I might hurt myself laughing."

"I'm trying to focus," she gritted out, those pains inside her growing worse. Then as delicately as she could, she lifted Lewis's hand to her mouth, seeking that same throbbing vein between the thumb and the wrist that she'd bitten into yesterday. Her fangs almost ached with need as she slowly slid them in, a little moan escaping her when that first hot taste met her tongue.

Kira forget about Vlad after that. Forgot about everything except the controlled bliss of feeding without damaging the fragile hand in her grip. By the time her hunger ebbed, she'd realized her eyes had closed in enjoyment . . . and when she opened them, Mencheres was in the room.

Mencheres entered silently, knowing what was going on before he saw Kira. Though the entrance of the house was almost impossible to see from the exterior of the mountain, once inside it, voices carried. Then he'd watched her feed from the human with a mixture of pride and arousal. Her expression was so sensual as she fed—and his trip to the hospital to secure those three blood bags had not been needed, it seemed.

Then her eyes opened and fixed right on his. For a moment, he felt as if everyone else in the room vanished. If they had truly been alone, he would have thrown himself on top of her and kissed her until her nails dug deliciously deep grooves into his back. His power swirled inside him, wanting to touch her as well. Everything about Kira made him come alive. He'd only been away from her for a few hours, yet that time dragged and burned across his subconscious until it was almost painful.

She pulled her mouth away from the male's hand, closing the holes as he'd shown her before more than a couple spare drops fell onto the floor. Then she rose, coming toward him with her gaze still dazzling green.

"Before the two of you get too far along, what did Veritas say?" Vlad asked.

Mencheres shook his head to clear away the images of all the different ways he was going to take Kira as soon as he had her back in the bedroom. "She'll come," he replied shortly. "Tomorrow."

"Afternoon or evening, right?" Kira asked, her sultry expression being replaced by one of stubbornness. "Not morning?"

He smiled faintly. "No, not morning." As if he didn't see *that* argument coming.

"Good." Her expression didn't change, however. "I'm going to take a shower. And then, after that, Mencheres, we need to talk."

It was clear from her tone, scent, and body language that he was not invited to join her bathing activities this time. He wasn't surprised. He'd known she would confront him about the ghouls. He'd only hoped Vlad might not be within earshot when she did.

He supposed it didn't matter. Whatever his plans were before to end his life, they'd changed. He'd have to be forced into the grave now instead of embracing it as he'd intended before. Death meant separation from Kira, something deplorable to him. It might come soon regardless, but not with his assistance anymore.

Kira left the room after murmuring thanks to the young man, who bowed to Vlad before he walked away. Mencheres exchanged a long glance with Vlad. His friend had a knowing curl to his lips.

"From the sounds of it, you're in trouble," Vlad drawled.

He shrugged. "I have it coming."

Chapter Twenty-seven

Mencheres waited in the bedroom he'd left Kira sleeping in hours before. Even though the hidden house inside the mountain was extremely spacious, it only had one shower, the water pumped from an interior well deeper back inside the dwelling. The shower was on the lower level, and the sounds were fainter, but he had heard Kira finish ten minutes ago, yet she was still not back.

After another ten minutes Kira appeared, re-dressed in the same sweater and pants she had on before, her hair still damp. She gave him a long, measuring look before she sat on the bed and then uttered one word.

"Why?"

He didn't bother to pretend ignorance about what she was asking. "For much the same reasons my sire had, I imagine. My line didn't need me anymore with my co-ruler to tend to it, Radje began spoiling for another fight, and I was tired. Furthermore, my visions of the future vanished except to show darkness approaching, so I knew my end was near. I decided to meet that end sooner rather than later, before Radje could conjure up charges against me that would ensnare my co-ruler as well."

Kira kept staring at him. "You forgot to mention that you were twisted up with guilt over your wife's death."

He smiled faintly. "I actually didn't realize that until recently, but yes. That also is true."

She lowered her gaze. "I ruined your plans, didn't I? I crashed the warehouse, then you saved both of us instead of letting the ghouls finish their job. After that week we were together and you let me go . . . were you planning to let someone kill you again?"

Below them, Mencheres heard Vlad grind out a curse, but he ignored that and kept his attention on Kira. "Yes. I still intended to, once another opportunity presented itself."

A tremor went through her, but she kept her head lowered, looking at the part of the blanket she crumpled and uncrumpled in her hand. On the floor below them, something smashed into a wall. Neither one of them reacted to that.

"And now?" she asked, her voice so soft he could barely hear her.

He wanted to go to her. To press her to him and promise they would never be parted, but that would be a lie. Instead, he'd give Kira the same unguarded honesty she'd shown him throughout their time together.

"No, I don't want to die now, but death comes for me regardless. I told you before that I wasn't long for this earth, Kira. It is not by choice, but my fate remains the same."

Her head snapped up at that, her eyes sparkling with

pink unshed tears. "Bullshit. I don't believe you're fated
to die any more than anyone else is."

He was used to his visions being questioned. Few believed in them until they'd seen them come to pass, and
even then, some still doubted.

"My visions are never wrong." How often he'd wished
they were.

"You ever heard of a self-fulfilling prophecy?" she
asked, jumping from the bed to stand before him. "It's
when people believe something so deeply that they do
things to *make* it happen. Maybe you saw this darkness
in your future because some part of you had already decided to throw in the towel, but your consciousness hadn't
acknowledged that decision yet. So when you looked, you
saw death in your future because, subconsciously, you'd
already decided to kill yourself."

He shook his head. "I looked again after I wanted to
live. Nothing had changed. The darkness was still there,
even closer this time."

"But that doesn't mean it's inevitable. Okay, you
changed your mind about killing yourself, but because
you saw death when you looked before, you're expecting
to see it again. And then you do, so you don't even bother
to fight to live, making death that much easier to sneak
up on you when Radje pulls something. It's just more of
the same self-fulfilling prophecy you need to snap out of,
damn it!"

Mencheres almost smiled. No one else had ever told
him to *snap out of* his visions before. "I wish it were that
simple."

"It is." She seized his arms. "You trust your visions
implicitly, but when did you lose the ability to see past
the darkness you're talking about? There's something
else that might be going on. Survivor's guilt. You're

all messed up over what happened with your wife. You blame yourself for every death she caused plus your part in her demise, so you might not see a future for yourself because you don't believe you deserve one."

"My visions cannot be altered due to emotional distress," he answered.

"Says who?" Kira replied sharply. "Just because it's never happened before doesn't make it impossible. After Pete died, I went to some group-therapy sessions to help deal with what happened. One guy whose family died in a car crash after the other car ran a stop sign all of a sudden couldn't see the color red anymore. Just couldn't see it! And yet you've blamed yourself for probably dozens of murders your wife committed, plus her death, yet you don't think that could freeze or alter your visions? The mind is an extremely powerful thing, and when it's paralyzed by grief or guilt, it can mess up just about anything."

"Kira . . ." Mencheres did not know what to say. He'd expected some form of denial from her over his fate. Sadness also, but this flat defiance that what he'd seen was not going to happen was somewhat startling.

"You've been through hell," she went on in that same intractable tone. "I'm sure I don't even know half of it, but I do know it would have broken most people. It almost broke you, too, because you were going to kill yourself, but I'm telling you that you are *not* doomed to die soon. I'd feel it if you were, just like I did with Pete, Tina, my mom, and even myself that night with Radje. Yet all of my instincts are telling me that you and I are long term, which means you'll be around. No matter what darkness you're seeing now."

She'd almost rendered him speechless again. Kira was barely thirty years old. How could she think her instincts were more accurate than over four thousand years of his visions?

"I've never been wrong before," he said. "Never."

"Then this will be your first time," she replied, touching his face. "Or you'll realize you misinterpreted what you saw. *I'm right*, Mencheres. I know it with my whole soul. Just like I know you love me, even if you're having trouble saying it."

For several moments, he could only stare at her, caught in her light green gaze as if he were a human ensnared by the mesmerizing glow of a vampire. Something freed inside him, a pressure released that he didn't know had been building, and the relief he felt was only matched by the certainty flowing through him that she was right—about part of what she said.

"I do love you," he said hoarsely, the words not an adequate representation of what he felt for Kira. She was everything that had been missing from his life, everything that made him want to stay in this harsh, unforgiving world that was somehow beautiful once more because of her.

She smiled, amazing him with the joy such a small gesture could generate inside him. "You see? I told you I was right."

"That does not mean—"

"Shush," she replied, putting her finger to his lips. He couldn't help but feel amusement slither through him. No one had *shushed* him in thousands of years, yet Kira did it without the slightest hesitation.

"I don't want you looking into the future again," she went on. "Not yet. You're a superpowerful vampire, but you're not a god. Until you work through the things that led you to feel like you'd rather be dead, *all* of them, you can't trust what you think you're seeing."

He still didn't think Kira was right about self-fulfilling prophecies, survivor's guilt, or misinterpretation when it came to his vision of impending death, but he was willing to heed her counsel. After all, his visions did come to an abrupt halt only after Patra's death. He might be far stronger than Kira on a power level, but emotionally, she stood on firmer ground. The events in the past few years had proven too much for him. He'd sought his own death—something he swore he'd never do after the pain of discovering Tenoch's suicide, yet he'd almost followed in his sire's footsteps. Only the beautiful, incredible woman in front of him prevented that when her path crossed with his that morning.

Fate. Was it possible his might not be only darkness after all?

"Tell me again what your mentor's credo was?" he asked, though he remembered her answer from before.

"Save one life," Kira said softly.

Mencheres drew her into his arms. "You did," he whispered before his mouth claimed hers. "You saved mine."

Kira slid a lazy hand along his back, her touch rousing him despite the past several passionate hours.

"This is such an interesting tattoo. What is it?"

"A *shenu*," he replied, rolling over on his side to face her. "The modern word is a cartouche."

She still traced the tattoo even though she wouldn't be able to see it anymore. "What does it say?"

"It is my birth name, Menkaure, in ancient Egyptian writing."

Her face clouded. "That's what Radje calls you."

He stroked her from her bare leg up to her lower back, and her expression eased once more.

"Were you named after that Pharaoh?" she asked.

His hand stilled. "What do you know of that Pharaoh?"

"When I was looking for you after you mesmerized my boss, I Googled 'Mencheres,' thinking it might lead me to you on the off chance that you had a Facebook page or something." Kira paused to chuckle. "You didn't, of course. All that came up under your name were links and articles about a Pharaoh way back when who was also called Mencheres, but he went by Menkaure most of the time." She gave him a curious glance. "Were you a descendant of his? Is that why you took one of his names?"

He uncurled himself from the bed, standing before her. It was time she learned all about him, even the oldest parts of his past.

"Menkaure had many names depending on the translation. Mycerinus, Mykerinus, and Mencheres, among others. I received this tattoo on the first day of my appointed reign when I was twenty-two years old, just six months before I became a vampire. I am not one of that Pharaoh's descendents you read about. I *am* that Pharaoh. I merely used the name Mencheres after I left Egypt."

Kira's mouth opened and closed, as if she had suddenly forgotten how to speak. He waited. After everything else she'd been through, he did not fear this revelation would prove too much for her.

"But that Pharaoh was from way, way, way back in ancient times. He has a pyramid in the Giza Plateau. That *can't* be you! You said you were older than dirt, but—"

"I was born in 2553 B.C.," he replied, watching her expression flit from denial to confusion to amazement. "I told you Radje and I came from a line of rulers who appointed a set frame for their heirs to reign over their human subjects. That was the line of Pharaohs from the first dynasty through the thirteenth. Radje and I were in the Fourth Dynasty. Radje is short for Radjedef, as you know, but Radjedef was more commonly known as Djedefre in Egyptian history. He was the half brother of Khafre, my father. My father and Radjedef were the sons of Khufu, the Pharaoh who built the Great Pyramid in Egypt."

Kira still did not look like she'd adequately absorbed this information. "Radje is your *uncle*? And you and your family made the pyramids? *The pyramids?*"

He shrugged. "They were designed for the retired Pharaohs to live in comfort among their people, presumed dead while a new Pharaoh reigned. But they were too costly. Our later heirs made the Valley of the Kings as a more efficient solution. All the underground passages and connecting tunnels—"

"You realize this is a little much to take in," she interrupted, shaking her head.

Mencheres raised a brow. "A month ago, you did not believe in vampires. Now you are one yourself, plus lover to another, and you're in the hidden mountain home of fiction's most famous vampire. I have every confidence that you will handle this latest revelation with minimal difficulty."

She still shook her head, but the disbelief left her expression. "Older than dirt," she muttered. "Who knew you were *under*exaggerating?"

He went to the foot of the bed, slowly crawling back on while sliding his body over Kira's from her feet up to her chest. When their faces were level, he stopped, letting his aura as well as his skin caress hers.

"Do I feel too ancient to you now?" he murmured. "Too different from the person you loved before you knew this?"

Her eyes were already glowing green, and her full lips parted. "No, you don't feel too ancient." Her voice was husky. "Or too different. You feel like mine. Whoever you were, whoever you are . . . you're mine."

Mencheres smiled, his fangs stretching to their full length. "So you have spoken, so it shall be decreed. For all eternity."

Chapter Twenty-eight

The Grand Canyon was ablaze with color in the setting rays of the sun. Rust, orange, vermilion, gold, indigo, and silver seemed to intersperse in an endless mural that was awe-inspiring. If Kira hadn't been so concerned about what the next hour might bring, she would have kept turning in slow circles to try to memorize the astounding beauty all around her.

But, of course, this wasn't a sightseeing trip, even though they were in one of America's most visited tourist attractions. The Grand Canyon was also a good place if they needed to run for their lives. The various caves, fissures, and hiding places were only exceeded by the canyon's enormity. Any pursuing Law Guardians or Enforcers wouldn't know whether to search for them in the skies or below, or so Mencheres had explained.

Kira stood between Vlad and Mencheres, the breeze coloring the air's natural bouquet with the different scents emanating from the two vampires. Mencheres's mix of sandalwood and dark spices was interspersed with Vlad's more unusual aroma of cinnamon and . . . smoke.

"Look," Mencheres said, pointing to the south.

She fixed her gaze in that direction, but all she saw was a blond teenager hiking up a trail about two hundred yards below where they were. She must be ahead of her tourist group, though Kira was surprised that tours ran at night. Maybe she should go down there and mesmerize the group into turning around so there weren't any innocent human bystanders who could get hurt if things got messy with the Law Guardian—

"Mencheres," the teenager called out. "I have come alone as promised."

"That's Veritas?" Kira blurted. The powerful Law Guardian that Mencheres and Vlad had spoken of in such cautious tones? She didn't even look old enough to drive a car!

The pretty young blonde looked right at her then, and even in the distance, Kira could see a flash of bright green in her eyes. Not human, without a doubt.

Vlad leveled his gaze on Kira. "You will quickly learn appearances are the most unreliable way to judge anyone in our world. Take, for example, me."

He held up a hand to Veritas, and it burst into blue flames. Kira's eyes widened. Neither Vlad's fingers nor his palm appeared the slightest bit burnt. The flames coated around his shirt cuff, but somehow that material didn't catch fire. Then when Vlad lowered his hand, the flames immediately extinguished without even a spark or singed hair to show for it.

"Now I know why you smell like smoke all the time,"

Kira muttered, adding *pyrokinesis* to her mental list of abilities that some vampires were capable of manifesting.

"Veritas," Mencheres called out. "I thank you for coming."

His voice was calm and confident, but Kira felt Mencheres's tenseness grating across her subconscious. He was braced for this to be an attack, ready to spring her away at the slightest hint of an ambush.

The blond Guardian increased her pace as she came toward them, moving now with a grace and speed up the steep incline in a way that made it obvious she wasn't human. By the time she was within fifty yards, Kira could feel the energy crackling off her. Power she'd only ever felt in such magnitude before from Mencheres.

"You have one hour to plead your case, Mencheres," Veritas said in a sharp tone. "That is all the grace the memory of our sire and our long association will buy you."

This doesn't sound promising, Kira thought. Veritas's Barbie-doll features were a mask of anger, and the energy swirling around her felt distinctly unpleasant.

Mencheres was not intimidated by the Law Guardian's attitude. He bowed his head in a respectful way and proceeded to detail in eloquent and compelling terms how he was in Wyoming with Kira and Gorgon while the club fire and murders occurred. He told Veritas she could pull his cell phone records to determine that calls were made from Wyoming, not Chicago, and that he would never leave behind evidence of their race's existence for humans to find, as evidenced by his destroying the cameras at Disneyland. He closed with his apologies for thrashing the Enforcers, but said he'd felt it was the only way to protect Kira from Radje's corrupt purposes later. Kira almost wanted to applaud when he was done.

If this was a campaign speech, he would've won over every voter.

Except one.

"And do you apologize for murdering an Enforcer, too? Or was that, too, beneath your notice in your zeal to defend your new lover?" Veritas almost spat at Mencheres.

His expression darkened. "What Enforcer? I killed none of them."

"Josephus chased after you in the skies along with six others, but he was later found shriveled on the ground," Veritas replied. Her gaze raked him. "You are indicted for murder of a Guardian Enforcer. Even your many allies will not be able to sway the council to mercy, no matter how powerful they may be."

She gave a pointed glance at Vlad when she made that comment, but Kira was too outraged to stay silent.

"Mencheres didn't do that! We went right from the skies down into the ocean, not anywhere on the ground. I ought to remember, because it scared the shit out of me."

"Kira . . ." Mencheres began.

"It's true," she replied, more to Veritas than him. The blonde's expression didn't change, but Kira didn't let that stop her. She was so sick of people assuming Mencheres did horrible things without once bothering to consider that someone else might be involved.

"Let me guess, you believe Radje's claim that Mencheres did all these things because he's lost his mind over me, right? And I'm just some wicked bitch who likes to incite him to murder? Could someone at least *meet me* before thinking that? I thought the human court system was messed up at times, but your vampire system is worse. At least we've got *innocent until proven guilty.* Not *guilty and sentenced* before even bothering to look at all the facts."

"Kira!" Mencheres's voice was harsher.

"You dare to insult the laws?" Veritas demanded, holding out her hand to Mencheres after it felt like he'd just snapped an invisible gag across Kira's mouth. "Do not interfere. Let her speak, or I leave now," Veritas growled.

Kira's lips were released from their sudden immobility. She gave Mencheres a single withering glare that promised severe consequences if he ever did that again, then addressed the steaming Law Guardian.

"I'm all for your laws to seek justice against whoever killed that Enforcer and leaked that tape, but I have to say I'm not impressed with how little investigative work has been done. Radje says Mencheres torched that club, so people just *believe* it, no matter that I was crazy from bloodlust those first few days and Mencheres was busy taking care of me. Then an Enforcer ends up dead after chasing Mencheres, so obviously, Mencheres killed him. No other explanation is considered even though if the sentence is so severe for one death, why wouldn't Mencheres have just killed them all? It doesn't make sense, especially if you believe he'd suddenly become whipped by a woman who likes him to murder people for her, as Radje keeps claiming."

Veritas had Kira by the collar of her shirt, her sea-blue eyes boring into hers.

"Perhaps Mencheres acted without your knowledge. Perhaps he forced you to participate. In this moment only I am offering you the chance to admit to the truth without fear of persecution. You have the word of a Guardian that you will not be charged. Did Mencheres do these things? Or did he ever leave your side during the evening of the fire, or after the Enforcers chased you, to be able to commit these crimes?"

"No to all the above," Kira answered steadily. "It wasn't him."

Veritas's gaze still pinned hers. "Are you willing to swear by your blood that he is innocent? To forfeit your own life if he is found guilty of committing even *one* of these acts?"

"Yes," Kira said, even as Mencheres burst, "She has been accused of nothing, you cannot expect her to forfeit her life based on the council's decision on me!"

"I can," Veritas said, releasing Kira. "And I will repeat her vow to the council once I return, so if you have guilt to confess, Mencheres, and you want to spare her, do it now."

Mencheres gave Kira such a tormented look that fear slid up her spine. He wouldn't confess to something he hadn't done, would he? Of course not. He'd be condemning himself to death just on the mere chance that the other Guardians would rule against him . . .

"Don't," she gasped, clutching his arms. "I know you think you're going to die anyway, but your visions are *wrong*, Mencheres! They're stalled and twisted from the guilt you felt over things that weren't even your fault. This is *not* the only way you can save me. Come on, if Veritas didn't in some way suspect more was going on, she wouldn't have shown up here. You didn't do any of this! Don't you *dare* say you did!"

Tears spilled out of her eyes, and her grip tightened until Kira heard bones snap in his arms, but fear made her unable to let up. Mencheres was about to slip away from her forever, she could feel it.

"Don't trust what those damned visions say," she whispered. "Trust me. We can beat Radje another way, I know it. Let me prove it to you."

His eyes, so dark and fathomless, stared into hers. Very

gently, he captured her hands and pulled them off his arms with a flex of his power. Then he brought them to his lips.

"I love you," he breathed against her skin.

"Don't, please," she begged, panic rising in her while tears continued to course down her cheeks.

Mencheres looked past Kira to Veritas. "I had nothing to do with the arson, the deaths of those people, or the Enforcer's death," he said in a clear tone. "The same person who accuses me is the one responsible. Radjedef."

Relief flooded Kira so strongly she thought her knees would give out. All her instincts screamed that Mencheres had been moments away from taking all the blame. Part of her wanted to throw her arms around him while the other part wanted to slap him for almost doing something so nobly, lethally stupid.

"Don't you ever scare me like that again," she ordered in a shaking voice.

His mouth curved in a grim smile. "Instead, I've terrified myself."

Kira knew what he meant, but she believed everything she said about finding a way to beat Radjedef. Veritas's expression when she looked at her only confirmed it. The Law Guardian appeared wary but thoughtful, that initial angry accusing light gone from her gaze.

"Mencheres, if you keep trying to throw your life away, I'll kill you myself," Vlad muttered. "You might not be needed by your people as much with Bones sharing your rule, but you are needed by your friends. Remember *that* the next time you hear the siren song of the grave."

"Most of the Guardians believe you killed those vampires and set fire to the club," Veritas said, speaking for the first time in several moments. "There was, however, a troubling find with Josephus's body. His head was taken off, but closer inspection revealed he might have also been stabbed in the back."

"Wouldn't it be obvious if he was?" Kira asked, frowning.

"No," Mencheres replied. "When a vampire is killed, the body decomposes back to its true age. Josephus was several hundred years old. There would have been little left of him except withered skin and bones."

Not a pretty mental image, but dead bodies seldom were. Kira still didn't understand the significance of the knife wound as being suspicious, unless the other Enforcers revealed that Mencheres left all their knives back at the park. Though Josephus could have grabbed his own blade before he chased them and later been killed with that . . .

"There you have it," Vlad said, sounding satisfied. "Vampire or ghoul, Mencheres doesn't use knives to kill. He simply tears someone's head off with his power. Radje would've needed a knife against an Enforcer, and the element of surprise, too. Explains why Josephus's wound was in the back. Poor bastard probably never saw it coming."

A flash of that day at the warehouse skittered across Kira's memory, and she grimaced. Mencheres had decapitated all of the ghouls with a mere thought, faster than it would have taken for him to gather up one of their knives. Why would Mencheres ever use knives when his telekinesis was a far faster and deadlier weapon?

"Radje must have taken Josephus's head off after he was dead to make it appear as if I'd done it," Mencheres mused. "Clever. He must not have thought anyone would look for a knife wound, or that evidence of one would remain. With an Enforcer's death blamed on me, most of my allies would fall away. He already knows I sought death before. This would leave me in a far more desperate position to give him what he wants first."

"What does he want, aside from your being dead?" Kira grumbled.

"My power. Cain was the father of our race, cursed by his god forever to roam the land as a fugitive in punishment for murdering Abel. But Cain pleaded that his sentence was too great, and his god took pity, marking Cain so none could kill him. Cain thus became the first vampire, dependent on blood for sustenance but beyond mortal death and possessing incredible power. Cain then made his own race to replace the family he'd been driven away from, but to only one of his offspring did he will out a portion of his incredible power. Enoch was that first recipient, and many centuries later, Enoch passed on Cain's legacy of power to his heir, Tenoch, who then passed it to me."

Veritas's blond brows rose. "How could Radjedef get that from you now? You gave that power legacy to Bones when you merged lines with him."

"So I did, and Bones cannot will the power to anyone else until he masters it completely. It took me several hundred years to do that. Radje has no intention of waiting that long. He wants me to will out all the power left in me. It's the only way he can be assured of finally possessing Cain's legacy."

"But if you will out *all* your power . . ." Kira's voice trailed off.

He gave a grim snort. "It will likely kill me. Or Radje will, once I'm weakened after giving it to him. If I live after willing him my power, I am the evidence of duplicity. If I'm dead, Radje could cloak his new additional power, and few would ever know he has it."

Veritas's face was very solemn. "You expect the Guardian Council to believe your charges against another Guardian of conspiracy, murder, exposing the race, and blackmail. All based on conjecture when your own adherence to our laws has been spotty at best."

"Spotty? He's done nothing wrong," Kira said in frustration.

"Rumors abound that Mencheres conjured wraiths to find and kill his wife. Black magic is expressly forbidden in the law, but of course, all those who witnessed Patra's death and the deaths of her guards are loyal to Mencheres and will not confirm this."

She gave a sharp look at Vlad as she spoke. He winked at her, his mouth curving in a sly smile.

"Did those same rumors mention how Patra summoned an army from the grave to ambush me and my people?" Mencheres countered.

"She sent *zombies* after you?" Kira asked, incredulous.

"Yes," Mencheres replied shortly. "And anything from the grave cannot be killed by normal means. Even my telekinesis was useless against them, for grave magic is not subject to the powers of the living, as Patra knew."

"You could have filed a formal complaint—" Veritas began.

"Which would have taken weeks to investigate," Mencheres interrupted. "Leaving me and most of my people dead by then because Patra would have conjured another form of grave magic to finish us after that one failed. It was only a lucky guess that saved us that time, but it was already too late for the dozens who had been cut down."

The Law Guardian's jaw was still set in a hard line. Kira could almost feel the tension between the three of them, and their infighting would only help Radje.

"I understand your reverence for the law, Veritas,"

Kira said. "You're a good cop. But if, hypothetically, Mencheres did conjure that spell against his wife, then he knows a surefire way to kill Radje. He also knows no one's willing to testify against him, either out of loyalty or fear. Yet Mencheres refuses to use this unbeatable power against someone who's pulling out all the stops to bring him down."

Kira leaned closer, and her voice dropped. "If he did use that power before, it only was in self-defense, and almost every law allows latitude for self-defense. He's not using it now even though it would be the fastest way to win, so isn't he then proving his utmost respect for the law?"

Veritas stared at each of them for a long time, her blue eyes far more ancient than her teenage appearance. Kira remained absolutely still. Praying the Law Guardian would see past Radje's house of cards.

"I may be inclined to believe you, but the rest of the Guardian Council will require proof, not conjecture, no matter how compelling," Veritas said at last.

And in the time it took them to gather that proof, Radje would be busy setting up more frame jobs for Mencheres, killing who knew how many more innocent people. Kira's teeth ground together. She'd helped catch a crooked cop once with Pete. Maybe she could do it again with Radje.

"I know a way to bust Radje," she said. Three gazes swung in her direction. "But we'll have to go back to Chicago to settle some business first."

Chapter Twenty-nine

Kira rode the Chicago Transit Green Line as if it were her first time. This was such a familiar route to her along the Loop, but now, everything about it was different. The multitudes of scents were overpowering, even more dominating than the roar of the transit car as it bulleted along the tracks. Aside from the harsher aromas of alcohol, urine, body odor, perfumes, and bad breath, the scents lingering on the car were also like fingerprints of emotions.

Of course, she could also smell traces of blood, either dotting the transit car or lingering on some of the people who entered and exited on their way to their next location. She'd recently fed again, so that scent didn't arouse hunger in her as much as acknowledgment. Blood was a part of her life now, no more a choice than her deciding not to breathe when she'd been human. In some ways, Kira couldn't believe how short a time had passed since she'd first woken up as a vampire. It felt far longer, much like the time since she'd first met Mencheres. Calendars, dates, and clocks were just not an accurate way to measure some things.

The voice announced that the Clinton Street stop was next. Kira shouldered her purse and stood, not needing to hold on to the back of the chair or the pole for balance. When the car stopped, she got off, headed now for the familiar streets that led to Tina's apartment.

So many times before, Kira had walked this part of West Loop after dark with her attention focused on any alleys opening up to her side, or extended patches of darkness where streetlights didn't penetrate. Or for the sound of footsteps following her too closely. Now she strode down the streets without looking anywhere but straight ahead, her steps brisk and confident. No patches of darkness, weapons, alleys, or lurking strangers could do her harm anymore. Everyone along these streets had heartbeats, making them vulnerable to *her,* not the other way around, should they choose to cross her path with malicious intent.

She made it to Tina's building just a little faster than she would have under normal circumstances. Couldn't attract unwanted attention by streaking up the streets with supernatural speed, after all. She used her key to get inside, then chose the stairs instead of the elevators to avoid any of Tina's neighbors who might happen to recognize her if she rode up with them. Kira already knew her identity had been leaked to news stations in the past several days. The last she called Tina, her sister had hung up without speaking. She didn't think Tina was angry with her. She assumed Tina's phone line was monitored, which meant her cell probably was, too. Kira didn't bother calling her brother; he almost never had a working number.

The stairwell was empty, allowing Kira to move at what was fast becoming a more natural speed to her. She reached the fourteenth level in mere minutes, brushing her hair behind her ear reflexively before entering the floor. Once outside Tina's apartment, however, she paused.

Two heartbeats were inside, not one. Kira inhaled near the door, but she couldn't distinguish anything overly helpful. She'd never caught her sister's scent as a vampire though the heavier citrus fragrance around the entrance probably belonged to Tina. Who was in there with her sister? And would whoever it was present a problem?

She couldn't afford to walk away now. She'd risked too much to come here. Kira knocked, again smoothing her hair to the side as she waited. First she heard footsteps, a heartbeat right on the other side of the door, and then a gasp before the door opened.

Tina stood on the other side, still blond and petite like always, but with a healthier glow to her complexion than the last time she'd seen her. Kira smiled. Mencheres's blood had brought her little sister back, and she now had the treatments for Tina's disease running all through her veins.

"Hey," Kira said. "Can I come in?"

Tina's blue eyes were wide, and her scent—yes, it was that citrus blend Kira had caught a whiff of outside the door, like oranges and cloves—soured ever so slightly even as her pulse sped up.

"Is everything okay?" Kira asked, tensing. Was a cop in the apartment with Tina? Good Lord, had they sent someone over after Kira called the last time?

"Kira?" Tina said tentatively, as if she didn't quite believe who she was seeing.

"Who is it, T?" her brother's voice called out from inside the apartment.

"Rick's here?" Kira asked, shaking her head. "Oh, Tina, you didn't let him move in, did you?"

"'S it?" Her brother appeared behind Tina's shoulder. His eyes were red and from the crease on his cheek, he looked like he'd just woken up.

"Kira, holy fuck!" he said, his eyes bulging when he saw her. "You're in big trouble, man. Like, huge," Rick finished.

"Hi, Rick," Kira said in a dry voice. "Joey finally threw you out?"

Tina stepped back mutely. Kira walked inside, one sniff revealing that Rick smelled like pot, some other drug, cigarettes, and alcohol. A glance showed he'd set up a bed on Tina's couch. It looked like he'd been there for days. Empty beer cans, an ashtray overflowing with butts, and a couple wadded-up bags of potato chips completed the picture.

Kira wanted to slug him, and not just for trashing Tina's place while he made himself at home.

"You're smoking around Tina? She's got CF, and she just got out of the hospital a few weeks ago after almost *dying*, but your goddamn nicotine habit is more important than her lungs? You couldn't even go outside to let her breathe some clean air in *her own* apartment, Rick?"

His face turned mottled red. "You're wanted by the fucking cops, the FBI, and maybe more, but you're going to bitch at me for smoking? Dude, you've got some nerve—"

"Oh be quiet," Kira snapped.

To her surprise, Rick stopped speaking. At once. His mouth opened, but nothing came out. Then his eyes bugged, and his hands started waving around like they were on fire.

Kira spun, expecting to see someone behind her, but no one was there except Tina. She'd just closed the door and stood staring at her.

"Your eyes . . ." she whispered.

Kira cursed. She'd kept a perfect grip on her emotions the entire way here, but five seconds in her brother's company had her dropping her normal disguise to glare bright green supernatural daggers at him. Now she had to fix this mess.

"Rick, sit down. Find a mental happy place or something," she directed him.

Rick sat on the floor, his frantic motions stilling and an expression of peace settling over his features. Kira found herself being grateful that she hadn't been a vampire when they were growing up and she'd had to babysit him for her father and his new wife. She might have taken horrible advantage of her mind-control skills. Rick had been a handful even as a child.

Then she turned to Tina, who had her eyes closed while a single tear slipped down her cheeks.

"Don't, Kira," Tina said, shaking her head with her eyes still squeezed shut. "Whatever you did to him, don't do it to me. I knew it. I saw that tape on YouTube, and even though I didn't want to believe . . . still, you never would have gotten involved in something like that, then just disappeared. Even if you did, Mom's *cross*. You wouldn't have let someone rip it off your neck and use it that way if it were only an act. You haven't taken her necklace off since she died, so when I saw that, I knew it had to be real . . ."

Kira's hand closed over the cross at her throat. It had shocked her knowing Mencheres used it to cut into his own throat and feed her his blood, but it never occurred to her that Tina would see that and be able to determine it wasn't twisted role-playing. Tina was right, though. She hadn't taken this necklace off, not since she'd unhooked it from her mother's throat and put it around her own the day before her mom's funeral.

"Tina . . ."

She wasn't sure what to say. She hadn't anticipated telling her sister this soon. Eventually, yes, but not tonight. Rick, she didn't think she could ever tell.

"The police found a bunch of blood vials in your apartment. They asked me if I'd known you were into vampire role-playing, if I'd ever seen that guy in the video before, or if I knew where you were." Tina's voice cracked. "I told them I didn't know anything, but I did recognize that guy from the hospital the night I came off the vent. The nurses kept going on about how it was a miracle I recovered like that. I've never felt better lately, either. Then when I saw the tape, him, what happened, and you vanished . . . all of a sudden, I knew why I was better."

Oh God, Tina had thought it *all* the way through. Kira wrestled with what to do. One flash of her eyes, and Kira could make Tina forget everything, but though with Rick, she didn't have a choice, Tina might be able to handle this.

"I met him by accident," Kira said, trying to sum up the past incredible few weeks in as short a way as possible. "Saw things that let me know he wasn't human, but he couldn't make me forget them like he could with most people. When I told you I had the flu, that wasn't true. He kept me with him, hoping that I'd fall under his power and that he could erase my mind of what I'd seen, but it never happened. Then he let me go, but I felt something so strong for him, I looked for him. That brought me to the club. You saw what happened there."

Tina didn't say anything, but her face went a shade paler. Still, her small frame was straight.

"He set fire to the place? Killed those people?"

"No," Kira said at once. "He was set up by that bastard who ordered my death. I may be away for a while, but I wanted to see you again and tell you . . . well, I didn't intend to tell you *this,* but I wanted to tell you that you don't need to worry. I'm okay, better than okay, and once this is taken care of, I'll be back in your life just like before."

Tina finally met Kira's gaze. Another tear slipped down her cheek. "I've been so scared. I thought you were gone forever because you were something *else* now. I don't know what all this means, and it's so hard to even believe, but when I heard you bitching at Rick, I knew it was still you inside."

Kira felt her own gaze grow moist. "Of course it's still me. It's nothing like the myths, Tina. I don't kill people. I don't hide out in a crypt during the day. You can see that I'm still wearing Mom's cross, so I don't recoil from religious objects, either. Most of what you've heard is wrong, in fact."

Tina still seemed a little dazed, but Kira remembered how overwhelmed she'd first felt, too, and that had been with more proof than Tina had seen.

"Do you have fangs?" Tina asked, looking both fascinated and hesitant.

"Yeah." Kira smiled wryly. "I'm still getting used to them."

"And the guy . . . you and he . . ."

"His name is Mencheres, and I love him," Kira replied

softly. "He's amazing. I don't have time to tell you how much, but he really is. You'll meet him soon, I promise."

Tina glanced over her shoulder, as if Mencheres would magically appear behind her through the door. "That'll be, ah, a little weird," she said with a catch in her voice. "I mean, you're my sister, so you don't feel like something *other* even if you are now. But he's all the way other. He even looks like a vampire, with that tall, dark, and hot thing going on. Does he live in one of those big creepy houses?"

"No, both places of his that I've been to were pretty normal," Kira replied while thinking, *aside from the house I haven't seen. The huge triangular one in the Giza Plateau.*

Tina's gaze flicked behind Kira. "You can't tell Rick. He loves you, but he rolled over on you as soon as the cops questioned him. Told them everything you've done since you were ten. If he knows about *this,* he'll go to the police, the news, you name it."

"No, I'm not telling Rick," Kira sighed, following Tina's gaze to her brother. Rick hummed to himself as he sat, looking far more relaxed than she'd seen him without being heavily stoned. "He won't even remember that I came here, either. But you will. If you want to."

Tina's expression was steady even though she was still pale. "I want to. You can trust me."

"I know I can, Tiny-T," Kira said, calling her the nickname she'd used since they were kids. She went to her sister, feeling Tina tremble just a little as she put her arms around her. Then her sister relaxed when nothing more happened except a hug, never knowing that Kira chanted "eggshells" in her mind so she wouldn't inadvertently squeeze too hard.

"I gotta go," she said at last, releasing Tina. "I had to

sneak away from Mencheres when he was out on business to come see you. He wouldn't have let me do it any other way, so I have to get back soon. He'll freak if he comes back, and I'm gone."

Tina touched her arm. "He keeps you from going out?"

"He's nothing like Pete," Kira said softly, knowing where Tina's worry stemmed from. "He's just afraid something will happen to me because of that other vampire who's after him. That's why I couldn't leave to see you until he was out. But once things are back to normal, I can go anywhere I want."

"I hope so," Tina said. "Don't call or e-mail. I think the police have my phone and maybe even my e-mails bugged or something, but be careful."

"I will."

Kira went over to Rick, staring at her brother. If only she could help him with his disease as easily as Mencheres had helped Tina.

"You never saw me tonight," she said at last, green flashing from her eyes. "You've been asleep. When you wake up in another few hours, you'll know Tina and I love you and we always will. You'll go to a Narcotics Anonymous meeting, and you'll get a sponsor, because you realize there's more to life than getting drunk or high. You'll know there's more to you than your addiction, Rick, and that you can beat this. Oh, and you won't smoke in front of Tina again," she finished.

Kira couldn't *make* her brother get clean and stay clean, but maybe, just maybe, this subconscious directive would set him on the path toward recovery. Ultimately, only Rick could save his own life. All Kira could do was try to give him a boost.

Then she turned, gave Tina a final hug, and walked out of the apartment. She took the stairwell again to go down, counting off the floors and missing Mencheres even though it had only been hours since she'd seen him. The stairwell was silent except for the clatter of her boots against the steps, but after she'd descended about a half dozen floors, tingles in the air brushed like invisible spiderwebs across Kira's skin.

She hesitated just a moment before resuming her pace. Six more floors to go until she reached street level. That spiderweb sensation increased, but Kira squared her shoulders and continued downward, ignoring the EXIT sign on her right that would lead her inside the building's sixth floor.

The vampires smashed into Kira before she reached the fourth floor.

Chapter Thirty

Mencheres's new mobile phone rang. He stared at the numbers showing that it was Bones calling for several seconds before answering. It took that long to compose himself so that his voice didn't betray the emotions raging inside him.

"Yes?"

"I just hung up with Radjedef," Bones began without preamble. "Told him I had no idea how to reach you and all that rot, but he gave me a number to repeat to you. Said you need to contact him 'before it's too late.' What the bloody hell does he mean by that?"

His power surged inside him, seeking someone to kill, but the only person Mencheres wanted to unleash that lethal force on wasn't here.

"More threats about the dead Enforcer, no doubt," he

replied coolly. "Give me the number—and then send a mass e-mail at once to all our people to forward to their property as well, repeating the number and message."

"I'll do it, but stop lying to me," Bones said in a flat tone before repeating the number. "What has Radjedef done now? Let me help you."

"When you alluded to the possibility that you've manifested more of my powers in the past year, was sensing a person's location part of those powers?" Mencheres asked, ignoring the other question.

Bones was silent for a moment. "No," he said finally.

"Then you can't help me," Mencheres sighed. "But you can help our people by not running afoul of the Guardian Council. Send that e-mail. Keep disavowing any knowledge of how to reach me. Renounce me if needed. That is what I require from you."

An exasperated snort sounded on the other line. "Now I know how frustrated my wife feels when I try to keep her out of things for her own protection."

"I'm glad you have Cat," Mencheres said quietly. "You believe I acted as I did in the past merely to secure her powers for our line, but I saw that you would love her. That, more than any other reason, was why I intervened."

"Why do I feel like you're saying goodbye to me?" Bones asked, his words edged with tension.

Mencheres closed his eyes, needing another moment before he could speak again. "You've made me very proud," he said at last.

Then he hung up even as Bones began to sputter out a demand to know where he was. When his mobile rang again with the same number flashing up, he didn't answer it. He'd wait an hour, enough time for Bones's e-mail to circulate—and Bones would send it, no matter how furious he was. Then Mencheres would call Radje and listen to the Law Guardian set terms for Kira's release that Radje had no intention of fulfilling.

He knew without a doubt that Radjedef had her. If any other Law Guardians would have snatched Kira, they would have been the ones to contact Bones, not Radje. The only question was whether Radje was smart enough to keep Kira alive.

Bones called five more times in the next twenty minutes. Mencheres ignored each one. Exactly sixty minutes after he'd hung up with Bones, Mencheres rang the number Bones had given him for Radje.

"Yes," Radje answered after several rings. He sounded angry.

"I am here," Mencheres stated.

"Menkaure, I am disappointed in your co-ruler. It seems he lied to a Guardian when he said he had no way to reach you," Radje purred, losing his hostile tone.

He almost smiled. "Bones was overzealous in attempting to deliver your message. He sent your number to all our people and their property, urging them to forward it to everyone they knew in an attempt to find someone who could reach me. You can spend your time searching through that list of thousands to see who was successful, or we can talk."

Radje let out a short laugh. "Clever. That explains all the recent hang-ups and anonymous threats. Your people are very loyal to you. And now I need to change this number."

"You have what I want," Mencheres said, too concerned for Kira to indulge in Radje's usual cutting banter. "I have what you want. Either we discuss a trade, or I end more than this call."

"I don't know what you're talking about," Radje said with feigned innocence.

"No need to pretend," he replied sharply. "If I went to the council to accuse you of taking Kira, they would only imprison me on sight, and you're too careful to admit to anything over the phone that I could record and play for them later. You have no audience except me, and I grow impatient."

A low whistle sounded. "Why, Menkaure, you sound like you lost your newest vampire. I wish I could help, but I haven't seen her since the night you changed her."

Radje was still taking no chances that their conversation was monitored, in person or by electronic device. Mencheres's power throbbed inside him with seething, lethal waves that were only matched by his fear for Kira. If Radje had killed her . . .

"You know I long to be quit of this world," he said in tones of ice. "I can accomplish that in two ways. One is to go straight to the Guardian Council to claim responsibility for all charges levied again me. My sentence will be death, and their justice will be swift. Or, I can go to you and exchange myself for Kira's safe release. I will do one of these things in the next twenty-four hours. Which will it be?"

Radje was silent. Mencheres waited while his rising anger and fear made the walls tremble around him. Radje had claimed that he was irrationally in love with Kira for his own purposes, but he'd never really believed it. Radje might have guessed he cared for her, but would his ignorance of Mencheres's true feelings mean the Law Guardian hadn't thought to keep Kira alive as blackmail? What if he'd killed her to incite Mencheres to rashness in an attempt to further turn the council against him?

Mencheres *knew* they shouldn't have returned to Chicago as she insisted. They could have acquired proof against Radje another way. If he hadn't agreed to Kira's plan, she would still be with him now . . .

"If you are to turn yourself in, as a Guardian and your only living family, I would urge you to come to me," Radje said at last. "I would hate for you to die beleaguered when I could give you ease before your demise."

Mencheres closed his fists while relief washed over him. Radje was still being cautious in his speech, but his meaning was clear. Kira was alive, and Radje was offering her in exchange for Mencheres's power—and death. Radje wasn't even pretending he would let Mencheres live afterward.

"Then the death I already sought will now be spent in barter for one of my people. Tell me, if you hadn't taken Kira, who else would you have leveraged against me for your purposes?"

"As a Guardian, I would never blackmail anyone, but if I *were* seeking leverage against you, Menkaure, it would not be difficult. You are never short on those you care for," Radje replied with cruel satisfaction.

"And you have never let yourself care for anything but power. Even with all of my many regrets, I would not trade my life for yours, uncle, no matter if it gained me another four thousand years."

"I weary of this exchange," Radje snapped. "I will see you at midnight tomorrow on the top of the Bank of America plaza in Atlanta. Come unarmed and alone."

"I require evidence that I will not be acting in vain," he countered. "Your word is not sufficient."

Radje chuckled. "If I *had* taken Kira, I would not bring her anywhere near you. You would simply kill me and any guards with that formidable power of yours. I take great risk meeting you alone to bring you before the council, but I console myself with the knowledge that should anything happen to me, actions will be taken later that ensure your punishment."

Or, if you don't check in with Kira's guards at an appointed time, they will kill her, Mencheres filled in cynically. He'd suspected as much. Ruthless Radje might be, but foolish he was not. No, Kira would be far away from the place where Mencheres met Radje. The only reason the Law Guardian didn't fear Mencheres's finding her beforehand was because his power to locate people had vanished along with his visions.

I'm coming, the dark underworld of Duat seemed to whisper to him.

Not yet, Mencheres told it.

"I trust you'll find another way to give me the proof I require. I will see you on the roof of the Tower at midnight tomorrow," he stated, and hung up.

Vlad walked across the room, his hands behind his back, his gaze hard.

"You don't *really* intend to go alone, do you?"

"To Radje?" Mencheres gave him a grim smile. "Oh yes."

Kira could hear Radje talking to Mencheres in one of the other rooms of the ancient complex he had secured her in. Images of plumed serpents, war, and warriors were carved onto the pale stone walls around her in this partially collapsed temple, providing the perfect eerie backdrop for the Law Guardian's twisted plans. Kira could almost imagine that she still heard the screams from unwilling sacrifices echoing through the ruins of the huge, formerly great Mayan city.

Iron manacles on her wrists and ankles were nailed to

the wall behind Kira. The shackles left her skin to chafe and heal in a repeated pattern every time she moved, but the manacles weren't responsible for the pain burning inside her. Her hunger was. She hadn't fed since before she went to see her sister.

After the trio of vampires kidnapped her from Tina's building and brought Kira here by plane to this huge site of ruins, Radje had systematically drained all the blood out of her with multiple slashes from a silver knife. Not because he was cruel, he'd explained with a cold smile, but this way, she'd be too weak to free herself. Radje even had the nerve to tell Kira she had no reason to fear that any of his guards would debase her while she was in her helpless position nailed to a wall. After all, he was a Law Guardian, and Guardians did not condone certain disrespectful activities.

Kira wondered if the pompous prick actually believed anything that came out of his mouth, or if he only thought *she* was stupid enough to believe him. She'd seen the looks thrown her way by some of the mercenaries Radje had inside this ancient structure, and none of them were respectful. Kira didn't need her instincts to tell her that Radje's guards were merely biding their time until their master gave them the okay. She knew Radje had no intention of letting her live, and he could care less if those callous men took a few moments of entertainment until they killed her as ordered.

"You have cause to rejoice," Radje said, sweeping into the room where Kira was. "Mencheres has agreed to trade himself for you. He really must be weary of life. Or he intends to set a trap for me with the other Guardians tomorrow night, but all they would see is me, risking myself to bring a condemned criminal in."

"You sure thought of everything," Kira replied in a

flat voice, hoping he'd leave so she wouldn't have to hear more of his self-aggrandizing.

Radje lasered his gaze into her, his dark eyes turning green. His long black hair was braided in a style that somehow still managed to look masculine, and those braids swung when he came closer to her.

"You are too pitifully young to understand how long I have waited, yet now at last it is time for me to claim my power."

"Don't you mean steal Mencheres's power?" she corrected.

He spread out his arms out in an annoyed manner. "That power was meant to be mine. Even the gods agree. Why else would Mencheres suddenly long for death? Why else would his visions and ability to trace people fail? Had not *all* these things come to pass, I couldn't act against him in this way. You see? Fate has intervened for my success!"

You narcissistic bastard, Kira thought, but she didn't push Radje's already-unstable temper by saying it aloud.

She knew why all those things had happened to Mencheres, and they had nothing to do with fate lending a helping hand in Radje's lust for power. It was centuries' worth of suppressed guilt, regret, and grief catching up with Mencheres, all coalescing into a wall of darkness that he couldn't see past and didn't think he had the strength to tear down. If Radje had a conscience, he'd be familiar with how strong inner demons could be. But, of course, the crooked Law Guardian was too empty inside to know anything about that.

"And you'll let me go after you get what you want from Mencheres?" she asked, only managing to contain the majority of her derision from the question.

Nothing altered in Radje's expression. "Of course. No

one would believe any tales you would tell, and even if some did, there would be no proof."

Except for your new power, Kira mentally added. Only an idiot would believe Radje wouldn't kill her to protect that secret from being told. Hell, she bet the mercenaries who guarded this place had their days numbered, too. She could guess that the only reason Radje was pretending he'd let her go was so Kira didn't scream any warning to Mencheres when he demanded to speak to her before giving Radje his power. Mencheres wouldn't give Radje anything until he knew she was alive. The Law Guardian would know that.

"So Menkaure took you as his lover," Radje said musingly, his gaze sliding over her in a way that made her long for a shower even more than blood. "I can smell him on you."

"Give me some soap and water, and I can fix that," she replied shortly. She didn't like the calculating gleam starting to appear in Radje's eyes, or the obviously explicit reference to Mencheres's scent on her. The sooner Radje left her alone, the better.

He came closer instead, stopping only inches from Kira. "When I first put a watch on your sister's residence, I wondered if it was futile. I sensed Menkaure had an affinity for you, so I did not expect him to let you return out of fear of a trap. If he didn't care where you went, then perhaps capturing you would benefit me nothing. Yet my guards heard you tell your sister that you had to sneak away from Menkaure to see her. That is why I knew you would be of use to me alive."

Kira suppressed a shudder as that disturbing gleam grew brighter in Radje's eyes.

"Tell me," he almost murmured, "how much did Menkaure claim to care for you?"

The last thing she'd do was tell Radje that Mencheres loved her. He'd only do even more terrible things to her to spite Mencheres, but she couldn't pretend that she meant nothing to Mencheres, either. That would be too obvious a lie. Even though Radje believed Mencheres had a death wish, he'd still agreed to trade himself for her.

"We didn't have a lot of time together, but the time we spent was promising," Kira said in as much of a noncommittal tone as she could manage. Anger and hunger competed in her. She wanted to smash the smirk off Radje's face . . . and she'd give every cent she had for a bag of blood right now.

"Do you know what the Greeks used to call Menkaure?" Radje asked with feigned casualness. "Eros, after the god of lust. As Pharaohs, we were both considered gods by our people. I have been a Law Guardian for almost three thousand years, but before then, when I spent my time seeking my own pleasure, as Menkaure did . . . my nights were spent in such a sea of flesh that I would never be able to number all the women I had."

That anger burned hotter inside Kira, but she sought to keep it down and her emotional shields up. It wasn't enough for Radje to frame Mencheres and ruin his life. Now he had to try and destroy his relationship with her, too, even though he fully intended to kill Mencheres as soon as he saw him.

"Good for you. With all those memories, sounds like you should direct a porno titled *Gods Gone Wild*," she replied, her voice almost sounding normal.

"Menkaure lived that way for well over two thousand years until he married," Radje said sharply, as if Kira had been too thick to figure out that Radje wasn't the only one swimming in a sea of flesh.

Kira blew out a sigh for effect. "Makes sense. All the

things he could do in bed about fried my circuits—and with that power of his, I mean that literally."

Radje gave her a contemptuous look. "It wasn't just women. Menkaure has had other men, too."

She shrugged as much as the metal clamps would allow. "So he experimented in his wild young vampire days. Lots of people have. Why, there was this one time in college with me and my girlfriend after a few tequila shots—"

"Are you too stupid to comprehend anything I have said?" he interrupted.

Kira gave him a hard stare, her anger escaping at last. "I understand a lot. Like how you're so obsessed with hating Mencheres that you'd stoop to even this. Go on, tell me more, but I don't care. Whatever hell Mencheres raised back then, I think he more than made up for it with over nine hundred years of celibacy, so you're not turning me against him with your dirty little anecdotes. Right now, all you're doing is boring me."

She saw his fist coming, but as she was bolted to the wall, all she could do was brace for it. Pain blasted through the side of her face, followed by a snap of her neck that she could feel *and* hear. For a few agonizing seconds, she couldn't see. And then the pain faded and her vision cleared so that Kira could notice every detail of Radje's wiping her blood from his hand onto her shirt.

"We will see how bored you are after I take Menkaure's power and kill him," Radje said crisply. "If you think he will find a way to defeat me, he will not. Menkaure knows he's already dead. If he didn't, he would have fought against me harder."

He swept out of the room with the curt word to one of the guards to make sure to eat in front of her while giving her nothing. Kira's mouth tightened into a grim line even as she fought to tamp down that searing hunger inside her. She had a task to accomplish, and she'd need a clear head in order to do it.

And a little time without any guards watching her.

Chapter Thirty-one

Mencheres lay on the bottom of the tub. The water had long since cooled, but he didn't add more to heat the temperature. He hadn't wanted to move lest it disrupt his concentration. For the past several hours, he'd stared at that looming wall of darkness in his mind, trying to tear it down brick by brick. Kira's location lay past it, if he could only find a way to breach its indomitable defenses.

But all that occurred was the darkness edging closer until it seemed to have already swallowed him. He replayed Kira's words in his mind as if they were talismans that could guide him. *You ever heard of a self-fulfilling prophecy? . . . When did you lose the ability to see past the darkness? . . . Survivor's guilt . . . you might not see a future for yourself because you don't believe you deserve one.*

None of that should matter now. He might not believe he deserved a future, but he knew Kira did. That should be enough to make him relinquish every bit of guilt that might have been blocking him before. Kira loved him, and she believed in him in a way that no one else had before, ever. That alone should be enough to enable him to rip down that wall of darkness within him.

Yet despite his channeling every fiber of his being toward destroying that wall to learn Kira's location before it was too late to rescue her and leave to meet Radje, the darkness didn't waver. Its denseness seemed to grow instead, and when the timer went off on the watch Mencheres had set, he knew with great sorrow that Kira was wrong. This wasn't a barrier he'd caused within himself, no matter how strongly her faith burned for him. It wasn't survivor's guilt, self-fulfilling prophecy, or his misinterpreting what he saw.

It was Duat, the dark underworld devoid of sky or land, and no one defeated death once its ferryman set his sights on them.

Mencheres rose from the tub, not even bothering to towel off before he pulled on his clothes. A calm purpose settled over him. Eternal darkness might await him, but before he entered Duat, he would bend that darkness to his purposes first. There was yet a way to save Kira.

Vlad's expression was somber as he waited for him outside the bathroom. He asked no questions, but he would know Mencheres had been unable to breach that wall inside him. Otherwise, he'd be urging them to leave, so they could retrieve Kira.

"Perhaps we can—" Vlad began.

"I know another way," Mencheres cut him off. His lips twisted into a sardonic smile. "Though you might not want to stay to see it."

* * *

Burning assailed her from the inside out even before Kira opened her eyes. Her mouth felt dry, her limbs ached, and somehow she had a stomach full of fire. For a few confused moments, she couldn't remember where she was, or why she was manacled to a wall. Then it came flooding back. *The three vampires ambushing her in Tina's building. Radje bringing her here. Mencheres, scheduled to meet Radje tonight to trade his life for hers.*

She didn't move or do anything else to rattle those metal clamps and alert the guards that she was awake. They hadn't left her alone once last night, to her dismay. Of course, Radje had been here, so perhaps the guards had put on a more diligent front for him. She heard them in the other rooms. They had humans with them, and those heartbeats sent Kira's hunger into overdrive. Though this building seemed to be closed to the public, the ruins were a tourist attraction, giving the guards an easy supply of food.

But no guards were in the room now. Radje might not be here either. He might be on his way to Atlanta to meet Mencheres. What time was it? How long had the dawn kept her asleep?

Kira glanced around, trying to see if any glimmers of sunlight streamed in the room past hers. She couldn't crane her neck enough to see any, or they weren't there, but it didn't *feel* dark yet. She still had time. The rapid thumping of those heartbeats called to her with a hypnotic lure, that burning in her stomach reminding her that she didn't have much time, either. If she couldn't control her hunger, it could drive her into a senseless blackout of bloodlust again.

Mencheres is counting on you, Kira reminded herself. She could do this. She wouldn't let him down.

As quietly as she could manage, she pulled at the iron manacle around her wrist. It creaked in an alarmingly loud way, making her eyes dart nervously to the open archway, but no one came. Kira gritted her teeth and tried again. The irons still groaned in a manner that sounded like alarm bells to her, but from the sounds in the other room, the guards were occupied with the humans. Who knew how long that would last? She had to hurry.

Kira felt the iron begin to wiggle back from the wall. Elation flooded her, but at the same time, she heard one of the guards mumble, "Did you hear that?"

She shut her eyes and sagged in her restraints just in time. The guard entered, waves from his aura increasing as he drew nearer. A large hand cupped her face, lingering far too long for her comfort. That same hand gave her breast a rough squeeze next, but Kira forced herself not to react.

"Still out," he muttered. Relief filled her as she heard him rejoin the others in the next room. She opened her eyes a slit, cautious just in case he'd pretended to walk out, but no one was in the room.

She might be able to pull the irons from the wall, but they were too noisy for her to get them out without alerting the guards. Kira gave her manacled hands and feet a ruthlessly analytical look. Broken bones would make a lot less noise than rattling irons. All she had to do was keep herself from screaming. She remembered the agony she'd felt when Flare had crushed her hand.

Easier said than done, but she had no choice.

Kira clenched her jaw shut, bracing herself. Then she slowly, mercilessly pulled her hand down, forcing not the iron from the wall but her hand through a circle far too narrow for it to fit.

Flames of throbbing pain shot through her hand as

her bones crunched together, sounding like someone grinding coffee beans for their morning brew. A shudder went through her, and she fought not to make any sound. When her hand cleared the iron clamp, it was twisted into an irregular shape for a few seconds; it hurt even worse as it healed. Then, even though the burning in her hand subsided, the one in her stomach seemed to increase.

She was running on fumes when it came to blood. She'd depleted more of her limited resources by injuring and healing herself, and she still had another hand and two feet to go.

Kira gave a bleak look at the room where the guards were. *You can do this*, she chanted to herself. Radje thought she was just an average new vampire, helpless against these restraints and his guards. She'd show him just how much he'd underestimated her—and Mencheres.

She looked at her other hand. Then, with gritted teeth, Kira began to pull.

Mencheres sat cross-legged inside a circle, his hands on his knees, his attention focused on the late-afternoon sun. He faced west, the direction from whence death came. Directly in front of him lay a silver knife and an empty cup. Vlad stood several feet from the circle's perimeter, his jaw flexed and the scent of smoke emanating from him.

"This is madness."

Mencheres picked up the silver knife. "I told you not to watch. You chose to regardless, but you must not interfere. You risk more than your life if you do."

"We'll go to Radje," Vlad all but growled. "You'll hold him with your power, and I'll burn him until he begs to tell you where he has Kira. *That* is a viable plan. Not attempting to summon a god from the underworld with a bizarre black magic ritual that will probably kill you."

"Radje is no fool," Mencheres replied. "He knows if he reveals where Kira is, I would kill him as soon as I secured her. Or Radje would refuse to reveal her location long enough to break whatever time limit he's set with her guards, so they would kill her. He's dared too much not to see this through, and even if I give him what he wants, he will still kill her."

"Kira could still get away. She's stronger than any of them realize. You do *not* have to do this."

Mencheres almost smiled. "Yes I do. In fact, I know now that it's been preordained."

Duat and the god of the underworld lay just beyond the edge of that silver knife. He picked it up, watching the blade flash in the moonlight. Then he picked up the empty cup with his other hand.

"Registered in their names, known by their bodies, engraved by their forms are the hours," Mencheres began to recite from the Amduat in his native Egyptian tongue. "Mysterious in their essence, without this secret image of the Duat being known by any person. This image is made in paint like this in the secrecy of the Duat, on the southern side of the Hidden Chamber. He who knows it will partake of the offerings in the Duat. He will be satisfied with the offerings to the gods following Osiris. All he wishes will be offered to him in the Earth."

When Mencheres finished speaking, he shoved the blade through his chest, directly into his heart. The silver burned with a fiery agony that felt like it filled his every vein in an instant. The last time he'd performed a dark ritual, he'd used steel instead of silver. But to summon the ferryman of the underworld, Mencheres required more payment than his blood and the bones of murdered comrades. He required the knowledge of sacred symbols drawn in blood that flowed from the edge of death.

"Aken," he chanted. "Ferryman of the dead, ruler of Duat. I summon thee."

He willed out his blood from the wound in his chest, holding the cup underneath it. His blood flowed in a steady, aching stream that felt like acid pouring from him. When the cup was full, Mencheres could barely move from the pain, but he needed to, even though the slightest shift of the blade would shred his heart and kill him. He couldn't use his power to hold the blade immobile, or to do what needed to be done next. His power was useless inside the circle.

He dipped his finger inside the cup, coating it with his blood. Despite the danger that jostling the blade would bring, he bent forward and began to draw the first of twelve symbols that would call forth Aken.

As soon as the first symbol was completed, shadows began to form inside the circle. *Akhs,* the damned souls of the underworld. If he wasn't strong enough to complete the ritual by drawing all twelve symbols, the *akhs* would consume him, sweeping his soul to Ammut, the Devourer goddess.

The darkness in his vision seemed to taunt him. Was it the endless River of the Dead that the ferryman would arrive on, if Mencheres were successful? Or was it the never-ending darkness of Duat, where he'd be condemned as one of the eternally restless *akhs*? Had his failure been fated long ago, and he'd spend all eternity trapped like the shadows that now encircled him?

"Mencheres," Vlad said, ignoring the warning not to interfere. "Stop this now."

"It is too late," he gritted, dipping his finger again in the cup of blood. Even that slight movement felt like it rammed the knife deeper into his heart. He tried to concentrate on the crimson liquid as he drew the next symbol instead, attempting to ignore the blistering pain and the overwhelming compulsion to pull the knife out *at once*. If he pulled the knife out, the *akhs* around him would immediately become corporeal and devour him. But the longer it took him to draw the symbols, the more power the *akhs* derived. They fed off pain, and with the silver in his chest, Mencheres was a feast for them. The stronger they grew, the more solid they would become.

Mencheres dipped his finger back in the cup. Kira's blood was part of him, her essence mixed together with the blood from the other donors he'd fed from. This would *not* be the closest he came to being with her again. She'd believed in him enough to risk her life with Radje, a person who'd already been responsible for her death once. He might have failed her that first time when he took her mortality, but he would not fail her this time.

He drew the third symbol even as the shadows of the *akhs* began to swirl faster around him. Mencheres shifted position to make the symbols circle him, the pain that caused almost making him convulse. He forced it back and slowly drew the fourth symbol. Each had to be precise; an error would nullify the ritual and condemn him. The silver in his heart felt like it began to grow tentacles, trying to destroy him with its own terrible will. He gritted his teeth, concentrating on the lines of the next symbol he drew. Seven more left before he was finished.

That pain continued to burn inside him in merciless waves. As the *akh* shadows increased their swirling dance around him, they lost their vaporous appearance to form hazy, manlike shapes, mouths opened in what looked to be snarls. Vlad muttered something, but Mencheres didn't listen. He was too focused on keeping his hand steady

as thunderbolts of pain wracked his body. The longer
the silver was in his heart, the more it would break him
down, shattering either his ability to draw or compelling
him to end it early by snatching the blade from his chest.
This ritual wasn't designed for the wielder to succeed. It
was meant for failure, which was why Patra never used it
against him when she sought to kill him through magic.

Six more symbols left. By the gods, he was only halfway there. He'd never finish in time.

Mencheres kept drawing regardless, his vision almost
hazy from the all-encompassing pain and the swirls of
akhs around him. They solidified with every passing
moment as they continued to feed off his pain. When they
were solid, they would feed off his flesh. It wouldn't be
long now.

A seizure nearly sprawled Mencheres into the carefully
drawn symbols before him. His hand shot out, stopping
his momentum, but coming within centimeters of smear-
ing one of those symbols. He closed his eyes, taking precious seconds to try to force the pain back into something
manageable, but it only continued to spread. His eyes
snapped open in growing dread. The more he concentrated on ignoring the pain, the more it grew, as did the
akhs, who now clearly resembled people instead of form-
less shapes.

"Kira will be dead by sunrise if you do not *finish this,*"
Vlad urged, sounding almost hoarse in his agitation.

Mencheres focused all his attention on drawing the
eighth symbol, letting the pain flow freely through his
body. It shook him, rustling the blade, sending more agonizing spurts through his limbs, but the only thing he
concentrated on was keeping his hand steady. His whole
body began to shudder, the suffering building to an intensity that made him wish for death so the pain would

cease. He would only need one rogue tremor to jostle that blade too forcefully. One smear in a symbol for it to all end. *It's inevitable,* the darkness whispered seductively. Why should he suffer trying to stave off something that could not be overcome?

Kira. Dead by sunrise.

He fought to keep his vision and his hand steady. Growls came from the *akhs* now, growing louder as they sensed their victory approaching. Mencheres forced himself not to look at them but to finish drawing the ninth symbol. Those growls grew louder, wisps of their fingers brushing him as the circle they flew around tightened further still. He didn't look up. He kept drawing even as the pain inside him grew to where all he wanted was to twist that blade in his chest to free himself from it.

"Hurry . . ." Vlad grated out.

Mencheres's hand wavered, and his vision clouded as he began to draw the tenth symbol. The *akhs* stroked him now, their hands flicking his back, arms, and shoulders, trying to get to the blade. He hunched forward as much as he dared, the searing anguish from that movement making his vision disappear completely for a moment. He forced himself to keep drawing, using his memory to form the lines, until very faintly, he could see again. His vision was narrowed to only the smallest space, but in that space, he could draw the eleventh symbol.

Fangs sank into his back, tearing at his flesh. He gave a hoarse shout. The *akhs* were solid enough that they had begun to feast.

He ignored the teeth slashing at him as finished the eleventh symbol. Then, using all of his strength to keep them away from the blade in his heart, Mencheres began to draw the last symbol. Agony exploded in him, darkness swam in his vision, and his hand shook while the *akhs* tore at him, but he kept drawing. Kira's face flashed in his mind, her full mouth parted in a smile. He focused on that with his last conscious thoughts.

Let the *akhs* devour him. Let the blade slip too deeply in his chest. Let the darkness of Duat come. He would still not stop drawing the symbol that led to Kira's safety.

A great roar filled his ears as Mencheres drew the final lines of the symbol. Then the blackness did claim him, drowning out that roar inside the eternal veil of darkness.

Chapter Thirty-two

Mencheres sat inside the circle, the knife still in his chest, the symbols finished around him, and the cup still in his hand. All of that was the same, yet he knew he was not on the same plane of existence anymore. The lack of pain was his first indicator. The utter void around the circle, absent of everything except piercing darkness, was the next.

Then the circle was pierced when a slim boat floated through. A tall figure stood at the helm, with the body and face of a man, yet the horns of a ram curled out from his head. Mencheres bowed as much as the knife protruding from his chest would allow.

"Ferryman," he said. "Lord of Duat."

When Mencheres straightened, Aken reached out and plucked the knife from his chest as if it were a bloom off

the ground. The huge horns neared Mencheres's head as
Aken then bent to lick the blade. All the while, Aken's
yellow eyes burned into his.

"You have paid your blood coin to summon me,
Cainenite. What do you seek?"

It had been thousands of years since Mencheres had
been referred to as a Cainenite, but the god of the underworld probably wasn't familiar with how that word
had been replaced with the more current one: "vampire."
After all, thousands of years were a mere pittance of time
to the gods.

Mencheres bowed again. "I seek another Cainenite
named Kira. She rose from my blood and her essence remains in me still. Use my blood to find her, and tell me
where she is."

"Give me your name," the ferryman commanded.

Names held power. Aken would bind their agreement
with his. "Menkaure," he replied, using the one he'd been
born with.

The ferryman gave him a toothless grin that looked
more like the open maw of the grave. Again, he licked
the knife that still had some of Mencheres's blood coated
on it.

"She is far from here," Aken stated. That smile widened. "It will take time to reach her."

The sun had been high in the sky when he began this
ritual, but he still might not have enough time. If Radje
and Kira were located on opposite sides of the world,
he would not have time to reach them both. Mencheres
didn't trust anyone else to secure Kira, either. No doubt
Radje left instructions for the guards to kill her at once
if there was an attack.

"Tell me where she is," he said.

The ferryman touched Mencheres's forehead. Images of a sprawling, decrepit city consisting of crumbling temples and monuments bordered by a vast jungle exploded in Mencheres's mind, combined with flashes of Kira manacled to a wall and guards milling in and around a large temple surrounded by pillars. His jaw tightened. He recognized those ruins. Kira was in Yucatán, Mexico, somewhere inside the Temple of the Warriors in the ancient Mayan city complex of Chichén Itzá. And he was in Chicago, over a thousand miles away, with an appointment to meet Radje in Atlanta at midnight or he'd order Kira's death.

Aken dropped his fingers from Mencheres's head and set the silver knife down in front of him. "Once summoned, my boat does not return to Duat empty. Either spill a worthy surrogate's blood on this blade before dawn, or I come for you."

"Agreed," Mencheres rasped.

Then the ferryman steered his boat out of the circle and disappeared into the blackness of the River of the Dead. As soon as he was gone, the circle dissolved, flinging Mencheres back in his own time. Vlad's amazed expression was the first thing he noticed, his friend's face bent close to his.

"I don't believe it, you're not dead."

Vlad grasped Mencheres's arms and pulled him to his feet. For a moment, Mencheres actually felt dizzy as the effect of traversing between two worlds clung to him. But then his mind cleared enough for him to notice that the sun was not quite as painfully bright as before.

"How long was I away?" he demanded.

"After those *things* tore half your flesh from you, you lay as if dead for over an hour," Vlad said, muttering, "If

I never see any creatures raised from black magic again, it will be too soon."

Mencheres grasped Vlad's arms. "I need a plane. Now."

Kira just finished pulling her final foot free from the ankle clamp when she heard someone coming. If vampires could sweat, she'd be covered in it. Her hands might have hurt when she pulled them free, but crushing her feet had been almost more than she could bear. It took all her will not to thrash around screaming at the top of her lungs from the pain. Freeing her feet took far longer, too. Especially adding in all the times the guards would wander in and she'd have to abruptly fake sleep while clutching the wrist irons and hoping the guards didn't look closely at them.

She tensed in a moment of indecision, the pain still radiating up her leg as her foot healed. Should she pretend to still be shackled and hope the guard didn't look at her irons closely—or at all? But then Kira heard the heartbeat accompanying those footsteps. Whoever was coming into the room was human.

She braced herself to let loose all the power she had in her gaze to shut the person up if Radje had human as well as vampire guards here, but then her jaw dropped when she saw who it was that edged inside. Only the knowledge that she'd give herself away kept Kira from gasping out her name.

Jennifer Jackson, the young girl Flare had forced into stripping. The same girl who'd gone missing from the club after Radje torched it and murdered those people.

Jennifer's eyes were wide as she crept into the room. No lights, she probably couldn't see much. Kira was torn. If the guards came looking for Jennifer, they'd find that Kira had slipped her irons. If she said anything to get Jennifer to leave, they'd hear that, too. And she had another problem. Jennifer's pulse was so tantalizingly near, her heartbeat sounding like nothing as much as the dinner bell. More pain twisted in her gut, and her fangs sprang from her gums. Only a few feet separated Kira from more blood than she could even begin to drink.

Jennifer gasped, her face lit in a pale green glow. Kira sprang soundlessly across the room, covering Jennifer's mouth. The contact with her warm, pulsating flesh was almost her undoing. An avalanche of need slammed through her, coating Kira like burning tar. She *had* to drink from Jennifer, but only a little. She'd stop before she took too much . . .

You'll kill her.

Her instincts shouted a clear warning that even her hunger-addled mind couldn't deny. She stared at Jennifer, forcing her attention away from that intoxicatingly pounding pulse only a few inches from her mouth, trying to listen for the guards over the sound of Jennifer's racing heart. She was too far gone to trust taking even a drop. If she started to feed, she wouldn't stop until Jennifer was dead.

You need the strength to get away, her hunger tempted her. *Taking one life is worth all the others you'll save later if you can just return to Mencheres. The guards will probably kill Jennifer anyway . . .*

Kira shook her head, forcing that hunger down with a strength that no normal new vampire would have. She would *not* murder an innocent girl, even if it did mean a better chance to get away. Radje treated life so dismissively. She wouldn't. Jennifer might die anyway, but it wouldn't be by her hand. Not while she still had an ounce of control left in her.

Kira put her finger to her lips in a gesture for silence, then slowly removed her hand from Jennifer's mouth. The sooner she wasn't touching her, the easier it would be not to sink her fangs into Jennifer's closest vein.

Jennifer didn't speak, but tears made her eyes shiny. She grabbed her hand when Kira tried to set her away, holding on with a grip that was surprisingly strong.

Take me with you, Jennifer mouthed.

Kira shook her head. Finding a way to slip past the guards would be hard enough alone. Trying to do that with a slower, louder, *weaker* human? She'd never make it.

Jennifer glanced back at the open doorway that led to the room where the guards were, then glanced back at Kira again.

I know a way out, Jennifer mouthed.

She wavered. Jennifer could be telling the truth. If she'd been here since the night of the club fire, she might be very familiar with the temple's layout or the expansive ruins beyond it. Kira had only gotten a brief look at the imposing temple, with its hundreds of pillars, stone warriors, and steep steps before Radje's guards hustled her into a pyramid hidden *inside* the crumbling pyramid. That had been a maze of corridors, inner vaults, and partially crumpled rooms that would be very difficult to navigate without alerting the guards to her escape.

But Jennifer could also be lying out of fear of being left behind. Kira couldn't blame her for that, but she couldn't risk taking Jennifer, either. She would still have a much better chance alone, even if Jennifer was telling the truth.

She shook her head no again, more emphatically.

The tears that had been welling in Jennifer's eyes spilled down her cheeks. *Please,* she mouthed, despair and desperation growing on her features.

Mack's voice rang in Kira's mind, just as strong and clear as it had been when he was alive. *Save one life.* She couldn't do anything to help the humans in the other room with the guards, but here was one person she might be able to save if she tried.

Kira grabbed Jennifer. No way would they make it if she limited herself to Jennifer's human speed; she'd have to carry her. Silently, she begged for the strength to do this without giving in to that overwhelming urge to feed. All her hunger saw was a bundle of juicy arteries in her arms, even if her mind recognized a terrified, traumatized girl who needed help.

Show me, Kira mouthed.

Jennifer pointed, and Kira darted off to the opposite side of the room, where Jennifer had snuck in from.

Mencheres drummed one finger on the armrest inside the Falcon 20 jet. It was the only visible sign of the tension boiling inside of him. It had been four hours since Aken told of Kira's location, and less than three of those hours had been spent flying. It had taken an hour alone to get to the nearest private jet charter company in Chicago and compel the humans into taking Vlad and Mencheres on an unscheduled flight immediately, but then more precious minutes ticked away while fueling and preparing the aircraft.

Then he couldn't force the pilots into pushing the plane to its maximum speed because the plane could only travel fifteen hundred miles before refueling—almost the exact distance from Chicago to the northern center of the Yucatán Peninsula, where the Chichén Itzá ruins were. If the plane burned more fuel going faster than its cruising speed of almost five hundred miles an hour, they would run out of fuel before reaching their destination.

But now, it was time to notify others where Kira was, just in case he failed to retrieve her in time.

"I need your phone," Mencheres said to Vlad.

He handed it over. Mencheres dialed Bones first, looking out the small window at the dark expanse of water far beneath them. The Gulf of Mexico. They were less than an hour away from Chichén Itzá.

"Tepesh," Bones answered his phone, not bothering to say hello. "Do you know where Mencheres is?"

"I am here," Mencheres replied calmly, even though he felt anything but calm.

"Bloody hell," Bones breathed. "When I last spoke to you, I thought—"

"I thought so as well," he interrupted with a hint of wryness. "But it appears I was not meant for that particular fate." His darkness might still find him, but not in the form of being trapped as one of the Devourer's *akhs* because he'd failed to complete the ritual.

"Where are you?"

"In a plane on my way to Chichén Itzá in the Yucatán Peninsula. That is where Radje has Kira. I need you to come here. If I am successful in freeing her, someone will still need to force one of her guards to confirm to Radje that all is well when I meet with him later."

"You need *him* for that?" Vlad looked mildly affronted. "I'm twice as old and twice as capable."

"Call Veritas and tell her where Kira is," Mencheres continued, not addressing Vlad's comment. He and Bones had always been at odds with each other, no doubt due to their similar natures. "Tell her to come but not to inform any other Guardians. I can't risk word getting to Radje."

"You're still trying to keep me on the good side of the Guardians in case you don't come back from this," Bones said in rasping tones.

"Yes," Mencheres replied shortly. "Our line must be protected, no matter what."

"Grandsire, I . . ." Bones stopped, his voice breaking off.

Mencheres smiled slightly. Bones might call him grandsire because he'd made the vampire who later turned Bones, but Mencheres knew he wasn't the only one who felt that their relationship was more father and son.

"It doesn't need to be said. I know."

Then he hung up, meeting Vlad's sardonic copper green gaze.

"Why you and Cat care so much for that street peasant, I will never know."

"Because we see deeper into him than you bother to look," Mencheres replied. "You were worse at his age. I remember; I was there."

"If you meant to send for Veritas and Bones, why didn't you call them in time to arrive with us?" Vlad asked, switching the subject.

Mencheres looked out the window again. "Veritas will be more interested in securing proof against Radje than in saving Kira's life. And now Bones and Cat will have the opportunity to mend fences with her by passing this on personally. Veritas is a valuable ally, but they have some history with her to overcome."

"You'll need to keep several guards alive. You don't know which one of them Radje is supposed to call later."

Mencheres gave him a measured look. "That's why I needed more than just you here once I leave to meet Radje—because I can't take Kira with me."

Chapter Thirty-three

Kira ran through the jungle with Jennifer clutched in her grip. The sun had set, but that only deepened the spots of shade in Kira's vision instead of plunging it into total darkness as it would appear to Jennifer. She had her arms around Kira's neck, which brought her throat within mere inches of Kira's mouth. The constant booming of her pulse from Jennifer's body pressed to hers was almost enough to make her delirious with need.

That burning pain within her was so constant, she couldn't remember a time when she hadn't felt it. Kira ran faster, trying to do more than elude the guards she could hear chasing her. She was trying to outrun her hunger, that mindless, clawing thing demanding to be sated on the person right beneath her mouth. *You can't help yourself,* her need all but screamed at her. *It's not your fault. You're a new vampire,* no one *could resist.*

I can, Kira told that hunger. She wasn't just a new vampire. She was a new vampire who had some of Mencheres's incredible power running through her veins. That's why Kira awoke hours before the guards expected her to. Why she could go almost two days without feeding and not be insane with hunger. Why she could smash all the bones in her hands and feet without making a sound, and why she could keep herself from tearing into Jennifer's throat now.

Mencheres said she would need extra power if Kira was to let herself be kidnapped by Radje. He flatly refused to agree to her plan otherwise, no matter that Vlad and Veritas insisted Kira was right, and it was the best way to provide indisputable proof of Radje's involvement to the rest of the Guardian Council. So though she'd objected, Kira had let Mencheres will out some of the power Radje had longed for over the course of thousands of years, albeit in a much smaller dose. Then all Kira had to do was wait to be kidnapped when she went to see Tina, cloaking that new power so Radje and the guards were lulled into a false sense of security, never knowing Kira had some of Cain's legacy running through her veins.

Now she was using that power to carry Jennifer through a dense overgrowth of Mexican jungle with who knew how many vampires chasing after them. If she had only the stamina of a new vampire, these guards would have caught up with her long ago, but she had strength and speed they could never have anticipated. She trusted Mencheres to break through that barrier in his mind and find her, but it would be better for both of them if he didn't have to battle through the temple to get to her.

Radje had left orders to kill her and the other humans if anyone attacked. Kira couldn't stay manacled to a wall and just expect Mencheres to be strong enough to stop every guard from following that directive while she hung limply there, waiting to be saved.

And if Mencheres couldn't find her through his power, then she needed to save both of them. She'd managed to get away. Now she had to stay away long enough for Mencheres to find them. Or for the guards to admit to Radje that they'd lost her when he called to offer Mencheres proof that she was still alive. Either would be enough indisputable proof for the other Guardians to fry Radje. Kira used that thought as extra incentive to go faster as she continued to race through the jungle. *Just evade them for a few more hours.* Mencheres would have his proof that way. She could do it.

Then Kira heard something in the jungle ahead of her. Something not animal or natural. She slowed, pulling Jennifer off her even as she warned her with a finger to her lips to be quiet. One of the vampires must have gotten ahead of her. They'd spread out to look for her, Kira had heard from their occasional shouts, but most of them were farther behind. Somehow, this one had made it past her. Maybe he could fly. That would explain it.

She couldn't hope to outrun him, not while carrying Jennifer. If she meant to get past him, she'd have to find a way to kill him.

The Yucatán Peninsula lay below them, the remains of the ancient Mayan city of Chichén Itzá tantalizingly near. Mencheres rose and instructed the two pilots to land on the first empty road or adequately long flat stretch of land they came across. He couldn't have the pilots land at an airport, not while Radje might have spies there as an extra precaution, watching for Mencheres or any of his people. Another flash of his gaze, and the pilots began to search for an unorthodox runway. The plane was small enough that it shouldn't take much to land on safely.

He was almost back at his seat when his mind seized with a pain he hadn't felt in several months—and never expected to experience again. Mencheres froze in disbelief, too stunned to reply even as a part of him registered that Vlad asked him what was wrong. Images filled his mind, somewhat dimmer than he was used to, but unmistakable.

Kira running through the jungle, a woman clasped in her arms. A vampire lay in wait ahead, others farther away but closing in. Kira set the woman down, turned and ran toward that vampire, grappling with him as she fought to strip away his silver knife . . .

He strode back to the pilots. "Go lower," he ordered them, his gaze lit up with green. "Fly over Chichén Itzá. When you are northeast of it, descend as low as you can."

"What are you doing?" Vlad demanded.

He swung around, determination and astonishment swirling inside him. "Kira's not in the Temple of the Warriors at Chichén Itzá anymore. She's in the jungle just north of it."

Vlad started to smile. "You saw that?"

"Yes." Mencheres's voice thickened with emotion. "In a vision."

The vampire rammed his knee into Kira's stomach. Pain blasted through her, but she kept her grip on his knife. His fangs tore into her shoulder next, ripping into flesh, but while that shot more searing pain into her, Kira reminded herself that he couldn't kill her that way. And she had fangs, too.

She twisted them over until she was on top of the vampire. All the training at police academy plus several years of defense classes came rushing to the forefront, mixing with her supernatural strength, Mencheres's power, and the hunger that still burned inside her. She slammed her elbow into the vampire's face, feeling bones break in both of them, but she didn't hesitate before ramming that same elbow into his face again. And again.

Her fourth blow blinded him. Then her knees smashed into his ribs before she scrambled lower, using her fangs to tear the knife from his grip. Before she allowed herself to think, Kira shoved that blade into his chest as hard as she could. His instant shout was cut off when she shook the blade roughly, feeling all his strength suddenly vanish. His body went limp, his head fell back, and that green light faded from his eyes.

Kira suppressed her urge to fling herself away from him out of repugnance. She had no time to second-guess the necessity of killing him. She yanked the blade out of the vampire's chest, clutching it as she doubled back to get Jennifer. With all the other sounds in the jungle, including the roar of an airplane flying overhead, Kira couldn't use Jennifer's heartbeat and breathing to track her. That was a good thing, though. It meant the other vampires couldn't, either.

Impatience, anger, and desperation unexpectedly filled Kira, almost overwhelming even the burn from her hunger. She ran faster toward where she'd left Jennifer. Had another vampire gotten to her? Was that why her instincts were all of a sudden going wild? Damn it, Jennifer had been through too much already! If one of those guards had found her, had hurt her again, Kira was going to kill him next.

Her grip tightened on the knife as she ducked, hurtling

herself through the dense undergrowth. That desperation grew stronger, throbbing inside her along with the painful hunger. Sounds jerked her head to the left, then the right, and even echoed ahead of her where Jennifer was supposed to be. Dread ran up her spine. The guards. They'd managed to surround her.

Kira slowed. She might have some of Mencheres's incredible power fueling her, but she couldn't take them all on. Her only chance was one at a time, and even those odds were slim. Still, she wasn't about to drop the knife and give herself up. She whirled, heading for the closest sounds to her, feeling almost consumed by the desperation inside her. *There!* her subconscious seemed to scream. *Right there!*

She felt a blast of electricity then, as sudden and overwhelming as a bolt of lightning. Kira froze so abruptly that it felt like she'd run into an invisible wall of cement. For a split second, she was panicked, looking down to see if she'd been pierced with multiple weapons to explain why she couldn't move. But then something else washed over her subconscious, replacing that former desperation with waves of relief and impatience.

That's when she realized what she was feeling weren't her emotions. They were Mencheres's. *He's here.*

Hard arms seized her in the next instant, swinging her up into an embrace that crackled with familiar power. Kira's paralysis vanished, allowing her to twist around to face him. Mencheres's eyes blazed emerald, his expression fierce as he stared at her. She yanked his head down before she could even think, glorying in the bruising passion as Mencheres kissed her like this was the last chance he'd ever get to do so.

All too quickly he drew away, reminding Kira that they were surrounded by enemy guards and now was not the time to show him how much she'd missed him. Mencheres stroked her face before he stepped back, then spread out his arms.

Rolls of invisible thunder shook the jungle. Kira's eyes widened as everything went silent with an abruptness that was startling. Even the sounds from the birds and animals ceased, leaving only the rustle of the countless leaves and trees to break the sudden awesome hush. A weight seemed to press on her, the vibrations from his power thickening the air into a denseness that was palpable.

"There you are," Mencheres muttered.

That weight lifted, and the animals resumed their nocturnal foraging and calls. The thick feel of his power still lingered in the air, though, and it didn't escape Kira's notice that her pursuers had fallen silent at the same moment that she'd felt like she was struck by lightning.

"Do you, ah, have them all?" she asked.

A tight smile crossed Mencheres's face, relaxing the fierceness in his expression only a fraction.

"Yes, I have them."

Then slow shuffling sounds came from around them. One by one, Radje's guards walked toward them, forming a circle. Their steps were perfectly synchronized, but the fear on their expressions made it plain that they weren't in control of their actions.

An eerie blue light broke through the jungle a hundred yards ahead. Kira glanced at Mencheres, but he didn't look alarmed, and the brush of emotion she felt from him was icy determination and relief, not fear. So she said nothing as that light came nearer. After a few moments, Vlad Tepesh appeared through the brush, his dark hair swinging with his strides, one of his blue-flamed hands wrapped around the throat of a vampire he half dragged alongside him.

"Hello, boys," he drawled as he entered the circle of vampire guards who were now standing still. The flames on his hands grew brighter, streaming down the vampire in his grip until the guard's body was engulfed. Vlad flung him into the center of the circle, not even a thread of his own clothing burned although the screaming vampire was writhing in a sea of flames.

"So then," Vlad said with pleasant cruelty. "Who wants to talk, and who wants to burn to death?"

Chapter Thirty-four

Mencheres wasn't surprised that it only took killing a few of the guards before the rest were all too eager to tell everything they knew about the rest of their numbers, their locations, which of them Radje was supposed to contact, and anything else he asked them. Radje hadn't picked older, seasoned mercenaries who would require far more incentive because they'd realize their fate was death anyway for their participation in these crimes. He'd picked younger, foolish vampires he'd changed himself in secret. Ones who would do his bidding without many questions asked and could easily disappear when Radje no longer had use for them.

Kira stayed with the human girl Mencheres recognized from the club, just out of eyesight. It was obvious she didn't care to witness the fiery interrogations, but she never questioned their necessity. She wanted to go back to check on the other humans at the temple where she'd been held, but Mencheres urged patience. They had to make sure no guards remained in other parts of Chichén Itzá who would alert Radje to their presence. His senses didn't pick up more than the seventeen vampires who'd chased Kira into the jungle, but he would take no chances.

Only after those still living revealed that they made up the entirety of Radje's guards on Kira did Mencheres venture back with Vlad and Kira to the temple ruins. Was it arrogance or paranoia that had made Radje leave so few of his people to guard Kira? Did he fear that larger numbers might betray him if one of his acolytes were loose-lipped, and word reached the Guardians of what he'd done? Or did he truly believe Mencheres cared so little for Kira that he hadn't expected him to take any measure possible to save her, knowing Radje would not release her as agreed?

Radje might have been correct had he taken anyone else *but* Kira. Only the knowledge that her life hung in the balance gave Mencheres the strength to finish the ritual to summon Aken. No soul's location was invisible from the ferryman of the dead, though Radje might not even know of the ritual to summon Aken. Few in their race knew the darkest magics. The only reason Patra knew how to wield the spells she'd used was because Mencheres taught them to her when they were together—a mistake he'd paid for dearly.

Yes, some knowledge was best left lost to the world. He cast a glance up at the moon. He'd have to leave in the next hour in order to make his meeting with Radje.

A familiar wave of energy reached across his senses. Only two days ago, there was just one vampire he could feel this way. But now that he'd shared a portion of his power with Kira, she was irrevocably tied to his senses as well.

"Bones is here," Mencheres stated.

Vlad raised a brow even as he nailed another guard to the walls of the temple with silver knives.

"He must have been farther south than we were when we first left. You called him less than two hours ago."

Kira appeared in the archway, her expression sad and angry. "I found six bodies here, but from what Jennifer said, there were even more people killed. The guards would dump the bodies in the jungle in shifts at night."

Vlad shoved another silver knife into a guard's wrist. Mencheres held them immobile now, but once he was gone, this would help secure them.

"Vampires like you piss me off," Vlad muttered. "Leaving a trail of bodies for humans to be suspicious over when there's no need to kill to feed. Ever had a mob of villagers armed with torches and pitchforks burn your house down while screaming 'death to the wampyre!'? I have, and it's irritating beyond belief."

"You know those old Romanians." Bones's voice drifted in from the entrance of the temple. "Just bloody unreasonable."

"You promised you wouldn't start with him . . ."

Cat's voice, speaking far softer than Bones had. Mencheres ignored both of their comments in favor of sliding his arms around Kira.

"I need to leave soon. You'll be safe with the three of them here."

Her green gaze pierced into his. "I'd tell you not to go because Radje's too dangerous, but you'd just repeat the same *indisputable proof needed* argument that I used when I talked you into letting Radje kidnap me from my sister's, wouldn't you?"

"As I've often said before, you are wise," Mencheres murmured. A strange exhilaration filled him, an excitement mixed with purpose that he hadn't felt in . . . he couldn't remember how long. His visions had *not* deserted him. The glimpse of Kira in the jungle proved that, and, if they hadn't, then he had a chance for a future after all.

What made the difference? Was it completing the ritual that, by rights, should have killed him? Or was Kira correct, and the wall of darkness blocking his vision was of his own making? Perhaps the touch of the god when Aken showed him where Kira was removed that block. Or he'd managed to tear it down earlier but didn't see the fruits of that right away. He didn't know. All he knew was that now, only one obstacle stood in his way from a life with Kira.

Radjedef. Mencheres intended to remove that obstacle.

"I smell Radjedef here," a voice he hadn't expected stated from the room outside theirs. "Something else, too. Old, and . . . familiar."

"Veritas," Mencheres said, surprise coloring his tone.

"She caught a ride with us," Cat announced, her brows rising as she came into the room and saw Vlad nailing the guards into the wall.

Vlad paused to give her a slanted smile. "I'd welcome you with a fond embrace, Cat, but as you can see, I'm a little busy. Bones, feel free to make use of the remaining knives on those three guards."

"At a time like this, you must miss your long wooden poles," Bones noted as he began to gather up knives, giving a cold glare to the guards who were waiting in the corner.

Vlad grunted. "Do I ever."

"Brought something for you," Cat said to Kira, holding out a shopping bag. "Didn't think they'd keep you fed while they had you."

Mencheres gave Cat a grateful look as Kira opened it to reveal several sealed bags of blood inside. She'd flatly refused to feed from any of the humans held captive, saying they'd suffered enough. Now he didn't have to take her to the hotel that bordered the ruins for Kira to slake her burning hunger on unsuspecting guests.

"Thank you," she said to Cat. Then she turned her attention to Veritas, who scanned the room with silent thoroughness.

"You smell Radje. His guards can verify that they were ordered by him to kidnap me. I can sure attest to Radje holding me here against my will, and he didn't tell any of the Guardians about it. Is that enough proof that he's gone rogue?" she asked in an unflinching tone.

"For me it is." Veritas approached the guards, giving them a critical evaluation. Then she turned around, sniffing again, her brow furrowed. "But for the rest of the council, some of whom are close friends with Radjedef, it is only circumstantial evidence backed up by questionable witness statements."

"You can't be *serious*," Kira began.

"Even if the council were satisfied, I would still go to Radje," Mencheres interrupted her angry response. He brushed her cheek. "Not only for evidence. For recompense."

Cat's nose wrinkled as she sniffed lightly near him. "Not to be rude, but what is that smell? It's like you bathed in dead bodies or something."

"I noticed it, too," Kira said. Her gaze clouded. "It worried me."

Vlad kept securing the guards, his face carefully blank. Bones raised a brow at Mencheres, waiting. He said nothing, but Veritas's gaze narrowed. She strode over to him, inhaling deeply near his chest, then as close to his head as she could reach without floating.

"Exactly *how* did you know where Kira was?" Veritas demanded.

"From a vision," Mencheres replied. That was part of the truth. Just not the entirety of it.

"I knew you could push past that block in your mind," Kira murmured, giving his waist a squeeze.

Veritas inhaled again, then she stepped back, her sea-green gaze turning hard.

"You smell of *Aken*."

Vlad muttered a curse. Cat and Kira asked, "Who's that?" at the same time. Mencheres said nothing, holding Veritas's stare.

She recognized the lord of the underworld's scent. There was only one way Veritas would be able to do that—if she'd previously summoned Aken herself.

It seemed he'd not been the only one Tenoch had shared the secrets of that ritual with. He and Veritas were at a stalemate. Summoning the ferryman was an act of black magic and a breach of vampire law. If she confronted Mencheres about his crime, she would have to confess her own.

"Now you know the other reason why I must go to Radje," Mencheres said evenly.

Veritas acknowledged their impasse with an inclination of her head. "I do. I wasn't always a Guardian." Then her gaze hardened again. "You must hurry. The ferryman does not tarry, and his boat never leaves empty."

"What are you two talking about?" Kira asked.

He kissed the top of her head. "I shall tell you when I return."

Cat cleared her throat. "I know I'm missing a ton of

subtext here, but I understand 'hurry.' The three of us came in on one of my uncle's new jets. You know that the government has access to the fastest planes available, so if you're in a rush, you can take my ride. You'll have to squeeze into the weapons area, so it's not comfy, but it's quick."

Mencheres mulled her offer. He preferred to stay away from anything to do with human governments, but he was running short on time. "I have a plane, but it needs fuel."

Cat smiled. "Mine doesn't—and did I mention it was *fast*?"

Chapter Thirty-five

The Bank of America building towered imperially over the rest of the skyscrapers in the Atlanta cityscape. Lights reflected off the gold-plated steel girders that crisscrossed in an open lattice design to form, of all things, a gleaming pyramid at the top. Mencheres stood on the roof of the nearby Symphony Tower, staring up at the thousand-foot skyscraper. How fitting that Radje chose this place. Their enmity had started on the sands of the Giza Plateau; but it would end here, inside the gleaming pyramid built not by ancient Pharaohs, but human industry.

He flew the other few hundred feet and landed on the exterior of the spire, sliding between the girders into its domed interior. Lights from the buildings below him paled against the dramatic golden glow that infused this metal cobweb of space. From this height, wind snatched at his clothes and hair as Mencheres spotted his old enemy standing on a beam forty feet above him, his back to Mencheres, looking out over the city spread below him.

"Do you remember when the tallest building was Khufu's pyramid?" Radje said, not turning around. "It took thousands of men and dozens of vampires to construct it. I used to sit at the top and look out over the people, marveling at how much smaller they appeared from that great height. Now look. The mortals make structures that dwarf Khufu's most magnificent accomplishment, and they erect them in under a year. How the world has changed."

Mencheres looked not at the dozens of impressive buildings Radje gestured to but at the man who'd been in his life since his birth. When Tenoch killed himself, Radjedef became the last person who'd known Mencheres since before he was a vampire. He and Radje were the last of the Fourth Dynasty Pharaohs still living. Pity Radje's insatiable jealousy and lust for power had brought them to this.

"The world has changed, true, and the past is buried under more than the sands of time," Mencheres replied. "I am content to let it rest there."

And he was. The weight he'd carried while focusing on his former sins had accomplished nothing except to burden him and endanger his people. That weight had even broken his power, shattering his visions and ultimately his will to live.

No more. He'd made mistakes—yes, many—but those he could not change. His future was yet unwritten, however. As Kira had proven, there was more to it than just oblivion, no matter how his despair had tricked him into believing nothing but darkness lay ahead.

"Menkaure," Radjedef said, turning around to face him. "It is time to finish this."

"Yes," he replied steadily, thinking back on the thousands of years of bitterness, blood, and strife between them. "More than time."

Mencheres jumped onto a beam across from Radje. The next gust of wind carried a hint of decay and magic mixed with the Law Guardian's scent instead of just the normal odors from the city. Mencheres inhaled even as Radje's mouth curled into an arch smile.

"You came alone as agreed, but I take no chances that you've surrendered so easily."

Mencheres let out a short laugh. Radje had coated himself with a spell of grave essence, the one thing that would negate Mencheres's telekinesis against him. Radje was cautious to the end, but it wouldn't be enough.

"Your concern flatters me, uncle," he said lightly.

Radje's gaze raked over him, calculating and expectant. "You're not the only one Tenoch taught the dark arts to. Now, take off your clothes. Then throw them over the side of the building."

Mencheres made a derisive sound as he began to strip off his shoes, trousers, and shirt. When he was naked, he threw everything over the side after a glance ensured no one was below. The clothes wouldn't injure any humans; the shoes would, from this height.

"You thought I would wear a wire? That is a human trick, Radje."

"Turn around," Radjedef said shortly.

Mencheres did, showing his back and stifling his scorn as he felt Radjedef roughly handle his hair, looking for any electronic devices.

"You know that vampires cannot hide wires beneath

their skin. Are you content that I have no means to record anything spoken between us?"

Radjedef considered him, the wind whipping the tight braids of his hair as he inhaled to pick up Mencheres's scent. "You smell impatient, Menkaure. Are you really this eager to die?"

He met his gaze. "Give me my proof that Kira lives, and let us be done with this business between us."

Radje took out his mobile phone, dialing. Mencheres waited, thinking how he'd hated to wash all traces of Kira's scent away before he met Radjedef, but it had been necessary. Any hint of her, Veritas, Radje's guards, or the ferryman would alert the Law Guardian to his defeat, and Mencheres didn't want him to know of it. Not yet.

Kira. Yes, he smelled impatient. He'd been too long without her. Even before that fateful morning at the warehouse, a part of him hungered for her. The same part that recognized her when they met, then later tormented Mencheres when he'd tried to forget about her.

"Shade, bring the phone to the prisoner. Force her to speak into it," Radje said curtly when his guard answered.

After several seconds, Mencheres could hear Shade tell Kira to speak, then Radje held the phone out, and her lovely voice flowed over the line to him even with the whirling winds. "Mencheres?"

"I am here," he said, meeting Radjedef's callously expectant gaze.

"I love you. Now, put Radje back on the phone."

Radje's brows rose, but he held the phone closer to his ear. "What?"

"Veritas is here," Kira said clearly. Radjedef's eyes widened. "There's an open position for an Enforcer since you killed Josephus," she went on. "Veritas said the training takes centuries, but I'm going for it. The vampire world can always use another good cop—"

Radje dropped the phone and leapt off the side of the building. Mencheres followed, his telekinesis unable to stop Radje, but his speed unhindered by the grave essence coating his enemy like an invisible shield. He caught him right before the Law Guardian slammed through the wall of the next building. Mencheres whipped them both upward, but even as he did, Radje twisted in his grip to face him. Fire erupted in Mencheres's belly in the next instant. That fire spread in a brutal arc upward, but he didn't loosen his grasp, even as he felt Radje rip his silver knife higher. He was almost there. Almost . . .

Mencheres flung Radje at the golden steel beams of the faux pyramid. Metal tore as the Law Guardian's body hurtled through it, ripping a hole inside the glowingly intricate structure. Mencheres flew through it, yanking the knife out of his stomach, to blast into Radje just as his uncle was about to leap out the side again. The two of them rolled in midair inside the spire, breaking more steel around them with their struggle.

Radje landed a ruthless knee in Mencheres's still-healing stomach, doubling him over, but again, he didn't let go. He drove Radje backward toward the object his uncle couldn't see—a bent steel beam sticking jaggedly out from the hole Radje's body had torn through the structure.

Radje screamed as that beam impaled him through the sternum. He tried to fling himself off, but Mencheres held him in a merciless grip. His eyes met the Law Guardian's for a second that seemed frozen in time before Mencheres ripped off several more gold-plated beams with his power, sending those hurtling into Radje's body.

The bespelled grave essence only worked on the wearer to negate his telekinesis. Radje had neglected to coat this structure in addition to his body.

More howls came from Radje as those ragged steel spears slammed home, pinning his arms, legs, chest, and stomach. Mencheres twisted them with another thought, curling the metal around Radje and through him, holding him in an unbreakable meld of steel and his strength. The glowing lights from the building shone on the Law Guardian's face as his blood turned the gold-leafed beams red around him, more blood dripping onto the floor almost fifty feet below.

Even with Radje's shouts, the wind whipping from different directions, and the noise from the city around them, Mencheres heard Kira's voice below them. She was screaming his name out from the cell phone Radje had dropped in his attempt to flee.

He sent a strand of his power downward, curling it around the phone to float it up to his hand. At the same time, he ripped off another steel beam, sending this one straight into Radje's throat. Gurgles replaced the Law Guardian's hate-filled screams, his voice barely audible over the keening of the wind.

"I am here," Mencheres said into the phone, interrupting Kira's frantic shouting.

"Thank God!" she gasped. "I could hear screams, but I couldn't tell if they were yours or his . . ."

"They were his," he replied, regretting the pain that would have caused her. "All is well. Radjedef cannot harm us any longer."

"I'm getting on a plane right now," she said, her voice still edged with anxiety even though relief shone through as well. "The one you flew in on is refueled and waiting. I'll be there in the next few hours. I love you."

Mencheres stared into Radjedef's eyes as he replied. "And I love you, my adored. I'll be waiting for you."

A shuffling sound later, and the female Law Guardian's voice flowed over the line. "Is he alive?" Veritas asked.

"No," Mencheres replied, the steel beam preventing Radje from making any sound Veritas could hear above the wind. "He tried to escape. I had to kill him."

"It matters not. This phone was on speaker before, so all of the Guardians heard Radje's complicity in kidnapping Kira and using her as blackmail against you. They also heard further testimony from the guards as to Radje's complicity in Josephus's death and in airing video footage that exposed our race to humans. You have been cleared of all charges, Mencheres."

"Thank you," he replied shortly, hammering another beam into Radje's throat when it had healed enough for him to begin to curse audibly. "I must go now, before humans stumble across this scene."

Veritas would know the real reason for his haste. The ferryman's boat never returned empty, and Mencheres had no intention of being the one to fill it.

He hung up on Veritas, then yanked the beam out of Radje's throat but kept the others where they were. After a few seconds, the gaping hole in the Law Guardian's neck healed until only blood remained to show for it.

Radje's gaze was green with seething hatred. "Was it all a trick? Did you never lose your visions? Never intend to seek your death? *Did you plan all of this?*"

Mencheres couldn't help his ironic laugh. "None of it was a trick, except tonight. You almost won, uncle, but somehow fate gave me back everything I'd lost—and even more."

"What now?" Radje hissed. "You intend to take my head?"

Mencheres cast his power from the torn-up lattice around them down to the roof of the Symphony Tower, where he'd stood earlier, waiting for the time to tick down to midnight. He curled it around the silver knife he'd left there, the same one from the ritual he'd performed earlier, and floated it up toward him.

He caught that knife with one hand, noting the fear in Radje's gaze when he saw it.

"I take nothing from you," Mencheres said, slicing that knife across Radje's chest and coating it on both sides with the Law Guardian's blood. At once, the brightly lit dome around them disappeared into the endless black of Duat, a lone boat floating toward them on an obsidian river. "He does," Mencheres finished, nodding at the ferryman.

Radjedef screamed as the horned figure of Aken appeared. Mencheres let go of Radje to back away, pulling out the steel beams from the Law Guardian and piling them in a heap below. Aken grabbed Radjedef with one long hand when he attempted to flee, that wide mouth open in a terrifying, toothless grin.

No one can outrun the ruler of the underworld, Mencheres thought grimly. Not even him. One day, he would be the one ferried to stand before Anubis, his sins measured on the scales against the Ma'at to see if the Devourer awaited him, or the peace of his eternal rest in Aaru.

But not today.

Radjedef was still screaming when Aken placed him in the boat. The horned head of the ferryman nodded at Mencheres.

"An acceptable surrogate, Menkaure. Tell me, did you find your darkness?"

A chill ran through Mencheres. "My darkness?"

"Kira," the ferryman said, pronouncing her name as the ancient Celts would.

Mencheres began to laugh. He'd had the symbolism all wrong. His visions showed darkness surging ever closer, destined to consume him. He'd thought it was death because his despair could anticipate nothing else, but it wasn't death. It was her.

Kira. Celtic for "dark."

"Yes, I found her," he said to Aken. His memory of that endless stretch of darkness in his vision, filling every aspect of his future, was suddenly the most beautiful image Mencheres had ever beheld.

He turned away from the ferryman. The black void disappeared, replaced with the glow from the damaged pyramid around him and the lights of the cityscape beyond. Radjedef's slowly shriveling body lay now on the bottom of the structure, lifeless, his soul in the boat of the ferryman on their journey back to Duat.

Mencheres had his own journey as well, but his was with Kira, into their future.

Turn the page

for a preview of

THE OTHER SIDE OF THE GRAVE

the next

Night Huntress novel

featuring

Cat and Bones

Available Spring 2011

From

AVON BOOKS

The vampire pulled on the chains restraining him to the cave wall. His eyes were bright green, their glow illuminating the darkness surrounding us.

"Do you really think these will hold me?" he asked, an English accent caressing the challenge.

"Sure do," I replied. Those manacles were installed and tested by a Master vampire, so they were strong enough. I should know. I'd once been stuck in them myself.

The vampire's smile revealed fangs in his white upper teeth. They hadn't been there several minutes ago, when he'd still looked human to the untrained eye.

"Right, then. What do you want, now that you have me helpless?"

He didn't sound like he felt helpless in the least. I pursed my lips and considered the question, letting my gaze sweep over him. Nothing interrupted my view, either, since he was naked. I'd long ago learned that weapons could be stored in various clothing items, but bare skin hid nothing.

Except now, it was also very distracting. The vampire's body was a pale, beautiful expanse of muscle, bone, and lean, elegant lines, all topped off by a gorgeous face with cheekbones so finely chiseled they could cut butter. Clothed or unclothed, the vampire was stunning, something he was obviously aware of. Those glowing green eyes looked into mine with a knowing stare.

"Need me to repeat the question?" he asked with a hint of wickedness.

I strove for nonchalance. "Who do you work for?"

His grin widened, letting me know my aloof act wasn't as convincing as I'd meant it to be. He even stretched as much as the chains allowed, his muscles rippling like waves on a pond.

"No one."

"Liar." I pulled out a silver knife and traced its tip lightly down his chest, not breaking his skin, just leaving a faint pink line that faded in seconds.

He glanced at the path my knife had traced. "Is that supposed to frighten me?"

I pretended to consider the question. "Well, I've cut a bloody swath through the undead world ever since I was sixteen. Even earned myself the nickname of the Red Reaper, so if I've got a knife next to your heart, then *yes,* you should be afraid."

His expression was still amused. "Right nasty wench you sound like, but I wager I could get free and have you on your back before you could stop me."

Cocky bastard. "Talk is cheap. Prove it."

His legs flashed out, knocking me off-balance. I sprang forward at once, but a hard, cool body flattened me to the cave floor in the next instant. An iron grip closed around my wrist, preventing me from raising the knife.

"Always pride before a fall," he murmured in satisfaction.

I tried to throw him off, but a ton of bricks would have

been easier to dislodge. *Should've chained his arms and his legs before daring him like that,* I mentally berated myself.

That arrogant smirk returned as the vampire looked down at me. "Keep squirming, luv. Rubs me in all the right places, it does."

"How'd you get out of the clamps?" Over his shoulder, I saw a hole in the cave that used to be from where the inch-thick titanium cuffs had dangled. Unbelievable. He'd ripped them right out of the wall.

A dark brow arched. "Knew just the right angle to pull. You don't install restraints without knowing how to get out of them. Only took a moment; and by then, I had you on your back. Just like I said I would."

If I'd still had a heartbeat, it would have been racing by then, but I'd lost that—for the most part—when I'd changed from a half-breed into a full vampire several months ago. My eyes turned bright green as fangs slid out of my teeth.

"Show-off."

He leaned down until our faces were only an inch apart. "Now, my lovely captive, with you trapped beneath me, what's to stop me from having my vile way with you?"

The knife I still held dropped from my hand as I wrapped my arms around his neck. "Nothing, I hope."

Bones, my vampire husband, gave a low, sinful laugh. "That's the answer I wanted to hear, Kitten."

Being underground in a cave wouldn't make most people's favorite last-minute accommodations list, but it was heaven to me. The only sounds were the smooth motions of the underground river. It was a relief not to have to tune out the background noise from countless conversations. If it were up to me, Bones and I would stay here for weeks.

But taking a time-out from our lives to get some R&R wasn't in the cards for us. I'd learned that the hard way. What I'd also learned was to grab moments of escape when we could. Hence the stopover to rest the dawn away in the same cave in which, seven years ago, my relationship with Bones began. Back then, it had been me in the chains, convinced I was about to be eaten by an evil bloodsucker. Instead, I ended up marrying that bloodsucker.

My cat gave a plaintive meow from the corner of the small enclave, scratching at the stone slab that served as a door.

"You don't get to explore," I told him. "You'd get lost."

He meowed again but began to lick his paw, giving me baleful looks the whole time. He still hadn't forgiven me for leaving him with a house sitter for months. I didn't blame my kitty for his grudge, but if he'd stayed with me, he might have gotten killed. Several people had.

"Rested enough, luv?" Bones asked.

"Um-hmm," I murmured, stretching. I'd fallen asleep shortly after dawn, but it hadn't been the instant unconsciousness that had plagued me for my first weeks as a vampire. I'd grown out of that, to my relief.

"We'd best get moving, then," he said.

Right. We had places to be, as usual.

"The only thing I regret about stopping to catch some sleep here is the lack of a normal shower," I sighed.

Bones snorted in amusement. "Come now, the river's very refreshing."

At forty degrees, "refreshing" was a kind way to describe the cave's version of indoor plumbing. Bones moved the stone slab out of the way so we could exit the alcove, putting it back before my kitty could leap out, too.

"The trick is to jump in," he went on. "Taking it slow doesn't make it any easier."

I swallowed a laugh. That advice could also apply to navigating the undead world. *All right. One leap into a freezing river, coming up.*

Then it was time to get to the real reason why we'd come to Ohio. With luck, nothing was going on in my old home state except for a few random cases of fang-on-fang violence.

I hoped, anyway.

The afternoon sun was still high in the sky by the time Bones and I arrived at the fountain of the Easton Mall. Well, a street away from it. We had to make sure that this wasn't a trap. Bones and I had a lot of enemies. Two recent vampire wars will do that, not to mention our former professions.

I didn't sense any excessive supernatural energy except a smaller tingle of power in the air that denoted one, maybe two younger vampires mixed in with the crowd. Still, neither Bones nor I moved until a hazy, indistinct form flew across the parking lot and into our rental car.

"Two vampires are at the fountain," Fabian, the ghost I'd sort of adopted, stated. His outline solidified until he looked more like a person and less like a thick particle cloud. "They didn't notice me."

Even though that was the goal, Fabian sounded almost sad at that last part. Unlike humans, vampires could see ghosts, but by and large they ignored them. Being dead didn't mean people automatically got along.

"Thanks, mate," Bones said. "Keep a lookout to make certain they don't have any unpleasant surprises waitin' for us."

Fabian's features blurred until his entire body disappeared.

"We were only supposed to meet with one vampire," I mused. "What do you think of our contact having a buddy with him?"

Bones shrugged. "I think he'd better have a bloody good reason for it."

He got out of the car. I followed suit, giving the silver knives concealed by my sleeves a slight, reassuring pat. *Never leave home without them* was my motto. True, this was a crowded, public place, but that didn't guarantee safety. The knives didn't, either, but they sure tipped the odds in our favor. So did the other two vampires parked farther down the street, ready to jump into action if this turned out to be something other than a fact-gathering chat.

Scents assailed me as I approached the courtyard fountain. Perfumes, body odor, and various chemicals were the strongest, but underneath was another layer I'd gotten better at deciphering. Emotions. Fear, greed, desire, anger, love, sadness . . . all those manifested in scents that ranged from sweetly aromatic to bitterly rancid. Not surprisingly, unpleasant emotions had the harsher aromas. Case in point: The vampires seated on the concrete bench both had the rotten-fruit smell of fear emanating from them even before Bones gave them a quelling glare.

"Which one of you is Scratch?" he asked in a crisp voice.

The one with gray streaks in his hair stood up. "I am."

"en you can stay, but he"—Bones paused to give a
of his head at the other, skinny vampire—"can

atch's voice lowered and he moved closer

to Bones. "That thing you're here to talk to me about? He might have some information on it."

Bones glanced at me. I lifted one shoulder in a half shrug. "May as well hear what our unexpected guest has to say," I commented.

"I'm Ed," the vampire spoke up, with a nervous look over Bones's shoulder at me. "Scratch didn't tell me he was meeting *you* guys here."

From Ed's expression, I guessed that between my crimson hair, the large red diamond on my finger, Bones's English accent, and the tingling aura of power he emanated, Ed had figured out who we were.

"That's because he didn't know," Bones answered coolly. His emotions were now locked down behind the impenetrable wall he used in public. Still, anyone could pick up on the edge to Bones's voice as he went on. "I take it introductions aren't necessary?"

Scratch's gaze slid to me, then skipped away. "No," he muttered. "You're Bones, and that's the Reaper."

Bones's expression didn't soften, but I smiled in my best I'm-not-going-to-kill-you way.

"Call me Cat, and why don't we find some shade to talk in?"

A French restaurant with outdoor seating was nearby, so the four of us found a table under an umbrella and sat down as if we were old friends catching up.

"You said your Master was killed a few years ago, and she left no one to look after the members of her line," Bones stated to Scratch, after the waitress took our drink orders. "A group of you banded together to watch out for one another. When did you first notice something odd was going on?"

"Several months ago, around fall last year," Scratch replied. "At first, we just thought some of the guys skipped town without telling anyone. We kept an eye on each other, but we weren't babysitters, y'know? Then, when more of us went missing, people who'd normally say something before taking off . . . well. It got the rest of us worried."

I didn't doubt it. As young, Masterless vampires, Scratch and others like him were on the bottom of the pecking order in the undead world. I might have some issues with the feudalistic system vampires operated under, but when it came to protecting members of their line, most Master vampires were pretty damn vigilant. Even the evil ones.

"Then, more ghouls started showing in the area," Scratch went on.

I tensed. This was why Bones and I had left our Blue Ridge home after we'd barely unpacked to come to Ohio.

"Hey, it's an undead playground here," Scratch continued, oblivious to my discomfort. "Lots of ley lines and fun vibrations, so we didn't think anything about all the flesh-eaters showing up. But some of 'em act real nasty to vampires. Harassing the Masterless ones, following them home, starting fights . . . it got us thinking maybe they were behind the disappearances. Problem is, no one gives a shit since we don't belong to anyone. I'm amazed *you're* interested, frankly."

"I have my reasons," Bones said in that same impassive tone. He didn't even glance at me. Centuries of feigning detachment made him an expert at it.

"If you're looking for money, we don't have much," Ed piped up. "Besides, I thought you retired from contract killing when you merged lines with that Mega-Master, Mencheres."

Bones arched a brow. "Try not to think too often, you'll only hurt yourself," he replied pleasantly.

Ed's face tightened, but he shut his mouth. I hid a smile.

Don't look a gift horse in the mouth—especially one that bites.

"Do you have any proof that ghouls might be involved in your friends' disappearances?" I asked Scratch, getting back to the subject.

"No. Just seems more than coincidence that whenever one of them went missing, they were last seen at a place where some of those asshole ghouls were."

"What places were those?" I asked.

"Some bars, clubs—"

"Names," Bones pressed.

Scratch began to rattle them off, but all of a sudden, his voice was drowned out under a deluge of others.

" *. . . four more hours until I get a break . . .*"

" *. . . remember to get the receipt for that? If it doesn't fit, I'm taking it back . . .*"

" *. . . if she looks at* one *more pair of shoes, I'm going to scream . . .*"

The sudden crash of intrusive conversation wasn't coming from the mall shoppers around us—I'd tuned that out even before we sat down. This was coming from inside my head. I jerked as if struck, my hand flying to my temple.

Oh shit. Not again.

THE NIGHT HUNTRESS NOVELS FROM

Jeaniene Frost

✝ HALFWAY TO THE GRAVE ✝

978-0-06-124508-4

Kick-ass demon hunter and half-vampire Cat Crawfield and
her sexy mentor, Bones, are being pursued by a group of kill-
ers. Now Cat will have to choose a side…and Bones is turning
out to be as tempting as any man with a heartbeat.

✝ ONE FOOT IN THE GRAVE ✝

978-0-06-124509-1

Cat Crawfield is now a special agent working to rid the world
of the rogue undead. But when she's targeted for assassination
she turns to her ex, the sexy and dangerous vampire Bones,
to help her.

✝ AT GRAVE'S END ✝

978-0-06-158307-0

Caught in the crosshairs of a vengeful vamp, Cat's about to
learn the true meaning of bad blood—just as she and Bones
need to stop a lethal magic from being unleashed.

✝ DESTINED FOR AN EARLY GRAVE ✝

978-0-06-158321-6

Cat is having terrifying visions in her dreams of a vampire
named Gregor who's more powerful than Bones.

✝ FIRST DROP OF CRIMSON ✝

978-0-06-158322-3

Spade, a powerful, mysterious vampire, is duty-bound to protect
Denise MacGregor—even if it means destroying his own kind.

Visit www.AuthorTracker.com for exclusive
information on your favorite HarperCollins authors.

At Avon Books, we know your passion for romance—once you finish one of our novels, you find yourself wanting more.

May we tempt you with . . .

- **Excerpts** from our upcoming releases.

- Entertaining **extras**, including authors' personal photo albums and book lists.

- Behind-the-scenes **scoop** on your favorite characters and series.

- **Sweepstakes** for the chance to win free books, romantic getaways, and other fun prizes.

- Writing **tips** from our authors and editors.

- **Blog** with our authors and find out why they love to write romance.

- **Exclusive content** that's not contained within the pages of our novels.

Join us at
www.avonbooks.com

AVON

An Imprint of HarperCollins*Publishers*
www.avonromance.com